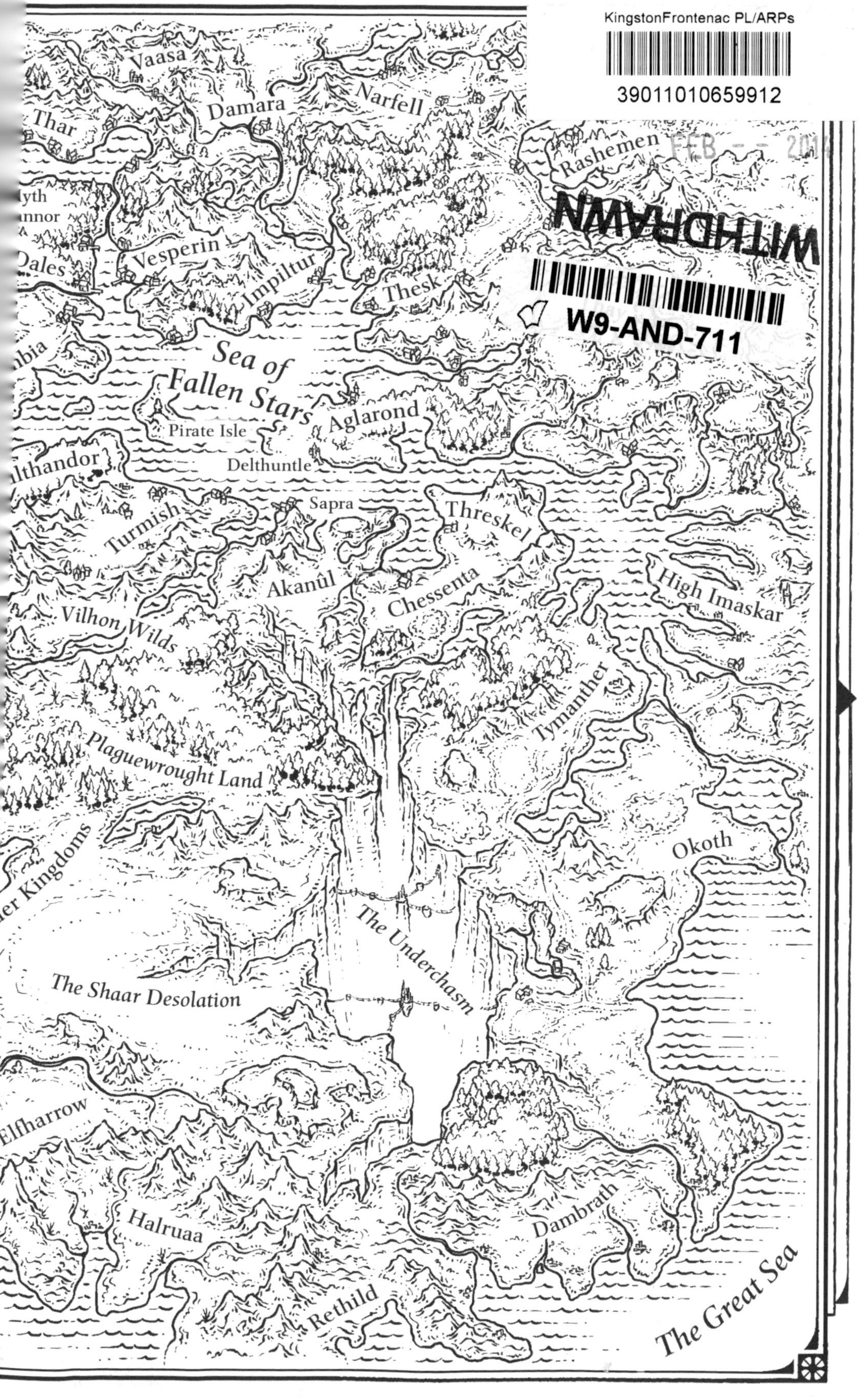
Vaasa
Damara
Narfell
Thar
Rashemen
Dales
Vesperin
Impiltur
Thesk
Sea of Fallen Stars
Pirate Isle
Aglarond
Delthuntle
Sapra
Turmish
Threskel
Akanûl
Chessenta
High Imaskar
Vilhon Wilds
Tymanther
Plaguewrought Land
Okoth
The Underchasm
The Shaar Desolation
Elfharrow
Halruaa
Dambrath
Rethild
The Great Sea

When the trials begin,
in soul-torn solitude despairing,
the hunter waits alone.
The companions emerge
from fast-bound ties of fate
uniting against a common foe.

When the shadows descend,
in Hell-sworn covenant unswerving
the blighted brothers hunt,
and the godborn appears,
in rose-blessed abbey reared,
arising to loose the godly spark.

When the harvest time comes,
in hate-fueled mission grim unbending,
the shadowed reapers search.
The adversary vies
with fiend-wrought enemies,
opposing the twisting schemes of Hell.

When the tempest is born,
as storm-tossed waters rise uncaring,
the promised hope still shines.
And the reaver beholds
the dawn-born chosen's gaze,
transforming the darkness into light.

When the battle is lost,
through quake-tossed battlefields unwitting
the seasoned legions march,
but the sentinel flees
with once-proud royalty,
protecting devotion's fragile heart.

When the ending draws near,
with ice-locked stars unmoving,
the threefold threats await,
and the herald proclaims,
in war-wrecked misery,
announcing the dying of an age.

—As written by Elliandreth of Orishaar, c. —17,600 DR

FORGOTTEN REALMS®

THE COMPANIONS
R.A. Salvatore

THE GODBORN
Paul S. Kemp

THE ADVERSARY
Erin M. Evans

THE REAVER
Richard Lee Byers

THE SENTINEL
Troy Denning
April 2014

THE HERALD
Ed Greenwood
June 2014

RICHARD LEE BYERS
THE REAVER

FORGOTTEN REALMS®

THE SUNDERING

Book
IV

THE REAVER

This book is protected under the copyright laws of the United States of America. Any reproduction or unau-thorized use of the material or artwork contained herein is prohibited without the express written permission of Wizards of the Coast, LLC

Published by Wizards of the Coast LLC. Manufactured by: Hasbro SA, Rue Emile-Boéchat 31, 2800 Delémont, CH. Represented by Hasbro Europe, 2 Roundwood Ave, Stockley Park, Uxbridge, Middlesex, UB11 1AZ, UK.

Forgotten Realms, Wizards of the Coast, D&D, and their respective logos are trademarks of Wizards of the Coast LLC, in the U.S.A. and other countries. All other trademarks are the property of their respective owners.

All characters in this book are fictitious. Any resemblance to actual persons, living or dead, is purely coincidental. All Wizards of the Coast characters, character names, and the distinctive likenesses thereof are property of Wizards of the Coast LLC.

Printed in the U.S.A.

Prophecy by: James Wyatt
Cartography by: Mike Schley
Cover art by: Tyler Jacobson
First Printing: February 2014

9 8 7 6 5 4 3 2 1

ISBN: 978-0-7869-6458-1
ISBN: 978-0-7869-6547-2 (ebook)
620A4358000001 EN

Cataloging-in-Publication data is on file with the Library of Congress

---

Contact Us at Wizards.com/CustomerService
Wizards of the Coast LLC, PO Box 707, Renton, WA 98057-0707, USA
USA & Canada: (800) 324-6496 or (425) 204-8069
Europe: +32(0) 70 233 277

Visit our web site at **www.dungeonsanddragons.com**

For Stacy

THE REAVER

CHAPTER ONE

Eleint, the Year of the Nether Mountain Scrolls (1486 DR)

Tʜᴇ ᴄᴏʟᴅ ʀᴀɪɴ ʜᴀᴍᴍᴇʀᴇᴅ ᴅᴏᴡɴ ʟɪᴋᴇ ᴀ ᴡᴀᴛᴇʀғᴀʟʟ. Cᴏᴍʙɪɴᴇᴅ with the gray clouds shrouding the sky from horizon to horizon, it was blinding. Peering around the corner of a peasant's cottage at more of the shacks, sheds, and pigpens that made up the ramshackle village, Anton Marivaldi took solace in the reflection that the enemy couldn't see him and his crew either.

Then darts of crimson light leaped out of the gloom and streaked at Atala. Like her captain, the pirate with the wheat-blond braids had been trying to spot the foe, and now she sought to duck back down behind the donkey cart she'd been using for cover. She was too slow, though, and a pair of the arcane missiles pierced her face. They didn't leave holes or any sort of visible wounds, but Atala flopped down in the mud, shuddered for a moment, and then lay still.

"I stand corrected," Anton murmured. "Someone can see." Perhaps the wizard had worked magic to sharpen his sight.

From beneath a broad-brimmed hat that shielded from the rain narrow gray eyes set in a long, dour countenance, Naraxes Corieth said, "I say we retreat before the wretches circle around and block the way back to the ship."

Anton snorted. "How likely is that?"

"How likely was it the child would turn out to have bodyguards," his first mate retorted, "and one of them a mage? How likely was it that all these farmers would risk their lives to protect him?"

3

Anton smiled. "It's the little surprises that make life interesting."

"Curse it, Captain, one man fell overboard before we even got here because you sailed us into the teeth of that storm—"

"We needed to reach this place before the boy moved on."

"—and now I count three more of our comrades lying dead!"

"You may count twenty before we're done. But the rest of us will be rich, and that's what matters." Anton turned to survey the crew at large.

His men were well armed for raiders living in the days of the Great Rain, when the perpetual downpour so quickly ruined bowstrings and rusted mail that many folk had dispensed with them. Their weapons coupled with the willingness to *take* what they needed filled their bellies and provided creature comforts in a time of want. Yet even so, like many people their captain had encountered over the course of the last several months, they had a haggard cast to their faces.

Anton raised his voice to make himself heard over the hiss and clatter of the rain. "We're going to split into three groups and charge. Naraxes and his squad will swing left. Yuicoerr will take his to the right. I'll lead mine straight up the center."

The pirates looked back at him with a sullen lack of enthusiasm. Then Yuicoerr, the second mate, an Aglarondan whose pointed chin and slanted eyes bespoke a trace of elf blood, said, "What about the wizard?"

"He can't throw spells in three directions at once," Anton said.

"Maybe not," Naraxes said, "but he might have more trouble hitting us if we wait until dark."

Anton grinned. "Excellent idea. Unless, of course, the villages sent a runner in the direction of Teziir, in which case, cavalry will arrive before nightfall to butcher us all."

"Still," the first mate said, "one blast of frost or vitriol—"

"Enough!" Anton snapped. "You heard my orders. Now, everyone who isn't craven, count off by threes!"

For a moment, no one spoke. But then Roberc squared his shoulders and said, "One." And perhaps the example of the sole halfling

4

in the company, an able fighter but one no bigger than the human child they sought, shamed the others into following suit.

Once the three squads formed up around their leaders, Anton took off his hooded cloak and hung it on a fence post so it wouldn't hinder him. The cold, stinging rain instantly plastered his inner garments to his skin. Suppressing a grimace, he drew his two curved blades, the long saber he customarily wielded in his left hand and the shorter cutlass, useful for parrying and close-in killing, he generally carried in his right.

The men around him still looked less than eager, but they did seem resigned. Some breathed heavily and glowered like madmen, summoning anger and the urge to violence. Others mouthed prayers, fingered lucky amulets, or guzzled from flasks and wineskins. In Anton's eyes, all such practices were equally pathetic. Still, whatever it took to steady the rogues so they could perform their function.

When he judged the crew ready, he said, "All right, charge on my signal, and whatever happens, keep going. Our first task is to kill the mage. The second is to seize the little boy. Alive, like Evendur Highcastle wants him."

He then turned in the direction of the foe, raised his saber over his head, swept it down, and lunged into the open. Scrambling out from behind the cottage, a cluster of nearby chicken coops, and a little shrine to Chauntea with a neglected-looking wooden statue of the Earthmother inside, the other pirates darted after him. Naraxes's and Yuicoerr's teams swung wide as instructed.

Anton's boots splashed up brown water from puddle after puddle. The mud alternately slid under his feet or clung to them like glue, threatening his balance either way. He squinted and blinked against the rain but still saw little sign of the enemy, just shadows in the dusky grayness up ahead.

Javelins plummeted at him and his companions.

But the folk who'd thrown them could, apparently, see no better than he could. Most of the weapons missed. On his right, though, a fellow renegade Turmishan, with skin the same mahogany brown and who still sported the long, black, squared-off beard his captain had long ago shaved off, caught a javelin where his neck met his shoulder and fell down thrashing. Another pirate tripped over him and pitched headlong in the muck.

Then a point of red light appeared amid the downpour. Even though Anton was looking for warning signs of hostile magic, it took him an instant to discern that the spark was moving, indeed, hurtling toward him and his companions fast as an arrow.

" 'Ware magic!" he roared. He sprang to the side and threw himself down to the ground.

Something boomed. Heat and yellow light washed over him, the ambient murk momentarily giving way to brightness. Men screamed, and when Anton raised his head, he saw them reel and drop as they burned like torches. The fires would go out quickly, dowsed by the rain, but likely not quickly enough to save them.

His striped purple sash, gold-trimmed crimson shirt, and the rest of his gaudy pirate finery now black with mud, Anton scrambled back to his feet. "Onward!" he screamed, charging once again, and as before, the survivors of the fiery attack raced after him, even though, as best he could judge, they only numbered half a dozen.

Anton watched for another spark, but none was forthcoming. Instead, thunder banged and a dazzling twist of lightning stabbed off to the left. Evidently satisfied with the harm he'd done to the pirates charging up the middle, the enemy mage turned his attention to Naraxes's squad.

Anton grinned and thought, Wizard, you should have finished with me first.

At last a line of armed rustics appeared amid the pelting rain and the gloom. Anton's respect for them increased a hair when he saw that they stood behind a low line of plows, horse troughs, and barrows. As barricades went, it wasn't much, but it showed somebody was thinking.

Two men pulled crossbows out of the sacks that had thus far protected them from the wet. The weapons clacked, Anton sprang to the side, and neither of the quarrels found him. He couldn't tell if all the freebooters behind him had been as lucky. Nobody screamed, so it was possible.

When he came within range, a boar spear jabbed at him. He knocked it out of line with the saber and leaped high enough to clear the makeshift barrier, slashing while in the air.

The saber sliced a farmer's face from his right eye to the left corner of his mouth and sent him stumbling backward, but not quite far enough to open a gap. As Anton landed, he slammed into the peasant, and the impact staggered him as well.

The foes to either side pivoted toward him. He bulled forward, shoving the stunned peasant with the gashed face ahead of him, and his assailants' initial blows, a swing with a mallet and a chop with a hoe, missed.

Anton heaved the man with the ruined features away from him and down into the mud. In so doing, he recovered his balance and cleared sufficient space to use both swords to good effect. He whirled and cut, and the saber slashed open the belly of the farmer with the hoe.

The man with the mallet screamed and rushed in with his weapon raised for a bone-crushing strike to the head. Anton stepped in, twisted, and the blow fell harmlessly behind him. He slid the point of the cutlass between the peasant's ribs.

As that man dropped, another villager rounded on Anton with a pitchfork. When the thrust came, Anton rammed the cutlass between the tines, jerked the fork to the side, and lunged. The saber tore open the peasant's throat, and blood spurted.

By now, the other pirates had reached the barricade, and, howling and hacking, swarmed over and pushed the defenders back. Satisfied, Anton turned to locate the wizard and spotted him—or rather her— too. But another of the boy prophet's actual bodyguards was in the way.

The barrel-chested warrior had proper martial gear, a broadsword, targe, brigandine, and a conical helm with a nose guard sticking down between brown eyes. Judging from his stance—feet at right

7

angles, blade high and slanting—he knew his trade and might well have learned it in Cormyr.

As he closed with the guard, Anton shifted to the left, then instantly back to the right. He feinted to the head, then whirled the saber low to slash beneath his opponent's shield.

Unfortunately, neither Anton's footwork nor his blade work deceived the warrior. The Cormyrean lowered the targe to deflect the true attack and cut over the top of it. Anton jerked sideways barely in time to keep the broadsword from cleaving his skull.

He grinned and tried a head cut of his own, but the targe jerked up and blocked it. Then he and his adversary traded attacks for the next few breaths. Neither scored, but the exchanges gave him the chance to take the Cormyrean's measure.

His initial impression was correct: The bodyguard was good. But like most swordsmen, he had a few favorite moves and an accustomed rhythm, and once Anton determined what they were, he likewise understood how to exploit them.

He waited for the Cormyrean to cut to the knee. When the attack came, he sidestepped and slashed at the other man's forearm.

But as he did, a stabbing pain in his gut turned the whirling extension of his arm into spastic flailing. The saber still reached the target but not squarely and not with the maiming force he'd intended.

A few paces behind the Cormyrean, the mage, a pale, slender moon elf whose blue cloak matched her tangled, rain-sodden hair, glared at Anton while holding a talisman over her head. He realized she'd cast a spell to cause the ongoing agony in his belly, and then the Cormyrean lunged and smashed the shield into him.

Anton reeled backward. The guard rushed him and bashed him again, this time knocking him down on his back in a puddle. His bloody right hand empty—Anton had evidently at least cut him badly enough to make him fumble the broadsword—the Cormyrean dropped to his knees beside his foe and raised the targe to smash the edge down on his head.

The preparatory action opened him up, and the need to strike *now,* now or never, spurred Anton into motion despite the ripping pain in his stomach. He stabbed the cutlass up underneath the bodyguard's ribs, and his foe flopped down on top of him.

To Anton's relief, his spell-induced torment subsided a moment later. Otherwise, he might not have found the strength to flounder out from under the Cormyrean's corpse. He scrambled up and looked in the elf's direction.

Another man-at-arms fought hard to protect her, but two pirates kept him busy. Anton had a clear path to the wizard, and he charged her.

Magic filled her hand with a short sword made of blue and yellow fire. Raindrops puffed into steam when they struck the blade. But unfortunately for her, whatever the supernatural virtues of the conjured weapon, her technique with it was rudimentary, and it only took an instant to cut past her guard and into her torso.

As she fell, Anton noticed the brooch pinned to her mantle, a rolled-up silvery scroll sealed with a round white moon and a circle of blue stars. It looked like a coat of arms, perhaps the symbol of some sect or knightly order, but he didn't recognize it.

Nor did he have time to wonder about it. He cast about and observed that although there was still a little killing going on, he and his fellow pirates were victorious. Naraxes's and Yuicoerr's squads had assailed the enemy's flanks to murderous effect, and it looked like all the boy's actual bodyguards were dead. The only folk still resisting the raiders were a handful of peasants too stupid to quit.

The pirates disposed of the dolts in a few more heartbeats, and then, panting, Naraxes hurried in Anton's direction. "We won," the first mate said.

"Yes," Anton said, "we defeated a rabble of pig keepers. It's a glorious moment."

Naraxes scowled. "The crew fought like demons to give you what you wanted."

"I want the boy. I don't see him."

9

"We just now finished fighting."

"Then start searching. Every hovel, dunghill, and woodpile. And while you're at it, round up all the peasants who are still alive."

Anton led one of the search parties himself. It would make the task go that much faster, and he wanted something to occupy his mind.

He relished combat even at those moments when he took some hurt or feared for his life. It whetted existence into something sharp and simple. But in the aftermath, he sometimes suffered a bleak despondency, and when he felt such feelings rising, activity helped to quell them.

He didn't find anyone who matched the description of the boy prophet or even any loot worth pocketing, just the cowering folk—children, mothers, the elderly and infirm—he flushed out of hiding. But when he marched them to join their fellow captives in the center of the village, he saw that some of the other searchers had been luckier.

In fact, one could argue they'd been too lucky. They'd found three little boys with blond hair and fair complexions, and on first inspection, there was nothing to distinguish the special one from the other two.

Anton could haul all three back to Pirate Isle and let Captain Highcastle identify the one he wanted. But what if *none* of them was the right child? It would be embarrassing to disappoint the self-proclaimed Chosen of Umberlee. It might even be dangerous.

He raked the prisoners with a menacing glare. "My name is Anton Marivaldi, and my ship is the *Iron Jest*. You may have heard of me."

Apparently they had. Some of them blanched.

"You have a choice," Anton continued. "Someone can point out the boy Stedd Whitehorn without further delay, in which case, all of you will live. Or you can keep mum until my men kill enough people to loosen somebody's tongue."

With that, he waited. While the rain beat down, the moments crawled by, and none of the peasants spoke up.

Perplexed, Anton shook his head. The rustics were clearly terrified. He could all but smell it on them despite the downpour. So why weren't they giving up an outsider to save themselves?

Maybe because, despite Anton's reputation, they hoped he wouldn't carry out his threat. If so, it was time to disabuse them of their optimism. He turned to Yuicoerr. "Have at it. Start with the babies and little girls."

"No!" an old man yelped. He was stooped and scrawny with brown spots on the backs of his wrinkled hands and the bald crown of his head.

Anton raised a hand to halt the second mate and the other pirates advancing with knives in hand. "I'm glad one of you is sensible. Keep talking, old man. Point out Stedd Whitehorn and save your grandchildren."

"I can't!" the elderly villager replied. "He isn't here! When the trouble started, one of his minders rushed him out of town!"

Anton's jaw tightened. That was what he'd feared might have happened, and he and his crew could hardly comb the countryside if riders from Teziir were on the way.

But was the story true? If he'd been commanding the other side, would he have believed he had to get the boy out of the village because he couldn't possibly win the battle to come? Why? The defenders had had wizardry and superior numbers on their side, and at least some of their fighters had been seasoned warriors of the scroll, moon, and stars.

"That's too bad," he said to the old man. "I explained the only way to save your village, but if the boy's no longer here, then obviously, you can't avail yourselves of the opportunity. Go on, lads. Kill everyone."

"Wait!" cried a woman with three small children clinging to her skirts. She had the sagging, loose-skinned look of someone who'd been stout before hunger whittled away the excess weight. "He's—"

"No!" cried one of the three golden-haired boys. "Don't say it! You don't have to." He turned to Anton, and even amid the downpour

11

and the gloom, his eyes were as blue as the clear skies and seas that no one had seen in a year. He swallowed, and in a voice that quavered just a little, said, "I'm Stedd."

Anton had to admit, the lad had courage. Although he might not know exactly what fate awaited him, he surely realized it wouldn't be pleasant. But then again, maybe he was simple or downright mad and believed the power he professed to serve would protect him.

"It's a pleasure to meet you," Anton said. "Now be a good boy and stand still while one of my men ties your hands and leashes you. Then we'll be on our way and let your friends here get back to slopping the hogs or whatever they need to do."

Yuicoerr looked to Anton. "What about our dead?"

"In my considered opinion, they're likely to stay that way."

"I mean, we should carry them back to the ship and give them to the sea."

"That would slow us down."

"Only a little, and we owe it to them."

Anton laughed. "When did you turn so sentimental? We owe it to ourselves—"

Something smashed into the back of Anton's head. He pitched forward onto his hands and knees, and, his skull ringing, turned his head to discover Naraxes standing over him. The first mate raised the belaying pin he used as a cudgel and clubbed him a second time.

The rain turned the streets of Immurk's Hold into streams rushing from the mountainous heights of Pirate Isle, past taverns, festhalls, fighting pits, chandleries, smithies, and sail makers' shops, and down to the harbor, where the rising waters of the Sea of Fallen Stars were drowning docks and shipyards. Umara Ankhlab hunched her shoulders against the downpour and tried to avoid wading through deep water. It slopped over the tops of her shoes and soaked her feet even so.

That was unpleasant, but not as much as her sense of Kymas Nahpret's amusement at her discomfort. Her superior had cast a spell to link their psyches, and in consequence saw, heard, and felt what she did, but not so intensely as to cause him distress.

One day, he said, speaking mind to mind, *if you serve me well, I'll make you as I am. Then you'll never be cold again.*

Or *forever* cold, she thought, forever cold and dead. Then she made haste to mask the thought before it bled across into Kymas's awareness. It would be unwise to let him realize she didn't want to become a vampire.

And actually, she needed to overcome her instinctive revulsion and desire it in truth. She came from a long line of tharchions and khazarks, but over the course of the last century, mortal Thayan nobles had declined in stature relative to the undead ones. The only way for even the daughter of an old and once-prominent Mulan family to achieve any measure of genuine status and influence was to become such a creature herself, and at least then she wouldn't have to bear the presence of a thing like a psychic tapeworm.

She splashed past scrawny, half-naked men setting up trident-shaped markers to line the street leading to the temple of Umberlee, Queen of the Depths. The rain made any sort of outdoor labor unpleasant, but the raiders of Pirate Isle evidently were no more concerned than Thayans for the misery of slaves, and the overseers with their coiled whips had taken shelter under the dripping eaves of nearby buildings.

Many buildings in Immurk's Hold were haphazardly constructed of driftwood, other flotsam, and the odd piece of plundered lumber. A few though, including fortresses and the mansions of the most rapaciously successful captains, were as imposing as any structure Umara had seen in any settlement bordering the Inner Sea. The house of the Bitch Queen was one of the latter, and thus proof that Pirate Isle was one of the few places where her priesthood had wielded considerable influence even before Evendur Highcastle proclaimed her new ascendancy. It was a pile of blue-green stone perched on a promontory overlooking the storm-tossed sea. Stairs and walkways snaked their way down the cliff face to vanish beneath the heaving surf where it smashed itself to spray against the rock.

Umara strode to the primary entrance, where two steps ascended to a recessed doorway with one of Umberlee's emblems, a double wave curling to both the right and the left, carved above it. A pair of sentries, novice priests in sea-green tabards, crossed their tridents to bar the way.

"I'm Umara Ankhlab," she told them, "Red Wizard and envoy of Szass Tam, master of Thay. The Chosen of Umberlee has agreed to receive me." As he certainly should have done after all the gifts Kymas's legionnaires had carried to the temple.

One of the waveservants said, "Yes, Saer. Follow me." And when he led her into the high-ceilinged, shadowy chamber beyond the doorway, her first thought was that it was a relief to escape the rain. She pushed back her scarlet cowl and wiped at the moisture that had blown inside it to dampen her face and shaven scalp.

But escaping the rain didn't mean she'd escaped water, or at least the idea of it. As one would expect, the keepers of Umberlee's house had adorned it with representations of sharks, eels, octopuses, and the goddess herself with her clawed hands, finned elbows, kelp hair, and cloak made of jellyfish dragging a ship beneath the waves. In addition, some acoustical trick filled the structure with the rhythmic hiss and crash of the waves below, while the cool air smelled of brine.

As Umara's guide conducted her deeper into the temple, she paid attention to the number and locations of other guards. She noted, too, the glyphs protecting windows and thresholds. Many of the symbols were unfamiliar to her, likely because they derived from divine magic rather than arcane. But even so, she could often sense the power lurking in them as a twinge of headache or a prickling on her skin.

Her escort ultimately brought her to a round chamber with several doorways leading out of it and what appeared to be a bottomless pool in the center. Given that the spacious room was above sea level, she inferred it was enchantment that drew the water up the shaft. Wet, splayed footprints suggested that some marine creature had recently clambered from it to confer with the waveservants or Captain Highcastle himself.

"Sahuagin," rumbled a voice at her back. "We're good friends."

Startled, she nearly jerked around. But it wouldn't do to appear nervous, and so she took a breath and turned with the composure appropriate to her alleged role as an envoy. At which point, she had to steady herself again.

Like most Thayans, she'd spent her life growing accustomed to the undead and in fact was obliged to consort with a vampire nearly every night of her life. Yet even so, the sight of Evendur Highcastle jarred her.

Plainly, he'd been a hulking brute of a man even when alive. The tendays he'd supposedly spent lying at the bottom of the sea before his goddess saw fit to reanimate him had swelled his bulk even larger just as they'd softened his features. Still, despite the bloated, mushy look of him and the bits the fish had nibbled away, the balanced solidity of his stance conveyed a sense of enormous strength.

His costly but mismatched attire accentuated the grotesquerie of his appearance. From his massive shoulders swept a pearl-bedizened, high-collared green cloak that was part of the regalia of a high priest of the Bitch Queen. Yet beneath it, he still dressed like a pirate with plunder to squander and an utter lack of taste, in a jerkin with alternating ruby and emerald buttons, an orange sash, black and white checked breeches, and high maroon boots inlaid with erotic imagery.

Spreading her hands, Umara gave Evendur a shallow bow, respectful but not servile. "Captain Highcastle, Szass Tam sends felicitations to his brother in undeath."

The pirate's face shifted, but his features were too puffy for Umara to tell exactly what expression he'd assumed. Her inability to read him gave her another twinge of unease.

"Does the lich understand that I am more than undead?" Evendur asked. "That I am the Chosen of the Queen of the Depths?"

Well, that's the question, isn't it? said Kymas, speaking inside Umara's head. *Use the talisman.*

Safely ensconced in the coffin concealed aboard their galley, his very existence unsuspected by any of the locals, the vampire could afford impatience. Umara was the one who'd suffer if Evendur caught her doing something he didn't like. She exerted her will to quiet her superior's urging and to keep the nasty sensation it produced, like an itch inside her skull, from showing in her face.

"He does indeed," she said to Evendur. "Who could doubt it, considering how quickly the church of Umberlee, under your leadership, is extending its influence around the Sea of Fallen Stars? That's why he sent me."

"To pledge me his fealty?"

Despite the gravity of Umara's situation, the question almost surprised a laugh out of her. Divinely anointed or no, the living corpse plainly didn't understand the ruler of Thay.

"Honestly, no," she said. "Only a small portion of Thay is coastline, and Bane is our patron deity. But Szass Tam offers an alliance between equals."

"I just told you: He and I are not 'equals.' "

"Captain, it's not for me to debate that. You and Szass Tam are both greater than I, so how could I even pretend to know which of you stands higher than the other? All I can do is deliver my master's message and hope that something in it meets with your favor."

The drowned man grunted. "Continue, then."

"Thank you. Szass Tam asks you to consider that he has the strongest army in the East, and you have a mighty fleet. Thayan traders have goods to sell—including crops grown in fields where continual rain doesn't spoil them—in Turmish, Impiltur, and the cities of the Dragon Coast if they can convey them to market without the sea wolves of Pirate Isle attacking them. They'll pay you for immunity . . . and for doing your utmost to destroy their Aglarondan competitors."

"What do I care about armies when I'm building an empire of the sea?" Evendur replied. "And as for the toll you propose, I already have something similar in mind, but I don't need an arrangement with your master to collect it. The day will come when every man who sails these waters or lives anywhere near them will tithe to Umberlee and her church."

"To answer your question about armies," Umara said, "may I show you something? I'll need to work some magic, but I give you my word, it's harmless."

Evendur spat a wad of something too dark and foul to be a living man's saliva. "I don't need your 'word', girl. You couldn't hurt me if you tried. Go ahead and cast your charm."

Inwardly, Umara bristled at his contempt, but, probably fortunately, she'd had a great deal of practice masking her resentment when undead beings condescended to her. She simply said, "Thank you," turned toward a clear space in the circular chamber, and began an incantation from *Six Lies and a Question,* a grimoire supposedly authored by the legendary illusionist Mythrellan.

As Umara crooned and whispered, she swept her hand back and forth like a child finger-painting. Gradually, a city square crowded with figures took form, and when the magic filled in enough detail, the figures began to move.

Soldiers wearing sea-green cloaks emblazoned with the image of a dolphin leaping over a seashell battled other men-at-arms clad in white surcoats bearing a purple dragon emblem. The major differences between the two factions were that the warriors of the dolphin were fully armored and attacking in squads, while as often as not, the men of the dragon wore no mail, carried no shields, and scurried to form up with their comrades.

The scene shifted to a tree-lined boulevard and then a shabby little marketplace in the shadow of a towering city wall. In each view, it was plain the warriors of the dolphin and shell had attacked the Purple Dragons by surprise and to deadly effect.

Evendur Highcastle had been an infamous pirate long before he rose from the waves as an undead monstrosity, and he studied the butchery with what Umara took to be professional interest. That meant it was time to use the talisman in her pocket. If she was lucky, his distraction combined with the magic already seething in the air would keep him from noticing another momentary pulse of power.

She wrapped her fingers around the carved onyx disk and mouthed the trigger word Kymas had taught her. Pain stabbed between her eyes as her perceptions shattered into paradox.

Evendur seemed to loom taller and also to spring toward her even though neither of those things actually happened. Rather, he became more massive and real than anything else, the crushing force of his presence diminishing the thick stone walls around him to something as wispy as the clash of shadows Umara had conjured to hold his attention.

Yet though he felt more solid and true than anything she'd ever experienced, at the same time, he was empty, absent, just a hole in the substance of the world opening on a realm of churning tumult and ferocity. It was actually the infinite violence of that place that made his mere existence so oppressive. That, and the intuition that at any moment, *something* might peer back at her from the far side of the opening.

No one claimed a place among the Red Wizards without facing fiends and other horrors that common folk could scarcely imagine. Still, Umara's heart pounded, and she had to bite back a moan.

She needed to get hold of herself before Evendur noticed anything amiss. She tried to let go of the talisman, but her fingers wouldn't stop clutching it. She took a breath, focused the trained will of a wizard on performing that simple action, and her digits slowly unclenched. Evendur reverted to the rotting hulk she'd first encountered, and vile as that creature was, she almost felt grateful to him for masking the greater horror that used him as a spy hole and a conduit.

"What am I seeing?" he asked.

"The defection of Daerlun," she replied. "With the beginning of summer, First Lord Gascam Highbanner betrayed Prince Irvel with the results you've now seen." Deprived of her concentration, the illusory struggle began to blur and fade.

"How do *you* know?" Evendur demanded.

She smiled. "Captain, you've made it plain you deem my powers weak compared to those granted by your goddess, and I don't contest the point. Still, Thayan scrying and divination have their uses."

"Maybe so," Evendur said, "but how does treachery in the war in the west concern me?"

"Prince Irvel and his army were the great hope of Cormyr," Umara said. "Now that they've come to grief, Sembia will soon win the war. Then it—and the conquered vassal state it will make of its foe—will be free to turn its attention to any power that threatens its interests anywhere around the Inner Sea. It will have a strong, seasoned navy *and* army to bring to bear, and this . . . tacit theocracy you're building may need allies to withstand them."

The pirate priest shook his swollen, all but neckless head; the dangling mustachios and strands of beard like black, slimy seaweed flopped back and forth. "I doubt it. By the time the Sembians and the shades pulling their strings turn their attention to me, the church of Umberlee will control every port and coast, no matter who the nominal lord may be. And if my enemies succeed in bringing a force against me even so, the goddess will give me the strength to smash them."

"I mean no irreverence, Captain, when I point out that the Queen of the Depths, mighty as she is, isn't the only deity in the world, nor is hers the only priesthood."

At last, Evendur's corpse face twisted into an expression Umara could interpret: a sneer. "They're the only ones that matter hereabouts. I'm making sure of it. Go home and tell Szass Tam that if he approaches me with the proper reverence, I may look on his petitions with favor. If not, Thayans can expect ill winds, sea serpents, and yes, the attentions of my pirates, whenever they set sail from Bezantur. The waveservant will show you out." He turned and strode out through one of the doorways along the wall.

Umara sighed and reached for Kymas with her thoughts. *Did you follow all that?* she asked.

Yes, replied the vampire mage. *The creature's an arrogant buffoon.* Even though the words were scornful, the underlying feeling wasn't. Kymas was impressed, perhaps even rattled, as his lieutenant had never known him before. Had they been conversing in the normal way, he likely would have concealed any trace of it beneath a facade of urbane imperturbability, but that was more difficult with their psyches linked.

Whatever you think of Highcastle's judgment, Umara said, *he manifestly is a Chosen. But now that we've established that, what are we supposed to do about it?*

You know, my dear. You know.

That's fine to say, but how are we supposed to manage it? Looking through my eyes, you saw how strong the creature is and, when I used the talisman, perceived his spiritual strength as well, but for argument's sake, let's say our wizardry could overpower him. We'd also have to contend with all the temple defenses, mystical and mundane, get off Pirate Isle, and escape across stormy seas that the raiders know how to sail better than our mariners ever will.

I'll think of something, Kymas said. *I haven't worked as long as I have and climbed as high as I have only to fail Szass Tam now.*

Umara might have found that dauntless attitude more inspiring if she hadn't suspected that only she and Kymas's other servants would have to pay the ultimate price for failure. She'd fall with a half-uttered spell on her lips, and the legionnaires would drop with bloody swords sliding from their hands, while the vampire slipped away to safety in the form of a fluttering bat or drifting mist.

It wasn't that Kymas was cowardly. She'd known him to brave considerable dangers when he judged circumstances warranted it. But never to spare or save one of his mortal agents. In his eyes, the living were so far beneath him that he sent them to their deaths with no more hesitation than a lanceboard player sacrificing pawns.

"Saer?" said a half-familiar voice. Umara blinked and discerned that in the moment when she'd turned her attention inward—or to the undead mage secreted on the Thayan vessel in the harbor, depending on how one cared to look at it—her escort had approached her. "The Chosen said it's time for you to go."

"Of course," she said, "lead on." The cleric—who had the hard, truculent look of a youth who'd been a pirate until recently—turned away, and she started whispering a spell.

She was trying to be stealthy about it, but the waveservant either heard her or simply sensed something amiss. He jerked back around with the tines of his trident dropping to threaten her.

Then she spoke the final word of the rhyming incantation, and the pugnacity in his face gave way to blinking confusion. That in turn melted into chagrin, and he hastily turned the points of his weapon away from her.

"I'm sorry!" he said. "I don't know what I was thinking."

Umara smiled. "It's all right. Something just startled you, I suppose."

The young priest shook his head. "I suppose. Still, if I hurt one of Captain Highcastle's guests . . ."

"If you want to make it up to me, how about letting me look around a little? I'll come back to the main entrance when I'm ready to leave."

He hesitated. "The Chosen said to show you out."

"That's exactly what you will do after I've looked my fill." Hoping he found her attractive—she'd observed that non-Thayan men sometimes did despite the shaved head and tattoos they deemed bizarre—she gave him a smile. "Please? The temple is magnificent, and I know you need to get back to your post."

The waveservant sighed. "I guess I do. Otherwise, I'd show you around myself. Just don't be too long, all right?" Resting his trident on his shoulder, he took his leave.

That was risky, Kymas observed. *What if the beguilement failed?*

It didn't, Umara replied, *and now I can search.*

For what?

Anything that will help us.

She skulked to one of the doorways behind the well. Beyond it was a smaller room where a cylindrical screen revolved around a greenish magical flame. The screen had shark shapes on it, and thus the light cast shadows of sharks circling the walls. Gold and silver gleamed atop an altar hewn from coral.

A common thief would likely have been happy to snatch the offerings and flee, and for a moment, her pride in her heritage and arcane accomplishments notwithstanding, Umara rather wished she was one. Then she thrust the feckless thought aside and prowled on into the next chamber, and the one after that.

Although she'd never visited a temple of Umberlee before, all great castles, palaces, and the like possessed certain features in common, and she soon discerned that she'd passed from the more public part of the structure to an area where important folk had their apartments and personal workrooms. That had its good side. She'd left the sentries and warding glyphs behind. But if anyone noticed her trespassing, it might well be someone less easily befuddled than her erstwhile escort.

In time, her search led her to a map room. Some hung on the walls, many were rolled up with their ends protruding from cubbyholes, and others lay spread on long tables where round brass weights kept the corners from curling up.

All the ones she could see were nautical charts. Spaces inland from the coasts were mostly blank, but the parchments were replete with information about the tides, reefs, shoals, and even the tiniest islets of the Sea of Fallen Stars. Some even pinpointed features in the uttermost depths like the sea elf city of Myth Nantar.

It occurred to Umara that the knowledge stored here might be even more valuable than the coins and jewelry she'd already left unpilfered. But it seemed just as irrelevant to her present needs, and so she began to turn away. Then dark spots caught her eye.

Specifically, greasy-looking smudges on one of the charts unrolled on a tabletop and the several smaller parchments scattered around it. In her imagination, Evendur traced lines on the map with a fingertip and held the papers before his eyes to read them, and exudate from his rotting skin left stains.

She headed for the table in question. When she was halfway there, she heard a faint creak of leather at her back. Someone was coming.

She hastily stepped aside so no one could see her from the other side of the doorway. But that wouldn't protect her for long, not in a room with nowhere to hide and no other exits. She whispered a spell, swept her hand from the top of her head down the front of her body, and cloaked herself in invisibility.

A moment later, Evendur himself strode into the chartroom, and she swallowed away a sudden dryness in her throat. In that instant, she found it all but impossible to place any faith in the basic magic she'd employed to conceal herself.

Yet if the spell was basic, her skills were not, and evidently even the Chosen had their limitations. Evendur stalked on past her.

That was good as far as it went, but if the Queen of the Depths chose this moment to peer out through Evendur's eyes, it was inconceivable that the charm would blind her. Breathing shallowly and holding still, Umara could only hope the deity had other matters to concern her.

Evendur moved to the same chart and notes that had snagged Umara's interest and studied them with the glum air of a man who, despite a lack of fresh facts or insights, had succumbed to the urge to resume picking at a vexing problem. Eventually, he tossed down a parchment to slide off the table and spill to the floor, made a disgusted growling noise, and turned back toward the door.

Umara started to relax at least a little, and then the Chosen stopped short. Frowning—another expression just barely identifiable despite the bloat and decay—he peered about.

He senses he isn't alone, Umara thought, and now that he's set his mind to it, he's going to spot me. If he can't do it by himself, he'll call on Umberlee to help him.

Strike first! Kymas said. He knew as well as she did how unlikely she was to prevail, but if by some miracle she did, he'd reap the benefit, and if she perished, he might learn something useful from the manner in which the Chosen opted to kill her.

She, however, had no intention of revealing herself by initiating combat or otherwise so long as any alternative remained. She whispered a cantrip, stretched out her hand, and shook it back and forth. The rolled maps in one of the floor-level cubbies rustled.

Evendur strode to the source of the noise, crouched down, and peered into the nook. Umara knew he wasn't going to find anything but hoped she'd allayed his suspicions even so. Mice were good at vanishing when larger creatures approached, and they infested nearly every manmade structure from time to time. With luck, the Temple of Umberlee was no exception.

Evendur snorted and stood back up. He took a last look around, then headed for the door.

Once she was sure he was truly gone, Umara let out a long breath. Her shoulders slumped, and her hands began to tremble. But she didn't have time to fall apart, so, scowling at her own frailty, she stifled the aftereffects of her close call by pure force of will and hurried to the table.

It took longer than she would have preferred to consider the chart and the papers, which proved to be dispatches from spies stationed at various points around the Sea of Fallen Stars. But no one else turned up to interrupt her, and by the end of the examination, she was smiling.

Thanks to their psychic link, she knew Kymas was smiling, too. She could even tell his fangs had extended thanks to a phantom sensation in her own mouth.

Easy prey, her master said, *yet a prize that will fully satisfy Szass Tam. We merely have to find the child first.*

CHAPTER TWO

ANTON AWOKE LYING IN THE DARK WITH NO IDEA WHERE HE WAS or what had happened to him. He only knew his head was throbbing and he urgently needed to throw up.

Instinct warned him he mustn't stay on his back lest he end up choking. He tried to roll over onto his side, but something prevented it. In his blind confusion, he couldn't tell whether it was simply that the agony in his head made him spastic or if something external restrained him.

He strained and finally flopped over just in time to retch out the contents of his stomach. Then he passed out.

When he roused again, it was to a telltale rolling beneath him and light shining through his eyelids. Squinting, he discerned that the glow came from a storm lantern in Naraxes's upraised hand. They were in the cramped hold of the *Iron Jest*. The lanky first mate stooped to avoid bumping his head.

Anton's hands and feet were tied, which had likely contributed to the difficulty he'd experienced turning over. Stedd Whitehorn, the boy prophet, was a few steps away and bound in a similar fashion.

Anton wanted to talk sitting up as opposed to lying in a sticky puddle of his own puke, but when he tried to lift himself, the pain in his head, which had subsided to an almost-tolerable ache, exploded back into full-blown pounding torture. "By the Maiden's kiss," he gasped, tears blurring the lantern light, "how many times did you bash me?"

"Just three," Naraxes said. "Just until I was sure you were out. But then the men kicked you around and stamped on you."

"Why? Why mutiny at all when I've led you to dozens of prizes and we'd just seized the biggest one of all?"

Naraxes hesitated as though he might be feeling the slightest twinge of guilt. "I didn't plan it. I just . . . lost my temper, and it went on from there. But it's been coming for a while. You throw our lives away and laugh as the corpses pile up."

"Maybe no one ever told you this, but a pirate's trade is inherently dangerous. And I never required anybody to run a risk greater than the ones I ran myself."

"Still, we've followed you as far as we care to."

"So why let me claim a captain's share of the price on the young preacher's head? I follow that much of your logic. But why bring me back aboard? If you're all so disgruntled, why not finish me off? Or leave me to the pig farmers?"

"You'll remember the gale you insisted on sailing through. There's a chance it's still blowing, or that another will rise, and if we give a life to Umberlee, maybe she'll show mercy to the rest of us."

Anton snorted. It made his head throb. "A little treachery is one thing, but now I'm truly disappointed in you. You've spent too many years at sea to believe you can bribe the weather, by tossing people overboard or otherwise."

Naraxes frowned. "Maybe I didn't always believe it, but I've changed along with the world. You haven't, and that's another reason to get rid of you. Only captains who truly revere Umberlee—and the crews that follow them—will prosper in the days to come."

"And reverence involves more than hunting someone down and trading him for a heap of Evendur Highcastle's gold. Fair enough. But maybe it's not too late for me. Perhaps you, with your deep understanding of spiritual matters, could instruct me in the mysteries of your faith."

Naraxes smiled a crooked smile. "Why settle for a mortal teacher when you'll meet the goddess herself soon enough?"

"Are we absolutely set on that? What if we don't run into a storm?"

"Then a sacrifice will show our gratitude and keep you from reaching Pirate Isle alive to complain you were ill used. The goddess knows, you have no friends there, not as such, but even so, other captains might object to a mutiny."

"And here I was consoling myself with the expectation that all Immurk's Hold would mourn my passing."

"Not likely. But it still seems easier all around if people believe the pig farmers killed you. Make your peace, Captain. We'll come and fetch you when it's time."

Naraxes turned, hung the lantern over his arm, and climbed the ladder that ascended to the main deck. The hatch creaked open, thumped shut, and utter darkness swallowed the hold once more.

"Well," Anton murmured, "that could have gone better." He tried to bring his feet and the hands tied behind his back together.

Pain stabbed down the length of his body. Until this moment, the hammering in his head had masked the full extent of his injuries, but now they announced themselves enthusiastically. He had broken ribs and a broken collarbone for certain, perhaps a broken hip and knee as well, and bruises and swelling everywhere.

But he'd always been strong and limber, and he couldn't afford to let the damage stop him. His breath rasping between his teeth, he strained uselessly until the self-inflicted torture wrung a cry out of him, and he had no choice but to relent.

Panting, he gathered the resolve to try again. Then he heard something sliding and bumping in his direction.

Still addled with pain, he needed a moment to remember his fellow captive and infer that the boy was crawling toward him. "What?" he croaked.

"I can help you," Stedd answered. "Just stay still."

Anton wasn't sure exactly why the boy wanted to help him, but in his current circumstances, he didn't care. He drew breath to instruct Stedd, and then small fingers brushed his forearm.

Surprise kept him from speaking as he'd intended. Stedd's touch was warm, but somehow, not in a way that suggested fever. Rather, the warmth felt right, natural, or at least that was as close as Anton could come to describing the sensation.

"The Morninglord gave me a lot when I was using it to help the village," said the boy. "I don't know how much more I can pull in right now. But whatever I get, you can have."

For a breath or two, nothing more happened, and Anton wondered how, without alienating him, he could convince Stedd to stop playing at being a holy man and do something practical. Then the child gasped, and the warmth in his fingers surged up Anton's arm and into the core of his body, while red and gold light washed across the hold. Because he and his fellow prisoner were lying back to back, Anton couldn't see the source of the glow but assumed Stedd was creating it somehow.

The tingling warmth and the light faded together, and as they did, Anton realized his many pains were dwindling, too. Even when he stretched, twisted, and pulled against his bonds, the resulting discomfort was insignificant compared to the torment he'd suffered mere moments before.

"By the fork," he murmured.

"You should thank Lathander," panted Stedd, a touch of childish exasperation in his voice, "not call out to his enemy."

Folk had gotten out of the habit of thanking Lathander since the god had supposedly disappeared a hundred years ago, but Anton saw no profit in remarking on it. A theological discussion wouldn't get him untied. "If you say so. Now hitch down until you can reach the top of my left boot. Unless my shipmates searched me very thoroughly, there's a skinny little blade riding in a hidden sheath. Pull it out."

Stedd fumbled at the task for a while. Then he said, "I found it, but I can't get it! They tied my hands too tight. My fingers are numb!"

"Never mind," Anton replied. "Roll back out of the way and let me do it."

This time, he managed to contort his body into the necessary position but then discovered his fingers were dead and clumsy, too. As he repeatedly tried and failed to extract the blade, he wondered why the power that had fixed his battered head and body hadn't relieved him of this impediment as well. Maybe it enjoyed spurring men on with false hope and the frantic, futile struggles that ensued.

But his own struggling wasn't futile, or at least not yet. Finally, his thumb and forefinger pinched the end of the knife hilt—really, just the portion of the needle blade that lacked sharp edges—and slid it forth.

He reversed the blade and sawed at the loops of thick, coarse rope constraining his wrists. With the knife in such an awkward attitude, it was impossible to bring any strength to bear. He had to rely on persistence and the keenness of the blade, and they seemed unlikely to get the job done before Naraxes and the other pirates came for him.

But eventually, one strand parted, then another, and then the remaining ones felt looser. Anton set down the knife and struggled to pull his wrists apart. That loosened the coils a little more, and he managed to drag his right hand out of them.

A moment later, his hands stung as though he'd stuck them into a nest of hornets. Teeth gritted, he rubbed them together to restore the circulation as quickly as possible, then picked up the knife and cut his feet free.

"That's got it," he whispered, "I'm loose. Speak up and show me where you are." He'd lost track of the boy's precise location while he was squirming and writhing around.

"Here," answered Stedd.

Anton crawled to him, and, working by touch, cut him free. The boy hissed as he too suffered the pain of returning circulation.

"That will pass in a moment," Anton said, "and then we need to go."

"Where?" Stedd asked.

"The only place there is to go. Up on deck."

29

The boy hesitated. "Aren't the pirates up there?"

"A couple, certainly, but most of them are in their berths asleep." Or at least Anton hoped so.

"But not all?"

"This is our one chance to get off the ship, and it's death for you to stay. Do you understand that?"

Stedd took a long, audible breath. "Yes. And the Morninglord will look out for us."

"*I'm* looking out for us. Follow my lead and we have a chance. Are you ready?"

"Yes."

Anton still had his bearings and thus experienced no difficulty guiding his charge to the ladder. "Wait here until I signal for you to come up," he whispered. "Then do it quietly."

Anton then climbed high enough to crack the hatch open and peek out. Nobody waited on the other side to shout an alarm or jab a spear in his face, so he scuttled on out into the cold, clattering rain, crouched down behind the main mast and the shrouds supporting it, and took a better look around.

He'd inferred from the absolute blackness in the hold that night had fallen, and it wasn't all that much brighter in the open air. The ever-present cloud cover blocked moon- and starlight even more thoroughly than it did sunshine. Still, he could make out enough to decide that his optimistic assumptions had been correct. Except for a helmsman on the quarterdeck and the lookout in the fighting top halfway up the foremast, the weary and decimated pirates were resting below deck.

For a heartbeat, he wondered if it might be possible to catch them all by surprise and somehow coerce them into putting him back in command. Then he snorted at his own foolishness and turned his thoughts to the practical question of how to escape the ship.

He had no way of determining the caravel's precise position but assumed it had traveled too far for him and Stedd to swim ashore.

Even in the unlikely event that he could make it, a child never would. They'd fare better in one of the ship's boats, but he could see no way to launch one without somebody noticing. Unless, that was, no one on deck was in a state to notice anything.

Head bowed and shoulders hunched, he shuffled astern and climbed the companionway to the quarterdeck. When he did, he saw that the current helmsman was One-Ear Grim, a stooped, grizzled fellow whose nickname was something of an exaggeration. He'd lost only the top half of his left ear when someone bit it off in a tavern brawl.

Likely tired of standing alone in the rainy night, One-Ear Grim gave the newcomer a sour look. Then his eyes snapped open wide as he registered who'd joined him at his post. He sucked in a breath and snatched for the cutlass hanging under his cloak.

Anton rushed the other pirate and thrust the narrow-bladed knife into his throat. One-Ear Grim stiffened with his warning cry unvoiced and his weapon only halfway clear of the scabbard. Anton stabbed him twice more, and then the helmsman's legs buckled and dumped him on the deck.

Anton peered down the length of the caravel. As best he could judge, the lookout was still gazing out over the bow, not back at the stern, and hadn't noticed anything amiss.

Anton appropriated One-Ear Grim's mantle, cutlass, dirk, coins, and baubles and manhandled the dead man's body over the rail. Then, still trying to look like he was in no hurry, he returned to the hatch, lifted it, and beckoned.

Stedd swallowed and gave a jerky nod. Despite the powerful magic he'd worked earlier, at the moment he looked like a scared little boy, not anyone's idea of the agent of a deity. But he climbed the ladder without needing to be coaxed.

Anton pulled the child close and wrapped one wing of his stolen cloak around him to conceal him. "Now we go astern."

"What?" Stedd asked.

"Up into the back of the ship."

The jolly boat hung from davits. Anton discarded the tarp that covered it, helped Stedd clamber in, and swung himself in after him. He then untied a pair of knots and let out the lines they'd secured. It was ordinarily a two-man job, but he managed to lower the small craft without simply dropping it into the sea.

Impelled by the moaning wind, the dark mass of the *Iron Jest* quickly receded from the jolly boat. Stedd watched it for a moment, then gave Anton a grin. "We did it!"

"Not yet," Anton replied. He lifted an oar from the bottom of the boat and set it in a rowlock. "Now comes the hard part. I row, and when the boat starts to fill up with rain, you bail."

As the night wore on, Anton discovered exactly how hard the hard part was. His back, shoulders, and arms ached. His hands blistered, and then the blisters broke. But, breath rasping, teeth gritted, he kept hauling on the sweeps, and when a trace of dawn filtered through the clouds on the eastern horizon, the light revealed a stretch of shoreline.

He smiled. But his satisfaction gave way to dismay when he saw that Stedd had set his bailing bucket back in the bottom of the boat and was staring at the eastern sky, whispering.

Anton was no priest, but like most people, he understood that folk with a connection to a supernatural power renewed their abilities through prayer and meditation. Judging from appearances, Stedd was doing that now.

If not for the boy's magic, Anton would still be lying broken and bound in the belly of his former ship, but that didn't mean it would be wise to allow Stedd further access to his talents. A prisoner who lacked the ability to cast spells was apt to prove less troublesome than one who could.

Yet it was also true that since fleeing the caravel, Stedd had seemed increasingly at ease in Anton's presence. Perhaps it was because a frightened child needed someone to trust, despite excellent reasons to the contrary. At any rate, if Stedd failed to grasp that his fundamental circumstances hadn't changed, perhaps it would behoove his sole remaining captor to keep him confused as long as possible. That too might make him easier to manage.

If that was the tack Anton intended to take, he needed an excuse for interrupting Stedd's prayers. He thought for a moment then barked, "Keep bailing!"

Startled, the boy jerked around to face him. "I'm supposed to pray at sunrise. And you take little rests every once in a while."

"I forgot you're a landlubber. Otherwise, you'd realize the boat's sprung a leak. We need one last long, hard push or we'll sink before we make it ashore."

Stedd looked down at his feet. Fortunately, with the rain constantly replacing the water he scooped out, it certainly looked as if the clinker-built hull might be leaking, and with a resolute scowl, he grabbed the pail again.

Stifling a grin, Anton took a fresh hold on the oars.

Not long after dawn gave way to morning, the jolly boat ran aground several paces away from a strip of mud and weeds, and the two fugitives waded the rest of the way ashore. Anton was poised to grab the boy if he tried to run, but there was no need. Stedd just looked around with a dazed expression that suggested he couldn't believe they'd actually reached land. Or that he was too exhausted to think or do anything more at all.

If it was the latter, Anton could sympathize, but he mustn't allow himself to slip into a similar condition. He scanned the gray, heaving sea and then the desolate shore with its windblown grasses and scrub pines slumped and dripping beneath the weight of the rain. To his relief, no threats were in sight. Not yet.

"Rest," he said. "On the ground, if you like, although if you're like me, those benches gave you your fill of sitting. Just don't fall asleep. In a little while, we need to look for food and shelter."

Stedd peered back, and Anton was struck again by how blue the captive's eyes were even on another dismal day. "Good," said the boy at length, "I'm hungry. But then what?"

"You mean, what am I going to do with you?"

"Well . . . yes."

"You know I'm a pirate," Anton said, "and I meant to collect the bounty on your head. But I give you my word, that was before you saved my life."

Stedd smiled. "The Morninglord told me to."

"So I could help you escape, I imagine. Anyway, you and I are comrades now—shipmates, thanks to our noble vessel beached yonder in the surf—and shipmates don't betray one another."

As soon as the words left Anton's mouth, he remembered that Stedd had only recently witnessed multiple demonstrations to the contrary. But likely punchy with fatigue, the boy gave every indication of taking the ludicrous statement seriously.

"Then will you go on helping me?" Stedd asked. "Can you help me go where I need to?"

"Where's that?"

"Sapra."

Inwardly, Anton winced. As a notorious reaver, he had nooses and worse awaiting him all around the Sea of Fallen Stars, and seldom did he permit the threat of them to deter him from plying his trade. But for the most part, he steered clear of his homeland; folk there recalled him with a special hatred.

Fortunately, he had no actual reason to take Stedd all the way to Sapra or anyplace else in Turmish. But he might as well say he would. Because then the boy would willingly accompany him on a trek east.

East made sense because Teziir lay in the opposite direction, and the city-state's patrols would still be on the lookout for sea raiders. Besides, if Anton failed to procure a ship or sailboat capable of reaching Pirate Isle before he came to Westgate, he could surely find one there. Westgate was a major port, and like any outlaw worthy of the name, he had contacts among its thieves' guilds and criminal fraternities.

"Yes," he lied, "I'll take you to Sapra. After all that's happened, I owe it to you."

THE REAVER

Umara tapped on a hatch carved with a scene of a Thayan fleet vanquishing an anonymous enemy armada. She wondered how long ago the naval victory had happened or if, in fact, it had ever truly happened at all. As she and Evendur Highcastle had discussed, Thay, for all its might, had never been much of a naval power, and its history was less than replete with glorious triumphs at sea.

"Come in, my friend," Kymas called.

She did and immediately had to detour around a folding screen positioned to block out every trace of sunshine. Even the sad, wan excuse for daylight currently sifting down amid the rain could sear a vampire's skin like flame.

Someone had secured the storm covers so the portholes couldn't admit any light, either, and only the greenish glow of cool magical fire illuminated the cabin, but that sufficed to reveal the clutter. Kymas hadn't required the displaced captain to remove his possessions before bringing in his own. A rack of staves stood shoved up against a suit of half plate on a stand like the bars of a torture cell; a spindly, jointed figure resembling an unstrung marionette made of black and scarlet metal sprawled across the lid of a sea chest; and volumes of arcane lore were jammed into the little bookshelf alongside rutters and a manual of naval regulations.

Tall, slender, and so pale that the viridian light turned him green as well, Kymas sat gazing at the end of his arm. There was no hand sticking out of the voluminous crimson sleeve of his robe, just wisps of vapor.

Umara had watched her master practice the trick a hundred times but still didn't see the point. What use would it ever be for Kymas to turn a portion of his body to mist while keeping the rest solid? Perhaps it was simply a pastime for idle moments.

He smiled at Umara, and the fog congealed into long, tattooed fingers and a thumb. "Have we left the harbor?" he asked.

"Yes," Umara said, "and the captain says no other ship followed us." From what she understood, it wasn't unknown for the marauders of Pirate Isle to cheerfully conduct business with outsiders who risked dropping anchor there, then attack them when they sought to depart.

"I doubted anyone would," the vampire replied, "given that we're supposedly carrying Captain Highcastle's answer to our lord and master. Still, it's helpful to be sure. It frees us to focus on the business at hand."

"We'll need to focus," Umara said.

Kymas arched an eyebrow, or rather, the smooth bit of alabaster skin where an eyebrow would be if, at some point during his mortal life, a barber hadn't permanently removed it. "That sounded grim. I trust you aren't having second thoughts about the plan that your own audacity made possible. Because I agree it's a better bet than trying to abduct the Chosen of Umberlee."

"That doesn't mean it will be easy. The church of Umberlee is already hunting for this Stedd Whitehorn. So are scores of pirates and, I'm sure, other knaves who hope to sell him to Evendur. Somehow, we need to find the boy ahead of all of them."

"And so we will. Watch and learn."

The undead mage snapped his fingers, and, clinking, the faceless black-and-red metal construct reared up from the lid of the sea chest. It then leaped to the top of a small table and proceeded to clear it, jumping to the floor with one item, setting it down, then springing back up for another.

Meanwhile, Kymas extricated a rutter from the bookshelf. He flipped through the first several pages, then put the book down on the table open to a chart showing the Inner Sea in its entirety.

"Now," he said, drawing a silver lancet from one of the many pockets in his ornately embroidered wizard's robe, "I need just a drop or two of mortal essence."

Inwardly, Umara flinched, but only inwardly. She gave him her left hand, and he pricked the tip of her middle finger. Nearly black in the greenish light, a bead of blood welled out.

Inhaling deeply—smelling the dollop of liquid life he'd just released from Umara's veins—Kymas stared at the bead long enough to give his lieutenant a pang of apprehension. Finally, however, he moved her hand over the open book and squeezed her finger below the tiny puncture. Drops of blood pattered down onto the map, and then he let her go.

Pinching with the thumb and forefinger of her other hand, Umara applied pressure to stanch the bleeding. All right, she told herself, it's over, and you're fine. Now do what he told you: watch and learn.

Kymas fixed his steel-gray eyes on the rutter and placed his hands just in front of and to either side of his face. It was a posture that always reminded Umara of a draft horse wearing blinders, but it was actually called the Window, and it was used for spying out that which was hidden.

Kymas then growled and hissed an incantation in the tongue of Thanatos, the Belly of Death, the layer of the Abyss where Orcus, Prince of the Undead, held sway. Now that liches, ghosts, and their ilk controlled the councils of the Red Wizards, the language had come into fashion for many sorts of magic, and Umara had perforce mastered it even though simply listening to it made her lightheaded and queasy.

It had an effect on Kymas, too. His upper canines lengthened, and his eyes became chatoyant, flashing in the emerald light like mirrors.

As his recitation continued, he invoked Orcus and the demon prince's vassals Glyphimbor, Sleepless, and Doresain the Ghoul King. He called on Kiaransalee and Velsharoon as well, extinct powers whose names nonetheless still exerted pressure on the fabric of All. Meanwhile, the sprinkled spatters of blood crawled toward one another like slugs.

As their paths converged, they fused together into a single writhing blob, which ultimately reared up in the form of a tiny humpbacked imp with stunted wings. The miniscule demon cast this way and that like a hound trying to pick up a scent, then scuttled across the map to the western stretch of the southern shore. There, it pointed repeatedly, jabbing with a clawed finger.

Kymas smiled. "The Black Lord is smiling on us. It won't take too long to reach that stretch of coast."

The blood imp looked up at its captor and gave a little cry like the cheep of a chick. There were no words in it, but no experienced mage would have needed them to understand what the creature wanted. It had done its summoner's bidding and now wished to return to the underworld.

"Later," Kymas told it, "when I have the child in my hands."

The captive spirit howled—which still sounded more like cheeping than anything else—and shook its fist. The vampire put an abrupt end to its tantrum by flipping the rutter shut and squashing it inside.

"Even spirits as lowly as this one will test you," Kymas said. "Never tolerate their impudence. Or defiance from any underling, come to think of it."

"Thank you for giving me the benefit of your wisdom," Umara said. "I'll tell the captain where we need to go."

"In a moment," the vampire replied. "First, I need your help with something else." He held out his hand, and her heart started thumping because it was clear what he wanted.

She felt a witless urge to remind him he had a ship full of servants he could use to slake his thirst but knew it would do no good. She was the mortal whose blood he'd seen and smelled with the vileness of the Abyss reverberating through his mind, and she was the one he craved.

She steeled herself with the certainty that he wouldn't kill her. Even in the grip of his thirst, he had a wizard's self-control, and she was useful. Nor would he transform her into a thing like himself. In his eyes, she hadn't earned it yet. Then she tugged her cloak and robe away from her throat and went into his embrace. There was nothing else she could do.

"I knew the trick had worked," Anton continued, "when I heard a great scraping and grinding, the Sembian ship lurched to a sudden stop, and her crew went staggering across the deck. Some even tumbled over the rail. As I'd hoped, the fact that they drew a finger length more than we did made all the difference. They had to stay hung up on those rocks and watch the *Iron Jest* sail away into the night."

Stedd grinned. "Tell another story."

"I can't think of any more," Anton lied. When he'd decided to play the part of the boy's friend as opposed to his captor, it hadn't occurred to him that the role would involve providing entertainment.

In fairness, he could scarcely blame the lad for seeking some distraction from the misery of trudging mile after wet, hungry, weary mile. Look as they might, they could find nothing growing wild that looked edible, nor even a forsaken cottage or shepherd's lean-to to provide a respite from the cold, stinging rain. The only structures that came into view were offshore, where the thatched rooftops of drowned villages resisted, for a little while longer, the shoving and dragging of the surf.

But curse it, Anton wasn't some wandering busker, and he was miserable, too. Too miserable to chatter endlessly for a child's amusement.

Stepping around a mud puddle, Stedd said, "Then what about things that happened to other pirates? There are a lot of you, aren't there?"

"I thought you were supposed to be holy," Anton growled. "Are you even allowed to enjoy tales of cutthroats preying on innocent folk?"

Stedd blinked. "I . . . I've liked tales of pirates and outlaws ever since I was little. Since long before Lathander spoke to me. Do you think it's bad?"

Anton reminded himself that he was trying to keep the child calm and cooperative, not upset him. "No, there's no harm in it. I doubt a few stories will twist you out of true." He smiled a crooked smile. "When I was your age, I relished tales of the brave heroes of the Turmishan navy hunting down fiendish pirates, so plainly, their influence was minimal."

Stedd mulled that over for several paces. Then he said, "Tell one of those stories."

Anton scowled. "Curse it, lad," he began, and then saw the boy had stopped listening to him.

That was because the landscape ahead had snagged his attention. Anton knew little about farming. He'd spent his childhood in Alaghôn, the capital of Turmish, and his adult life at sea. But now that Stedd had drawn his attention to it, even he could see a difference between the terrain they'd covered since coming ashore and what lay before them.

The marshy fields at their backs were either abandoned or had never known cultivation in the first place. Up ahead, somebody was still trying to grow barley and peas, even though the combination of meager sunlight and relentless, battering rain made both crops look anemic.

"Good eye," Anton said. "Someone still lives hereabouts. Farther along this very trail, I imagine." He drew his new cutlass an inch to make sure it was loose in the scabbard, then slid it back. The curved brass guard clicked against the mouth of the sheath.

Stedd frowned. "Why did you do that?"

"I have some coin, and I'll buy food and a cloak for you if the folk up ahead will sell them. But I've heard reports of people hoarding food who won't part with it at any price."

The boy frowned. "We can't just steal it."

Clearly, Stedd was in little danger of growing up to be a pirate. "Aren't you an important person?" Anton asked. "Don't I need to get you to Sapra, no matter what it takes?"

"It . . . it doesn't work like that. I'm not special, just my work is, and anyway, you can't walk the wrong path and get to the right place."

"Whatever that means. Look, I'm not an idiot. I'd prefer *not* to have to take on the task of terrorizing an entire hamlet all by myself. Why don't we just walk on and see what we see?"

The boy nodded. "All right."

As they advanced, the village gradually took shape amid the rain. The rising waters of the Inner Sea had nearly encroached on its northern edge, and a few small boats were beached there, but nothing capable of weathering serious storms, eluding the *Iron Jest,* and reaching Pirate Isle. If the locals had ever possessed a proper fishing vessel, they'd lost it in the upheavals of the last few years.

Closer still, and Anton caught the clamor of raised voices. Though it was difficult to make out words amid the hiss of the rain, he didn't think he and Stedd were the cause of the excitement. So far, he could see no sign that anyone had spotted their approach. Still, he made sure the boy prophet walked behind him, lest he lose Evendur Highcastle's bounty to a nervous peasant's sling stone or javelin.

The noise subsided to a degree before Anton peeked warily around the corner of a house and found its source. Maybe that was because the gaunt, white-haired woman slumped in the grips of two strong men had screamed pleas and vilifications until her voice gave out. Now she simply watched with tears steaming down her wrinkled face as a line of her neighbors carried a stool, a spinning wheel, garments, a wilted-looking cabbage, and some ceramic jars that likely held preserved or pickled foodstuffs out of her cottage. An Umberlant priest armed with a trident and wrapped in a blue-green mantle patterned to resemble fish scale watched the despoliation, too, but his square, middle-aged face with its wide mouth and fringe of beard wore a smirk of satisfaction.

Anton's mouth watered at the sight of the food, but the presence of the waveservant interested him even more. Had the cleric heard about Stedd? Did he know that the new leader of the church of Umberlee wanted him?

Unfortunately, it was possible that even a priest in this obscure little settlement knew about every aspect of the situation, the bounty included, and would be happy to claim every copper of it for himself. After being betrayed once, Anton was reluctant to seek help from anyone else who might do the same. He needed to find his own way back to Immurk's Hold and deliver Stedd to Evendur Highcastle with his own two hands.

He wondered if the waveservant would recognize the lad on sight. Maybe, their hunger notwithstanding, it would be wiser to withdraw and—

Stedd rendered such deliberations moot by darting around Anton and out into the open. "Stop!" he cried, his child's voice shrill.

CHAPTER THREE

STARTLED, THE VILLAGERS GAWKED AT STEDD. ANTON HURRIED up to stand beside him. "This is none of our business," he said from the corner of his mouth.

Although he didn't mean for anyone but the boy to hear it, the warning made the waveservant sneer. "Indeed it isn't, stranger. Indeed it isn't. You and the child stay out of it. Unless you care to come to the shore and offer with the rest of us."

Perhaps it was the fact that Anton had only just escaped the identical fate that made him feel a pang of disgust. "You're going to drown the old woman?"

"We are. She's feeble and useless. She takes food from the mouths of those who still contribute to the village. She needs to die."

"No," said Stedd, "you mustn't do it. It's wrong."

The priest's mouth tightened. "No, child, it isn't. Listen and learn. Umberlee has become the greatest deity hereabouts, and, I truly believe, in all the world. The wise know this because the sea keeps rising to demonstrate her power. Thus, her will—her creed—is right by definition. And she teaches us to love strength, hate weakness, and worship her before all other gods or goddesses. Those who follow her path will thrive. Misery and death await all others."

"But that isn't true," argued Stedd, addressing not just the waveservant but everyone within earshot. "Umberlee *isn't* making it rain. The world is being reborn, and the Great Rain is part of the birth pains. Like all such pains, it will come to an end, and when it does, we can live in a time better than any we've known before. But it depends on how we act now. If we hold onto kindness and hope even when it's hard, tomorrow will be good. But if we turn vicious and hurt even our own neighbors, then it won't matter that the sun is shining and the crops are growing, because we'll still be like wild starving dogs on the inside."

Anton's eyes narrowed in surprise. Aboard the *Jest*, Stedd had demonstrated a remarkable ability to heal, but in the time since, he'd mostly seemed like a normal little boy. Now, however, the wandering prophet who'd annoyed the church of Umberlee by preaching a doctrine diametrically opposed to its own stood revealed, with a confidence in his stance and a conviction in his voice that lent weight to his words despite his youth. In fact, it was possible the contrast served to make his entreaty all the more impressive.

Certainly, some of the villagers looked interested if not dumbfounded. The waveservant, however, laughed a nasty laugh. Before the Great Rain, he'd likely lived a relatively unassuming life. The other villagers would have turned to him when it was time to sacrifice to his savage goddess for a safe voyage or good fishing but wouldn't have tolerated him trying to tell them what to believe or order them around. Now, however, he seemed confident—indeed, arrogant—in his new leadership role.

"Madness," he said, "madness and impudence. *I am a priest.* The wisdom of a deity informs every word I say. Can you say the same, little boy? If not, I suggest you shut your mouth."

"Yes," Anton said, "do that." He took hold of Stedd's shoulder to pull him back.

But the boy twisted away with surprising strength. "I can 'say the same.' Because *Lathander* speaks through me."

That declaration brought another moment of quiet, and then the waveservant laughed again. "If you're going to trade in blasphemy, you should at least bring your lies up to date. The Morninglord died a hundred years ago."

Stedd shook his head. "He didn't. For a while, he had to stop being what he was, but now he can be again. He can shine the light he shined before."

"Gibberish." The priest shifted his gaze to Anton. "But blasphemy nonetheless. Take your lunatic ward away from here before my duty obliges me to take him *from* you."

"Everyone is looking at me," said Stedd, once more addressing the crowd at large. "Don't. Look in the eyes of the kinswoman and neighbor you're about to kill. And if you're too ashamed to do it, learn from that. It's the good part of your soul trying to stop you from doing something awful."

Villagers muttered to one another. Then a woman who held a couple of the ceramic pots said, "I don't . . . I mean, Aggie *is* kin to me on my mother's side."

"To me, too," said a runt of a man bundled up in gray. With a deferential if not apologetic demeanor, he turned to the waveservant. "I know we complain, Saer, but we're not starving yet. We catch some fish."

The priest sneered. "And how long do you think *that* will last if you fail to honor the Queen of the Depths?"

"We could sacrifice something else," the small man said. "Maybe a chicken. I have an old hen that's stopped laying."

"Quiet!" the cleric snapped, and the word carried a charge of magic like the crack of a whip. The runt jerked and made a choking sound as the command momentarily deprived him of the power of speech. Other villagers flinched.

"Don't be afraid," said Stedd. "The waveservant is trying to bully you into doing what he wants. But if you say no, the Morninglord will protect you."

The priest scowled. "Let's put that lie to the test. Let's see your dead god protect *you*." He snatched a little seashell from a pocket of his cloak and squeezed it in his fist until it cracked. Three streaks of greenish blur wavered into being in the air before him, then, in just a heartbeat, put on definition and solidity.

45

The sahuagin were the size of men, with shark-like heads complete with fangs, crests of fin running down their spines, and tridents in their clawed, webbed fingers. Gill slits dilated and contracted in the sides of their scaly necks, but they were entirely capable of surviving out of water long enough to make an example of a "blasphemer" and his hapless companion.

Somehow comprehending without being told what their summoner desired, the sea devils lumbered forward. Peasants screamed and scrambled to distance themselves from the creatures.

Anton shot Stedd a glance. "You said your god would protect us."

"Yes," said Stedd, his blue eyes wide, "but not through me! I couldn't get my magic back because I had to bail out the rowboat."

For an instant, Anton imagined himself stepping aside and waving the sahuagin on by to stab and claw the boy to pieces. But satisfying as that might be, it would mean giving up the bounty.

He yanked his cutlass from its scabbard. "Stay back!" he said, and then the sea devils shambled into striking distance.

In his experience, these brutes were strong, ferocious, and skillful with their chosen weapons, but not especially agile on land. That appeared to be the only advantage he possessed, but maybe if he maneuvered constantly and forced the sahuagin to keep turning back and forth, it would be enough. He parried an initial trident thrust, dodged right, and slashed.

His target jerked back from the blade, and a cut that might have been lethal merely split the leathery hide above its ribs. He lunged to make a follow-up attack, but the sea devil blocked quarterstaff-style with the shaft of its trident, then jammed the length of wood into him and heaved him staggering backward.

Anton struggled to recover his balance as his feet slipped in the mud. He was still floundering when his adversary's trident leaped at his face.

Incapable of any other defense, he threw himself down in the muck, and the three-pointed weapon shot over him. He rolled to one knee and slashed. The cutlass sliced the sea devil's leg, and it staggered and roared.

By that time, the other two sahuagin had circled their comrade to threaten Anton anew, but they faltered for a heartbeat as though his dive to the ground had surprised them. It gave him time to jump up and scramble left, obliging them to change their facing once more.

He scored twice more in the moments that followed, once on the hobbling foe he'd wounded initially and once on a fresh one. But, armored by their scales, neither dropped.

Curse it, he had to dispatch the enemy faster than this or they'd surely kill him instead. Energized by combat, he no longer felt weary and hungry but recognized that for the illusion it was. Soon, he was going to slow down, the sea devils would finally succeed in surrounding him, and that would be that.

Time to take bigger chances, then. He extended the cutlass and hurled himself forward.

The all-out running attack might well be his last if the sahuagin he'd targeted—the lamed one—simply shifted its longer weapon into line to spit him. But it reacted a hair too slowly, and the cutlass punched into its throat and half ripped its head off as he sprinted by.

Grinning, he wrenched himself around. Then his momentary elation gave way to dismay.

One sea devil broke away and started toward Stedd. Sidestepping, its fellow positioned itself and leveled its trident to keep Anton from rushing in pursuit.

Anton stepped into the distance, inviting an attack, and drew one in the form of a stab to the belly. He parried with all his strength, and that was forceful enough not merely to deflect the trident but to make the sahuagin fumble its grip on it. He lunged, cut, and the creature reeled. He charged around it.

By then, the sea devil that was after Stedd had backed him up against a wall. Either the idiot boy hadn't had sense enough to run out of the village or else the shacks and ring of spectators had hemmed him in.

Anton cut into the sahuagin's spine with its spiny, scalloped fin. The shark man stumbled, shuddered, then fell down into a puddle.

The resulting splash almost covered the sound of footsteps charging up behind Anton as he'd rushed behind the creature he'd just dispatched. Almost, but fortunately, not quite. Realizing that, despite the wound he'd given it the sahuagin that had attempted to bar his path was still on its feet, he whirled to face it.

Sure enough, here it came, with blood pouring down from the gash on the top of its head. Hoping the flow was getting in its yellow eyes and blinding it, he decided to feint high and cut low. But then a strangling pain erupted in his chest, and he doubled over retching brine.

Well behind the creature, the waveservant grinned and brandished his trident over his head. In his struggle to best the shark men, Anton had all but forgotten the foe who'd whisked them to the battlefield, but now he realized Umberlee's servant had cast a spell on him.

The sahuagin poised its trident for a thrust. Anton feebly waved his cutlass but could do nothing more. Until he finished expelling the conjured seawater from his airways, he'd be as incapable of self-defense as any other drowning man.

Then a high voice screamed, and a different trident pierced the sea devil's flank at the spot where a human carried his kidney. His face contorted, Stedd worked to shove the heavy, triple-pointed spear deeper into the sahuagin's flesh. The creature hissed and swung its own weapon high for a counterthrust down at its assailant.

Anton's chest and throat still burned, and he couldn't stop gasping. But gasping was breathing, and if he could breathe, he could fight. He hacked the sahuagin's leg out from under it and finished the job of splitting its skull when it fell.

Then he straightened, smiled at the waveservant, and took satisfaction in the flicker of alarm in the other man's expression. "What's the matter," he rasped, "all out of summoning spells?"

The waveservant looked to his parishioners. "Kill him!" he cried. "While he's still weak!"

After a moment, three of the rougher-looking villagers started forward. But with a theatrical flourish, Anton slowly swept the cutlass, now gory from point to guard, in their direction. They balked.

"For your own sakes," said Anton, "don't. Leave the priest and me to settle this between ourselves." He strode forward, and the rustics scurried to clear his path.

For a moment, the waveservant looked like he was considering turning tail. Then his square face twisted. He hissed words that sounded less like human language than breakers curling and foaming toward a shore, and on the final syllable, jabbed his trident in the direction of his oncoming foe.

Nothing seemed to happen. But intuition prompted Anton to glance back. Streaming up into the air from a puddle, rippling water gathered itself into the shape of a floating trident. If he hadn't turned, it would have struck him down by surprise. As it might spear him yet, for as he knew from past experience, he couldn't destroy such a manifestation of magic by any means at his disposal.

He ducked its first thrust, whirled, and ran, zigzagging to throw off its aim. The trick enabled him to reach the waveservant unscathed.

That accomplishment meant he'd now have to contend with two stabbing tridents instead of one, but he didn't care. All that mattered was that at long last, his true foe was finally within reach.

Anton cut at the waveservant's head, and the priest blocked the stroke with his trident. The pirate then sprang to the side and discovered an instant later that he'd timed the trick properly. The flying trident streaked through the space he'd just vacated toward its creator.

Unfortunately, though, the three tines splashed harmlessly against the waveservant's chest. Then the scattered droplets flew back together to reform them as the trident spun itself around. Evidently, the magic couldn't harm the man who'd worked the spell. But at least for the moment, both tridents, the one of steel and ash and its counterpart of solidified water, were in front of Anton. That was better than having to worry about a stab in the back.

He beat the mundane trident hard enough to loosen the Umberlant's grip on it. As he'd known it would, the action opened him to a thrust from the flying weapon, but he pivoted back in time to defend with an equally forceful parry. The trident splashed apart, then flew back together as it had before.

But before it could finish reforming, Anton rushed the waveservant. Scrambling backward, the priest dropped the trident and opened his mouth, no doubt to attempt more magic. Happily, to no avail. The cutlass slashed his face and then pierced his heart before he could even start the prayer.

As the waveservant collapsed, Anton spun back around to face the trident of water. He had to dodge one more thrust, and then the weapon fell apart and splashed back onto the ground.

Anton was panting, and his blade shook in his hand. But he couldn't relax yet. He had, after all, just killed the village priest, and although he'd intimidated the locals previously, they might yet find the nerve to try to avenge one of their own.

He turned around to find them gawking at him. He couldn't tell how they felt about what had just happened. Maybe they were still deciding.

Then Stedd walked forward several paces, perhaps so everyone in the crowd could see him clearly. "I'm sorry for this," he said. "We didn't come here to hurt anybody. But the priest brought it on himself. He wanted to prove Lathander couldn't help me, and he paid for his disbelief.

"That means," the boy continued, "he gave his life to teach you all a lesson, but the lesson wasn't what he expected. Will you learn it? Will you choose a different path than the one he was pushing you down? This is the time to decide!"

A big, middle-aged man with shrewd, deep-set eyes squared his shoulders. He looked like the sort of fellow who might have been a village elder or even mayor before hard times and the desperation they engendered allowed the waveservant to usurp everyone else's authority.

"Let Aggie go," the big man said, "and put her things back where they belong."

His body slumping, Anton let the cutlass drop to his side.

THE REAVER

At some point, a sailor, likely at the displaced captain's command, had rigged a little awning stitched from sailcloth to project out from the edge of the quarterdeck over a bit of the main deck. The cover provided some shelter, and Umara had taken refuge beneath it to eat her biscuit and mug of fish stew out of the rain.

It was a decent supper by the low standards of shipboard life. The cook had paid an exorbitant price in Thayan silver for flour while the galley sat at anchor in the harbor of Immurk's Hold, and as a result, the ship's biscuits were currently fresh and soft. A sensible person would enjoy them before they petrified into the usual flavorless, tooth-breaking lumps.

But the best Umara could manage was a few nibbles, even though her body presumably needed nourishment to replace the lost blood. Lingering revulsion robbed her of her appetite.

People claimed a vampire's kiss could induce rapture. With a mix of wistfulness and thankfulness, she wondered why Kymas never bothered to manipulate her emotions in that fashion. Maybe he assumed she already enjoyed the sting of his needle teeth and the suck of his cold lips—she'd certainly been too prudent to indicate otherwise—or perhaps the nature of her experience simply didn't matter to him.

She could only hope that when she herself was undead, predation would feel different from the other side. Because if the act still revolted her, and yet she had to perform it over and over down the centuries of her extended existence . . .

With a scowl, she shoved such anxieties away. Of course, she'd relish drinking blood. Her transformation would sweep away her squeamishness along with any other weak mortal feelings and notions that might otherwise keep her from thriving. It would solve her problems and make her better than she was, and, fixing her mind on that reassuring truth, she slurped in another mouthful of fish, carrots, and lentils.

The taste still failed to stimulate her appetite.

With a sigh, she stuck the remains of her biscuit into a cloak pocket in the hope she'd want it later. Then she walked to the gunwale and flicked the contents of her cup down into the black, benighted sea.

Moments later, the hatch below the quarterdeck clicked open, and Kymas emerged in a red hooded cloak like her own. With his thirst slaked, he looked every inch the mage as courtier, moving in unhurried fashion with a subtle smile on his face. It had taken Umara years to learn to recognize the bare hint of tautness in his posture that revealed something had displeased him.

Fortunately, it didn't appear that the something was her. Kymas gave her a smile and said, "There you are. Good. You can help me sort this out." He raised his voice: "Captain!"

Ehmed Sepandem was an aging Mulan with two missing fingers, a pockmarked sour face, and a disposition to match. Umara sometimes wondered if his bitterness arose from the growing suspicion that his masters deemed his lifetime of service insufficient to merit the supreme reward of undeath. Whatever the cause, he was a tyrant to the crew but came quickly as any common swab when a Red Wizard called him.

"Yes, Lord," Ehmed said.

"Good evening, Captain," Kymas replied. "Do you know, I believe I'm growing accustomed to life at sea. Though shut up in the cabin you were generous enough to lend me, I somehow sensed the ship was making little headway. So I came on deck to see for myself, and sure enough, it's so."

Ehmed glanced back at the lateen sails. "The wind's still from the east, Lord. We're beating into it, but it's slow going."

"That makes sense on its own terms," Kymas said, "but I was under the impression that it was precisely for occasions like this that we have oars."

The captain hesitated. Umara suspected that, like many an underling faced with a superior's unreasonable demands, he was calculating how to explain the realities of the situation without appearing insubordinate.

"The oarsmen rowed all day," he finally said. "They have to eat and rest, or they'll be of no use tomorrow."

"I see your point," Kymas said, "and I apologize. Here we are, Lady Ankhlab and myself, wizards of Thay, guests aboard your vessel, and we should have taken an interest in your problems before this. Let's go down to the first bank."

The first bank of benches was below deck, and the reeking, whip-scarred wretches shackled behind their oars were slaves. Kymas looked around, and then, pointing, said, "I'll have that one."

Even skinnier than his fellows, truly emaciated, the man the vampire had indicated sat slumped motionless and perhaps unconscious over the shaft of his oar. Ehmed grunted. "I don't know what you have in mind, Lord, but that man won't last much longer even with proper use."

"That's why I chose him," the wizard replied. "I like to think I'm a good Banite overall, but I confess to a preference for mercy within the bounds of practicality."

With that, he headed down the aisle between the benches, and Umara and the captain followed. Either sensing something uncanny about the vampire or simply leery of any Red Wizard, slaves shrank from him to the extent their leg irons would allow.

The dying oarsman, however, remained oblivious until Kymas took hold of matted hair crawling with lice and lifted his head. The rower then yelped and tried to slap the Red Wizard's hand away, but Kymas held onto him without difficulty.

The vampire stared into the slave's eyes. "I'm going to set you free. Do you believe me?"

His struggles subsiding, the oarsman stared back. "Yes," he murmured.

"Good." Kymas glanced around at Umara. "Could you do something about these?" He gestured to the cuffs securing the slave's ankles.

Umara didn't have a key to the leg irons, but she didn't need one. Trying not to breathe in the stench of the filth under the benches, she kneeled down and spoke a word of opening, and the magic popped the shackle open.

"Now come along," Kymas said. Hobbling, the mesmerized slave followed him, Ehmed, and Umara up back up onto the main deck.

The upper bank of oars was the responsibility of free men, mariners who performed other duties besides rowing. Naturally, they weren't chained to their benches, but some were resting there even so. In the close confines of the ship, it was a place to sit or stretch out. Others stood in line waiting for the cook to ladle out their evening meals.

"I'd like everyone's attention!" Kymas called, and the crew turned to look at him. "Gather round."

After a moment of nearly universal hesitation, all hands except those occupied with some essential task came closer. Umara had seen such reluctance countless times before. Many Thayan commoners preferred to keep their distance from Red Wizards, especially undead ones.

"Thank you," Kymas said. "Now I don't have to shout to ask who among you understands what I'm trying to accomplish by chasing around the Inner Sea."

Nobody answered.

Kymas nodded. "That's what I thought, so allow me to explain. Over the course of the last couple years, individuals with special gifts have been appearing in various places around Faerûn. Allowed to run wild, these Chosen, as they're called, pose a threat to Thayan interests. But conversely, if someone could lay hands on one of them and fetch him to Szass Tam, our monarch could harness his power to do great things."

Based on her own understanding of magic and all the stories she'd heard about the ruler of her homeland, Umara suspected the prisoner in question wouldn't survive the harnessing. Or else would wish he hadn't.

"So that's my mission," Kymas continued, "and I'm not the first of our master's servants to undertake something similar. I'm told he dispatched an expedition to the Star Peaks but it failed to accomplish its objective, and those agents had to bear the weight of his disappointment."

The vampire ran his gaze over his listeners. "I would very much regret finding myself in the same position, and yet the obstacles in my way are considerable. I've identified a target, but others are seeking him, too. I need to scoop him up before they do. Thus, it dismayed me to learn that the combination of contrary winds and human frailty has slowed our progress to a crawl.

"I can't do anything about the former. I never studied that form of magic. But I can address the latter." Kymas turned to Umara. "Kill the slave."

She felt a twinge of distaste. As every Thayan understood, the lowly lived and died to serve their betters, but unlike some aristocrats, she took no pleasure in the gratuitous mistreatment of slaves. But she supposed it wasn't gratuitous if her superior commanded it, and it might actually be an act of mercy to put the wretch out of his misery.

She murmured rhyming words that filled her mouth with a metallic taste, then breathed on her hand at the end of the incantation. The taste departed, and her hand changed. Catching the light of a nearby storm lantern, her skin glinted. Her fingertips tapered into points, and a ridge like the edge of a knife protruded along the bottom of her hand from the tip of the little finger to the wrist.

As it did, the slave finally shook off the dazed passivity Kymas's gaze had induced and realized what was about to happen. Goggling, he tried to recoil, but the vampire and Ehmed were in the way, and the latter shoved him stumbling back in Umara's direction. She sliced the side of his neck.

Blood jetted, and the slave fell. Kymas waited for him to stop shuddering and then said, "My turn."

The senior wizard made a little snapping motion with his arm, and a wand carved of bone slid out of his voluminous sleeve and into fingers just as ivory-pale. He raised the implement over his head and chanted in the language of Thanatos.

The words and the feeling they engendered, as though the night was a huge black fist closing around the galley, made Umara's ears ache and her temples throb. And she was not alone in her distress. One onlooker vomited. Another sailor scurried into the bow to get as far away as possible. His retreat represented a breach of discipline, but he was evidently willing to risk a flogging.

The corpse twitched, then shuddered. A pale yellow luminescence flowered in its eyes.

"Stand up," Kymas said, and the zombie did. "Everyone, behold an improved oarsman. It doesn't need nourishment or rest. If I wished, it would row without stopping for years on end, until its joints simply fell apart. If I filled the benches with others like it, I would no longer have to worry about making good time."

One of the sailors clenched his fist and touched it to his heart. It was a way of asking the Black Hand to shield him from misfortune. No doubt his fellow mariners likewise recognized that Kymas was threatening them and not merely the slaves.

Kymas smiled. "But alas, the transformation involves a tradeoff. As living men, you possess skills that would depart your bodies along with your souls, and I would hate to see my mission fail for lack of access to those abilities. For that and other reasons, I'd prefer to leave you as you are provided you can muster the will to row for longer periods at a stretch. Can you?"

For a moment, no one answered. Then a man said, "Aye."

Kymas smiled. "Splendid. By all means, have your suppers before you return to the oars." He turned to the zombie. "You, come with me back below."

Where, Umara reflected, the gruesome sight of the creature would provide the same sort of motivation to the slave rowers, and after that, Kymas would bid it return to its station. She wondered how well its bench mate would tolerate having to toil beside it.

When Anton tried to rise from the pallet Aggie had made for him, his body was as stiff as an iron bar. That, along with exhaustion and the relief of resting warm, clean, and dry at last, made him as disinclined to stand up as ever in his life.

Grunting, he struggled to his feet anyway, then contemplated the garments hung near the fire. Any item he put on now would likely still be damp come morning. He supposed it didn't much matter. The rain would find its way inside his cloak soon enough, perhaps before he and Stedd had even left the village.

Still, he simply pulled on his breeches, threw his mantle around his shoulders, and drew up the cowl. Then he opened the cottage door, slipped out, and eased it shut behind him.

Every step squished mud up between his toes, but at least the rain had let up some and merely pattered on his shoulders. He was glad, but months into this sodden catastrophe he knew better than to take that as cause for hope that the precipitation might actually stop. The weather was simply teasing him.

When he reached the shore, he sheltered beneath an apple tree. Except for a couple of stunted green pieces of fruit rotting on the branch, it wasn't bearing. Maybe salt water, diffusing through the soil from the encroaching sea, had poisoned it.

He gazed out across the waves rolling in beneath the cloud cover. Everything was black except for the flicker of lightning far to the northwest.

That dark vista was essentially what he'd hoped to see. Yet for some reason, it set a hollow ache inside him. He supposed it was just another manifestation of his fatigue.

Still, tired as he was, it would be more prudent to stand and watch for a while than just take a single look and return to the cottage. He knuckled his eyes, and then a voice said, "What are you doing?"

Anton turned to see that Stedd, wrapped in the hooded mantle the villagers had given him, had crept up behind him. "You're supposed to be asleep."

"I woke up and saw you sneak out," Stedd replied. "What are you looking for?"

"The lights of the *Iron Jest*. Or of any other ship that might be hunting us. Now go back to bed."

Instead, the boy moved up to stand and look out over the waves beside Anton. "Are you angry at me?"

"I was for a little while," Anton admitted, and then, mindful of his resolve to stay on good terms with his unwitting captive, added a lie: "Not anymore."

"Because I got you into a fight? You didn't want the waveservant to drown Aggie, either. I could tell."

"That doesn't mean I would have chosen to risk my life—and yours—to save her."

"People have to help each other. It's what Lathander wants. It's what Umberlee *doesn't* want."

"If you say so."

Stedd frowned up at him. "Don't you believe Lathander's back?"

Anton shrugged. "How would I know one way or the other?"

"Because I healed you."

"And the magic had to come from somewhere. I follow the logic. But healers aren't all that uncommon, they claim to derive their abilities from many different sources, and in my experience, some of them aren't especially nice people."

"Do you think I'm 'nice'?" Stedd replied.

Anton snorted. "I didn't let the sahuagin have you, so apparently I don't mind you all that much. But here's the nub of it. I'm helping you for your own sake, not some god's. I don't care if Lathander has returned or not. I don't believe any deity is going to put himself out to make my little mortal existence any better. To the extent they notice us at all, the gods want us to serve them, not the other way around."

"That's the bad powers like Umberlee. It's not Lathander, or why did he save Aggie?"

"*I* saved Aggie after—skip it. I don't want to hear that the Morninglord inspired me or gave me strength or whatever rebuttal it is that just popped into your head. I want to know if you understand how lucky we are that this dismal little place is so completely out of touch. If the waveservant had been on the lookout for you, or if any of the locals knew about the price on your head, our afternoon could have turned out very differently."

"I have to speak up for Lathander even when it's dangerous."

"Who'll speak for him if Evendur Highcastle gets his slimy dead hands on you?"

"Maybe somebody who heard me speak before."

"Curse it, boy, do you *want* to die, or do you want to reach Sapra?"

"Sapra. You know that."

"And do you believe it's the will of your Morninglord that has you traveling with a scoundrel who's survived for years with all the navies of the Inner Sea trying to hunt him down?"

"Yes."

"Then mind me. When I tell you it's safe to climb up on a stump and preach, do that. But when I say you need to keep your mouth shut, or tug your hood down, turn, and walk away, you do that, too. Agreed?"

Stedd hesitated, then said, "I can't just turn my back if something truly bad, like what was happening to Aggie, is going on right in front of me."

"The rise of the Church of the Bitch Queen notwithstanding, I doubt we'll find ourselves constantly stumbling across attempts at human sacrifice. That would be bad luck to say the least. Will you follow my lead in less drastic circumstances? I swear on Lathander's sword—"

"He has a mace: Dawnspeaker."

"Fine. I swear on his mace Dawnspeaker that heeding me will increase the likelihood of your reaching Turmish alive."

Stedd frowned, pondering, and then held out his hand. "I promise."

Anton shook the boy's hand and, yielding to a pang of curiosity, said, "What's special about Sapra, anyway? Why is it important that you go there?"

Stedd sighed. "I don't know yet. I wish Lathander would just tell me everything at once, but it doesn't work like that. He lights up things—the things I can see—a little bit at a time."

"Like a sunrise," Anton said.

Stedd grinned. "Yes! At first, when I got out of the camp—"

"The camp?"

The boy waved his hand, seemingly to indicate that "the camp" was far enough behind him that it no longer mattered. "I only knew I had to come south. And even with a war blocking the way, I made it. Then, when I saw the Great Rain, I understood I had to tell people the rise of the sea didn't mean they needed to bow down to Umberlee and follow her teachings. They could still be good and put their trust in Lathander. Then, last month, I realized I needed to go to Sapra."

Anton smiled. "And do . . . something."

"I guess. Anyway, I think that somehow, Sapra is where a thing that's supposed to happen, will. Or won't, if I can't do what I'm supposed to. But I'm going to!"

Anton had to admit, Stedd made it sound interesting. For a moment, it almost seemed a pity that the boy was never going to get within a hundred miles of Sapra.

CHAPTER FOUR

STEDD PEERED ABOUT WITH FASCINATION AT HUMANS, HALF-ELVES, halflings no taller than himself, and even the occasional brown-skinned, fair-haired gnome pushing past one another in the cobbled streets and at vendor's carts, shops, tenements, towers, and flags and banners that, though soaked with rain and hanging lifeless, still lent splashes of color to another gray day. Westgate was plainly larger than Teziir, and that made it the biggest city Stedd had ever visited. He'd been born on a farm, and though he'd passed sizable towns on his journey south and east, the Moonstars had kept him clear of them as a way of keeping clear of the war.

As usual, the thought of the benefactors who had, for reasons they'd said involved some sort of prophecy, spirited him away from the camp and protected him thereafter brought a pang of mingled grief and guilt, the latter because he'd made friends with the very man responsible for their deaths. But he still needed *someone* to help him, and it seemed clear that, despite his past crimes, Captain Marivaldi was Lathander's choice for the task. Stedd could only hope that, as they looked down on him from the afterlife, Questele and the others understood.

Anton interrupted his sad reflections by stopping abruptly. "What is it?" Stedd asked.

"Look," the pirate answered, gesturing toward the block they were about to enter.

Stedd did and saw that many of the doors ahead had trident shapes chalked on them. Frowning, he said, "Those people must all worship Umberlee."

"Or feel a need to placate those who do," Anton said. "Either way, it's a warning to stay alert."

"Or turn around and go somewhere else," Stedd suggested. Actually, the sight of the Bitch Queen's emblem drawn over and over again made him want to denounce her lies and proclaim Lathander's truth in their place. But there was sense in his companion's view that it would be stupid to do so where it was likely to bring about his death.

Anton shook his head. "We assumed the waveservants would have a strong presence in Westgate; they had a decent-sized temple here even before their church started its climb to power. But in this town, there are ways to avoid the attention of those who wish you ill, and I guarantee I can finally get us a suitable boat."

"Aren't we more likely to have trouble with the *Iron Jest*—or some other pirate ship—if we travel by sea?"

Anton took a breath in the way that indicated he was making an effort not to grow impatient. "I've explained to you, I can avoid that, too."

"On horses, we could make good time traveling overland. Couldn't we?"

"With rivers in flood and trails washed out? Don't count on it. Just trust me. Haven't I kept you safe so far?"

That was true enough. Since leaving Aggie's village, Anton had successfully dealt with hungry wolves and a trio of would-be adolescent bandits lying in ambush for whoever happened along.

"Yes," Stedd said, "and I do trust you. Just tell me what to do."

To his surprise, for just an instant, Anton's mouth appeared to tighten ever so slightly, like he was sorry Stedd had conceded the argument. But that made no sense, and the flicker of expression vanished in an instant if it had ever even been present in the first place.

"Just stay close," the Turmishan said, "keep your eyes open, and for weeping Ilmater's sake, resist the urge to preach."

Stedd sighed. "Don't worry about that."

He himself couldn't help fretting, though, as he and his guardian prowled onward and additional signs of the Umberlant church's tightening hold on the city came into view. Bakers, masons, and hatters, folk whose trades had nothing to do with the sea, wore seashell pendants or garments patterned with scales or dyed blue-green. Someone had broken into a potter's establishment, the only shop on its block without a trident on its door, and smashed the crockery. Mostly distressingly of all, perhaps, a shrine to Sune, with caryatids depicting Lady Firehair bracing its crimson door, *did* have a trident scratched on the panel; apparently, even the heartwarders within were conceding the primacy of the Queen of the Depths.

It was wrong and had to stop! Stedd steadied himself with the thought that it would—somehow—when he reached Sapra.

The wet streets took him and Anton gradually downhill until they started catching glimpses of the harbor. According to the pirate, Westgate had once been the third busiest port on the Sea of Fallen Stars with the facilities one would expect of such a hub of trade. The harbor was still busy, but it was also a beleaguered improvisation. The waves surged through the ground floors of partially submerged buildings while, farther out, warning buoys marked the locations of structures the sea had swallowed entirely. The docks had a rickety look because they were temporary, designed to be dismantled, moved, and reassembled when that became necessary to keep them above water.

Eventually, Anton led Stedd down a street so narrow that the two of them nearly blocked it walking side by side. Even to a boy who knew little of city life, the shops had a shabby look to them. A fat man took a wary look around, pulled down his hat, and turned up the collar of his cloak before hurrying away from an apothecary's doorway with a little bottle clutched in his hand. The bent-backed scribe in a cramped box of a shop reflexively hid the document he was working on behind his hand and forearm when Stedd glanced in at him.

Anton stopped in front of a door decorated with a picture of a golden helmet topped with a crimson plume. Or at least, the colors might have started out as vividly yellow and red. Now, the paint was so faded and flaking that it was difficult to be certain.

The pirate said, "Wait here. Keep your hood up and don't talk to anyone. Understand?"

"You're going inside?"

"To procure our transportation."

"Can't I come with you?"

"It's better if you stay put." Anton squeezed Stedd's shoulder, then turned and opened the door. Voices murmured from the dimness beyond until the Turmishan slipped inside and closed the door behind him. After that, there was nothing to hear but the rain drumming on rooftops and cobblestones.

Stedd took shelter under a pawnbroker's eaves and leaned against a grimy brick wall. While trying not to be obvious about it, he watched the visitors to the various shops, the pedestrians who simply traversed the narrow street on the way to someplace else, and a skinny black cat that kept coming near, perhaps in the hope of a handout, but scrambled away whenever he bent down to pet it.

It passed the time until four men, all clad in shades of blue and green, turned down the street.

Stedd could tell they weren't waveservants. They weren't wearing vestments, just outfits thrown together from random garments approximating the proper color. Nor were the tridents they carried the consecrated weapons of the church of Umberlee. Rather, they were pitchforks or implements for fishing. Still, the foursome looked more dangerous than the common worshipers who contented themselves with a shark-tooth pendant or some other simple token of devotion, and such being the case, maybe they were on the lookout for Lathander's boy prophet.

Swallowing away a sudden dryness in his mouth, Stedd told himself that couldn't be the case, or they'd be rushing him already. Then it occurred to him that at a distance, on a disreputable street where children didn't belong, they might take him for a grownup halfling instead of what he was.

Unfortunately, he doubted they'd remain confused if they saw him up close. Trying not to look like he was in a hurry, and praying there was nothing in the way he moved that would give him away, he ambled to the door with the crumbling painting and pulled it open.

As he'd suspected, the space on the other side was a tavern, with kegs and jugs on the sagging shelves behind the bar and outlines of human figures drawn on the walls. The gashes left by throwing knives mottled the targets like sores, especially in the vicinities of the hearts and eyes.

The room smelled of beer, smoke, and a sweaty crowd packed in tight, although that last stink was a sort of ghost of last night's carousing. At the moment, only a handful of glum-looking, possibly hungover folk sat drinking at the mismatched tables. Intent on their own solitary thoughts or desultory conversations, none paid any attention to Stedd. If they noticed him at all, maybe they too thought he was a halfling.

Good. But he felt like a cornered animal until enough time passed that it was clear Umberlee's followers weren't going to follow him inside.

Once he judged he'd given them enough time to prowl on by, he wondered if he should go back outside. But even the tavernkeeper, a barrel-chested fellow with pouchy, bloodshot eyes who looked as morose and withdrawn as his patrons, didn't seem interested in demanding that the newcomer buy a drink; he was busy pouring himself a cupful of clear spirits. So perhaps, Anton's instructions notwithstanding, Stedd was better off biding where he was.

Thinking of the pirate made Stedd wonder where *he* was. Then he noticed a curtain that evidently shielded some sort of secondary room or alcove. It seemed likely Anton was on the other side conferring with his contact.

Stedd decided to take a seat close enough to the curtain to eavesdrop. After his brush with the Bitch Queen's bravos, it might settle his jangled nerves to verify that he actually did know where his protector was and that arrangements for the boat were proceeding as they ought. With luck, he'd be able to tell when the palaver was drawing to a close and be back on the street before it did, and then Anton would never know he'd disobeyed him.

Making sure the legs didn't scrape on the planks beneath the sawdust on the floor, Stedd pulled out a chair. He caught Anton's voice: ". . . these years working together, you know I'm good for it."

"Times are hard," replied someone who sounded like a talking bullfrog.

"Surely not for a gang with ties to Jaundamicar Bleth," Anton said.

In a colder tone, the bullfrog said, "We don't talk about that."

"Sorry. I was just looking for a way to remind you you're not dealing with a simpleton."

"Neither are you. Do you think it hasn't even occurred to me to wonder why you need a boat? Where's the *Iron Jest*?"

"Busy elsewhere with a chore that's none of your concern."

"All right. Fair enough. And I suppose that in light of our years of friendship, you can settle up after. The voyage will just cost a little more that way: one thousand gold in lions, nobles, or a mix."

"One thousand doesn't strike me as a notably friendly sum."

"To sneak Anton Marivaldi safely to his destination despite all the port officials, navy men, and rival pirates who live for the chance to lay hands on him? You're right, that's not friendship, more like a brother's love."

"Fine, my gold-grubbing brother. I agree."

"Understand, that's payment due as soon as the voyage is over. You might think you can just scarper off and leave the captain holding out his hand like a fool. From what I know of you, you might even get away with it. But ask yourself if you want to be at feud with the Fire Knives forever after."

"I already said I agree. What captain are we speaking of?"

"Do you know Helstag Deepdale?"

Anton snorted. "I know he doesn't take that worm-eaten tub of his out of sight of shore. I believe it's the only intelligent decision he ever made."

"He'll make the crossing to Pirate Isle if I tell him to."

Stedd felt shocked, like someone had unexpectedly slapped him in the face.

But maybe things were really all right. Maybe Anton had only told the bullfrog he intended to go to Pirate Isle because that was what the other man would expect.

No. No matter how hard Stedd tried, he couldn't make himself believe that. As a reaver, Anton ranged all around the Sea of Fallen Stars, so why would he need to claim that he was headed for Pirate Isle to avert some sort of suspicion? And why would he reject Helstag Deepdale's coaster if his objective was Sapra? Stedd was scarcely an expert on the geography of the region, but the Moonstars had taught him enough to know that a person could reach Turmish by hugging the southern shore. In fact, that was pretty much the only way to do it if one actually wanted to *avoid* sailing close to the pirate stronghold.

Once again, Stedd remembered Anton killing Questele and her brothers-in-arms, then threatening to murder the captive villagers, and felt grinding shame at his own idiocy for ever trusting him. That feeling, though, immediately gave way to a stab of panic. He had to get away from the pirate, and this moment was likely his only chance.

He rose and hurried toward the door. His departure finally evoked a halfhearted "Hey!" from the tavernkeeper, but he ignored the call and kept going.

No ruffians with tridents were lying in wait on the street. That was a minor relief, but where was Stedd supposed to go in a city full of strangers, any one of whom, out of greed, piety, or fear, might see fit to hand him over to the agents of Umberlee? Perhaps if he found a safe place to pray, Lathander would help him figure it out, but for now, he needed to keep putting distance between Anton and himself.

Struggling against the urge to run outright, he strode past the pawnshop and onward. He turned right at the first corner and left at the next one.

"Or more likely drown me trying," said Anton. "Please, tell me there's another choice."

Perched on the high stool he needed to sit at the table comfortably, Dalabrac Bramblefoot smiled. The halfling dressed decently but with a sober lack of ostentation, carried no visible weapons, and with his round, avuncular face, looked more like a modestly successful tradesman than an officer in Westgate's most powerful criminal fraternity. Where externals were concerned, his one exceptional feature was the guttural voice that had no business issuing from such a small body.

"Helstag would be hurt," he croaked, "that you don't trust his seamanship. But have it your way. What about Falrinn Greatorm?"

Anton smiled. "Falrinn will do. Where and when do I board?"

"Don't worry about that. Stay here, have another drink or two, and I'll send word to him to make ready. Come evening, we'll sneak you down to the harbor, and you and Falrinn can sail with the tide." Dalabrac smiled and picked up the brandy bottle. "For a thousand gold, I take good care of you."

"Thanks," Anton said, "but I need to attend to other business before I embark. I'll meet Falrinn on the dock."

In other circumstances, he would have been happy to let the Fire Knives hide him until it was time to sail. But he didn't want them seeing Stedd before it was necessary lest they realize a prize worth far more than a thousand Cormyrean lions stood before them for the taking. It would be better to rendezvous with Falrinn after dark with the boy prophet disguised as well as was practical, board the smuggler's vessel, and cast off before anyone had time to wonder about Stedd's identity.

Dalabrac shrugged. "Suit yourself. He still ties up on the east end of the harbor, but of course, everything is different with the flooding. Look for a boat with gray sails and a blue light shining in the bow."

"I remember him signaling with that blue lantern." Anton lifted his dented pewter cup in salute to Dalabrac, drained it, rose, and pushed back through the curtain into the tavern's common room.

As he strode toward the door, he told himself that the difficult part of his enterprise was over. Falrinn's boat was nimble enough to evade the *Iron Jest* and any other seafaring hunters. At some point, Stedd might realize where they were truly headed, but it would be too late for him to do anything about it. If need be, Anton would tie him up to keep him out of mischief.

Although imagining that made him feel vaguely uncomfortable. He didn't know why. A man did what was necessary to make his way; if he balked, some more enterprising soul would only knock him down, walk over him, and commit the selfsame act he'd been too squeamish to perform. With that truth held firmly in mind, he pulled open the door.

Stedd was gone.

Hoping that the rain and gloom had momentarily deceived him, Anton cast about. To his growing dismay, he still saw no sign of the boy. He paced along the narrow street and peered into the various shops. Stedd wasn't inside any of them.

Had waveservants or other hunters recognized the child and snatched him away? Possibly. But wouldn't Stedd have scurried into the Golden Helm in search of his protector if he saw trouble headed his way?

Not if he'd been taken by surprise. Not if someone struck him down before he had a chance to act. Anton imagined the little boy sprawled facedown with Umberlant priests standing over him, and the surge of rage the picture evoked surprised him. No doubt it was anger at the thought of someone else snatching his prize away from him.

Although he didn't know for certain that was what had happened. Maybe Stedd finally realized his traveling companion remained what he'd always been, an enemy resolved to sell him for the bounty.

But if so, how? Anton was confident he'd given the boy no reason to suspect him. To the contrary; he played the part of a true guardian and friend. At first, the pretence had required effort, but as the days wore on, it had become habitual, perhaps, in some sense, even natural.

Still, maybe Stedd had discovered the truth with magic.

On their first morning together, Anton had deemed it prudent to prevent the boy from renewing his abilities. But it had proved impractical to do the same with each new sunrise, and so, although he'd kept interfering when circumstances provided a good excuse, the boy nonetheless possessed some magic. It might only be healing of the sort that had aided Anton aboard the *Jest* and sick folk they'd met along the trail. That was all the Turmishan had witnessed so far. But for all he knew, when turned to the purpose, it might also yield warnings and revelations.

With a jaw-clenching spasm of frustration, Anton decided there was no way to guess with any degree of confidence why Stedd had disappeared. There were too many ambiguities involved. In any case, what mattered was finding him, but how was a lone pirate, himself a fugitive, supposed to find a single missing child in the teeming sprawl that was Westgate?

Plainly, he couldn't. But the Fire Knives had eyes throughout the city. He was just going to have to tell them the truth and cut them in for a full share of the bounty.

He strode back into the Golden Helm and ripped open the curtain screening the alcove. Startled, Dalabrac peered at him.

"I need your help with another problem," Anton said.

"What?" the halfling asked, perhaps a shade too quickly, or with a bit too much concern. At any rate, something about his reaction gave Anton a twinge of unease. But that didn't alter the fact that he needed help.

"I had a boy with me," he said, "born and raised on Pirate Isle and unfortunately, unhappy there. He stowed away aboard a ship, and his father has posted a reward . . ."

Dalabrac grimaced. "Stop. I know you were traveling with a child. I also know who the child truly is."

Anton blinked. "How?"

"I warned you I'm not a simpleton, and neither are the new leaders of your former crew. They've been in touch to tell me you absconded with the boy prophet that Evendur Highcastle wants and might turn up here to ask for help."

"In which case," Anton said, "they wanted the Fire Knives to return the two of us to their keeping instead."

"Of course," the halfling said, "I wouldn't have turned an old friend over to be killed."

"Of course not," Anton said, making no effort to conceal his skepticism.

"But once the boy was actually standing in front of me, it's possible I would have proposed that you and I renegotiate our arrangement. And that, I infer, is the problem. You wouldn't even have told me there is a boy if you hadn't just discovered that you've lost him."

"Unfortunately, yes. He was right outside in the street, and now he's disappeared. I need your help finding him."

"But do I need your help?" Dalabrac replied. "The Fire Knives know Westgate far better than you ever could. At this point, what can you contribute to the enterprise?"

"The lad trusts me"—Anton hoped that was still true—"and I know how he thinks. I can also fight if need be. You may remember, I'm pretty good at it."

Dalabrac hopped down from his stool. "I remember having to stab that Shou son of a troll in the arse and save your hide. But still, yes, you are. So, a new arrangement. One third of Evendur Highcastle's bounty for you, two thirds for the Fire Knives, and no need to cut in your former crew. Agreed?"

"Yes," Anton said.

"Then let's get moving."

Despite the rows of stalls, the marketplace, a plaza where three streets came together, felt relatively open, and despite the scarcity of goods and the high prices that periodically elicited cries of amazed disgust, a fair number of folk were shopping. It all made the skin between Stedd's shoulder blades crawl like someone was about to stick a dagger there.

But on the trek from the Star Peaks to the Sea of Fallen Stars, Questele had told him that sometimes, the safest place to hide was in a crowd, and whether or not this was one of those occasions, he hadn't figured out anywhere else to go. So he drifted from one vendor's stand to the next and struggled not to constantly look around for signs of pursuit like the fugitive he was.

Hooves clattered and wheels rumbled and threw up water as four wagons rolled into the marketplace. Someone had painted a white hand clasping a blue rose on the side of each, and the men driving them or riding in the backs wore livery marked with the same symbol.

The wagons headed down one of the busier aisles, busier because, despite the paucity of harvests out in the countryside and the reluctance of farmers to send produce to market that they might end up needing to eat themselves, the grocers had some fruit and vegetables to sell. Some of their customers had to scurry out of the way of the draft horses with their jingling harness.

A thin man with a weak-chinned but keen face like a weasel's hopped down from the bench of the lead wagon, and ignoring those who'd arrived ahead of him, started talking to a grocer. At the end of the exchange, he tossed her a purse and his associates loaded up her bushel baskets of cucumbers and ambercup squash, not stopping until they stripped her area clean.

By that time, the weasel had moved on to a second grocer. After another brief bit of haggling, he purchased all of that vendor's wares, this time, radishes and pears.

The other shoppers—reduced to would-be shoppers now—were glowering and grumbling among themselves. The weasel ignored them and moved on to a stand selling sacks of flour. But before he could begin another transaction, a big woman in an apron with a wicker basket hanging on her arm grabbed him by the shoulder and pulled him around.

Stedd was too far away to hear the exchange that followed, but he could imagine it. The woman was saying it didn't matter how rich or important the weasel's master was; the nobleman or merchant had no right to buy *all* the food. And, sneering, the weasel was replying that what he was doing was entirely legal, and if she didn't like it, that was her problem, not his.

The weasel attempted to end the altercation by turning back to engage the flour vendor. But the woman with the basket grabbed him and pulled him around more roughly than before.

The rich man's factor jerked free of her grip, shouted, and waved his hand. Two men wearing the hand-and-rose emblem left off loading a wagon and strode in his direction with the obvious intent of forcing the woman to leave him alone.

But the woman had plenty of sympathizers among the onlookers, and several of them planted themselves in the way of the weasel's subordinates. By calling for help, he'd only succeeded in creating a second confrontation.

Other servants moved to reinforce their beleaguered fellows. Their problem was that they couldn't do that and look after the wagons, too, and a boy a year or two older than Stedd darted toward the one with the radishes and pears. His mother yelled for him to stop, but he didn't.

Perhaps it was her cry that alerted the servant who lurched back around. He rushed the boy, tackled him just short of the wagon, and bore him down on the wet cobbles. The man's fist swept up and down as he repeatedly punched the child in the face.

Someone shouted, "Get him!" and people rushed to drag the servant off the boy and beat him in his turn. They were so eager to vent their outrage that no one offered further aid to the child. In fact, his rescuers stepped on him as, dazed and bloodied, he tried to crawl away.

Stedd missed seeing where violence erupted next. Seemingly in the blink of an eye, it was everywhere.

People punched and tried to grab the servants in livery, who, outnumbered, fought back desperately. But there was more to the fracas than that. Following the thieving boy's example, other folk shoved their way toward the wagons or overran the vendors' stalls and battled one another for the spoils to be found there, overturning bins and baskets in their frenzy and tumbling onions and snap beans to the ground.

Horrified, Stedd realized his own precarious circumstances didn't matter; this situation was bad enough that he felt compelled to intervene.

Ahead of him, an itinerant vendor simply abandoned his pushcart and ran before the spreading chaos could overtake him. Stedd dashed to the cart and climbed on top of it. Trinkets, including starfish on thongs, trident badges, and similar ornaments, snapped and crunched beneath his feet.

All right, now what? Stedd couldn't just start preaching the way he had dozens of times before. With all the yelling and crashing going on, no one would even notice, let alone stop looting and brawling to pay attention.

He pictured a golden sunrise and reached out to the god enthroned at the heart of the light. And an idea came to him, although not in words. He'd never heard Lathander's voice as such. It was more like the Morninglord's grace quickened his own capacities to perceive and to plan.

He took a long breath and raised his hand to the sky. Flowing from east to west, a wave of light and warmth swept across the marketplace and the dozens of vicious scuffles in progress there.

The glow didn't stop the rain, and the cloud cover walling away the sun remained unbroken. But it was still daylight brighter than the folk of the Inner Sea had experienced in a year. Startled, the brawlers stopped fighting to look around.

When they did, they beheld Stedd on his makeshift dais with his arm still dramatically upraised. He was no mountebank, but since coming south, he'd addressed enough crowds to learn a little showmanship, and as long as it helped him deliver Lathander's message, he didn't see any harm in it.

"Please," he said, "for your own sakes, don't fight one another, and don't steal. It's not who you are nor who you *want* to be."

"Did you make the light?" called a woman with blood trickling from a split lip. She clutched a half-gobbled pear in her hand.

"Lathander made it," Stedd replied. "He's come back to tell us the Great Rain won't last forever, and we don't need to turn on each other to survive it. In fact, the way to make it through is to do the opposite: Stand together, and help folk in need."

"That's not what Umberlee teaches!" shouted one of the men wearing the blue-rose emblem. His eyes were so wide that white showed all around, and the whip he'd likely grabbed from one of the wagons trembled in his grip.

"Umberlee's just one power among many," Stedd replied, "and you can choose which one to follow, the same way people always have. She'll never be supreme in Westgate or anywhere else unless people lift her up with their belief and their obedience."

"That's blasphemy," declared the man with the whip, "and everyone who's watched the sea rise knows it! Just like anybody who's even heard the name knows Lathander's dead. He died in our great-grandfathers' time with a dozen other gods."

As the servant offered his retort, the magical light faded. It did so simply because it had burned through all the power Stedd had channeled to make it shine, but the timing was unfortunate. The returning gloom felt like validation of the Umberlant's assertion.

Mouths twisted and scowled as disappointment and disgust replaced the hope that had momentarily brightened haggard faces. A major port like Westgate no doubt saw too much magic to be easily impressed by it, and, deciding Stedd was simply a charlatan or deluded wretch with a mystical trick or two at his disposal, people went back to the grim business of snatching any food within reach, which sometimes devolved into playing tug of war with bins, baskets, and even individual pieces of produce. Subjected to such rough handling, a sack split and poured flour onto the pavement, depriving both contenders of the contents. A man cried out when, shying at all the commotion pressing in around it, a draft horse set its hoof down on his foot.

It was plain that renewed violence was only a breath or two away, and this time, some of it was likely to involve Stedd. The servant with the whip started toward him, and so did two other men. Either they'd heard something about a reward offered for a boy prophet or they simply meant to punish him for proclaiming a message they considered pernicious nonsense.

When Stedd reached out to Lathander, the contact clarified his thinking and buttressed his faith. But it didn't turn him into a different person, and on the human level, he was as alarmed as any child would be at the prospect of three grown men pummeling him, flogging him, or worse. His heart pounded, and his mouth was dry. The fear made it hard to think about anything but running away. But that would mean leaving his work undone.

Should he lash out at his assailants with magic as the village waveservant had struck at Anton? It might be possible, but he didn't know for sure. He'd never tried to use his gifts for fighting. From the beginning, he'd sensed that the Morninglord wanted him to give people help and hope, not punishment.

That, he decided, was what he still needed to do, and he thought he saw how. Once again, he fixed his inner eye on the dawn that flowered eternally if a person only knew where to look, and prayed for an infusion of its glory.

Lathander answered with such an abundance of power that for the first time, the channeling hurt. Stedd's insides burned like fire. Only for a moment, though, and then the pain became ecstasy. That, however, made it no less imperative that he turn the force he'd received to a sacred purpose, and with a strangled cry and a flailing wave of his arm, he hurled it forth.

At the same instant, the whip curled through the air and lashed him across the chest. The stinging blow staggered him, and he fell off the pushcart onto the cobbles. The impact smashed the wind out of him.

He tried to scramble up. The lash cracked down across his shoulders, and the stroke knocked him back down onto his hands and knees. He lunged, and a hand caught hold of his cloak and threw him back to his starting position. Dazed, he cast about for a way past his tormentors but couldn't spot one. The bullies' legs and the pushcart had him surrounded.

The whip snapped down again. He jerked with pain and bit his tongue. That, however, was the last stroke. As the lingering burn of it subsided, excited babbling replaced the shrieks, grunts, curses, and pounding noises of the riot.

Stedd raised his head. Fruit and vegetables lay heaped here, there, and everywhere in such profusion as to bury whatever baskets remained intact. As he'd intended, the magic he'd cast across the plaza had multiplied the foodstuffs ten times over.

A few folk were frantically snatching all they could. But more simply goggled at the abundance, or turned in his direction with the same astonished wonder in their eyes.

Someone offered Stedd a hand. When he took it and clambered to his feet, he saw he'd accepted the help of the man with the whip.

"I'm sorry," the servant said.

"It's all right," Stedd answered. Talking made his tongue hurt as much as the places the whip had struck, and his voice was thick. He tried to spit away the coppery taste of blood.

"I didn't *know*," the man persisted.

"Hardly anybody does. Spread the word. Tell people Lathander's come back, and he'll help us if we take care of each another, too." Stedd stumbled as his legs threatened to give way beneath him.

The man with the whip caught him by the arm. "I did hurt you!"

"It's not that," said Stedd. He gave the man what he hoped was a reassuring smile. "Praying that hard just pulled the strength out of me."

"Sit." The servant hoisted him onto the pushcart, and people gathered expectantly around.

That meant that much as he would have liked to, Stedd couldn't just relax and recover. He needed to reiterate the Morninglord's message now that they were ready to receive it. He even healed the folk worst injured in the brawl, although that drained every last iota of his mystical strength and attenuated his feeling of closeness to his god.

As it did, his anxiety returned. He supposed that Anton alone couldn't snatch him from this crowd of well-wishers, but what if the pirate showed up at the head of a gang of toughs, or what if waveservants and their knavish-looking followers appeared? Could the ordinary folk who were Stedd's new friends stand up to them, or would they simply get hurt or killed trying? He didn't want to be the cause of that.

But he was also reluctant to scuttle off in an obvious display of fear that might undermine the hope he'd just kindled in their hearts. He was still trying to think of a graceful way to take his leave when five men-at-arms tramped into the marketplace. Each wore a blue surcoat embroidered with a yellow sun and carried a round shield bearing the same device. The maces in their gauntleted hands had blue-stained handles and yellow-enameled spiky heads.

Their leader was a tall man in his middle years with a dangling black moustache that reminded Stedd of a horseshoe. He smiled and nodded his thanks as he approached the pushcart and folk cleared a path for him and his men.

"My name is Niseus Zoporos," he said, "and I serve the temple of Amaunator. The priests sent me because word reached them that a boy drew down the light of the sun to do something wonderful. Is that boy you, young Saer?"

"Yes," said Stedd, thinking for an instant how odd it felt for someone to address him like he was the son of a nobleman. But of course, that bit of deference didn't matter.

What did matter was that Amaunator, the Keeper of the Yellow Sun, and Lathander were the same deity, give or take. To the extent that Stedd understood it, Amaunator, the celestial timekeeper, was the role the god assumed when the universe required a force for stability above all else. Now that that era was passing, and the need for hope and new beginnings was paramount, he was becoming the Morninglord once more.

Given that they all served the same power, surely the sunlords would help Stedd on his way. They'd be true friends and allies, like the Moonstars.

"My master asks that you come to the House of the Sun," Niseus said. "He says the two of you clearly have much to discuss. To that I would add that whether you know it or not, you aren't safe on the streets, not even in the midst of these good people."

"I do know it." Stedd hopped down off the pushcart. His welts gave him another twinge, but at least he'd recovered enough of his physical vigor that nobody needed to hold him up. "Please, take me there."

CHAPTER FIVE

UMARA KEPT IMAGINING HER WIG WAS ASKEW, BUT PROBABLY, WITH her cowl up, it didn't matter even if it was. It was likely better to leave it alone than to risk somebody noticing her fussing with it.

The wig was only part of her disguise. A stain covered the tattooing on her hands and neck, and she'd exchanged her red robes for nondescript garments of brown and tan. Nothing marked her as a wizard of Thay.

The drawback to that was that she wasn't intimidating. No one in the crowd gathered before the temple of Amaunator with its huge sundial—a rather pathetic monument in a city where the sun never pierced the clouds—cleared a path for her. She had to twist and squirm her way closer to the twelve steps leading up to the four arched golden doors.

So far, it was a waste of effort. She wasn't observing anything she hadn't already noticed from the periphery of the throng. But she was enjoying Kymas's discomfort. Like the firewalkers of Kossuth and the doomguides of Kelemvor, the sunlords of Amaunator were staunch foes of the undead, and even when the vampire was merely a psychic passenger peering through Umara's eyes, it pained him a little to approach their consecrated stronghold.

In a murky sort of way, she could even sense Kymas resisting the urge to order her to retreat lest he appear weak. Taking care to mask her own thoughts, she smiled at his predicament, and then one of the golden doors opened.

People caught their breaths and craned for a better view, but groaned and slumped with disappointment when a grown woman in gold and blue came out.

She raised her hands for silence. "We of the temple understand why you're here," she called. "You want to see the boy from the marketplace. But he's conferring with the hierophant, and after that, he'll need to rest. So there's no point standing in the rain. Go home. We hope the lad can speak to you tomorrow."

Some folk shouted angry retorts. Ignoring them, the sunlady gave the crowd a perfunctory blessing by sweeping her hand through an arc, then went back inside. Afterward, some people did indeed turn to leave, but others stubbornly stayed put.

Very good, said Kymas, conversing mind to mind. *That verifies the rumor. The Chosen is in the temple. We've caught up with him at last.*

And all it took, Umara reflected, was working six oarsmen to death, whereupon the senior wizard turned the corpses into zombies and made them row some more. She told herself the end justified the means, but something about it was still distasteful.

What do we do now? she asked.

We go in and fetch him, of course. Well, to be precise, you do. I'll meet you as soon as you exit, and we'll take him to the galley together.

With a twinge of sardonic amusement, she supposed the dangerous solo task was her just reward for secretly laughing at her superior's inability to tread on sacred ground.

Hundreds of years old—it had begun life as Morningstar Haven, a house of worship devoted to Lathander—the temple of Amaunator was a treasure trove of stained glass windows and skylights. Of late, Niseus Zoporos rarely noticed them without experiencing a pang of sadness at the memory of how brightly they once shined.

Perhaps they were the reason he heard the start of the chanting despite the thick stone walls: "Show us the boy! Show us the boy! Show us the boy!"

A small man with a balding crown and bushy gray eyebrows, Randal Sweetgrove, First Sunlord of Westgate, sat with his collection of sundials, hourglasses, calendar stones, shadow clocks, candle clocks, and dripping clepsydras arrayed behind him. He'd been smiling at Stedd, who was sitting on the other side of his desk, but he scowled at the noise from outside. "I thought I told Miri to send those people home."

"She tried," Niseus said from his station by the door. "Some went. Some didn't."

"I can talk to them," said Stedd, meanwhile beginning the process of squirming out of an ornate chair that was rather too deep for him. "I feel better now, and the waveservants won't be able to get me with Sir Niseus and the other guards protecting me."

"Please, rest," Randal said. "There'll be time for speeches later."

"But I told you," said the boy as he completed the process of planting his feet on the floor, "I have to deliver Lathander's message *and* keep traveling toward Sapra. So really, I shouldn't waste time."

"Sit back down!" the sunlord snapped.

Stedd didn't resume his seat, but he did falter in surprise.

"I'm not your enemy, son," Randal continued, "quite the contrary, and sitting here talking to you, I've weighed your words carefully in the hope of discovering that your notions aren't heretical after all, just awkwardly expressed."

Stedd shook his head. "Heretical?"

"Yes, and to my regret, after giving them a fair hearing, I can interpret them no other way. The sun god didn't change from one incarnation to another only to revert to his previous persona a mere century later. The cycle takes millennia. It always has and always will. It can never vary because it reflects the order Amaunator embodies above all else."

"You're wrong," said the boy. "Lathander came back because we need him."

"Lad, I started my priestly training when I was as young as you are now. I've spent forty-five years contemplating the mysteries. Don't you see how foolish, how insolent it is to claim you understand them better than I do?"

"I understand how it could seem that way," Stedd replied with bitter disappointment in his voice, "and if it makes you angry, I'm sorry. But I still have to do what Lathander wants. I thought you'd help me, but if you don't want to, I'll go."

"Niseus," said the sunlord, "block the door."

To thwart and intimidate a mere child who'd come here willingly at a temple knight's invitation? It seemed like dishonorable behavior to say the least. But Niseus had sworn an oath of obedience, and he sidestepped to place himself in front of the exit.

"Let me out!" said Stedd.

"It will be all right," Niseus replied. He hoped that was true.

Stedd pivoted and evidently spotted the smaller door in the back wall amid all the water clocks and such. He started to scramble around Randal's desk.

The First Sunlord rattled off an invocation and swept his hand through the arc that symbolized the sun's daily passage across the sky. Stedd's muscles clenched into rigid immobility, and he pitched off balance and fell.

Randal looked to Niseus. "The paralysis won't last long," the high priest said. "Put the boy where he can't get up to mischief. Lock him up with his hands tied and his mouth gagged."

As predicted, Stedd's muscles unlocked before Niseus finished securing him, but the boy didn't offer any resistance. He plainly possessed his share of courage, but even so, this unexpected reversal, arriving just when he imagined he'd found friends and sanctuary, had hammered the fight out of him.

Niseus tramped back through the temple to Randal's study. "It's done."

The sunlord sighed. "I take it you disapprove."

"Explain why it was necessary."

"Where to begin . . . with the obvious, I suppose. Do *you* think the boy's right about our god, and I'm wrong?"

"Of course not, Saer. But if you'd seen the piles of vegetables in the marketplace and the way all the people were looking at him—"

"Creating food out of thin air is fairly basic clerical magic. If you recall, you've seen me do it."

I never saw you create that much, Niseus thought, but his instincts warned him that saying so would only irritate his superior. "Then are you saying the boy really is channeling the divine?"

"He's made contact with something. It isn't necessarily the god we worship, and even if it is, that doesn't mean he isn't confused about the nature of what he's experiencing. The higher powers are mysterious. If they weren't, the world wouldn't need priests."

Niseus frowned. "All right. I see that. But does it mean we had to deal with him so harshly?"

"Considering that he refused to cooperate, yes. We live in harsh times, and a time when people can't even see the sun. Do you think we can afford to let some illiterate farm boy wander around preaching nonsense and possibly produce a full-blown schism among the faithful?"

"I suppose not. But what do we do instead? Keep him here and teach him to believe what he ought to believe? Train him to be a true sunlord?"

Randal grimaced. "That could be seen as the waste of an opportunity."

Niseus felt a pang of foreboding. "How so?"

"The church of Umberlee is becoming far and away the most powerful faith in Westgate. You and I can wish it were otherwise, but wishing won't change the reality. The day may soon come when the prosperity, the dignity, indeed, the very survival of other temples depends on reaching an accommodation with Whitecap Hall."

"And now you have something the waveservants want."

"Judging from all the sniffing around they and their agents have done of late, they want him quite a lot. Enough, I hope, to guarantee tolerance for the House of the Sun in exchange."

"You had this in the back of your mind from the start, didn't you? Why didn't you tell me before you sent me out to fetch the boy?"

"I didn't want to take the time lest he disappear before you reached him. And, I confess, I hesitated to burden you with knowledge you'd find distasteful even though I knew the moment would arrive soon enough."

" 'Distasteful' is a mild word for it."

"Believe me, I know. But we'll be sacrificing a single troublemaker for the greater good. For the life of the church to which you and I have both given our lives. Can I count on you to stand by me as I carry it through?"

Niseus took a breath. "I'm your faithful servant, First Sunlord, the same as I've always been."

"You're my friend, Sir Knight, and for that, I will always be grateful." Randal picked up a quill. "I'll send a missive to the shark lovers informing them we have the boy, and then we can open negotiations."

Anton had asked Dalabrac to procure a new saber for him, and the halfling had delivered a weapon that exceeded his expectations, exceptionally sharp and well balanced and with a subtle glimmer of enchantment in the curved steel of the blade. But wearing a sword on both hips, the saber on one and the cutlass on the other, made it harder to conceal the weapons under his new yellow mantle, or at least he suspected that was the case. He flipped the wings of the garment outward in the hope of eliminating telltale bulges.

Clad in his own sunlord disguise, Dalabrac looked up at him. "You keep doing that. Are you nervous?"

"All but petrified," Anton answered drily. "Yourself?"

The Fire Knife grinned. "The same. Mind you, I wasn't quite counting on a crowd of our young prophet's admirers loitering in front of the temple. But if we collect him without raising a commotion and haul him out the same way we're going in, it shouldn't pose a problem."

"Then let's get to it," Anton said. They'd waited long enough that, with any sort of luck at all, most of those who resided in the House of the Sun should already be in bed.

But as he, Dalabrac, and two other similarly disguised Fire Knives emerged from their lurking place behind an adjacent building and headed up an alley toward the rear of the temple, he realized Tymora might not be smiling in his direction tonight. Lightning flared, and the flash illuminated two men-at-arms guarding the unassuming back door.

Thunder boomed as Anton and his companions faltered. When the echoing crash subsided, the pirate said, "You neglected to mention guards."

"They aren't usually there," Dalabrac replied. "The boy must have convinced the sun priests that someone might try to abduct him."

"How right he was," Anton said. "Well, I suppose this is where we put our mummery to the test. Everyone, keep moving before it registers on the guards that we balked."

They did, and made it within several paces of the temple guards before the next blaze of lightning. The warriors, bundled up in their cloaks against the rain, goggled and lifted their maces. Evidently the wavering light had revealed the newcomers' vestments for the hastily created counterfeits they were.

The man-at-arms on the left shouted, but another peal of thunder drowned out the sound. Anton snatched out his saber, charged, parried a mace strike, and cut down the sentry before the echoes died.

At once, he pivoted to engage the other guard, but there was no need. The warrior already lay crumpled on the ground.

Dalabrac slipped a blowpipe back into his sleeve. "That was unfortunate."

"Yes," Anton said. "Tell your tailor I won't be recommending him to anyone else in need of a disguise."

Still, the way lay open before them, and if they made haste, perhaps they could finish their business and be gone before anyone came to relieve the two dead sentinels. Anton eased the door open.

The rooms beyond the doorway were nearly as dark as night outside, but a few oil lamps cast pools of wavering yellow light in the gloom. The intruders prowled past a laundry and a kitchen, both deserted at this hour, and then came to a point where they could go left or right.

Dalabrac pointed left. He claimed to have the plans to every major structure in Westgate at his disposal, and Anton could only hope he really did know where the high-ranking sunlords had their personal quarters. They presumably housed honored guests like a boy who professed a special connection to their god in the same area.

The way led up a staircase on the west side of the building and then down a gallery that had doors on one side and on the other overlooked a spacious shrine complete with pews, a white marble altar gleaming beneath a hanging golden sphere aglow with magical light, and statues of Amaunator and the exarchs in his service.

Anton tried the first door. It was unlocked. The space beyond was all one room, with no partition to separate the desk, chairs, table, and bookshelf on one right from the washstand, wardrobe, and cot on the left. But it looked cozy enough to a reaver who'd spent years living in an even smaller cabin aboard a caravel. Snoring rattled from the man in the bed.

Anton crept to the sunlord's bedside, slipped his cutlass from its scabbard, clamped his hand over the sleeper's mouth, and set the blade against his throat. The man jerked awake.

"Stay still," Anton whispered, "and stay quiet. Otherwise, I'll kill you. Nod if you understand."

After a moment, the priest did. Anton warily lifted his hand away. The sunlord, a man with a prominent, deeply cleft chin and eyes wide with fear, didn't attempt to cry out.

"Good," Anton told him. "Keep doing as you're told, and you might survive this. Where's Stedd Whitehorn?"

The cleric had to swallow before he could reply audibly. "On the other side of the temple."

Anton frowned. "Why not on this one? My friend says this is where all the nice living quarters are."

"The First Sunlord locked the boy up to keep him from spreading heresy."

"It grieves me to think a holy man would lie," Dalabrac said, "but nobody's proclaimed the lad a heretic." He turned to Anton. "Kill this fellow, and we'll wake the one in the next room."

"I'm telling the truth!" the cleric said. "Would *you* denounce the boy with that mob gathered outside the temple? Sweetgrove is waiting for everyone to calm down."

"That does make sense," Anton said.

The halfling shrugged. "Maybe. I suppose, then, that the lad is in one of the Towers of Enlightenment?"

"Yes," said the priest.

"Which?" Dalabrac asked.

"I don't know. I haven't been up there to see."

"Is he under guard?"

"I just told you—"

"You haven't been up there to see," Anton said. "So it appears you have nothing more to tell us." Employing the curved brass guard of the cutlass like a knuckleduster, he drove it into the priest's temple. The man jerked then lay motionless.

"Not exactly a credit to his faith," Dalabrac said in his deep croak of a voice. "We barely started scaring him before he babbled everything he knew. You should have cut his throat on general principle."

"If anyone else looks in here," Anton replied, "he'll see a sleeping coward as opposed to a dead one with blood all over his nightclothes."

The Fire Knife grinned. "There is that. Should we take the time to question anyone else, do you think?"

"No," Anton said, "not if you know where the Towers of Enlightenment are. There can't be that many of them, can there, or prisoners shut away inside them?"

"I wouldn't think so."

"Then let's collect the boy and get out."

One of the limitations of invisibility was that while people couldn't see a mage who shrouded herself in such an enchantment, they certainly would notice a door that opened seemingly of its own accord. Thus, Umara had come prepared to neutralize the two sentries watching over the rear entrance to the House of the Sun and was surprised to discover that someone had performed the task before her.

That surely meant somebody had invaded the temple to retrieve the boy prophet ahead of her. Curse it, anyway! But at least there was no indication that the rival hunters had accidentally roused the sunlords. Despite their head start, Umara might still be able to find the boy first. It was a big temple, and she had magic to facilitate her search.

So use it, said Kymas, speaking mind to mind.

I was just about to, she replied.

She slipped through the door into the quiet gloom beyond. It was a relief to escape the pounding storm and even pleasanter to feel that she was suddenly alone in her head. The sanctity of even the mundane work areas of the temple had proved sufficient to break her psychic link to the vampire.

She let out a long sigh but knew she mustn't stand idly savoring the sensation. She skulked to the halo of light shed by the nearest oil lamp, willed her veil of invisibility to fall away, took the scroll Kymas had given her from under her cloak, and read the trigger phrase. The words that followed glowed red and vanished in quick succession as the spell they composed cast itself.

A shimmer danced through the air and silvery floating orbs, each the size of a human eyeball, appeared before her. They lacked pupils or any other external feature to suggest they were peering in a particular direction or capable of perception at all, but because she'd created them, Umara could feel them watching her expectantly.

"There's a little blond-haired boy somewhere in this temple," she whispered. "Find him, then return to me."

The orbs flew away in a swarm that dispersed rapidly as one seeker after another veered off to investigate what lay beyond a particular doorway. Meanwhile, Umara shrouded herself in invisibility once more.

Unfortunately, that protection didn't extend to the orbs. But they were small and darted around quickly. That should make them difficult to spot. And while Umara knew almost nothing about the inner workings of the Church of the Yellow Sun, she doubted that many of Amaunator's servants were up and about conducting observances in the dead of night.

Still, as time dragged by, she had to resist an old nervous habit of biting her nails. Because if some resident of the temple *did* notice one of the flying eyes, or worse, if her competitors had already spirited her prize away, life would become a good deal more difficult.

Finally, one of the orbs hurtled back into view. It oriented on its maker despite her invisibility, and when she held out her hand, it settled into her palm and started dissolving. A cool tingling ran up her arm as the searcher's memories unfolded before her inner eye.

Umara blinked in surprise to see that the boy prophet must actually be a prisoner, not the honored guest that she'd supposed. But it was good. She could use that.

The final image presented itself, and the orb faded out of existence. Umara headed deeper into the temple, where sculleries and pantries gave way to spaces that smelled of frankincense and where rows of columns with golden capitals supported vaulted ceilings. Images of the Keeper of the Yellow Sun gazed down with placid indifference, as though even he couldn't see her, but she didn't encounter anyone mortal.

Though the orb had looped back and forth and up and down in the course of its wanderings, its memories had still provided Umara with a fairly clear notion of where the prisoner was and how best to reach him. She proceeded to the east side of the temple, and when a staircase provided the opportunity to ascend to a higher level, she took advantage of it.

Eventually, her prowling brought her to a place where a bored-looking temple guard armed with a mace and garbed in blue and yellow stood beside one in a row of little doorways. On the other side, a cramped little staircase corkscrewed upward.

Umara whispered an incantation and flicked out the fingers of her left hand. Shafts of blue light streaked from her fingertips and plunged into the sentry's chest. He grunted and pitched forward with a thump that echoed off the nearby stonework.

Umara didn't think the noise was loud or distinctive enough to rouse any of the sleepers in this cavernous place. She was more concerned by the fact that she'd just popped back into view of anyone who might happen to be looking. It was another limitation of invisibility that casting combat magic generally ripped the mask asunder.

She scurried to the fallen guard, and, teeth gritted, dragged the body bumping far enough up the spiral stairs that no one who simply wandered by on the landing below would see it. Then she pulled the iron key from the warrior's belt and climbed onward.

At the top was a locked grille of a door, and on the other side of that, a little chamber occupying the top of a stubby tower rising from the temple roof. Umara could tell it was a tower because the walls and even the ceiling were mostly clear crystal window. Perhaps the original idea had been to place priests in need of correction in an optimal setting to contemplate the glories of the sun. And if the cell became oppressively bright and hot, that too might encourage the occupant to mend his ways.

Of course, no one incarcerated here since the start of the Great Rain had needed to worry about glare or heatstroke. Still, even asleep on his side on the floor, the boy looked miserable enough with his hands and feet tied and a gag in his mouth.

He looked ordinary, too, and perhaps before Umara went to the trouble to steal him from the temple, she should double-check that he truly was what she sought. She reached into her pocket, gripped the carved onyx talisman, braced herself, and breathed the word of activation.

As before, she felt a twinge of headache as her perceptions altered. But after that, the experience was different.

Seen for what he truly was, Evendur Highcastle had been like a stone so heavy its mere existence threatened to grind her into nothingness. Whereas the boy felt like a vista of endless sky that pierced a person with its beauty and inspired both exultation and calm in equal measure.

And despite the looming, crushing spiritual bulk of him, the Chosen of Umberlee had simultaneously possessed a sickening quality of absence, as though, even if he failed to realize it himself, he was no more than a hole in the fabric of the world through which the Queen of the Depths could work her will. The child remained entirely a person, individual and free-willed, yet also shining with the promise of joy and resounding in the mind like a trumpet call to some heroic endeavor.

It was that call that soured the momentary bliss of revelation when it came home to Umara that, in relation to her life at least, the spirit of optimism the boy embodied was fundamentally a lie. The undead ruled her homeland and always would. In the years to come, she would either grovel, scheme, and kill her way into their pestilent ranks or remain forever subservient, and neither future seemed all that joyful or heroic.

With a scowl, she released the onyx disk, and her perceptions reverted to normal. As a gust of wind clattered rain against the tower, she unlocked the grille with the key she'd found, kneeled down beside the boy, and touched him on the shoulder. He woke with a gasp and, squirming, tried to recoil from her.

"Easy," she said, "I'm a friend. I heard about what you did in the marketplace, and I've come to set you free." She pulled the gag from his mouth. "What's your name?"

"Stedd," he croaked. "Stedd Whitehorn."

"And I'm Wydda." It would have been unwise to give her true name. He might have recognized it as Thayan and questioned

92

whether anyone hailing from Szass Tam's realm, particularly a wizard, could truly wish him well.

"Can you really get me out of here?"

She smiled, drew her dagger, and sawed at his bonds. "I got in, didn't it? And I have a ship waiting in the harbor to take you away from Westgate."

"I need to go east."

"Then you will." All the way to the Thaymount, she suspected. "My friends and I are here to help you however we can."

"Thank you." He rubbed his wrists and then his ankles.

"Ready to stand?" she asked.

He nodded and she hoisted him up. He gave a little hiss of pain, but after that he seemed to be all right.

She kept hold of his hand. "I'm going to cast a spell to help us sneak away," she said. "It might make you feel strange for a moment, but it won't hurt you."

Stedd nodded. "All right."

He trusted Umara, and while that was what she wanted, something about it gave her a twinge of disgust not unlike what she'd felt when killing the dying rower. Pushing the useless emotion aside, she cast another enchantment of invisibility.

Just as she finished, a fork of lightning flared across the sky. The illumination alleviated the gloom in the tower and gave Stedd a good look at his body fading away. He shot her a grin that reminded her of how wonderful wizardry had seemed when she first started learning it as a girl no older than he was.

She repeated the spell and veiled herself. "Remember that we still need to be quiet," she said, "and hang onto my hand so we don't get separated. Now let's get moving."

It was awkward negotiating the dark, cramped, twisting stairs while, in effect, towing the boy behind her, especially when they had to maneuver around the corpse. Stedd sighed in a way that made her wonder if he was sorry she'd killed the guard. If so, she couldn't imagine why.

Once they left the little tower behind, the going was easier. She hoped Stedd wouldn't want to leave by the front way and join his true followers when they reached ground level. If he did, she'd have to persuade—

A horn blared from the spaces below, the brassy note echoing through the temple. In its wake, a thick voice called out, and a door banged open.

Scowling, Umara wondered what had gone wrong. Maybe someone had found the two dead guards outside the back entrance. Or spotted the rival hunters sneaking around. In any case, somebody had raised the alarm.

"What do we do?" Stedd whispered.

"Keep making our way out," Umara replied. "We're still invisible, and there can't be that many guards. This is a temple, not a fortress." She gave his hand a gentle tug. "Come on."

They made it a few more steps. Then golden light shined through the dimness, and silvery figures shimmered into being in the lofty open space in the middle of the temple. They looked like women forged of metal. Feathery wings beat slowly to suspend them in midair, and long, straight swords gleamed in either hand.

Like many Red Wizards, Umara knew more about devils, demons, and elementals than she did about the denizens of the so-called higher planes. But she took the silver creatures to be angels, archons, or something comparable. Someone, most likely the First Sunlord himself, was doing his utmost to make sure Stedd didn't escape; he'd summoned supernatural help to prevent it.

It was possible, though, that the temple's celestial allies were no more able to see the invisible than were its mortal protectors. Umara crept onward, and to her relief, Stedd moved with her. Despite the fearsome spectacle that had just materialized, he hadn't frozen.

The entities peered this way and that. Then one with a golden circlet on her brow abruptly looked straight at Umara and Stedd. She pointed with the sword in her right hand and extended the one in her left behind her back.

A beam of argent light leaped from the blade aimed at the mortals. A hot prickling danced over Umara's skin as the ray caught her, and from the corner of her eye, she saw Stedd pop back into view. No doubt the winged outsider's magic had just put an end to her own invisibility as well.

Wings beating more rapidly now, all the flying women oriented on her and the boy. Rattling off hissing, crackling words of power, Umara hurled fire at the entity crowned with gold. The blast rocked the spirit and charred patches of her silvery body black. But afterward, she flew at the fugitives, and her sisters followed.

Anton and the Fire Knives had been about to ascend a staircase when the winged women appeared. Now they stood motionless. The creatures had spotted them immediately but seemingly dismissed them as of no importance, and they were reluctant to do anything that might prompt the entities to reconsider that initial judgment.

But they couldn't stay put much longer. Voices were calling, and footsteps were scuffing and thumping. The temple's human guardians would arrive soon, and now that they were on alert, they were unlikely to take Anton and his companions for anything other than the trespassers they were.

He was still trying to decide what to do when a silver spirit cast light from one of her swords. The beam cut across a bit of the gallery above, and suddenly, Stedd and a tall, slender woman in a brown hooded cloak were standing there. Presumably, they had been all along, and countermagic had just ripped a charm of invisibility away.

The sight of Stedd resolved Anton's uncertainty. He drew his blades and charged up the stairs, and after a moment of hesitation, Dalabrac and the other two Fire Knives pounded after him.

A booming burst of flame engulfed one of the winged beings. Apparently, the stranger in brown was a mage, and Anton was glad of it; his chances were at least a little better than they'd seemed a moment before.

When he reached the top of the stairs, there were five brown-cloaked women, the original, presumably, and four illusory duplicates that mirrored her movements perfectly to flummox the silver creatures. It worked, too. She pierced one of the flying spirits with ragged shafts of shadow, and when the being sought to retaliate, her sword simply popped one of the phantoms like a bubble.

But while the mage's two winged assailants kept her occupied, another swooped across the balcony at Stedd. The boy turned tail and dodged as he ran, but his pursuer compensated.

Anton sprinted, leaped, cut, and caught the silver creature's wing. He half expected the stroke to ring like metal striking metal, but it didn't. Rather, the saber scraped on bone. The celestial being slammed down on the gallery floor and started to scramble to her feet, but he slashed the side of her neck before she could. The blood that sprayed from the wound was clear as spring water.

Anton pivoted. The mage in brown, Dalabrac, and the other Fire Knives were busy fighting silver spirits and seemingly holding their own. But more foes were winging their way toward the gallery. The gods only knew how many the high priest had summoned altogether.

Anton turned to Stedd. "Get back against the wall!"

Stedd balked. In the excitement of combat, Anton had forgotten that the boy no longer had any reason to trust him.

"Do it!" the pirate urged. "It's the only way we can protect you. The creatures won't be able to use their wings or get around behind you."

Stedd stared back for another heartbeat. Then, evidently seeing something in Anton's face that persuaded him, he gave a jerky nod and scurried to put himself where his former traveling companion wanted him.

Anton spun back around, and a silver woman lit in front of him. Her eyes blank and her sharp features expressionless, she advanced with her swords spinning.

He cut to the chest, but the saber glanced off. She was wearing armor, but of the same color as her flesh and feathers, which made it difficult to see. One of the twin swords whirled at this head, and he parried with the cutlass. The straight blade caught on his guard, and he tried to twist it out of her grip, but she spun it free before he could.

For the next few breaths, they traded sword strokes, neither scoring, and then Anton went on the defensive. It was scarcely his preferred style of fighting, especially when enemy reinforcements were surely on the way, but the winged spirit was too formidable. He needed to study her and find a weakness to exploit.

Possibly mistaking his attitude for fear or flagging strength, she pressed him hard, and his tactics nearly cost him a split skull and a maimed leg. After that, however, he recognized what he was looking for.

The creature's swordplay was deft and forceful, but it had a symmetry and regularity to it that reminded him of banks of oars sweeping in unison or chanting mariners hoisting a sail. When his opponent attacked with one weapon, she invariably followed up with a cut from the other at the same tempo, provided that circumstances allowed.

Now that Anton saw the pattern, he was happy to allow it. He parried a clanging stroke with the saber but didn't riposte. The silver woman started to swing her other sword, he sprang in, and her cut fell harmlessly behind him.

He thrust the cutlass up under her jaw, where her armor didn't cover her. Her features still as immobile as those of the statues adorning the temple, she collapsed.

Anton looked around to see what else was happening. One of Dalabrac's Fire Knives—a black-bearded man with chipped yellow teeth—recoiled from a sword stroke and bumped into the railing at the edge of the gallery. His adversary cut with the weapon in her other hand, and the gang member's head tumbled into space. Meanwhile, his cheeks bulging, the halfling blew a plume of dark vapor from a pipe, and, brushed by the discharge, a silver spirit fell to her knees and pawed at her face.

Suddenly, Anton glimpsed movement at the periphery of his vision. He whirled to find a celestial foe plunging into the distance, one of her blades already cutting at his head. He raised his saber in a frantic attempt to parry.

Then the spirit lurched off balance, and it was plain her flailing stroke would miss. Thus, Anton didn't need to parry. He simply sliced her, once and then again.

As the creature fell, Anton spotted the wizard in brown—who'd run through her supply of phantom decoys—standing with hands outstretched at the conclusion of some cabalistic gesture. Evidently, he had her to thank for tripping his attacker, and he gave her a nod before pivoting to engage the next silver warrior.

That one turned out to move and fight in exactly the same manner as the first one he'd killed, and he disposed of her in a similar fashion. Afterward, when he looked around again, no other spirits remained, and he hadn't lost any more of his allies, although Dalabrac's remaining underling, a wiry, walleyed fellow, was squeezing a gash in his forearm in an effort to stop the bleeding.

Unfortunately, that didn't mean their troubles were over. Anton strode to the railing and looked over. On the ground floor, the temple guards and the sunlords with martial training had their shields on their arms, their maces in hand, and had just about finished forming up to climb the stairs and engage the intruders.

Stedd scurried up to stand beside Anton. "You can't just kill them all," said the boy. "They're only doing what they think is right."

Anton snorted. "I appreciate the implied compliment. But given the numbers involved and the quantity of priestly magic on their side, the trick will be to keep them from slaughtering us." He turned to Dalabrac. "There's not much point in worrying about being quiet anymore."

"Sadly," said the halfling, "that's true." Of them all, he was the only one who didn't look sweaty, out of breath, or generally disheveled. His fraudulent vestments still hung straight on his child-sized form. He picked up a dead spirit's fallen sword and took a step toward the nearest stained glass window.

"Let me," the wizard said. She placed herself before the window and gave a shout that boomed like the thunderclaps crashing outside.

The glass mosaic shattered, and despite the drumming of the storm, Anton heard the pieces smashing again on the cobblestones outside. Cold rain blew in through the window frame.

Anton shot the mage a smile. "Nicely done."

It took her an instant to smile back. "I can be useful from time to time."

The wounded Fire Knife hurried to the opening, produced a coiled rope from under his disguise, and dropped the line over the edge. Meanwhile, Dalabrac took out a lump of something spongy, kneaded it a few times, and pressed it to the stonework. His confederate then stuck the end of the rope into it.

"Don't worry, it will hold." Dalabrac grinned at Anton. "My alchemist does better work than my tailor."

"Stedd and I don't need a rope." The wizard took the boy by the hand and led him to the drop. "Just jump."

The boy took a breath, then stepped off the edge with her. Presumably, a word of command would cushion their fall.

Anton slid down the rope. The wounded Fire Knife followed. Dalabrac simply scurried down the wall like a lizard, somehow never needing to fumble or grope for the next finger- or toehold despite the dark and the wet.

The five fugitives hurried away from the temple. Judging that the disguises were no longer useful, Anton and the Fire Knives stripped their outer garments away. Then a figure stepped out of a shadowy doorway.

Stedd gasped, and, hands darting for their weapons, Anton and the gang members pivoted to face the potential threat. "It's all right!" said the mage in brown. "He's on our side."

"Indeed I am," said the newcomer. Like his confederate, he was tall, slender, and had an oval of fair-complexioned face within his cowl, although in the dark, Anton couldn't make out much more than that. "That is, if you're helping to rescue the Chosen. My—"

"They're not!" said Stedd. "This man"—he pointed—"is Anton Marivaldi, a pirate! He wants to sell me to Umberlee's church on Pirate Isle!"

Anton wracked his brain for a lie that Stedd—and the mage and her friend—might conceivably believe. "That's over, Stedd, I promise. The halfling here believes in Lathander, and he made me a better offer."

"It's true," said Dalabrac, joining in without hesitation. "I've seen the Lord of the Morning in my dreams."

Seemingly not certain what to think or say, Stedd looked from one of his would-be deceivers to the other.

"Look," Anton said, "if we don't keep moving, the rest of it won't matter anyway."

"That's true," said the pale stranger, "and my friend's wizardry will protect you if it turns out that these three aren't what they claim to be. Let's—" He frowned. "Drat."

For a moment, Anton couldn't tell what the other man was reacting to. Then something leaped from the broken window and soared on lashing wings.

The flying creature glowed with an inner light, and thus, even though he had to squint, Anton could tell at once that the new threat wasn't another silver woman; perhaps Randal Sweetgrove had given up on those. The male angel's wings were snowy white, and his lithe, mostly naked body, golden-bronze. He carried a flanged mace in his hands.

"What is that thing?" asked the mage in brown.

"An astral deva," the pale man replied.

"Hide us," said Stedd, looking up at the wizard, "before it spots us!"

"I can't," she replied. "I used up all my invisibility spells. I didn't expect to need so many." She squeezed Stedd's shoulder. "But it will be all right."

"Indeed," said the pale man. "Our wizard will stay behind long enough to kill the angel and then catch up with us."

The wizard shot her associate a startled look that seemed to ask, You want me to fight this thing *alone*? But she didn't express the thought aloud. Instead, she swallowed and answered, "Yes, Saer."

"Now that that's settled . . ." Dalabrac waved his hand to indicate the rain-spattered street before them.

Everyone but the mage started running. Red light gleamed from the curtains of rain and the drenched cobbles beneath them as she threw an initial spell at the oncoming astral deva. Meanwhile, Stedd scrambled to put himself beside Anton.

"You can't just leave her!" said the boy.

Watch me, Anton thought.

"She can't beat it by herself!" Stedd persisted.

Anton didn't need the wizard to win, only delay the creature long enough to cover his and Stedd's retreat. Still, in his way, the lad had raised a disquieting point.

Long ago, in a life he'd thrown away, Anton's teachers had stressed that a combat wizard was often the most powerful weapon in a battle . . . right up until the moment a single cut or thrust silenced the spellcaster in mid-incantation. Thus, a sensible officer never left such assets unprotected.

The woman in brown had coped without anybody playing bodyguard when she and her allies were fighting the silver spirits, but it was plain from her reaction that the astral deva was significantly more powerful. What if, battling alone, she couldn't even slow it down? What, then, would the remaining fugitives do without her?

Besides . . . besides . . .

Anton had another thought in his head, but it wouldn't come clear, and he didn't have time to pick at it. "Dalabrac!" he called, hoping by that one word to somehow convey that he was trusting the Fire Knives to follow through on the plan and wait for him. Even though he didn't trust them in the slightest. Then he turned, snatched his blades out of their scabbards, and charged back toward the wizard.

The wizard hurled a pale flare of cold from her outstretched hands. The magic froze raindrops, which for a moment then clattered on the cobbles with a sharper note. But as far as Anton could discern, the astral deva endured the freezing blast without even flinching, let alone suffering genuine harm.

The winged man brandished his mace. Floating lengths of golden phosphorescence shimmered into being around the mage. Recognizing the spell, Anton sprinted even faster than before. He plowed into the wizard, and despite the impediment of the weapons in his hands, wrapped his arms around her and bulled her forward. The clumsy tackle sufficed to carry her clear of the blades of force just before they finished materializing and started spinning.

Anton and the wizard splashed down together in a puddle. He hastily disentangled himself from her and looked up to check on their foe. Who was seemingly no longer interested in that role. The astral deva had seen fit to strike a blow at the mage when advancing in the teeth of her harassment, but now, intent on pursuing Stedd, the spirit was simply flying over her head and Anton's.

Anton scrambled to his feet. "If you put the angel on the ground, I can kill him with my swords!"

The wizard jumped up. "There's one spell that might do it." Swirling her hands through a complex figure, she hissed and snarled words of power. Anton had no idea what they meant, but he'd heard it said that mages sometimes conjured in the language of dragons, and by the sound of it, this might be such a spell.

On the final syllable, the mage clenched her fists. The astral deva's wings flailed asynchronously and then stopped beating altogether. The resulting plunge to the ground would have killed a human being, but he rolled to his feet with just some scrapes on his golden skin. Like that of the silver women, his blood was clear.

Anton charged, and the astral deva spoke a word that made the whole world ring like a giant bell. The resonance filled his head and made him feel on the verge of fainting. But he clung to consciousness and drove himself onward, and after a staggering step or two, he shook off the effect.

As he closed, he feinted to the head, and the angel's mace leaped up to parry. Meanwhile, Anton cut to the knee and scored there, too. But it was like trying to slice into seasoned oak, and the resulting wound was just a scratch. Though Dalabrac had loaned him an enchanted saber, apparently it wasn't enchanted enough to overcome the astral deva's holiness or whatever quality it was that armored him.

The spirit struck back, and when Anton parried, the force of his opponent's blow nearly knocked the cutlass from his grasp. In addition to his other advantages, the astral deva was stronger than a human being.

As they traded attacks, Anton looked for some regularity he could exploit, only to find that the golden man didn't share the silver spirits' predilection for steady tempo and symmetrical patterns. Still, the saber scored twice more, but once again, the resulting wounds were superficial.

Circling several paces away, the wizard cast darts of blue light at the angel and called writhing shadow tentacles up from the ground to wrap around his legs. Unfortunately, the former didn't appear to hurt him, and the latter simply frayed away to nothing on contact with his shining flesh.

All we're doing, Anton thought, is delaying the creature. But that was enough to persuade the astral deva to use more of his own magic. He spoke another word, and a flash of light dazzled Anton and stabbed pain through his head. The combination slowed him, and his foe nearly caught him with a follow-up blow to the ribs.

"Throw me the saber!" the wizard called. Anton heard pain in her voice. Evidently, the astral deva's last magical attack had battered both of them.

He wondered if it had, in fact, unhinged her. It certainly seemed like a mad idea to partially disarm himself when he was barely holding his own as it was.

"Why?" he answered.

"Trust me!"

Well, he thought, with sudden recklessness, why not? Nothing else is working, and it should at least be interesting to find out what she has in mind.

He tossed the saber in the direction of her voice, and it clanked on the cobblestones.

The astral deva attacked savagely, relentlessly, and Anton retreated, dodged, and parried. It was difficult enough simply to defend himself, but he had to do more than that. He also had to keep the spirit away from the woman in brown while she cast what he hoped was the highly efficacious spell requiring the saber.

He managed for a breath or two, and then parried with imperfect technique. The mace snapped the blade of the cutlass an inch above the guard.

The astral deva whirled his weapon up for a blow to the head. Anton retreated a step, dropped the useless remains of the cutlass, opened his hands like a wrestler, and wondered why he wasn't turning tail. Then something bumped his forearm.

It was the hilt of the saber. The wizard had finished with it, and now she was giving it back.

He snatched it, sidestepped the mace, and cut at the astral deva's forearm. As he did, he had a sudden sense of ferocity, as if the saber was alive and waking up. As if it hated the angel and lusted to destroy him.

Despite that, the astral deva managed to yank his arm back in time to avoid the initial slash. But Anton instantly stepped and cut again. The saber was light and eager in his hand.

The second attack caught the angel across the knuckles and sliced his fingers through. The digits and the weapon they'd gripped fell away. The astral deva's eyes and mouth gaped, and inside Anton's head, he heard the saber laugh.

He poised the sword for a chest cut, then glimpsed motion at the edge of his vision. He dodged, and the mace streaked past his head and flew into the astral deva's undamaged hand.

But as the angel's fingers closed on the haft, Anton rushed in and cut. The saber sheared between two ribs and deep into the creature's chest. The astral deva shuddered, and the mace slipped from his grasp. Anton yanked his sword free, made another cut, and the celestial warrior fell with clear blood gushing from what was left of his neck.

The saber's exultation was so intense that for an instant, the silent howl drowned out Anton's own thoughts. Then the blade either fell back asleep or reverted to normal altogether.

Anton grinned at the wizard. "When you simply handed the saber back to me, I had a certain sense of anticlimax. But that was neatly done."

The mage smiled back. "I infused the weapon with . . . well, the metaphysical principle antithetical to entities like our foe. Don't worry. The taint will pass."

"I don't know if that's good or bad. Someday I might want to kill another . . ." A door on the ground floor of the House of the Sun flew open, and guards and priests poured out. "Run!"

It was more difficult to catch scents in the rain. But the walleyed man was bleeding despite his efforts to stanch the flow, and if there was anything a vampire could smell even in adverse conditions, it was blood. In fact, even though Kymas wasn't particularly thirsty, the aroma had been tantalizing him ever since he'd come into contact with the mortal.

When the smell thickened, it told him the man was sneaking up behind him. He whirled to discover a dagger in the wretch's hand.

The remainder of Kymas's time in Westgate might run more smoothly if Stedd didn't realize his true nature until they left port. So he took the trouble to block the thrust. He didn't do it particularly skillfully. The blade would almost certainly have cut his hand if common steel were capable of doing so. But he hoped Lathander's Chosen couldn't tell that.

Kymas looked into his assailant's eyes and froze him in place. Only for a moment, but that was time enough for a vampire to draw his own dirk and stab the mortal in the heart.

The red, coppery scent in the air intensified from piquant to maddening. For a moment, Kymas positively ached to grab the mortal and at least taste him before the alchemy of death transmuted the precious elixir in his veins to worthless dross. He willed the urge if not the desire away and pivoted toward his remaining companions.

Obviously, Dalabrac had trusted his confederate to dispose of Kymas; he was hovering over Stedd in case the outbreak of violence prompted the lad to bolt. But as the walleyed man collapsed to the cobbles, the halfling snatched one of his blowpipes from its hiding place.

Meanwhile, Stedd looked wildly back and forth. It was entirely possible he hadn't noticed Dalabrac's partner creeping up behind Kymas and didn't know which of them had been the aggressor.

Kymas flicked his tongue over his fangs to make absolutely sure they weren't extended, then gave the boy a reassuring smile. "It's all right, son. As I'm sure you suspected, Anton Marivaldi lied to you. He and these other knaves still meant to sell you to the church of Umberlee. But I won't let them."

"Don't believe him," Dalabrac said. "One of my friends died to rescue you. By now, there's a fair chance Anton has, too. And if that weren't sacrifice enough, this pasty squirt of dung just murdered Darstag. You saw it for yourself!"

"I acted in self-defense," Kymas replied with a twinge of amusement. As things had worked out, that assertion was actually true.

"No. *This* is self-defense." Dalabrac blew into the blowpipe.

Kymas expected a poisoned dart or some other mundane weapon to which vampires were impervious. But to preserve his masquerade of mortality, he twisted to the side.

A puff of dust emerged from the end of the pipe. Then, with an earsplitting screech, it instantly congealed into a floating chain. Still shrieking, the links hurtled at Kymas, and he recoiled another step. The chain spun around the space he'd just vacated and yanked itself tight. As it had nothing to bind in its coils, the result was simply to jerk itself straight.

Because he recognized the spell, which some enchanter had seen fit to store in dust-and-blowpipe form, Kymas knew the magic had yet to run its course, and as expected, the screaming chain lashed at his head like a flail. He raised his arm to block.

The impact stung, but it didn't stagger or stun him as it might have a lesser being. As the chain whirled back for a second stroke, he rattled off the first words of a counterspell to expunge it from existence.

Dalabrac puffed into another blowpipe, and the vapor that sprayed out gathered itself into half a dozen pairs of fanged jaws. Like the chain before them, they streaked at Kymas.

He swatted two away and dodged another, but the rest bit him. In the aggregate, the pain he was now experiencing was enough to spoil the precise cadence and articulation spellcasting required. The half-formed magic dispersed in a useless hiss and shimmer.

He could attempt another counterspell and probably succeed, but he decided he didn't care about preserving his impersonation if it meant standing and enduring more punishment like a slave bound to the whipping post. He dissolved into mist and flowed out of the middle of the gnashing, flying jaws and shrieking, swinging chain.

He resumed solid form as soon as he'd drifted far enough that his magical attackers wouldn't instantly reorient on him. His fangs were out, and inside his newly torn garments, his wounds were healing with supernatural rapidity. Some of his Red Wizard tattoos were likely on display as well, though he doubted the goggling, horrified mortals noticed the latter.

Dalabrac's hand shot inside his jerkin, surely to bring out yet another blowpipe. No, you don't, Kymas thought. He sprang and bore the halfling down beneath him, then drove his fangs into his prey's neck.

The first mouthful of blood was ecstasy so keen it bordered on delirium. The fact that Dalabrac had had the insolence to defy him, to inflict pain and indignity on him, made the taste all the sweeter.

"Get off him!" Stedd shrilled, his voice barely audible over the still-screaming chain. Then light blazed through the dark and the veils of rain, and Kymas's skin charred and blistered.

As he averted his face, Kymas supposed he should have been prepared for this. After all, Stedd was the Chosen of the god of the dawn. But up until now, he'd simply acted like a normal child, as if he was currently incapable of manifesting divine power. Perhaps the threat of an undead night stalker, the very antithesis of everything Lathander represented, had stirred him to a supreme effort.

However it happened, Kymas didn't want to suffer another flare of holy sunlight. As soon as the first one faded, and he could bear to look in Stedd's direction again, he leaped up, grabbed the dying Dalabrac, and threw him.

The halfling's body slammed into the little boy and knocked him down. Kymas charged, pounced, and pinned Stedd on the ground.

Then he had to struggle not to bite him. Stedd had hurt him worse than Dalabrac, and drinking him would be even more satisfying. But the thought of Szass Tam, and the prospect of the lich's displeasure, steadied him.

He slapped Stedd in the temple and knocked him unconscious. Then, his burns still smarting, he tossed the boy prophet over his shoulder and hurried onward.

Anton took another look over his shoulder. Though it was difficult to be certain with only the occasional lightning flash and trace of yellow candle glow leaking out one window or another to light the night, it appeared that he and the wizard in brown had shaken any pursuers off their trail.

That arguably meant his companion had outlived her usefulness. In fact, now that the half-drowned harbor lay ahead, she was apt to become a hindrance. It was time to dispose of her as the Fire Knives had surely already rid themselves of the long-legged associate to whom she'd deferred as "Saer."

Given her mystical talents, the safest way to do it would be with a saber slash or dagger thrust from behind. But he found himself reluctant to kill her. He supposed it had something to do with the fact that they'd fought the winged spirits together. Sourly amused at his unaccustomed sentimentality, he slowed down to let her get a pace ahead of him. After that, he gripped the hilt of his knife. The pommel was heavy enough to make a good bludgeon.

He was just about to draw the weapon when two recumbent forms, one half as long as the other, appeared in the gloom. Casting about for signs of a lurking threat, Anton nonetheless quickened his stride, and the wizard did the same.

The smaller body was Dalabrac, and the larger was his walleyed henchman. The rain had washed away most of the blood that would otherwise have pooled around the corpses, but judging from the tears in his neck, the halfling must have bled copiously. Anton wondered what had made the wounds. A savage dog?

"I guess more angels or sunlords must have caught up with our companions before we did," said the mage. "Your friends died—sorry—but until we know otherwise, let's hope Stedd and my master got away."

It was more likely that the Fire Knives had attacked the pale man in an effort to take sole possession of Stedd and he'd somehow killed them instead, and Anton wondered if the woman in brown failed to see that. She struck him as shrewd enough to put the pieces together. But it would be counterproductive to challenge her version of events.

"If so," he said, "they surely hurried onward to your ship. Let's do the same."

She hesitated. "I will. You don't have to."

He cocked his head. "Meaning?"

"Just . . . the halfling hired you, and he's dead. Stedd mistrusts you. The ship's crew likely won't welcome an infamous pirate. You might be better off if we part company."

"I appreciate your concern. But it isn't about coin anymore. Believe it or not, I actually like the boy—well, sometimes—and I like to finish what I start. And if he truly is a messenger from a god, well, perhaps a man who's lived as I have could use a friend in the highest of high places. I'll tell you what. Let me escort you all the way to your vessel and see for myself that Stedd made it there safely. Then, if there truly isn't a berth for the likes of me, I'll take my leave."

The wizard sighed. "Have it your way."

As they hurried onward, Anton was glad he'd persuaded her to lead him to Stedd's present location but unable to imagine what he was going to do when they arrived. What could he do against a whole ship? He told himself he'd think of something, but when a rickety length of temporary pier came into view, and the wizard gasped and faltered, he realized he wasn't even going to get the chance.

There was no ship tied up at dockside. The pale man had cast off and left the mage behind. Straining, Anton peered out to sea, but the vessel had already vanished.

"May he burn in the Abyss forever," the wizard growled.

"If you're talking about your superior," Anton said, "I second your opinion. But we can't just stand here cursing him. By now, the sunlords, the church of Umberlee, and the watch—the entire city, give or take—are all seeking us. Fortunately, I have a fast boat of my own ready to sail, the one in which *I* intended to carry Stedd to safety."

The wizard studied him. "And you'd take me with you?"

"After all we've been through together? Certainly."

Obviously, they *had* indeed fought side by side, but more to the point, he might need her. She knew what her master's ship looked like. He didn't.

"Then thank you," she said.

"Come on," he said, "it's this way."

At least he hoped it was. He didn't think Dalabrac had been lying about that particular detail, but then, he hadn't discerned the halfling's true intentions during their first conversation in the Golden Helm, either.

110

As he and his companion hurried along the shaky docks, he noticed yet another corpse, one that presumably had nothing to do with his own endeavors, bumping against one of the piles. Rats skittered through the gloom, and he reflected that they at least appeared to be prospering during the Great Rain. Evidently they knew how to find and take what they needed even when other creatures were going hungry. Maybe they too were pirates in their way.

Finally, and to his relief, a point of blue light appeared in the darkness ahead. "Wait here until I call you," he told the mage. "The captain doesn't like surprises."

As he prowled forward, he wondered if he was the one about to get a surprise in the form of Fire Knives lying in wait. But he couldn't see any such lurkers aboard the long, low sailboat with the blue lantern hanging from the stern. Although really, it wasn't easy even to make out the vessel herself. When the rains came, its master, lifelong smuggler of contraband and fugitives that he was, had dyed the sails and painted the hull to blend with gray skies and seas.

In any event, only one figure looked up at Anton from the deck, and that one was only a bit taller than Dalabrac had been. His skin was dark like the Turmishan's, but the close-trimmed beard framing his sharp-nosed face was so silvery a blond that it seemed to glow in the darkness.

"Where's everybody else?" asked Falrinn Greatorm.

"I'm bringing a wizard I met along the way," Anton answered. "Dalabrac won't be joining us, nor will any other Fire Knives."

The gnome snorted. "First, Dalabrac sends word that we wants to use my boat to set a trap for you." He hesitated. "You understand, it was nothing personal."

"Just business."

"Aye. But then the next message tells me he and I are setting sail and you may or may not be coming along."

"Depending on whether he decided it made more sense to deal fairly or betray me."

"So I assumed. But now you're here, and he isn't."

"I'm sure it's frustrating for a methodical fellow like you when things keep changing. But at least somebody turned up, and I still need transport."

"As I need payment," Falrinn said.

"Dalabrac didn't pay?"

"He isn't you."

Anton frowned. He didn't have time for an extended palaver. He and the wizard needed to set sail before anyone showed up to stop them, an imperative that tempted him to simply steal the sailboat. But the *Footloose Maid* was a unique vessel, and he might need her master to get her out to sea quickly or make the best possible time thereafter.

"Look," he said, "you must have heard about Evendur Highcastle's bounty on the boy preacher."

"Aye, but so what? The child's right here in Westgate under the protection of the sunlords."

"Like the various messages you had from Dalabrac, that information is out of date. The boy set sail tonight, and if you help me chase him down, I'll cut you in for half."

Scowling, Falrinn stood and pondered long enough that Anton started to reconsider the idea of stealing the boat. "Curse it, Marivaldi, if it was anyone but you . . . But I won't deny that over the years, I've made a fair amount of coin off your crazy schemes. Fetch your wizard and help me cast off."

"She doesn't know my true intentions. You'll need to watch what you say."

"Oh, that sounds promising. But don't worry. I'll follow your lead. If I didn't know how to lie, some harbormaster would have hanged me long ago."

CHAPTER SIX

EVENDUR HIGHCASTLE SAVORED THE GLEAMING AND CLINKING OF the gold and platinum pieces spilling through his fingers back into the coffer. He'd claimed his share of plunder as a pirate, but the sums were paltry compared to the treasure that came to the hierophant of a thriving religion.

Flecks of his spongy fingers dropped along with the coins, but noticing things like that no longer troubled him. He'd come to understand that no matter how thoroughly he rotted, he'd remain as strong as ever, and he didn't care that his appearance was horrific. To the contrary. Even as a mortal man, he'd liked inspiring fear. It was as pleasurable as it was useful.

Although if Imbras Ilshansa was frightened, the pudgy, brown-haired young Impilturian concealed it with the aplomb of an accomplished envoy. "I hope the gift is satisfactory," he said.

Evendur turned away from the coffer and the eight others like it and back toward the emissary and the deep, round pool at the center of the chamber. "It'll do for a start. But the proper term is 'offering'. Or 'tribute'."

"I beg your pardon," Imbras said. "*Offering*, of course. And, I trust, the first of many. If Impiltur thrives, it will naturally pay homage to the goddess who nurtures it."

Evendur grinned. "Just what kind of nurturing are you looking for?"

The envoy hesitated. "Well, Wavelord, if you would have me speak frankly . . . Folk in my land are turning to the worship of Umberlee in increasing numbers, and that, plainly, is exactly how it should be. Unfortunately, in many cases, they're the same people most dissatisfied with the Grand Council. Thus, their faith often becomes a justification if not a vehicle for riots, rebellion, and anarchy."

"Yet if Impilturian waveservants preached their sermons just a little differently, they could channel all that anger in a useful direction."

"The people have the right to be angry," Imbras replied. "The Grand Council has failed them, and the reason is that such a body is by its very nature incapable of effectively governing a realm. Impiltur needs to restore the monarchy."

Evendur grunted. "Before my rebirth, I didn't pay much attention to royal bloodlines. But I believe House Ilshansa claims such a tie to old Imbrar II."

"I freely acknowledge," Imbras said, "that my uncle hopes to take the throne. Why shouldn't my family assert our claim when it's by far the most legitimate? And once we've united the realm, we'll finally drive out the demon cults that have plagued us for decades."

"If Umberlee gave Impiltur—and House Ilshansa—such a glorious future, 'homage' wouldn't be enough. Your folk would have to worship her before all other deities."

"The Queen of the Depths will be the patron deity of the royal family and any noble or merchant who hopes to find favor in our eyes. Her temple will be the grandest in every town."

"In that case—"

A roar sounded from the center of the room and echoed off the wall. Startled, Evendur and his petitioner jerked in the direction of the noise.

A whirling column like a waterspout rose swaying from the well. Such a manifestation unquestionably involved one of the forces or intelligences to which Evendur was attuned, and he focused his will to probe it.

But before he could begin, the water spun outward and swept him up along with Imbras. They tumbled in an impossible whirlpool that filled the chamber but evidently refused to spill out the doors and windows.

As Umberlee's Chosen and an undead besides, Evendur had no fear of drowning, but it enraged him to have the element of which he was the rightful master turned against him. He grabbed for the source of the disturbance with his thoughts, his intent now less to comprehend or communicate that to rend and smash.

An opposing power slapped—or perhaps flicked—his awareness back inside his skull with an effortless violence that jolted him. He belatedly realized there was only one entity that could do this, and that might mean he was in real trouble after all.

When he reached out again, his psychic tone was deferential. Unfortunately, it made no difference. The Bitch Queen rebuffed him again, and with equal brutality.

The watery vortex slammed and scraped him against the chamber walls until he feared that even his preternaturally powerful body would come apart. He felt a pang of dread at the possibility of enduring eternity as a detached head or something similarly broken and helpless.

Then, at last, the whirlpool drew in on itself and dumped him on the floor. A waterspout rising from the central pool once more, it took on definition until it was the looming torso of a blue-green woman with seashell ornaments and a cloak made of jellyfish.

Common sense suggested that the water couldn't simultaneously hold the steady form of a woman and swirl, but even so, Evendur felt that somehow, he could still see the raging tumult of the waterspout as he looked at her. Or maybe the violence was in her smile, all but unbearable with an infinite love of ruin.

Not unbearable to her Chosen, though, and given that, unlike Imbras, Evendur was still intact, he dared to hope he retained that status. He clambered onto his knees and bowed his head. "Goddess," he said.

In response, pain ripped through him, and he cried out. The torment was Umberlee's way of telling him she was angry. And that he would be wise to hold his tongue.

"I tasked you to be my hunter," snarled the Queen of the Depths. "To seize the Morninglord's Chosen and offer him up to me. And instead I find you playing at *diplomacy.*" Her malice lashed him again, and then again.

Jerking, Evendur endured the bursts of agony as best he could. A part of him wanted to protest that on other occasions, the deity herself had commanded him to forge alliances like those he'd been pursuing in Impiltur, but he sensed such a plaint would only further enrage her. Reason and fairness were alien to her nature.

After perhaps twenty strokes of the psychic lash, the punishment stopped, although the lingering anger in her voice made it sound as if she might yield to the urge to resume at any moment. "Because of your blundering," she said, "Red Wizards have seized the Chosen of Lathander. They're sailing east from Westgate to give him to Szass Tam, who will then put him to death."

Inwardly, Evendur flinched. This truly was bad. *He* was supposed to kill the boy prophet in a sacrificial ritual that would both augment his mystical power and discredit the reborn faith of Lathander in the eyes of those who might otherwise have credited its message. According to Umberlee, it was the one sure way to ensure the supremacy of her church across the Sea of Fallen Stars, and it obviously couldn't happen if the infamous lich lord of Thay slew the child instead.

"Seize the boy," the goddess said. "Do it with your own hands, and do not fail. You can catch the Thayans' galley in the straits between Pirate Isle and Gulthandor."

The towering figure of water lost cohesion as she ceased inhabiting it. With a splash that soaked Evendur all over again, the brine plunged back down into the well.

Though he no longer needed air to survive, the habits of life still lingered, and he took a long, steadying breath. Linked as he was to the Queen of the Depths, he generally rejoiced in her transcendent ferocity. But not when she directed any measure of it in his direction.

He strode through the temple until he found one of the senior waveservants. He told the priest what he wanted done in his absence, then returned to the pool.

There, he roared words that sounded like a raging gale and surf pounding against rocks. Unlike common waveservants, he'd never studied the secret languages of the sea or any form of magic. But his ascension had put the knowledge in his head.

The spell didn't agitate the pool below him in any visible fashion, yet he could sense it changing. It felt like a door opening, and when it finished swinging wide, he jumped in.

He then swam down the shaft as quickly and agilely as any squid or eel. That was another of Umberlee's gifts. So was the inhuman sight that allowed him to see despite the rapidly gathering gloom.

The well twisted just where it always had, but shortly thereafter, he swam across a kind of threshold. He couldn't see the discontinuity, either, but he felt it as a surge of exhilaration. Grinning, he kicked and stroked faster, until he shot out the end of the passage.

The mouth of the tunnel was likewise invisible when he glanced back around. The whole of Pirate Isle was gone. Instead of emerging adjacent to the promontory on which the temple rose, or near any other land, he was in open water.

Specifically, he was floating in the heart of Umberlee's watery realm. He had only to open his mind to sense currents flowing endlessly on through a thousand reefs teeming with huge, brightly colored fish and the dark gliding or lurking things that preyed on them. Before his transformation, he might have felt alarm upon perceiving the latter, for the least of them could have gobbled up a mortal man without difficulty. But now, fearing them would have been like fearing himself.

In other places, the sea floor dropped away to frigid gulfs where different predators dangled glowing lures on fleshy tendrils, and blind things crawled and slithered in the ooze. Those creatures were Evendur's kindred, too, and their grotesqueries made him smile like a child beholding a clown's capers.

In fact, had he permitted it, he could have drifted for a long while marveling at the wonders swimming or scuttling on every side. But that was unlikely to please Umberlee, so he thrust the temptation aside.

Thanks to the esoteric lore the goddess had implanted, he knew that every body of water in the mortal world linked to this ultimate ocean. More, he knew a further secret, one that ordinary priests and mages might never discover in decades of study: *Any* spot here connected to *every* place in or on the mundane world's seas. But only if a mystic possessed the might and skill to force open the way.

Evendur pulled his rotting hands in gathering motions and croaked words that made it sound as if he were drowning all over again. At first, intrigued by the power they sensed accumulating in the water, gigantic hammerheads and rays came swimming close to investigate. Before long, though, the alternating waves of hot and cold became intense enough to alarm them, and they fled.

On the final word of the incantation, awareness pierced Evendur like a hundred arrows hurtling from as many different directions. It was like possessing countless eyes and using each one to peer through a different porthole.

But people, even undead Chosen of Umberlee, were meant to possess only two eyes and use both to look in a single direction. Evendur could make no sense of his jumbled perceptions and felt as if they were punching holes in his mind.

He imposed order by willing his ethereal eyes shut one at a time until only one still peered at a stretch of the rolling gray surface of the Sea of Fallen Stars. He cast about. When certain no ship was in view, he closed the first eye and opened another on a vista that was nearly identical.

The third perspective revealed squawking seagulls perched on the floating carcass of a pilot whale and pecking and tearing at the meat. But still no ship.

Evendur wasn't counting on spotting the Red Wizards' galley. That would take considerable luck. But he needed a vessel of some sort. Feeling increasingly impatient, he opened more eyes in quick succession.

On his twenty-seventh try, he found what he was seeking, a caravel on a starboard tack off the southern coast. In fact, it was the *Iron Jest,* a vessel that had sometimes cooperated with his own now-sunken *Abattoir* in raids on ports and merchant convoys.

That was good. The *Iron Jest* was a fast ship, and the hard men aboard should be eager to help him catch Lathander's Chosen and collect the price on his head. In fact, she'd be ideal if not for her captain.

Evendur had never liked Anton Marivaldi. He'd never liked any of the rare men who refused to defer to him, even in subtle ways, as tougher and more cunning than themselves, and the Turmishan was one such. On occasion, he'd even made his fellow captain the target of his jibes.

But now, surely, those days were over. Because Anton was the same little mortal he'd always been, and Evendur was a demigod. Thinking that it would be satisfying to make the knave grovel, he allowed all his other ethereal eyes to wither out of existence.

Then he focused his will on the connection to the *Iron Jest*'s vicinity and set about transforming it from a spy hole to a passage like the one that had brought him from Pirate Isle to Umberlee's ocean. He visualized his hands gripping the edges of the opening and pulling them apart.

When the gateway was wide enough, he swam through then kicked and stroked upward until his head broke the surface. Rain pounded down on him, and the seas were heavy enough to dismay any human swimmer, but he took pleasure in the heaving peril that was no threat whatsoever to him.

He looked around, found the *Iron Jest*, and swam after it. A trailing line hung off the stern, and he caught hold of it and climbed hand over hand.

As he started to clamber over the railing, a shaven-headed pirate with rings in both ears noticed him and gave a squawk of alarm. The fellow looked wildly about, found a belaying pin, grabbed it, and rushed Evendur with the obvious intent of knocking him back into the sea. Maybe he'd mistaken the newcomer for one of the marine ghouls called lacedons.

Though it was awkward when he was straddling the rail, Evendur ducked the makeshift cudgel, caught the human by the throat, and gave him a single brutal shake. Combined with the pressure constricting his windpipe, the jolt was enough to make the pirate falter.

Evendur pulled his assailant close and glared into his eyes. "Do you recognize me now?" he asked.

"Yes," the pirate croaked.

"Good." He gave the mortal a second, harder shake, heard his spine break, and tossed him overboard.

Then he finished climbing onto the deck and ran his gaze over the other men who by now were gaping at him. "Is there anyone else who doesn't know me?" he asked.

A man with a long, somber face under a broad-brimmed hat cleared his throat. Evendur thought he ought to recognize the fellow, and after a moment, the memory came to him. The rogue was Naraxes Corieth, the *Jest*'s first mate.

"We know you, Captain," Naraxes said. "Or am I supposed to say Wavelord?"

"Captain will do," Evendur said. "Where's Marivaldi?"

"Gone. I'm captain now."

Well, perhaps that was better. Naraxes might prove more tractable than Anton would have. But why did the fool seem so nervous?

"But the trouble is," Naraxes continued, "when Anton left, he took the boy with him."

The words were so unexpected that it took Evendur a moment to truly comprehend them. "You're telling me you had the child? The one who preaches that Lathander's returned?"

"Well, yes. Isn't that why you're here?"

Evendur decided it wouldn't look especially demigod-ish to admit he didn't know the apparently tangled tale of how the paths of the Morninglord's Chosen, Anton Marivaldi, his estranged crew, Red Wizards, and the stars only knew who else had converged and diverged over the course of the past tenday or so. Fortunately, he didn't need to know to address the current situation.

"It is," he said, "but not in the way you think. I've decided to catch the false prophet personally, and it's your good luck that I've chosen your ship to do it. Once we take the boy to Pirate Isle, the temple will pay you the promised bounty."

Naraxes nodded. "We'll help."

Evendur sneered. "I hope you didn't think I was *asking.*"

"No, Captain! Of course not!"

"Good. Now come about. We're looking for a Thayan galley, and I plan to catch her in the straits."

Naraxes turned to relay the commands. Strolling toward the bow, enjoying the way the crewmen tried to cringe from him without being obvious about it, Evendur began a first inspection of his new ship. It felt good to have a deck rolling under his boots again, and better still to be on the hunt for a prize.

Anton woke up cold, wet, and stiff. More promisingly, though, he also woke to the smell of cooking. He opened his eyes, and for an instant was surprised to find himself aboard a vessel considerably smaller than the *Iron Jest.* Then he remembered capturing Stedd and all that had followed, including the flight from Westgate with Falrinn and Wydda the wizard.

Well, no doubt he'd have ample opportunity to find out. At the moment, she was in the bow, and he was lying under the low shelter amidships that had manifestly done an unsatisfactory job of keeping the rain from blowing in on him. He crawled out and headed for the stern to attend to one of the cruder requirements of nature as far away from her as possible.

Still a gentleman, he thought with sour self-derision. Father would be proud.

Falrinn was in the stern adjusting the tiller, which attached to greasy brass gears that, he claimed, allowed him to do so with exactitude. He made similar boasts about the unconventional arrangements of pulleys, ratchets, and such he'd incorporated into the rigging. Anton remained skeptical that all the various contrivances would do a knowledgeable human mariner any good, but on previous voyages, he'd seen how they allowed one small gnome to trim sail and pilot the boat with ease and efficiency.

As Anton buttoned up his breeches, Falrinn proffered a spyglass. The human accepted it with the care such a valuable tool deserved.

"The wizard says we're looking for a galley," Falrinn said. "But she doesn't know what style of galley, the port or realm the ship calls home, or even exactly where it's heading."

Anton grinned. "You'd almost think she doesn't trust us."

He ducked back under the shelter to scoop some breakfast—eggs scrambled with chopped fish—from the frying pan on the little wrought iron stove. He wolfed them down and then, feeling more vital and alert, headed into the bow. The mage gave him a nod.

The exertions of the previous night had left her looking bedraggled and weary, with dark smudges under bloodshot eyes. But except for that, her skin was smooth and creamy, a little rosier atop the high cheekbones, and the eyes were a vivid green. Anton realized for the first time that she was comely.

"You know," he said, "from one secretive soul to another, there really isn't much point in not telling Falrinn and me exactly what vessel we're chasing. We're going to sight her from far away." He showed the wizard the spyglass. "That first look will tell us a great deal about her, and the gnome will turn our boat around if he doesn't like what he sees."

The mage frowned. "Don't you think I'd tell you more if I could? I want to catch up with my fellow Lathanderians quickly. But my . . . superior only hired the galley a short time ago. I never got around to learning much about her. Nor did he choose to tell me exactly where he planned to take Stedd. He truly is a 'secretive soul,' and he must have thought it safer for me not to know."

Anton smiled. "Nonsense. You're the kind of person who never stops observing and discovering, especially information that bears on your own well-being. You'd ferret out the details of your lord's plans whether he wanted you to have them or not."

The wizard hesitated. "You give me too much credit." She lifted her hand to flick stray strands of brown hair off her cheek, and her sleeve slid partway down her forearm. In so doing, it exposed marks on her forearm. They looked faded, but Anton discerned that was because they were actually peeking through a layer of pigment she'd spread on top of them.

The sight of the tattoos made him take reflexive note of the location of his weapons. He only had his dagger and skinny hidden boot blade on his person; he'd left the saber under the shelter. He considered, too, the feasibility of simply lunging at her and shoving her over the side. Yet he realized he was no more inclined to kill her now than he had been on the street in Westgate.

"Actually," he said, "I didn't give you enough credit. Until this moment, it hadn't occurred to me that you might be one of the wicked tattooed wizards of Thay." He gestured to indicate the exposed sigils.

She gave a start and peered at the telltale marks. He could all but hear her thoughts as she quickly considered whether she could possibly convince him that the arcane symbols weren't what he believed them to be. Then, grimacing, she said, "The Black Hand take it, this stain is supposed to be waterproof!"

"Take it from a sailor," Anton replied, "nothing is truly waterproof over the long haul. And we've had a very wet night and morning."

"Well, at least I can stop wearing this nasty thing." She pushed her cowl back, pulled her brown wig off, and gave the shaven scalp beneath a vigorous scratching. A hint of stubble grayed the ivory skin of her scalp.

Somewhat to Anton's surprise, baldness didn't mar the mage's looks. Rather, it made her exotic, like the occasional sea elf women he'd encountered over the years, though he suspected the latter would have mightily resented the comparison.

When she finished scratching, she said, "But you have to understand—"

"Please," Anton said, "allow me. You and your master are *virtuous* Thayans, expatriate because you can't bear your native land's depravities. You only disguise your nationality to avert prejudice, and you truly do mean to help Stedd. It could scarcely sound more plausible, and naturally I believe it all implicitly."

A grudging smile tugged at the corners of the wizard's generous mouth. "As I fervently believe the halfling really did hire you, one of the most infamous reavers from Suzail to Escalant, to help whisk a little boy to safety."

Anton grinned. "It sounds like neither one of us is able to lie to the other anymore."

"I wouldn't jump to *that* conclusion."

"Fair enough. But in this interlude of relative candor, will you favor me with your real name? I doubt it's Wydda. That's not Thayan."

"It's Umara Ankhlab."

"Well met, Umara." He offered his hand, and she shook it. She had the soft skin of someone who'd never performed manual labor, but her grip was firm. "I assume you and your leader—"

"Kymas Nahpret."

"—you and Kymas are actually hoping to collect the bounty on Stedd the same as I was."

Umara frowned. "You're wrong there. Kymas and I are in service to Szass Tam. The Lich King tasked us to find Chosen and fetch them back to Thay."

"And Stedd's a 'Chosen'? He doesn't call himself that, or at least he didn't while we were traveling together."

"But he is. The champion of reborn Lathander, as Evendur Highcastle is the hand of Umberlee." She sighed. "With each, I employed a talisman to be sure."

"If you knew all that, it might have been more sporting of you to go after the undead pirate lord instead of the wandering farm boy."

The wizard scowled. "And it might have been more 'sporting' for you to win your gold attacking cogs and round ships like pirates are supposed to."

"I imagined the lad would be older, and likely a lunatic or char-latan who wasn't doing anybody any good . . . but as we're being honest, I'll confess it wouldn't have mattered if I had known the truth. Evendur's offering a *lot* of gold. Which, given that Stedd is now in the hands of your fellow Thayans, I suppose has now passed beyond my reach. Unless, of course, you care to help me pluck the boy from Kymas's clutches. You, I, and Falrinn can split the bounty three ways, after which you can live out your days in luxury as a genuine expatriate."

Umara hesitated just long enough to make him wonder if she was actually considering the proposition. "I'm afraid not. My family is Thayan nobility going back for centuries. I know my path, even if . . . That is to say, I know my path, and it isn't treason."

"Even though your superior left you behind in Westgate?"

"With the sunlords pursuing us, he set sail as expeditiously as possible to safeguard the success of our mission. It was just what I should have expected of him, and I don't hold it against him."

Anton suspected that wasn't wholly true. But he also sensed that pursuing the matter wouldn't subvert her loyalty. "Well," he said, "in any case, I can't honestly recommend treason as the gateway to a happy life."

"How's that?"

"Nothing." He raised the spyglass and scanned the seas before them, meanwhile reflecting that truth was overrated. He and Umara had only been indulging in it for a few breaths, and, ridiculously, here it was already trying to rekindle regrets grown cold long ago.

He didn't see any ships, Thayan or otherwise. When he lowered the telescope and turned back around, it annoyed him a little that the wizard appeared to be studying him. But if her scrutiny had afforded any insights, she didn't see fit to remark on them.

Rather, she simply said, "If you and Captain Greatorm get me back aboard the galley, I'll see to it that Kymas pays you for your trouble. It won't be a fortune like Evendur Highcastle's bounty." She smiled a crooked smile. "As you've already observed, my master plainly doesn't consider me indispensable. But I am a Red Wizard of Thay, and it will be something."

He wondered if she truly believed he'd settle for that. She might if she didn't know his reputation for boldness and relentless pursuit of an objective. But even if she didn't believe it, the suggestion was a reasonable tactic given that, landlubber that she was, she needed Anton and Falrinn to sail the boat. Better, then, to come to a false accord now and defer a fight until they caught up with the other Thayans.

And, Anton realized, pretending to agree to her offer now and saving hostilities for later made just as much sense for him. She knew what Kymas's ship looked like. He didn't. Her magic might prove useful as they pursued it. And if she truly did believe he was willing to settle for whatever payment Kymas might offer, she'd presumably prevail on her superior to welcome him aboard the Thayan ship, which should simplify the task of spiriting Stedd off it.

He sighed with what he hoped was a convincing imitation of resignation. "Whatever your master is willing to pay for you, I suppose it will have to do."

Throughout the morning, a favorable wind carried them eastward. Meanwhile, fiddling with his various mechanisms, Falrinn repeatedly trimmed the sails and reset the rudder. Umara, whose curiosity apparently outweighed any tendency to aristocratic aloofness, alternately pestered the gnome with questions about his innovations and sought to make conversation with her fellow human.

For his part, Anton found that he didn't much mind the distraction. Trustworthy or not—almost certainly not—she was pleasant enough to talk to. Perhaps it was because she had manners and an education, even though acquired in her sinister necromantic homeland, and it had been a long while since he'd conversed with a lady. Generally, the reaver's life restricted his choice of womanly companions to festhall bawds and female pirates as coarse as . . . well, he supposed, as coarse as he himself was.

He pointed out landmarks when the mainland became visible, despite the grayness and the rain, and taught Umara to fish with trailing lines. They grilled the sea bass and dolphinfish they caught, and ate them at dusk.

Afterward, they returned to the bow and Anton peered out into the moonless, starless blackness hoping to spot another vessel's lanterns. Sitting beside him, Umara asked, "Why do you even need to chase Stedd?"

Anton snorted. "I thought we covered that. For the coin."

"But why do you need any more treasure?" She tugged her hood down in an effort to keep the rain out of her face. "I mean, I know why my family has a proud name and little else. The great War of the Zulkirs devastated much of Thay, and it certainly blighted our land. And in the decades since, Szass Tam hasn't much concerned himself with providing opportunities for folk who are still alive. But you . . ."

"But I'm Anton Marivaldi. The madman who plundered the spice fleet out of Telflamm. The fiend who burned the harbor at Delthuntle. Why is it I'm not already rich as a merchant prince and long retired from the sea?"

"Well . . . I wasn't going to say 'madman' or 'fiend.' But yes."

He shook his head. "It's a good question. Somehow, the coin and gems always run through my fingers in a heartbeat. Cormyr could fight Sembia for a year on the treasure I've squandered standing drinks for taverns full of rogues who'd knife me for a shaved copper. Maybe it's because I can't imagine going away and living a different life."

"Is being a pirate truly all that grand?"

He thought about it. "No. Not really. But it's what there is. For me."

Her tone wistful, Umara said, "I can understand that."

The sailboat bucked almost like a horse as it met the waves, but as she gazed into the dark and the rain, Umara no longer feared being bounced around on her bench or, worse, being bounced overboard. After several days at sea, she was accustomed to the motion of the vessel.

In fact, she was surprised at how relaxed she was in general. At first, a mage's disciplined patience notwithstanding, she'd experienced bouts of frustration that a galley that had left port only shortly before Falrinn's sailboat should prove so elusive. But it wasn't long before impatience faded, and resignation that actually felt rather peaceful took its place.

She supposed it was because there was nothing she could do to influence the outcome of events. She needed to rejoin Kymas and participate in the final phase of their mission. It was both her duty and the only way she'd receive any measure of the credit for its successful completion. But Falrinn and Anton were the mariners, not she, and they'd catch the galley when they caught it. Meanwhile, for essentially the first time since the start of her adolescence, she had no responsibilities and no walking dead man of a teacher or superior ordering her around. Certainly, her two current companions made for pleasanter company, and she hoped she wouldn't have to kill them when her time aboard the sailboat came to an end.

Falrinn, she thought, might well be content to accept whatever payment Kymas was willing to offer and go away. The gnome was a practical sort. Anton, however, had a reputation for recklessness, and that accorded with her own impression of him. He might well make another play for Stedd no matter what the odds against him.

She told herself that if he did, he would have only his own stubborn folly to blame for what ensued, but that didn't make her feel any happier about the prospect. Frowning, she resolved to think about something else, and then a point of orange light appeared and disappeared in the darkness off the port bow, like a firefly that had only chosen to glow once.

But a ship's lanterns wouldn't blink. They'd shine steadily. Uncertain whether she'd seen something real or just a trick of the night, she leaned forward and peered intently.

For several breaths, nothing happened. She decided she had been mistaken and started to settle herself more comfortably. Then light pulsed again, but a different light, a hair-thin, crooked white line accompanied by a tiny snap like the crack of a distant whip.

Now Umara knew what she was seeing. "Come here!" she called.

Falrinn had been snoring in the shelter amidships, and Anton had been dozing beside the rudder. They both stood up and made their way into the bow.

"What do you see?" the pirate asked.

"Nothing now," Umara asked. "But somewhere ahead of us, a wizard threw a blast of flame and followed it up with a thunderbolt."

"I assume," Anton said, "that Kymas Nahpret has those spells in his repertoire."

"Yes."

"Then we're finally catching up with him. Good."

Falrinn spat over the side. "He wouldn't be throwing battle magic unless somebody else had caught up with him, too."

Anton smiled. "Don't tell me the Inner Sea's cleverest smuggler is afraid of a little scrap."

"Smuggling's not like piracy. Pirates make trouble, smugglers avoid it. But I'll get us close enough to see what all the fuss is about. You two keep watch." The gnome made a minute adjustment to the headsail, then went to trim the mainsail.

Umara waited. Nothing else flickered in the blackness ahead. After a time, she said, "There truly were spells discharging. I may not be a sailor, but I know magic when I see it."

"I'm sure you do," Anton replied.

"So why aren't we seeing any more of it?" Umara asked.

"It's possible," the reaver said, "that a fiery blast and a bolt of lightning were enough to scare off or even destroy an enemy vessel. Or that Kymas discovered it's still out of range, and now he's conserving his power. Or that an enemy archer shot back at him and took him out of the fight."

"That last is doubtful," she said.

"Why?" Anton asked.

Umara belatedly remembered she hadn't told Anton that Kymas was a vampire. His ignorance on that particular point might hinder him if he did try to steal Stedd, and in any case, she preferred he have no reason to suspect she herself was occasionally obliged to submit to such a creature's embrace. She didn't want the pirate imagining her in that degraded attitude.

"If there was any danger from bowmen," she replied, "Kymas likely would have armored himself with enchantment."

"Ah."

"How long, do you think, before we get close enough to know what's really happening?"

Anton shrugged. "Obviously, I can't know when I'm not even the one who saw the flashes, but perhaps a long while yet. Maybe not even until after daybreak."

"If it takes that long, the fight will definitely be over."

"Not necessarily. Ships can maneuver and chase each other around for ridiculous amounts of time before they start fighting in earnest. I've spent some of the most tedious days of my life just standing on a deck waiting for a battle to start."

But Umara didn't find the watching and waiting tedious. She strained her eyes peering, and pictured all the situations she might discover when the sailboat finally drew close enough. Surely, given Kymas's supernatural might and the mettle of the marines in his service, the galley would prevail in a sea battle. Yet what if it didn't?

She imagined the broken vessel sinking and carrying Stedd down with it, and the mental picture made her wince. It would be a sad, ugly way for the boy to die.

Then, scowling, she pushed the soft, foolish thought away. Stedd was fated to die no matter what. It was her task to make certain that his death was useful, to her monarch, her master, and herself.

After a while, she and Anton both spotted another wink of red-orange fire. He called out, "Two points to starboard!" Falrinn adjusted the rudder and cold rain drummed on the deck.

Sometime after that, the eastern sky started lightening, revealing massed gray thunderheads like floating mountains. Beneath them, still far apart and small with distance, Kymas's galley and a caravel emerged from the falling sheets of rain and the gloom. Umara frowned because it appeared her master was running from that one lone ship and it was giving chase. Given equal odds, she would have expected the undead wizard to seek battle as quickly as possible, before daybreak drove him under cover.

Something else surprised her, too. The caravel's sails bellied with the same blustery westerly that was blowing Falrinn's sailboat along. But the crew aboard the galley had taken down her sails and were relying on the churning oars for propulsion.

"By the fork," Anton murmured, "that's the *Iron Jest*."

"Your ship?" Umara asked. He'd told her the story of his mutinous crew.

Falrinn came scurrying forward. "When did the *Jest* acquire a weather worker?" he asked.

Anton shook his head. "When I took my leave of her, she didn't have one."

"Well, she does now," said the gnome. "He's stolen the wind from the galley. If not for the rowers, she wouldn't be making any headway. As it is, I judge she's struggling against an unnatural current."

"It looks that way to me, too," Anton said.

Umara had no idea how her companions could tell, but she didn't doubt they were right, and proof that there was some manner of spellcaster aboard the *Iron Jest* came just a moment later. Making use of the time remaining to him, Kymas hurled a spark at the pirate vessel that roared into a burst of yellow fire when it struck the bow. Despite the rain, the forecastle caught fire. But at once, water leaped up from the surface of the sea, washed across the bow of the caravel, and extinguished the blaze.

Moments later, the water beneath the galley heaved, lifting it high and dropping it back down. A sailor fell overboard. Oars snagged on one another, a couple snapping, and in the wallowing aftermath, some rowers made haste to free the tangled ones and jettison the broken stubs for replacements, but others remained stationary. The zombie oarsmen, Umara realized, couldn't take the initiative to perform that or any task. Someone needed to command them.

"The Thayans," Falrinn called from the stern, "are lucky the sea mage hasn't just sunk them outright. It looks like he's got the power."

"He won't," Anton shouted back. "The church of Umberlee wants Stedd alive. He's risking flinging the boy overboard as it is, but he's probably right that Kymas has him stowed securely." He turned to Umara. "So in the end, it's apt to come down to grappling hooks, boarding pikes, and cutlasses, and with both ships locked together, tricks with the wind and the waves won't be useful anymore. Can your people hold their own in a fair fight?"

Possibly not. Not if Kymas had already shut himself away and the pirates' wizard had any useful spells left for the casting. "I don't know," she admitted. "Kymas may have used up most of his power already. We should help them if we can."

Help? For a moment, Anton wasn't sure what to make of the idea, for by any sane estimation, both his former crew and the Thayans were rivals trying to abscond with the prize that was rightfully his. So why risk his own life aiding anybody?

Because he was in the straits. Pirate Isle was just a day or two away, while Thay was still hundreds of miles to the east. So if Umara and her folk ended up with boy, he'd have more time to work out a way to steal him.

Besides, he had a score to settle with Naraxes and the other mutineers.

He grinned at the Red Wizard. "I'll be honored to assist if I can." He looked back at Falrinn. "Let's catch up to the galley."

"Sail my little boat into the middle of a fight between two warships?" the gnome replied. "Aye, Captain! When ice burns and wolves play the whistlecane."

"Come on! It'll be fun."

"Why don't you should swim over? That will be even more fun."

The muscles in Anton's neck tightened. Falrinn was being entirely sensible, but that didn't make his recalcitrance any less frustrating. "My old friend—"

Umara touched Anton on the arm. Surprised, he fell silent.

The mage then smiled at Falrinn. "What if we were invisible?" she asked.

The gnome scowled, considering. "Well, no one aboard the *Iron Jest* would throw spells or shoot crossbow bolts at us. But can you hide the whole boat?"

"I think so. I have a knack for concealment and illusions."

Falrinn shrugged. "If it works, I suppose I'm game."

Umara took a long breath. Anton assumed she was clearing her head. She started to speak, and then a notion popped into his head.

"Wait," he said. "Suppose we do get aboard the galley. Are you certain you'll then be able to out-spell the weather worker?"

The Red Wizard frowned. "No. How could I be? But I have to try."

"Maybe not. Not if you can wrap you and me in invisibility that lasts even after we leave the sailboat." He looked down the length of the vessel. "Not if Falrinn can take us to the *Jest* instead of your ship."

"I *can*," said the gnome, "but the idea is stupid."

Anton grinned. "Probably. But I have a plan." He turned back to Umara. "Would you like a tour of the proud vessel I once commanded?"

She smiled. "Why not?"

Anton retrieved his saber from under the shelter, and Falrinn hastily trimmed the sails. Eyes closed, Umara raised her hands over her head and recited words that somehow echoed even without any walls to bounce off. A scent like that of lilies suffused the air.

Then the entire sailboat and those aboard it faded from view. Anton laughed.

Falrinn, however, cursed. "You didn't warn me I wouldn't be able to see us, either! How am I supposed to pilot the boat?"

"By touch," Anton answered. "If you can't do it, you're not the sailor I always took you to be."

Still swearing, the gnome stamped around the deck. Ratchets clacked as he made further adjustments to the sails. Meanwhile, Anton took stock of just how hidden they were.

Plainly, the concealment was less than total. The boat's wake extended behind it, and a keen eye could make out the rain splashing against surfaces that were themselves invisible. But in the feeble light of an overcast dawn, with everyone aboard the *Iron Jest* intent on the galley ahead of them as opposed to anything astern, it should suffice.

Once Anton determined that, he had nothing to do but wait while the sailboat made its approach. Fortunately, the smaller, lighter vessel was faster than its quarry, and, still growling obscenities from time to time, Falrinn was managing it with a deftness that justified Anton's faith in him.

When they were racing along beside the caravel's stern, the smuggler said, "This is as close as I can get."

"How do we cross over?" Umara asked.

"You're a mage," Anton said. "I hoped you'd have a way."

She laughed. "As planners go, you aren't as impressive as you could be." She recited another rhyme, and for a moment, he felt like mites were crawling on his skin.

Then a line trailing from the *Jest* lifted itself up out of the water and snaked through the air in his direction. He caught it, and then it slumped in his hand, lifeless as any other rope.

"Have you got hold of it, too?" he asked.

"Yes," Umara answered.

"Then here we go." He jumped over the side, and she, presumably, did the same.

The caravel dragged him through the cold brine, and he pulled himself hand over hand along the rope until he could haul himself out of the water and swarm up toward the deck. He noted the *Jest* was about due for scraping and recaulking, then grinned at his outmoded way of thinking. The condition of the ship was no longer his concern. If he had his way, it soon wouldn't even be Naraxes's.

Anton swung himself over the rail just below the quarterdeck, where a different helmsman stood in the same spot where One-Ear Grim had breathed his last. This close, Anton had more concerns about the rain spoiling his invisibility, but so far, the helmsman plainly hadn't noticed him. Nor had the archers in the fighting top or the men clustered at the bow waiting to board the galley.

The hanging line swung and creaked as Umara climbed up behind him. Looking down, he could just make out the ghost her spell and the raindrops made of her. He took hold of her arm and pulled her onto the deck.

"Thanks," she gasped.

"Are you all right?"

"Just winded. Crawling up a rope half drowned was harder than I expected. What now?"

"I'll show you."

As they skulked forward, he peered in an effort to spot the sea mage Naraxes had recruited. He couldn't, though. The spellcaster was probably all the way forward, where it would be easiest to target the galley, and masts, cordage, and assorted reavers were in the way.

Well, if the fellow was at the far end of the ship, perhaps that was just as well. Anton took a cautious look around, then undogged a hatch. The ladder beneath it descended to a different section of the hold than the one where he and Stedd had been imprisoned.

With the hatch lowered again, the cramped, cluttered compartment was too dark to see anything more than shadows. Then Umara murmured a charm, and a patch of bulkhead glowed silver, revealing a miscellany of casks, crates, and tools.

"I take it," she said, "you were counting on me to take care of this detail in the master plan as well."

"Why not? Whoever heard of a wizard who couldn't make light?"

"Now that I have, what are we looking for?"

"This." He gestured to a box with cabalistic sigils painted on it, then remembered she couldn't see him do that or anything. Smiling, he indicated the container by giving it a little shake inside the netting that held it securely on a shelf.

When Umara spoke again, her voice sounded from right in front of the crate. "These are signs of cold and quiescence."

Anton sawed at the netting with his dagger. "And I paid a wizard plenty to draw them. Many a captain has doomed his own ship by bringing incendiaries aboard. Until this morning, I didn't intend to be one of them."

When he finished cutting the netting away, he pried the box open and lifted off the frigid lid. Nestled in straw, the round black catapult projectiles inside had arcane symbols of their own inscribed on them.

"It looks they're all here," Umara said.

"They are. A pirate can't make much profit burning up the very prize he's chasing. They were only for an emergency, and lucky me, I finally have a suitable one. Can you set them off from up on deck?"

"I can, but will it matter? The sea wizard put out one fire already."

"Yes, but surely he was expecting Kymas to throw more flame. We can hope a surprise explosion ripping through the guts of the ship will befuddle him. Even if it doesn't, flooding the hold to put out our blaze ought to pose its own problems."

Topside once more, the pair of them phantoms in the rain, she whispered, "When I cast fire, I'll reappear. I'll veil myself again immediately, but still."

"I'll watch your back," he told her.

She murmured hissing, popping words that had no business issuing from a human throat, then swept one vague, transparent arm down at the open hatch. A red spark shot from fingertips that simultaneously became opaque flesh and gleaming nails once more.

A detonation boomed, and a tongue of flame leaped higher than Anton's head. He just had time to think, Not bad, and then a far louder explosion jolted the caravel from bow to stern and sent him reeling. The initial blast had only been Umara's spell birthing flame, while the one that followed an instant later had been the incendiaries detonating in response.

Staggering, ears ringing, he struggled to recover his balance. A part of him was appalled at what he'd done. But the ship he'd just scuttled didn't belong to him anymore and never could have again. He thrust such sentimentality aside, pivoted to see how Umara was faring, and cursed.

The Red Wizard sprawled on the deck next to the hatch and had evidently bumped her head when she fell. Her eyes were open and her mouth was moving soundlessly, so perhaps she wasn't entirely unconscious, but she was near enough that she wasn't even trying to shift away from the heat of the flames shooting up right beside her.

She was useless in that condition, a liability, and Anton started to turn away. But then he hesitated. For all he knew, she might come to her senses in a moment. And he needed her to convince Kymas Nahpret to welcome him aboard the galley.

The *Iron Jest* was already listing to port—maybe the blast itself had punched a hole in the hull without the fire needing to burn through—and Anton dragged Umara until he could deposit her at the foot of one of the shrouds to keep her from sliding over the side. Had any of his fellow pirates been paying attention, the knave likely would have realized that an invisible agency was hauling the stunned woman along. But the crew had plenty of other matters to distract them, like their own falls and resulting injuries, the yellow flame leaping and black smoke billowing upward in various places— remarkably, somehow fire was already licking at the mainsail—and a first panicked scramble for the lifeboats.

Anton crouched beside Umara and patted her cheek. "Wake up," he said, "we have to go."

The green eyes blinked, but she still seemed dazed. She certainly wasn't trying to get up.

"Come on," he growled, "or I swear by every devil in every hell, I'll leave you behind." He pinched her cheek as hard as he could.

She pawed clumsily at his hand in an effort to push it away. Then he sensed a figure standing over them. He looked up and caught his breath.

Anton had known Evendur Highcastle was now undead. But he didn't frequent any deity's temple, even Umberlee's, and he'd only glimpsed the Bitch Queen's new hierophant at a distance in the streets of Immurk's Hold. And now, even though he'd never liked the swaggering bully his fellow captain had been, it was revolting to finally, truly behold the slimy, swollen horror his transformation had made of him.

Evendur glared down at Umara. "You again," he snarled. "You did this." He bent to seize her in hands whose rings were all but buried in puffy rot.

Anton sprang up, whipped out his saber, and slashed.

The rapid motion compromised his concealment. Sensing something whirling at him through the rain, Evendur jerked backward. The tip of the saber still sliced him across the forearm, but the cut was scarcely the lethal stroke Anton had intended. It was, however, a sufficiently aggressive action to make opacity race up the blade from the sludge-smeared point to the guard and then on into his hand and arm.

Evendur peered at his newly revealed attacker with a mix of fury and surprise. "Marivaldi!"

"Wait," Anton replied. Even as the request left his mouth, he recognized it as likely the most useless word he'd ever uttered.

"Kill him!" Evendur bellowed, and though many of the reavers were too busy trying to fight fires or abandon ship to heed even Umberlee's Chosen, several came running.

The first one thrust with a boarding pike. Anton sidestepped, and momentum impelled his opponent another step down the slanting deck. That brought him into saber range, and Anton slashed his leg out from under him.

That was one adversary down, but Anton had to pivot instantly to confront the next. This time, the treacherous footing made *him* slip, and, off balance, he only just managed to parry a cutlass cut to the head and riposte with a slash that opened the other pirate's belly.

The wounded man dropped the cutlass to clutch at his stomach. As the weapon started to slide and tumble away, Anton stabbed the tip of the saber into the loop defined by handle and guard, flipped the captured blade into the air, and caught it in his off hand.

That bit of panache made his other assailants hesitate, but only for an instant. Then they resumed their advance, and in a more organized fashion than before, spreading out to flank him. Meanwhile, seemingly untroubled by the fresh gash in his arm, Evendur unlimbered the boarding axe slung over his back, stroked a fingertip along the edge, and made it glow a sickly green.

A figure at the edge of Anton's vision hacked with a broadsword. Anton whirled, parried with the cutlass, and saw that his attacker was Naraxes. He cut with the saber, and the former first mate blocked with a buckler. Steel bit into wood.

Anton heard or perhaps simply sensed motion at his back. With a hollow feeling in his gut, he realized it was likely suicide to turn away from Naraxes and suicide not to. He opted to turn and found Evendur rushing him with the boarding axe raised above his head.

Anton lifted the cutlass into a high guard and whipped the saber in a stop cut to the ribs. He scored, but it didn't matter. The Chosen started to swing his weapon anyway.

Then, however, two luminous spheres leaped through the air to strike Evendur from behind. On impact, one vanished in a burst of flame, while the other winked out of existence with an earsplitting screech that flensed gobs of rotten flesh off his bones. He jerked, and the slanted deck betrayed him and sent him staggering, too. The flailing axe cut missed.

Anton spun back around toward his other foes. Though he was too late to witness it, magic had plainly attacked them, too. The front of his body encrusted with frost, Naraxes looked like a helplessly shuddering snowman. Two other pirates lay dead, each burned in one fashion or another, one with patches of flesh still bubbling and melting.

Traces of phosphorescence fading on the fingers that had cast the spell, Umara gripped the shroud and dragged herself to her feet. "You said we need to go," she panted.

Anton grinned. "Now that you mention it."

"No," Evendur said. "Stay and die with your ship like a captain should." He ripped the burning jerkin and shirt from his back and moved to place himself between his foes and the port edge of the deck.

Anton had just about reached the unhappy conclusion that while he and Umara might be able to slow the Chosen of Umberlee down for a breath or two, no power at their command was likely to stop him. But they might as well try. Hoping Evendur was unfamiliar with the stance and the combinations that flowed out of it, he raised both blades high in a guard his father's master-of-arms had taught him.

Then the *Iron Jest* gave another great lurch as the sea surged into another breached compartment below deck. This time, the stern dropped, while the bow lifted out of the water.

The motion sent nearly everything and everyone, Evendur included, sliding, reeling, or tumbling helplessly aft. Umara, however, was still hanging onto the shroud, and, dropping the cutlass, Anton managed to snatch hold of a halyard.

Anton rammed the saber back into its scabbard. "Come on!" he said. "Evendur won't give us another chance." He made a floundering run at the port side of the caravel and dived into the sea. Umara splashed in after him.

Despite the best efforts of the saber that seemed intent on fouling the action of his kicking legs, he swam away from the *Jest* as fast as he could. When a ship sank, it created a suction that could drag swimmers under. He'd seen it happen.

Finally, unsure if he truly deemed himself out of the danger zone or was just too spent to swim any farther, he halted, turned, and started treading water. Umara was still with him.

"As you should be," he rasped, "after the trouble I took on your behalf."

The Red Wizard didn't ask what he meant. She was intent on the *Iron Jest,* and why not? It was quite a spectacle.

The back third of the caravel was underwater. The rest was canted even higher, and much of it covered in roaring flame that made a mockery of the rain. The spars and sails were trees of fire, and as best Anton could tell, most of the boats were burning, too. Some men risked setting themselves alight in what must be an agonizing struggle to lower the smaller vessels into the water. Others, clinging precariously to whatever support they could find, stabbed, chopped, and wrestled for a place aboard them. A gray-black wave of rats flung themselves over the side of the *Jest* to attempt the impossible swim to land.

Then, with a horrible, sudden smoothness, the rest of the caravel slid under the sea, leaving only smoke above the waves. It was almost as if Umberlee, who supposedly loved sinking ships above all things, truly had taken the *Jest* in her colossal hand and pulled it down.

The submersion raised a wave that lifted Anton and Umara and dropped them back amid charred scraps of flotsam. A scrabbling rat pulled itself aboard a broken section of ribband and claimed it for its raft.

Hoping for more comfortable transportation, blinking against the water trickling down from his hair into his eyes, Anton peered about and found Falrinn and his sailboat, visible once more, off to the left. "Falrinn! Here we are! Come get us!"

"I'm working on it," the gnome answered. He threw a line and it plopped down in the water.

Anton used the rope to clamber back inside the sailboat. Umara sought to do likewise, but likely thanks to her knock on the head, exhaustion, and saturated garments, struggled unsuccessfully. Anton took her arm and, with a grunt, heaved her aboard.

"So," Falrinn said, "on to the galley?"

Umara gave him a smile. "Of course."

She kept smiling, too, as the gnome adjusted their course, and she and Anton slumped on benches. The Turmishan, however, felt a bleak anger rising inside him.

It wasn't simply the bitter melancholy that sometimes overtook him after a battle, although that might be a part of it. It was the realization of just how thoroughly he'd wrecked his own schemes.

His intent had been to eliminate a shipload of rivals and then sell Stedd to Evendur. But instead, he'd attacked the undead captain himself and sent him to the bottom.

How was Anton supposed to collect the bounty now? He supposed he could still try selling Stedd to the Umberlant church, but would the waveservants even want the boy now that the leader who'd declared his apprehension important was gone? Even if they did, would they deal fairly with a man who'd assailed Evendur Highcastle with fire and blade?

Curse it, anyway!

Perhaps the most galling aspect of the whole affair was that Anton hadn't needed to reveal himself to Evendur. He could have preserved his invisibility and then salvaged the situation somehow. But he hadn't. He'd swung his saber because . . . he wasn't even sure of the *because.* Maybe just because the new Evendur was so hideous to look at, and he and the old one had so seldom gotten along.

In any case, he supposed that now he'd simply have to accept whatever payment the Thayans offered for sinking the *Iron Jest* and Umara's safe return and go on his way. It surely wouldn't be enough to buy a new ship, and the prospect of serving aboard some other pirate captain's vessel, as he had in the early years of his exile, had little appeal. But what was the alternative?

As the sailboat approached the galley, Umara, still looking annoyingly pleased at the "success" of their foray against the *Iron Jest,* stood in the bow with her head bared. She hadn't shaved her scalp during her time with Anton and Falrinn, and her black hair had started to grow out. But plainly, she still trusted the other Thayans to recognize her, and apparently, they did. No one shot at the smaller vessel, and a sailor dropped a rope ladder over the side.

Falrinn waved Anton toward the larger vessel. "Go collect our pay," the smuggler said.

"You're both welcome aboard the galley," Umara told him.

"Thank you, lass," Falrinn answered, "but I'll be fine down here." Where, Anton thought, he'd have a better chance of escape if Kymas Nahpret proved less appreciative of their efforts than Umara had promised. Other than the unsavory reputation of Thayans in general and Red Wizards in particular, he saw no reason why that should be the case, but it didn't surprise him that the gnome felt he'd taken enough chances for one day.

It *did* surprise him that when the moment came to board the galley, Umara's air of exhilaration fell away from her. She stopped smiling, took a long breath, and squared her shoulders in the manner of someone resignedly taking up a chore. But maybe she was simply wrapping herself in the dignity the crew expected of her.

She climbed the rope ladder first, in the slightly hesitant manner of someone unaccustomed to them, and he followed. He reached the deck just in time to find her countrymen still standing at attention.

The living ones, at any rate. Three, currently armed for battle like the rest, were slouching zombies with slack gray faces and a yellow sheen in their sunken eyes. By the essentially intact look of them, they hadn't been dead, or undead, more than a tenday or two.

Umara waved her hand, and, while casting some curious glances in Anton's direction, most of the mariners returned to the task of making the galley shipshape after the tossing Evendur had given it. But a middle-aged man with a pocked, sour face and the last two fingers missing from his left hand approached the wizard.

"Captain," Umara said.

"Lady Sir," the officer replied. "Did *you* sink the pirates?"

"With the help of this warrior"—she nodded to Anton—"and his friend."

"After we abandoned you in Westgate," the captain said, a note of disgust in his voice.

"We all have to follow orders," Umara said. "Speaking of which, is Lord Kymas in his cabin?"

"Yes," the other Thayan said. "He rushed in there as soon as it became clear the pirates wouldn't be bothering us anymore."

Anton wondered why. It was strange behavior for any commander in the wake of an engagement. But perhaps Kymas was a landlubber like Umara and realized that, though nominally in charge, he had nothing to contribute to the task of setting the galley to rights.

Umara looked at Anton like she wanted to say something but didn't know what. After a moment, she settled for, "I'll go talk to Kymas." She turned toward the hatch under the awning projecting out from the quarterdeck. Likely knocked loose by the shaking the galley had weathered, the left side of the sailcloth rectangle drooped.

Then an oarsman cried out. Together with Umara and the captain, Anton hurried to the larboard side of the galley to see what had alarmed the man. By the time they got there, other folk were peering, pointing, and exclaiming.

A bowshot away, a shadowy form stood on the surface of the sea. In the gloom and the rain, Anton couldn't see it particularly clearly, but he had no doubt it was Evendur Highcastle.

And why, Anton thought bitterly, wouldn't it be? The living corpse was the Chosen of the Queen of the Depths. He felt like an idiot for imagining he could dispose of such a monstrosity just by sinking a caravel out from under him.

"Still," Umara breathed, "he doesn't have a ship or a band of followers anymore. Perhaps he'll give up for today."

As if in response, the sea heaved beneath the galley and sent it crashing down, throwing the decks into confusion once again. Oars lurched in the thole pins, battering rowers with bone-breaking force. Arms flailing, a marine toppled over the side. For a moment, it looked as though Umara might tumble after him, but Anton grabbed her arm and steadied her.

"Kill the creature!" Anton bellowed. "Kill him!"

He'd momentarily forgotten he wasn't the captain aboard this vessel, but the Thayans heeded him anyway. Arrows and crossbow bolts arced in Evendur's direction. Rattling off words of power,

Umara thrust out her arms and sent darts of blue light streaking after them.

Some of the arrows and quarrels fell short or flew wide. Waves leaped up to block the others. Even so, two or three actually pierced the bloated, decaying flesh of their target, and Umara's magic did, too. But they evidently didn't do much damage, because Evendur started forward.

The sea raised the galley and dropped it into a trough. For a heartbeat, the sea streamed across the deck, and someone screamed.

Then the tall, pale man Anton had met on the benighted street in Westgate strode out of the cabin in the stern. He now wore an intricately embroidered scarlet robe and cloak. "What is this?" he demanded.

Umara stared at him. "You—"

"I know a spell to shield me when I absolutely require it. Now, why is the ship still being tossed about when our attackers are burned alive or drowned?"

"Not quite all of them are." Anton pointed to the figure advancing atop the sea.

Kymas Nahpret smiled a grim little smile. "The fool doesn't know when to give up, does he? But if he insists on perishing with his vessel, I'll oblige him."

The wizard pulled a slender ebony wand from his sleeve. He hissed an incantation that filled Anton with instinctive revulsion even though he didn't understand a word of it, then flicked the wand in Evendur's direction as though miming a teacher's admonitory tap on a daydreaming pupil's head.

The air around Evendur darkened. Then vapor puffed from the dead man's body, and Anton realized it was the rain that had truly darkened in the course of changing from water to something that seared like vitriol.

And, to Anton's excitement, it appeared to be hurting Evendur more than anything else hitherto. The dead man flailed, staggered, and then plunged down into the sea as, perhaps, the magical assault broke his concentration.

145

Some of the Thayans cheered. Until, like an invisible cable was drawing him up, Evendur rose above the surface once more.

By then, though, in a manner that momentarily reminded Anton of Dalabrac and his countless blowpipes, Kymas had traded the ebony wand for one made of glass or crystal. He shouted a word that sounded like crockery smashing and stabbed the instrument at the Chosen.

At the same moment, Evendur shook his fist at his attacker. The wand shattered, and a wave of transformation ran up Kymas's hand and on into his arm, turning the limb as clear as the mystical weapon had been. Immediately after the first wave flowed a second that made the wizard's altered substance crack and crunch.

Wincing, Anton expected to see Kymas's whole body break into hundreds of glittering shards. But Kymas arrested the change by dissolving his whole arm into mist, in effect amputating it above the highest point to which the infection had spread. When he willed it back into solidity, it was pallid flesh and blood-red sleeve once more.

Anton thought it an impressive defense, but Kymas still looked rattled that Evendur had reflected his own attack back on him. The Red Wizard pivoted to the captain and said, "Why aren't we moving?"

"Same reason as before," the officer answered. "The rowers aren't ready to row, and the current and the wind are both running against us."

Now that someone had drawn Anton's attention to it, the pirate felt the wind gusting from bow to stern driving spattering rain before it. At least, he thought, it was doing Falrinn some good. Unwilling to bide dangerously close to the Thayan ship while Evendur bounced it up and down, the gnome was fleeing westward.

Anton hoped Falrinn would get away, and it actually looked likely. The Bitch Queen's Chosen appeared to be devoting all his attention to the galley.

All his attention and all his power. The ship rose high and smashed down. The mainmast snapped at the base and fell toward the stern with broken cordage streaming out behind it.

Anton sprang in front of Umara and raised his arm to protect his face. A line whistled past his ear, but nothing struck him. The mainmast slammed into the smaller mast aft, snapping it as well, and both hammered down on the quarterdeck.

"Much more of this," the captain said, "and the hull's likely to start coming apart."

Umara turned to Anton. "You said Evendur wants Stedd alive."

"We may have made him so angry that he's willing to settle for drowning without the frills as opposed to ritual sacrifice. Or else he wants to force us to surrender."

"Then he's going to be disappointed," Kymas said, and Anton had to give him credit. He'd seemed shaken for an instant, but he was all resolve now. "Umara and I are more than a match for any jumped-up zombie, especially if we work together." He turned to the other mage. "Let's try some necromancy. We'll command him to pull his own head off."

Whispering in unison, the Red Wizards whispered words that set Anton's teeth on edge. But they didn't make Evendur decapitate himself or even break stride, and a moment later, the sea heaved the galley up and down. The tangled wreckage of the two masts bounced and shifted, and sailors scrambled to keep from being crushed, or swept overboard.

"All right," Kymas said, "more acid. He didn't like it before."

True, Anton thought, but the corrosive rain hadn't stopped Evendur, either, and he suspected it would have even less effect the second time around. He turned to the captain and asked, "Where are you keeping the boy?"

"The lower rowing deck," the Thayan said. "But . . ."

Anton looked around and spotted a companionway that looked like it ought to lead to the lower banks of oars. Weaving around injured men and trying not to trip over snapped rigging, dropped weapons, and other litter, he dashed in that direction.

The next upheaval came when he was partway down the steep little flight of steps. It pitched him forward to splash down into bilge water that sloshed back and forth with the rocking of the boat.

Near the companionway, a mariner had jammed himself in a corner. The captain probably expected him to command the oarsmen, but at the moment, his eyes wide with fear, he didn't seem to working on anything but making sure the tossing of the galley didn't throw him around.

Beyond the sailor were the rows of benches with an aisle running down the center of them. There was just enough wan gray light leaking in through the outriggers to illuminate the creatures occupying them. But even if there hadn't been, Anton would have known them for what they were by the rotten stink that suddenly assailed him.

Like the zombies topside, these looked relatively fresh and had likely started the voyage as living slaves. They still wore their leg irons, and the shackles had held them more or less in place as the galley slammed up and down, although jerking oars had battered them and left them sprawled and twisted in peculiar attitudes.

Stedd lay in the filthy water between two of the central benches. To Anton's relief, the boy's face wasn't submerged, but he wasn't moving, either.

As Anton splashed toward him, the nauseating stink of corruption intensified, and the air grew colder even as the light dimmed. Or was it? Anton suddenly wondered if it was actually his eyes that were failing.

He *might* be going blind. He realized he felt weak and sick in a way that his exertions and bruises didn't explain. He was stumbling, dizzy, and his pulse pounded in his neck. Was the beat irregular? He wasn't sure, but he thought so.

Then, mere shadows in his murky sight, the dead men started to turn in his direction. They were about to rise and swarm over him. He knew it.

Except, he realized, that he didn't.

Common mindless zombies wouldn't do that, or anything, without being ordered to, and besides, these were shackled in place. A curse had evidently poisoned his mind with terror and nonsense. Resisting its influence as best he could, he reeled onward.

Another upheaval sent him staggering, and the lurching end of an oar nearly caught him in the kidney. Then a final stride brought him to Stedd, who didn't react to his arrival.

The boy's eyes had rolled up, with white showing all across the bottoms, and he was shaking. Cast in the form of a skull, an amulet made of black metal hung around his neck.

Anton pulled off the medallion and threw it as far as he could. Stedd's shuddering abated immediately, and so did the Turmishan's own feelings of illness and dread. Plainly, Kymas Nahpret had used magic to render the boy prophet helpless. Perhaps the amulet had somehow focused the innate vileness of the zombies, the undeath that was antithetical to the life-giving light and warmth of the sun, on him.

"Hey!" called the Thayan braced in the corner. "You're not supposed to do that."

Anton didn't bother to look around. "One more word," he said, "and I'll kill you." And then, to Stedd: "Wake up, lad. Come back to me."

Stedd's eyelids fluttered then his eyes focused on Anton. "You . . ." he croaked. "I was having nightmares . . . "

"They're over now," Anton said.

"I remember, the bad man made me wear the black skull . . . did you come to help me?"

Anton felt a twinge of discomfort or something akin to it, but there was no time to pause and wonder why. "We need to help each other. Evendur Highcastle, the 'bad man' who put a price on your head, is attacking us. Nobody has been able to hurt him, or at least, not enough for it to matter. But maybe you and your sun god can."

Stedd shook his head. "I couldn't pray with the skull around my neck. I couldn't even think."

"You have to—"

The world, or at least their little bit of it, heaved up and down. Zombies flailed back and forth as though trying to dance despite the impediment of their leg irons. In the aftermath, Stedd looked shocked, and Anton realized that was only natural. The boy hadn't been conscious for any of the previous tosses.

"As I was saying," the pirate continued, "you have to use your power, and that's the reason why. Evendur will sink us if you don't."

"But I'm weak!"

"What matters is, is Lathander weak? That's not what you told me when we were hiking to Westgate."

Stedd swallowed. "All right. I'll try."

The boy had trouble standing, so Anton helped him. Then they hurried to the companionway and up into the rain.

With commendable discipline, those marines who hadn't yet tumbled overboard or suffered some other mishap were loosing arrows and crossbow bolts as fast as they could shoot. Still casting magic in concert, Umara and Kymas conjured a fiend with the curling horns of a ram and the leathery wings of a bat and sent it flying at Evendur with its barbed spear leveled.

Yet none of the defenders' efforts were helping very much. Evendur had a couple more arrows sticking in him, and a couple more charred and torn places in his flesh, but he was only a javelin cast away now and still inexorably advancing. Waves leaped to block the missiles streaking at him; one momentarily assumed the form of a gigantic fish to swallow the bat-winged devil whole.

Stedd gawked at Evendur, then took a deep breath and closed his eyes. Hoping the boy was reestablishing a broad, clear channel down which his god's power could stream, Anton positioned himself so as to screen him. If the Bitch Queen's Chosen hadn't already noticed Stedd on deck, there was no reason to give him a second chance.

The ship wallowed. Anton had the feeling that the unquiet water beneath her was getting ready to fling her into the air once more.

"Take all the time you need," he said to Stedd. "But if that's more than another heartbeat, hang on to something."

"I'm ready now." Stedd stepped into the open and thrust his hand at Evendur.

The undead pirate's head jerked in the boy's direction. Whitecaps broke across the surface of the sea. But before the water could do whatever its master wanted it to, a ray of brilliant light streaked from Stedd's fingertips, struck Evendur in the center of his massive chest, and set him ablaze—not with fire, but painting him with radiance.

Evendur's will brought waves leaping over him, but they failed to extinguish the dazzling halo. Then he roared words of power that included the name "Umberlee." When they too failed, he dived beneath the surface and hurtled along for some distance like an undersea shooting star. And then, at last, the glow went out.

Unfortunately, that meant Anton could no longer see him in the depths. He waited tensely to find out if the undead reaver would return to the fray. Time dragged until it seemed likely the answer was no. A breath later, a sailor let out a cheer, and his fellows joined in.

The moment after that, Stedd collapsed to his knees.

Anton crouched beside him. "Are you all right?"

"Yes," the boy whispered. "Just . . . that was harder than making all the food . . . it was the hardest thing yet . . . "

"I'm glad to hear it," Kymas said. "You won't feel tempted to make a fuss when we put your amulet back on and restore you to your friends in the lower tier. This time, I think we'll tie you up as well."

"Hold on," Anton said.

The senior wizard turned to him. "I can see you and Umara have come to a genuine understanding, and I appreciate all you've done this morning. I look forward to welcoming you as you deserve. But it will have to wait until the prisoner's secure. As he just demonstrated, he's dangerous."

"The pirates and sunlords both managed to hold him without torturing him."

Kymas shrugged. "He's growing more powerful, and in any case, what's the difference?"

Anton didn't know, and the prudent part of him urged him to let the matter go. Unfortunately, another part was set on having its way.

"Make me the boy's warder," he said. "I'll manage him without breaking his mind or making him sick. That way, you can be sure he'll reach Thay alive and fit for whatever you mean to do with him when you get there."

"An interesting proposal," Kymas said, "but I prefer the existing arrangements. Now, please, stand aside." He gazed steadily into Anton's eyes.

For a moment, Anton felt lightheaded, and then his sensible side finally came to the fore. He drew breath to tell the Red Wizard he could have it his way but then recalled the malaise that had afflicted him among the undead oarsmen. Kymas Nahpret had created that enchantment, and Anton's sudden willingness to give way likely derived from a similar source.

The Turmishan clenched his fists. "Stay out of my head, you piece of dung."

Kymas sighed. "This is so perverse of you. I truly did intend to honor whatever promise Umara made you, but by your pugnacity, you've forfeited any claim on my good will. Surrender your weapons."

Anton whipped out his dagger, lunged, grabbed the wizard by the collar, and poised the blade at his throat. "No. You put the boy and me ashore. Or else you and I can die together."

"You should have opted for your enchanted weapon," Kymas replied. "Then murdering me would at least be possible, albeit unlikely. My dear, would you please put an end to this farce?"

Umara rattled off rhyming words and pointed at Anton. Pain ripped through his chest, and, gasping, he stiffened.

In that moment of incapacitation, Kymas wrenched himself free. Then he punched Anton in the head.

CHAPTER SEVEN

ANTON FELL TO THE DECK UNCONSCIOUS, AND UMARA LOOKED down at him with a knot of emotions pulling tight in her chest. She couldn't untangle them all, but she did know she was angry.

Why did you make me do that? she silently asked. Why were you such an idiot?

Kymas gave her a sardonic look. "That was *marginally* helpful," he said, "but if I'd been in the mood to brawl, I could have broken free at any time. Why didn't you cast something a bit more lethal?"

Because she herself wasn't sure, she made up a lie that ought to satisfy him: "I expended much of my power aboard the pirate ship and nearly all the rest when you and I were fighting the Chosen of Umberlee. I don't have any lethal spells left."

"Hm. Well, perhaps it worked out for the best." The vampire turned to Ehmed Sepandem. "Now that the wizards have attended to all the difficult and dangerous tasks, maybe your men could at least muster the wherewithal to carry our two prisoners down to the lower oars."

"Yes, lord," the captain said.

When they all arrived there, Kymas had the mariners drag Stedd to the center of the rowing benches and bind him hand and foot. Then the vampire retrieved a skull-shaped medallion made of black metal from the bilge water and hung it around the boy's neck. Umara could see Stedd straining to resist the talisman's influence, but he quickly lapsed into a sort of twitching, shivering trance state nonetheless.

Kymas then glanced around at the zombies. The attack on the galley had so thoroughly battered a couple of the creatures as to rob them of animation. Others had suffered broken bones that would hinder them as they sought to row.

"Put our new guest behind an oar," Kymas said. "He can take up some of the slack."

"Yes, lord," said a marine. "Uh, should I kill him? So you can make him like these other things?"

"No," Kymas said, "just lock him down, and chain his hands to the oar while you're at it. He can work himself to death here in the dark and the stink with the magic of the amulet gnawing away at him. It will give him the opportunity to reflect on his insolence."

Umara watched the marines carry out their master's instructions. Until, surprising herself, she blurted, "Is this truly necessary?"

Kymas regarded her quizzically. "The wretch didn't just argue with me. He insulted and threatened me. I see no reason to grant him the mercy of a quick death."

She took a breath. "I was thinking, must we kill him at all? I recognize his transgressions, but I also see that if not for him, we might neither of us be alive or have Lathander's Chosen in our possession. Doesn't it—"

"Balance the scales?" Kymas shook his head. "I'm disappointed in you, Red Wizard. What a very un-Thayan way to think.

"The lowly owe the high respect and obedience," the vampire continued, "whereas the high don't owe the lowly anything at all. Certainly not fairness, whatever that weakling's notion actually means."

Umara realized she'd pushed as hard as she dared. Bowing her head, she said, "Yes, Master. I understand."

"I hope so. Let's get out of here."

Back on deck, Kymas strode briskly toward the cabin under the quarterdeck, but not quite briskly enough. Suddenly, wisps of smoke puffed from his hands and face, and, sizzling, patches of alabaster skin charred black. His protective charm was failing, and despite the clouds and the rain, the light of the hidden sun was burning him.

He sprinted toward the stern, dodged through the wreckage of the fallen masts, threw open the hatch to his cabin, scrambled inside, and slammed it shut behind him. Umara scurried after him, hesitated, then rapped on a detail of the naval battle carved into the panel, a warship stuffed from prow to stern with spearmen.

"Come in," he said, the hint of an edge in his cultured voice. "The screen is in position to block the light."

It was, and by the time she stepped around it, his burns were already healing. "I'm glad you're all right," she said.

"You should be," he replied, "considering that it was your foolishness that delayed me below deck."

"I apologize."

"The principle I just explained to you—that I shouldn't have needed to explain—applies at every point up and down the great long ladder that is the world. It applies every bit as much between you and me as it does between your Turmishan friend and me."

"I know that, lord."

"Then come 'apologize' with your blood."

As he bared her neck, he murmured, "I know you dislike this. I've always known. Do you know why I don't change your loathing to pleasure?"

She hesitated. "Because a Red Wizard needs to learn to endure that which is difficult?"

"Well, yes, partly. But mostly because your aversion increases the pleasure for me."

Anton gathered that he must, in his own bellicose and imbecilic fashion, have impressed the Thayans, for they hadn't contented themselves with chaining down his feet. They'd also looped a set of manacles around his oar before locking them on his wrists, a hindrance that prevented him from reaching the narrow blade hidden in his boot.

The manacles clinked every time he and his zombie benchmate with the skin sloughing off its grub-infested arms and torso hauled on their oar. After a while, he'd realized he was croaking out his reminiscences, tall tales, and sea shanties in time to the beat.

"So the sea giant said, 'If that's the Pool of Love, why does it bubble and smoke?' And *I* said . . . "

Curse it, what *had* the clever original hero of the story said to convince the wicked giant to dive into the lava? Anton's mother had told him the tale dozens of times, but now he couldn't remember.

Blame exhaustion, the fetid air, or the debilitating aura of the skull medallion. Perhaps because Anton wasn't currently attempting to remove the amulet from around Stedd's neck, the effect wasn't hitting him as hard, but he could still feel it in his body and mind alike.

He wracked his brain for several pulls on the oar, then gave up and started a new story. "You may have noticed that unlike many another pirate—or all these Thayans—I don't have any tattoos. But I used to. I was covered from the neck down. And this is the story of how I lost them.

"The *Iron Jest*," he continued, "had been through a storm so terrible it left every sail in tatters. If we didn't mend them, we'd never make port. But when we checked the ship's stores, we discovered we'd forgotten to stow any thread.

"So I took my dagger and picked at a bit of the tattooing on my left big toe until I dug the end of a line of ink out of my skin. Then I pinched it between my thumb and forefinger and started pulling very carefully."

"What?" Stedd mumbled.

Anton grinned. He'd talked and sung his throat raw in an effort to rouse the boy despite the power of the skull talisman, but he'd nearly given up hope of it working.

"Never mind," he said. "Just wake all the way up. But don't squirm around."

He didn't want the overseer of the lower tier to realize Stedd was awake. Fortunately, the Thayan had already proved to be a lackadaisical supervisor, happy to stay by the companionway outside the aura of the amulet so long as Anton kept rowing. And if the pirate and the boy prophet kept their voices low, the creak of the oars should cover the sound of their conversation.

Stedd's eyes fluttered open. "I'm sick . . . "

"You're exhausted and wearing that filthy skull again. But you have to raise the power to free yourself."

Stedd grimaced. "I don't think I can. Not like this. It's just too much."

There was a demoralizing certainty in the lad's voice, but Anton struggled to keep any hint of defeatism out of his own. "Surely not too much for the fighter who destroyed Evendur Highcastle."

"I didn't destroy him. He'd already used up a lot of his own strength, and you and the wizards had already hurt him some. So I was able to hurt him more. Enough to chase him off. But that was all."

"If we're not done with him, that's all the more reason for you to get us free."

"All right, I'll try." The boy stared at the planking over their heads as though hoping by sheer force of will to peer through it to the sky beyond. His lips moved as he whispered his entreaties. But Anton couldn't see anything happening in response, not even the faintest, briefest flicker of conjured light, and finally Stedd said, "I'm sorry."

Anton sighed. "So am I."

"But this isn't the end. As long as we don't give up, we'll find a way."

A muscle in the Turmishan's back gave him a twinge and made him suck in a breath. "Boy, I *don't* give up. Ever. But I don't care if you are Chosen, whatever that really means; you need to get over thinking that destiny or some friendly god is going to make everything come out all right. That's not how the world works."

"I don't think that. Not exactly. But—"

"Show me the divine hand manifest in what's happened to you so far. *Everybody* lied and betrayed everybody else. *Everyone* wanted to kill you or peddle you to those who would. It's not exactly the sort of inspirational fable the priests like to tell. It's what that dastard Kymas called it: a farce. A bloody, random comedy of errors."

"Everything *is* different than I thought it would be, back when Lathander first spoke to me. I'm scared a lot of the time. But I need to go east, and you know what? I am. You took me part of the way, and the Thayans are taking me farther."

Anton frowned. He hadn't looked at the situation like that. Probably because it was a ridiculous perspective.

"It's not going to help you," he said, "that Thay just happens to lie at the eastern end of the Inner Sea. You won't even lay eyes on Sapra as the galley sails on by."

"Maybe. But it isn't true that nobody's really my friend. There were Questele and the other Moonstars, and now there's you."

"By the fork, mooncalf, haven't you figured me out even now? I didn't sneak into the House of the Sun or chase after the galley to rescue you. The sordid truth is, I never stopped intending to sell you to Evendur. It was just another droll twist in the plot of the farce that put him and me on opposite sides today."

"I did figure that out," Stedd answered, "and I don't like it. But then you tried to help me when the Red Wizard said he was going to hang the skull on me again."

"And I have no idea why. But you can rest assured that if I had the moment to live over again, I'd cheerfully drop the chain over your head myself."

"I don't believe that. Why do you *want* to be bad? You try so hard that when a good feeling pushes you to do something, you don't even see that's the reason why."

Inwardly, Anton flinched. "Has your Morninglord been telling you the alleged secrets of my innermost heart?"

"No. It doesn't work like that. But sometimes I understand things I wouldn't have before."

"Well, this isn't one of those occasions. I don't have to try to be bad. I *am* bad, and I have a string of outrages and atrocities to prove it."

"That doesn't mean—"

"Enough prattle! Pray. Meditate. Find some magic to set us free."

Lying in filthy bilge water, Stedd presumably resumed trying to do precisely that, albeit, to no more effect than before. At least the absence of twitching and jerking provided reassurance that he hadn't slipped back into nightmare-ridden delirium.

Meanwhile, Anton felt pains flower throughout his body. He was strong and fit but lacked the calluses and specially developed musculature of a galley slave, and he was paying for it. The ordeal would have been even more taxing if he hadn't figured out how to let his putrescent but indefatigable benchmate do more than its fair share of the labor. Unfortunately, he couldn't let the zombie do too much more than half, lest the overseer take notice.

In time, Anton also learned that even with the sun hidden behind the rainclouds, he could guess the passage of time by the way the feeble daylight shined through the outriggers. Thus, he judged it was late afternoon when, robed in scarlet and magenta, her head newly shaved, her cheek bruised where he'd pinched it, Umara descended the companionway.

"Be quiet and keep still," Anton whispered. He suspected the wizard intended a closer inspection than any the overseer had made of late, and he didn't want Stedd to give himself away.

Somewhat to the pirate's surprise, Umara gave the Thayan mariner permission to vacate his post for a while, and the man clomped up the steep shallow steps. Then the mage headed down the central aisle.

She gazed down at Stedd with a somber expression that hinted at regret, but her jaw tightened as she stepped around him to reach

159

Anton. She backhanded the reaver across the face; her rings tore his cheek.

"Idiot!" she snarled.

For some reason, Anton could only laugh, even though it made his sundry aches hurt worse. "Is that how Thayans apologize?"

"I have nothing to apologize for!"

"No," he said, "you don't." Deciding she likely wouldn't object if he let the zombie do all the rowing, he uncurled his raw fingers from the oar. Even that hurt; they didn't want to straighten out.

"What possessed you to defy a Red Wizard and a squad of marines standing ready to assist him?"

"I relish a challenge? It seemed like a shrewd idea at the time? Truly, I can't explain the impulse. Some passing madness, I suppose."

"And now you have to die for it."

"Are you here to do the honors?"

She scowled as though he'd bruised her feelings. "Kymas doesn't mean to let you off that easily."

"I can't say I'm surprised. Why did you come, then?"

She reached into a concealed pocket and brought out a little silver flask. When she offered it, he drank without hesitation, for after all, who would waste poison on a man in his situation?

The liquid burned like some unfamiliar sweetish liquor, but its analgesic properties took effect far more quickly than that of alcohol alone. One mouthful made Anton's assortment of pains dwindle significantly.

Umara reclaimed the flask and screwed the cap back on. "You won't wake up stiff, either."

"You mean they're eventually going to let me rest? I'd just about concluded your crew can't repair the rigging to raise a sail."

"They can't. In fact, Evendur Highcastle crippled the galley in several ways. We lost one of the side tillers, and we're taking on water as fast as we can pump it out. Captain Sepandem plans to limp to the coast and, if possible, find a shipyard and put in for repairs. If it's not possible, we'll continue our journey on land."

"Through the wilds of Gulthandor? That should be entertaining. Perhaps Lord Kymas will let me tag along as a porter."

Umara put away the flask and produced a split biscuit with a slice of fried fish in the middle. The aroma flooded Anton's mouth with saliva, and he took the food and gobbled it down. The bread was stale and hard, and the fish cold and greasy, but he was too hungry for it to matter.

"That was all I could bring," the wizard said.

"I'm sure it was tastier than whatever scraps my keeper will eventually toss my way."

"And it's all I can do for you."

"It's more than I expected."

"I mean it. I won't be back. Not like this. My duty is my duty, my path is my path, and that's all there is to it."

"Truly, I understand. You have a respectable place among your people. Ambitions, too, I imagine. You can't just throw them away."

"No," she said, "I can't." She looked at him for another moment, then turned away.

Stedd said, "Wait!"

Startled, Umara gaped down at the boy, and Anton felt an impotent urge to grab him and smack him. Didn't the empty-headed child realize that the possibility of him eventually channeling more magic, however remote that possibility might be, was the best chance they had? And he'd just thrown it away.

"You're conscious," Umara said.

"Yes." Stedd tried to sit up despite the impediment of his bonds.

After a moment, Umara helped him lift his upper body out of the bilge water and settled him against the end of a bench. "How?" she asked.

"Anton talked to me to help me wake up. And maybe I'm getting used to the skull. I mean, just a little. I can't reach out to Lathander, so don't worry about that."

"Then why reveal you're awake?" the wizard asked.

"So I can talk to you," Stedd replied. "You and Anton are just alike. He thinks he has to be bad. You think you have to be what you are. But you don't. You can change."

Umara sighed. "You're a bright boy, Stedd. I could tell the moment I met you. But you're talking about things a child can't understand."

"You're wrong. Even with the skull around my neck, I still see things."

She hesitated. "Like what?"

"Like, you don't even want to go where you're going. Not really. You like magic, but hardly anything else about your life."

"So I should throw it all away to help you? No. I'm not a traitor."

"Lathander doesn't want you to be. He wants you to make your country better."

Umara blinked. "What, now?"

Even in the gloom, Stedd's blue eyes seemed to shine. "It's . . . you're right. I don't understand everything. How could I, when I've never even been to your land? But it's like there are two Thays. A real one, and one you dream about."

"I don't *dream* about it. Like any educated person, I know that a hundred years ago, Thay was different. But I'm not obsessed with the past. I'm getting on with my life."

"Anything that changed once can change again. There's a new dawn every day, even when people can't see it behind the clouds."

"That may be, but it's ridiculous to tell me to go change Thay. I'm one person!"

"You can't do it all yourself, but you can be part of it. Maybe a big part. Only, not if you just keep doing what you're told no matter how low or mean it is. You have to start listening to your heart. Then Lathander can help you."

Umara snorted. "Why would he? The old Thay, the Thay you imagine I'd want to restore, was his enemy."

"But it was still better than the land you have now. And if it came back, maybe it could get better still."

162

The Red Wizard stood silent for a breath or two, then shook her head. "It was a good try, child. But some lies are just too absurd for anyone to believe."

Stedd frowned up at her. "I don't lie. That's the two of you."

"Well, I'm truly sorry I ever deceived you, and sorrier still for what's coming. But I can't do anything about it." She turned and waded back up the aisle with her scarlet robes dragging in the bilge water.

As she disappeared up the companionway, Anton said, "It *was* a good try, but also a rotten choice of tactics. There was never any hope of persuading her."

"I guess," Stedd said, and now he simply seemed like a sad, tired little boy, without even a hint of divine inspiration in his manner. "At least she didn't make me go back to sleep."

Frowning, Anton realized that was true, she hadn't, and for a while, he wondered if Stedd's plea actually might have struck a chord with Umara. But as he toiled through the night and into the following day, exhaustion made every pull on the oar a torment, and the power of the skull medallion scraped away at his manhood and obliged him to struggle against recurring urges to weep and beg the overseer for mercy, he decided it plainly hadn't.

But then, when it was afternoon once more, the mariner abruptly slumped, slid off the little seat built into the corner, and started snoring. And a moment later, Umara descended the steps with Anton's saber and a cutlass tucked under her arm.

She plucked an iron key from the overseer's belt and hurried down the aisle. She then pulled the chain from around Stedd's neck, flung it away like Anton had, and unlocked the Turmishan's manacles.

"I don't know why I'm doing this," she growled.

Anton grinned. "Blame the lad. Clearly, his greatest magic is the ability to rob folk of their common sense."

Evendur floated in the endless green waters of Umberlee's other-worldly ocean. Enormous eels and sawsharks came swimming to inspect him.

He didn't recall passing from one level of reality to another to reach waters that would douse Lathander's burning light and help him recover his strength. Maybe he'd done it instinctively. But it was also possible the Queen of the Depths had drawn him here, and not for healing but for judgment.

Suddenly, she came swimming out of nowhere—or rather, out of another hidden doorway from one place to another—with gigantic great whites, krakens, jellyfish, and sea dragons swimming in attendance. Huge and terrible as the apparition that had risen from the pool in the temple had been, it barely hinted at the awful majesty of the goddess in her latest form, the trident tall as a tower in one clawed and scaly hand, the least of the shells that made up her jewelry as big as wagon wheels, and her mane of kelp and gelatinous cloak streaming and swirling around her. Evendur felt like a speck of plankton drifting in front of a whale.

As in the temple, he struggled against the urge to plead that if the goddess would only give him the chance to finish his task, he could still capture the boy. In all likelihood, excuses and assurances would only anger her further, and in truth, for the fearful part of him that a man kept hidden from the world, it was easier to remain silent in the face of her transcendent malice and disgust.

A colossal shark glided closer to him and opened its jaws. Umberlee's eyes followed it. They were like immense black pearls, yet at the same time, whirlpools spinning down into annihilation.

Evendur steeled himself against the terror howling inside him. He meant to perish without letting it out. That, it seemed, was the only thing left to him.

Then, however, the shark veered off just before its toothy maw would otherwise have engulfed him. Had Umberlee really only ever meant to scare him? Or, at the final instant, had his display of courage blunted her fury? He had no way of knowing, nor, at this moment of reprieve, did he care.

"I made you my vessel," the Bitch Queen said. "You are the fangs that tear, the jaws that clamp, the tentacles that snare and sting. Yet a *child* bested you. Fail again, and you will pray to me through endless eons to send a hungry beast to end your suffering."

With that, she wheeled, and her monstrous entourage turned with her. The flukes of her scaly mermaid tail were as long as many a city street, and when she swept them downward, the motion created a surge that tumbled Evendur through the water.

Umara gave Anton the key, the saber and cutlass, and the silver flask containing what remained of the analgesic elixir. As he bent to unlock his leg irons, she drew her dagger and crouched down in the bilge water to cut Stedd's bonds, while the reeking zombies rowed obliviously onward.

By the time she finished freeing the boy and helping him to his feet, Anton was rising, also. She frowned to see that despite drinking what remained of the elixir, he had difficulty straightening all the way up and flexing his fingers with their broken blisters.

He gave her a crooked smile. "If my condition distresses you, you should have come to your change of heart sooner. Or brought another dram of potion. You didn't, did you?"

She shook her head. "There wasn't any more."

"Well, I'll be all right." The pirate drew his saber and cut at the air. "Once I move around enough to work the kinks out. What's the plan?"

"One that I hope won't even require you to fight. Kymas is a vampire—"

"Oh, splendid!"

"I hope that for us, it will be. It's afternoon. He ought to be sound asleep in his coffin. I'm going to stab a stake through his heart and then cut his head off."

"And afterward, the crew won't think anything about it?"

"Afterward, I'll be the only Red Wizard left aboard." She smiled. "And where I come from, killing one's superior is an acknowledged way of climbing the 'great long ladder.' "

Anton smiled back. "It's reassuring that you actually aren't doing this because the boy's blather drove you insane or, worse, moral."

"Hey!" said Stedd.

Anton stayed focused on Umara. "Make me invisible again and I can come with you."

"I thought of that, but no. For pure sneaking, one is better than two even if the second sneak is veiled in magic."

"I suppose. Especially in the rain. Then what do you want me to do while you're busy staking and beheading?"

"Just stay here. It will be as safe as anywhere. Come running if you hear a commotion. Or, if you see that it's too late to help me, do whatever you can for yourself and Stedd."

"All right. Good hunting. And thank you."

"Thank me when it's done." She gave Stedd a smile, squeezed his shoulder, and headed for the companionway.

Her heart pounded as she stepped back up into the rain, agitated by the irrational fear that somehow, all the sailors and marines would perceive she'd just gone from being Kymas's faithful lieutenant to his would-be murderer. But no one gave her a second glance.

She took a deep breath, looked around, and found Ehmed glowering at the crewmen laboring to repair the damaged side tiller. She beckoned to him as she approached, and he strode to meet her.

"Lady Sir," he said, "how can I serve you?"

"You know," she said, "what manner of being Lord Kymas is. So you know that unless he works magic to transcend his normal limits, he sleeps—and sleeps deeply—during the day."

"If you say so. You're the mage. You understand the nature of . . . of gentlemen like that better than I do."

"I also understand," Umara said, "why under normal circumstances, Lord Kymas prefers to keep his precise resting place a secret

166

even from me. But unfortunately, our situation isn't normal anymore. The ship could go down at any time."

Ehmed frowned. "The men and I will get you to shore."

"I believe you will if anyone can. Still, if we do sink, Kymas may well require my magic to save him. So I need you to tell me where his coffin is."

The captain cocked his head. "How would I know?"

"Because it's your galley. You must know where the secret compartment is."

"I would if there was one, but there isn't. I never saw a coffin come aboard, but I figured it was in my . . . I mean, in *his* cabin. Haven't you seen it there?"

"No." Nor could she imagine how he could have fit such a large object in amid all the clutter. "But you know what? I'm fussing over nothing. We *aren't* going to sink, certainly not before nightfall, and when Kymas wakes, I'll ask him where the box is."

"That makes sense to me, Lady Sir." Ehmed paused. "Is there anything else?"

"No, Captain, thank you."

"Then I'd better get back to directing the men."

Ehmed returned to the damaged tiller, and she made her way past a pair of mariners working a pump and followed the hose down into the cargo hold aft of the lower banks of oars. Despite the pump team's dogged efforts, water sloshed around her feet and partway up her calves.

She was now underneath Kymas's cabin, and she could imagine him retiring there at daybreak, then changing to mist and passing through some tiny opening down to this space, where his coffin actually resided. But when she whispered a charm and set a patch of bulkhead alight, she didn't see it.

That didn't actually surprise her. If the box was down here, it was surely either invisible or wrapped in illusion. She murmured a counterspell to strip such concealments away.

Nothing changed.

It was possible she simply hadn't mustered the force necessary to disrupt the original enchantment, but she doubted it. Kymas was the more powerful wizard overall, but she fancied herself his equal at casting and penetrating veils.

If he wasn't down here, he must actually be in the cabin. Somehow.

She climbed back topside and headed for the carved hatch under the still-drooping awning. No one would suspect anything amiss if she passed through readily. But if somebody noticed her having difficulty, he might realize she was entering without permission.

She turned the handle and pulled. The hatch shifted minutely, then caught in the frame.

So she whispered a word of opening. The lock clicked, and the hatch hitched open. She slipped inside and closed it behind her.

The magical candles and torches were still burning as they would for centuries unless some spellcaster went to the trouble to extinguish them. The greenish light gleamed on the rack of staves, Ehmed's suit of half plate on its stand, the little metal automaton, currently draped motionless atop the sea chest as it awaited a new command, and all the rest of the jumbled articles Umara had seen on previous visits. Rainwater dripped through a pair of new leaks in the timbers overhead.

Umara recited the same spell of revelation she'd cast in the hold, and with the same lack of results. Nothing hitherto unseen popped into view, and everything that had already been visible remained as it was.

Yet, she reflected, scowling, if the coffin was here, wizardry had to be hiding it somehow. Whirling her hands in spiral patterns, her fingertips trailing crimson phosphorescence, she recited a spell intended to indicate the presence of any sort of magic.

In response, the entire cabin seemed to glow with rainbow colors, because so many of the articles before her bore enchantments. Kymas must have enchanted nearly every item he'd brought on the journey—or had some underling attend to the chore—at least in one petty fashion or another, and even the evicted Ehmed had left a couple magical belongings behind. There was simply no way to pick out the spell concealing the coffin from all the others.

Umara wondered how much time remained before sundown. Not much, she suspected. Perhaps not much at all.

She started picking through the articles in the cabin, examining the cramped space by feel as well as sight. Her mouth was dry, and her pulse quickened. The jangling tautness in her nerves demanded that she rush, but she forced herself to remain methodical.

Yet even so, she nearly passed over the oblong carnelian box on one of the built-in shelves. She was already turning away when it struck her how exactly it resembled a certain type of Thayan sarcophagus.

She found that she couldn't simply lift the lid and look inside. A ward was holding it in place, and she'd have to disrupt it. But as she drew breath to do so, she was already certain what she'd find.

Magic could change the size of a person or object. To a shapeshifter like a vampire, such spells likely came easily, and she was glad of it. She liked the thought of her proud master perishing while shrunk to the size of a doll.

Metal clinked, and then something bumped between her shoulder blades and clung there, yanking her cowl off her head as it scrabbled for purchase. A shrill brassy tone like the blare of a glaur horn jabbed into her ears.

Startled, she faltered, and something sharp stabbed into the skin on the left side of her neck. An instant later, a little hinged arm of red and black metal whipped around the right side of her head, and tiny fingers with needle points clawed at her eye. She flinched away, and they tore her cheek instead.

She reached behind her and yanked her small attacker from its perch. She felt a twinge as its fingers pulled free of her neck and hoped she hadn't just ripped her own skin too badly.

Grunting, she threw her assailant against the screen in front of the hatch. Still emitting the brassy wail, it fell with a clatter and then rolled to its feet.

As she'd realized as soon as she saw its arm, it was Kymas's little metal golem. It hadn't been inert after all. It had been surreptitiously standing watch and sprung into action when she touched the shrunken stone coffin.

The automaton poised its hands to claw and grab, flexed its knees, and sprang upward. She backhanded it and knocked it flying into the rack of staves.

Once again, the metal puppet scrambled up as soon as it fit the floor, but this time, she was ready for it. Backing away to the minimal extent the close quarters allowed, she rattled off words of wrath and thrust out her arm. Her fingertips throbbed, and darts of blue light shot out of them to pierce her attacker and tear it to shreds. The blaring died.

She felt a surge of satisfaction. Then other fingers, full-size this time, grabbed her from behind and threw her face first into the screen. The collision made it fall back into the hatch and then crash to the floor. She fell right along with it.

She was half stunned, but instinct made her flounder over into a sitting position to face the new threat. No doubt roused by the racket the marionette had made, Kymas loomed over her. She thought dazedly that she was sorry she'd missed seeing him emerge from the coffin and grow to normal size. That would have been interesting.

"I can respect the desire to eliminate me," he said, exposing fangs that had already extended, "but not your judgment. You should have waited until you were stronger." He stooped and reached for her.

She was certain that no attack she could cast in the instant remaining would stop him. Investing it with every iota of willpower she could muster, she screamed the word of opening instead.

With a crash, the hatch flew open. Banging, the storm covers did, too. Gray daylight shined through the openings, and Kymas's hairless head and alabaster hands burst into flame.

The vampire roared and flailed. Umara snatched for the stake concealed in her robe. If she could stab it into his heart, that would be the end of him.

But despite the fiery agony he was suffering, Kymas caught the stake in mid-thrust. He jerked it away from her, reversed it, and swept it down at her.

She flung herself to the side, and the stake made a cracking sound as the point slammed against the floor. She scrambled out onto the deck before he could try again.

The hatch slammed shut behind her, and with a ragged clattering, the storm covers did the same. Kymas apparently possessed a charm of closing as potent as her word of opening.

Umara knew what would happen next. The blaze consuming the vampire's substance would gutter out. He'd shield himself against the sunlight and perhaps take another moment to start healing his burns. Then he'd come after her.

The sailors had heard the racket in the cabin, witnessed her frantic, scuttling withdrawal, and now they were gaping at her. She drew herself up straight and attempted to cloak herself in the haughty aura of command proper to a Red Wizard.

"Kymas," she shouted, "is a traitor and means to kill us all. When he comes out, attack him!"

She couldn't tell if anyone believed her or meant to obey, nor did she have time for persuasion. She raised her hands to conjure a blast of fire, spoke the first crackling word of the incantation, and then realized that any magic that further damaged the already crippled galley might result in her death even if Kymas's retribution didn't.

Anton, she decided, had been right. Stedd really had robbed her of every trace of sense.

Despite the rain pattering on the deck overhead, Anton heard a brassy note cutting through the air. Next came banging, and then the sound of Umara shouting.

Stedd asked, "What was she saying?"

"I couldn't make the words out, either, but she told us to consider noise the call to battle. Can you blast Kymas the way you blasted Evendur? Or work *any* magic to hurt him or slow him down?"

"I don't think so. Not yet."

"Then keep hiding. If neither Umara nor I come back for you . . . well, you'll have to think of something."

With that, Anton climbed the companionway. He half expected crewmen to start shouting and rush him the moment he slipped up onto the desk, but they didn't. Everyone was busy staring at the galley's stern—

—where Kymas Nahpret stood casting about with the carved hatch to his cabin standing ajar behind him. The vampire had charred patches on his ivory face and hands but the failing, feeble light of an overcast dusk wasn't inflicting any new burns. He must have shielded himself against the sun.

Unlike those who served him, Kymas oriented on Anton immediately. The undead mage stared, and despite the intervening distance, the pirate felt a surge of lightheadedness. He couldn't remember why everything had seemed so dangerous and urgent just a moment before.

Then crimson light rippled over the vampire's body. Above and behind him on the quarterdeck, Umara appeared with her hand outstretched. She'd breached her invisibility by making a mystical attack.

Unfortunately, the spell didn't appear to have harmed Kymas, but it did make him whirl in Umara's direction. When he did, Anton's head cleared.

The Turmishan drew his blades and charged down the strip of deck that ran between the upper banks of oars. Now lashed in place, the fallen mainmast took up part of the walkway.

Anton's dash snagged the attention of some of the Thayan mariners, distracted though they were. A couple oarsmen—two of the ones who were still alive instead of zombies—started to scramble up from the benches onto the deck with the manifest intention of blocking the way. But then someone called, "Belay that!" Whereupon the rowers faltered.

Meanwhile, the capacious sleeves and voluminous folds of his robe billowing like the wings of a huge red bat, Kymas sprang from the main deck onto the quarterdeck. The crewmen who'd been adjusting the stern rudder recoiled.

So did Umara. But when Kymas plunged down on top of her, she vanished.

A heartbeat later, a second Umara appeared in front of the drooping awning and the entrance to the vampire's cabin. She too had her hand outstretched, and with a crackle, a twist of lightning leaped from it to burn into Kymas's back. The vampire shuddered.

Anton grinned. By combining illusion and invisibility, Umara had kept the other Red Wizard from attacking her for a critical moment. Better, she'd maneuvered him to a place where she could smite him with a powerful destructive spell without risking further damage to their already leaking, floundering ship.

But neat as the trick was, it didn't end the fight. When the spear of lightning winked out of existence, Kymas spun around toward Umara, snarled words in the innately repellent conjuring language Anton had heard him use before, and slapped at the air.

Seething into view, already in motion as it emerged from nothingness, a disembodied hand as long as a man was tall and seemingly made of shadow slapped at Umara. She jerked backward and avoided the blow but nearly pitched herself overboard in the process.

Her murky attacker instantly reversed direction for a backhand swipe. Meanwhile, an orb of gray-black crystal appeared in Kymas's fingers, and he brandished it over his head as he started another incantation. Distorted faces appeared, stretched, and split into new visages inside the dark but gleaming sphere.

Flanking the entrance to the cabin and the strip of sagging sailcloth that shaded it, two companionways ran up to the quarterdeck. Umara was in front of the one to starboard, so Kymas was looking in that direction. Hoping to avoid notice, Anton sprinted for the larboard steps.

But to his disappointment, though not his surprise, the undead wizard pivoted in his direction, shouted a word of power, and stamped his foot. The cry became a roar loud enough to jab pain into Anton's ears and jolt through the larboard half of the quarterdeck and the steps the pirate ascended.

Staggered, he felt the risers breaking apart under his feet. In another moment, they'd give way, and he'd fall, perhaps over the side. He made one more bounding, ascending stride, leaped, and landed teetering on the very edge of the ragged hole his foe had just torn in the planking above his cabin.

Anton windmilled his arms and the blades in his hands, caught his balance, stepped to safety, and then, as he came on guard, shot Kymas a grin. "That was foolish," he said. "Now it's going to rain in on all your things."

"It truly is sad," the vampire replied, "that you didn't know your place." The crystal orb vanished, he held out his hand, and a red staff flew up out of the hole in the deck and slapped into his palm. Taking it in his other hand as well, he shifted into a trained staff fighter's middle guard and shuffled forward.

When facing a staff fighter, Anton liked to cut at his adversary's fingers. Taking care not to look into the vampire's eyes, he advanced and feinted low. As he'd hoped, the staff snapped down to block, and then he made the true attack, a slash at Kymas's right hand.

An instant before the saber would have sheared flesh and bone, Kymas's extremity burst into mist. Striking right through the gray vapor, the blade rebounded from the staff. Spinning his weapon one-handed, the Red Wizard caught the saber in a bind and nearly tore it from Anton's grasp before he could twirl it free.

At once, Kymas snapped the staff at Anton's head. Anton parried with the cutlass, and though he knew by a telltale glimmer deep in the steel and the light, somehow eager feel of the weapon that it

174

too was enchanted, the impact still jolted his arm to the shoulder. Plainly, the vampire had extraordinary strength and skill to match; otherwise, he couldn't have wielded a staff to such vicious effect with two hands, let alone one.

That was unfortunate. So were most aspects of this situation, including Anton's physical condition. He'd promised Umara he could fight if need be, and in fact, at the moment, energized by combat, he felt more or less like himself. But it was likely he wasn't moving as quickly or surely as he would in better circumstances, and likelier still that he'd tire soon.

Still, he thought, I'm not pulling an oar or breathing zombie stink, so why am I complaining?

He tried to hook the staff with the cutlass and yank it aside to clear the way for a saber cut to the chest. Both hands solid and gripping his weapon again, Kymas stepped back just far enough for the cutlass to fall short, then clubbed at Anton's forearm with a stroke that would surely have shattered bone if the pirate hadn't evaded in his turn.

They traded attacks for the next several heartbeats, neither quite managing to penetrate the other's defense. Anton was too busy fighting, avoiding Kymas's gaze, and trying not to step in the hole to spare a glance to see how Umara was faring. He could only hope she was still alive. Or rather, he hoped she'd destroyed the shadow hand and was about to strike Kymas with another spell.

The vampire whispered words that made wood creak, crack, and crunch all around him although that was apparently incidental to the incantation's actual purpose. Hoping to at least spoil the casting, Anton rushed in and cut to the head. Kymas parried and nearly knocked the saber out of his hand.

As Anton fumbled to recover a firm hold on the hilt, Kymas hissed the final word of his spell. Likewise hissing, only louder, a scaly length of flesh burst out of the wizard's abdomen and through the scarlet folds of his robes. Eyeless, it spread its fanged jaws wide and struck at the man in front of it.

175

Caught by surprise, Anton just managed a thrust with the cutlass. The short blade stabbed into the pallid roof of the tentacle snake's mouth.

The thing's jaws snapped shut anyway, and only the cutlass's curved brass guard kept its fangs out of Anton's hand. The violent action in defiance of the weapon drove the blade deeper, and the bloody point popped out of the snake-thing's dorsal surface.

Surely, Anton thought, that had hurt it badly, and if Tymora favored him at all, hurt the undead mage who'd grown it out of his belly, too. But apparently Lady Luck *wasn't* smiling in his direction. The tentacle ripped itself free of the impalement, nearly yanking the cutlass from his grasp in the process, and then both it and Kymas attacked as fiercely as before.

Swaying back and forth and up and down, alternately trying to bite Anton or loop around an ankle or wrist, the tentacle serpent added a new complication to a duel that hadn't been going notably well as it was. Step by step, Kymas pushed him back, and the cramped confines of the broken quarterdeck wouldn't permit him to back very far. Another retreat or two would drop him over the side.

Having evidently rid herself of the shadow hand, Umara crept up the remaining companionway, which put her at Kymas's back. Her lips moved as she whispered something too faint for Anton to hear. She whipped her hands through diagonal clawing motions.

Kymas jerked and stumbled. Though Anton couldn't see the wound from his vantage point, he surmised that Umara's spell had produced an invisible something that was tearing at the vampire from behind.

Anton sprang forward to take advantage of Kymas's incapacity. But, unaffected by its creator's distress, the tentacle snake whipped itself into the way and struck. Anton knocked the gnashing jaws to the side and swung the saber at the writhing arm behind them. The stroke sliced off the eyeless head, and both it and the member to which it had been attached melted away.

The demise of the tentacle serpent constituted progress of a sort, but by the time Anton followed up with a flank cut, Kymas had recovered from the shock of the unexpected assault from behind. Once again wielding the staff one-handed, the Red Wizard parried, and at the same moment, the dark orb reappeared in his off hand. Snarling a word of command, he threw it down on the deck.

The globe shattered, and a dozen misty, elongated figures rose from the shards. Moaning, half the phantoms flew at Umara. The rest swarmed on the unseen thing she'd evoked to rip at Kymas; they evidently perceived it without difficulty.

They kept it away from their master, too, and, freed of the danger it posed, he drove Anton backward again until the pirate had the jagged hole in the planking on his left and the sea just a step or two behind him.

Anton hitched to the right, and Kymas whirled the staff in a murderous horizontal arc. He'd been waiting for the Turmishan to dodge in that direction, for after all, where else was there to go?

But the blow didn't connect. After that initial feinting shift, Anton actually leaped left, over the hole. At last he could see his adversary's back—bare, burned, and shredded thanks to Umara's lightning and her invisible minion—and he slashed it as he fell.

He couldn't focus on making that clumsy stroke count and land gracefully, too, so he crashed down on a miscellany of hard objects. The impact knocked the wind out of him, but he made himself flop over onto his back.

Rain stung his upturned face. At some point during the fight, it had started coming down harder, and he'd been too preoccupied to notice. Squinting against it, he peered upward and rather to his surprise saw only cloud beyond the splintered hole, not Kymas jumping after him or throwing a spell at him. That last saber cut must have finally slowed the undead wizard down.

But it surely hadn't destroyed him, and left to his own devices, he'd quickly shed his wounds and be as strong as ever. Anton sucked in a breath, jumped up, and scrambled out of the cabin and up the surviving companionway.

On what remained of the quarterdeck, Umara was alive and armored in crimson light. Unfortunately, she was also still busy contending with the apparitions from the broken orb.

Kymas was likewise still on his feet, but it was no longer just his fangs that looked bestial. His ears were pointed, and his eyes, red. He'd dropped the staff to seize the rudder man—the poor wretch must have been cowering up here the whole time—in clawed hands, yank him close, and bite his throat out.

Yet despite his newly demonic appearance, Kymas retained the ability to speak. He proved it by bellowing, "Kill the pirate! Umara, too!"

"Yes, lord!" called Captain Sepandem from somewhere to the fore. "Get them, men!"

That was an unfortunate development, but Kymas was still the primary threat. Anton rushed him.

His mouth and chin smeared with gore, Kymas dropped the dying crewman, hissed a word of power, and thrust out his hand. A bolt of ragged darkness flared from his claws. Anton twisted, and the power missed him by a hair.

But as he dodged, he inadvertently met the vampire's crimson gaze. His thoughts dissolved into confusion. Uncertain why he was running, he broke stride. Kymas lunged at him, grabbed him by the shoulders, and opened his gory mouth wide.

Perhaps it was the suddenness of Kymas's action, or the threat implicit in it, that jolted Anton out of his daze. The Red Wizard was too close for him to easily use the saber, but he managed to jam the cutlass between their bodies and rip his assailant's belly open.

Kymas shoved Anton away and staggered backward. His body steamed as it started melting into mist. So he could slip away and hide.

"No," Anton gasped. He darted forward and swung the saber. Kymas's head flew from his shoulders and tumbled into the sea. His body rotted even as it fell.

Anton turned, but nothing else required his immediate attention. With a shouted word and a clap of her hands, Umara destroyed the last of the phantoms. It unraveled into nothingness in a way that reminded him of his mother pulling apart an unsatisfactory bit of knitting. And while some of the marines and sailors had armed themselves, they were no longer advancing on the quarterdeck.

Panting, Anton grinned at Umara. "What was that you said about no fighting?"

"Well," she said, "maybe just enough to make it interesting."

CHAPTER EIGHT

THE GALLEY LISTED TO PORT A BOWSHOT OFFSHORE WHERE IT HAD run aground. Men and zombies waded from the ship to the beach with bundles slung on their backs.

Sheltering beneath the branches of an oak that did a fair job of keeping off the rain, Umara watched the unloading alongside Anton and Ehmed. A short distance away, Stedd stood out in the open with his face upturned. Dawn had come and gone, and as usual, the sun was hidden behind the clouds, but it didn't matter. After his captivity in the bowels of the ship, the boy was hungry for the open sky.

But if Stedd was elated in a quiet, mystical sort of way, Ehmed's expression was glummer than usual. Presumably, the death of his vessel was to blame.

"You were as good as your word," Umara told him. "You got us ashore."

The captain sighed. "Yes, Lady Sir."

"I also appreciate it that none of your men quite managed to intervene in my fight with Kymas before the whole thing was over."

For a moment, Ehmed's lips quirked upward. "Well, you know sailors, Lady Sir. Useless and undependable. Lord Kymas told me so on more than one occasion, when he wasn't driving the rowers of the upper tier like they were slaves." He turned his head in Stedd's direction. "I didn't take any pleasure in seeing a child treated the way we treated that one. But no guard nor any sort of restraints? He could run off."

Umara took a breath. "He won't because he's no longer our prisoner. The notion that he ought to be was at the heart of Kymas's treachery. Our purpose now is to take Stedd to Sapra. By so doing, we'll cement an alliance that will serve Thay well in days to come."

Ehmed frowned as though he would have liked to ask the questions her unexpected assertions evoked. But after a moment's hesitation, all he said was, "Yes, Lady Sir. I'd better go check what's come off the ship and what still needs to."

As the captain strode toward the waterline, Anton murmured, "Eventually, you'll have to tell him that none of you can go home."

Umara shook her head. "I told you, I'm a loyal Thayan. I have no intention of spending the rest of my life in exile. Besides, Stedd says I'm supposed to go back."

"Stedd says a lot of things. But I haven't heard him explain how to justify your failure to carry out your orders."

Orders handed down from Szass Tam himself. Umara imagined standing before that legendary terror and felt a pang of dread.

"I'll figure out something," she said.

"If they understood the actual situation, Ehmed and the others might not care to gamble their lives on your glibness."

Anxiety gave way to irritation. Scowling, she said, "I'm not Kymas. I have a reasonable amount of concern for my underlings, and I hope that if worst comes to worst, my superiors will only punish me. But I'm entitled to the crew's service by virtue of who and what I am, even if they come to grief because of it."

Anton smiled. "Spoken like a true Red Wizard."

Still vexed, although she wasn't entirely certain why, she said, "Anyway, who are you to say these things to me? When did you ever hesitate to lie or put other folk in harm's way to accomplish your ends?"

The Turmishan's eyes—eyes a rich, shining brown like polished agate—blinked, and then he burst out laughing. "Well, now that you mention it, never once in all my years of plundering. What in the name of the deepest hell has gotten into me?"

Stedd, she thought, and perhaps their time aboard Falrinn's sailboat, an interlude when neither of them had needed to fight, scheme, or tell too many lies, had exercised some small influence as well.

"I'm more concerned about whether your newfound regard for honesty will last," she said aloud. "If I knew, perhaps I'd know how far to trust you."

He grinned. "What a cold thing to say to the comrade who helped you kill angels *and* a vampire. How many folk share a bond like that?"

That tugged a smile out of her. "Nonetheless. You know I truly mean to help Stedd. Otherwise, I wouldn't have rebelled against Kymas. But it was different for you. You had to stand with me to be free."

"And now you wonder if I'm still looking for a way to re-kidnap Stedd and turn a profit on him."

"Can you convince me you're not?"

"Well, I suppose it's not beyond the realm of possibility that I could carry the boy off from the midst of you and your followers, that he and I could survive alone on this desolate shore, and then I could find someone besides the church of Umberlee willing to buy him. Maybe a different band of Thayans. But truly, I'm bored just thinking about it. How many times have you and I and other scoundrels like us pursued the poor brat, taken him prisoner, and then lost him again to bad luck or a rival? I'd rather play a new game."

"Escorting him to Sapra?"

Anton hesitated. "I don't go to Turmish. But I'll tag along as far as the border."

She wondered why he shunned the land of his birth. She assumed his fellow Turmishans had put a price on his head, but so had the rulers of Teziir and Westgate, and that hadn't kept him out of their territories.

She drew breath to ask him about it. Then, down on the beach, somebody shouted, "Ship ho!"

Umara looked out to sea. Beyond the galley and farther to the northeast, tiny with distance, she could make out square-rigged sails bobbing up and down as the vessel beneath them cut through the waves.

"Curse it," Anton said. "That's the *Octopus*."

Umara didn't know how he could identify the ship from so far away, but that was scarcely the important question. "Is it a pirate ship?"

"Yes, and her master was always one to truckle to Evendur Highcastle even before the stinking piece of offal came back from the bottom of the sea. I guarantee you he's hunting Stedd the same as we were."

"Is it possible he knows Stedd's with us?"

"Given Evendur's magic, how can you rule it out? Even if he doesn't know, he might think a wreck and a bunch of castaways are too easy a prize to pass up."

Umara scowled. "We're not easy."

"No, we're not. But we're exhausted from the fighting yesterday and then nursing the ship to shore. Have you had a chance to rest and renew your powers?"

"I napped."

"I'll take that as a no. The *Octopus* has a sorcerer aboard. If you were fresh, I'd say he isn't much compared to you. But as you're not . . . " Anton spread his hands.

"All right. I'll give the order." She hurried after Ehmed Sepandem.

Anton started to follow Umara, then remembered that no one here had any reason to take direction from him. If he ventured closer to the tide line and the salvaged supplies piled up there, it would only encourage folk to urge him to load himself up like a pack mule.

On impulse, he headed over to Stedd instead. Oblivious to the scurrying commotion breaking out on the beach, the boy was still gazing raptly up at the clouds.

Anton put his hand on Stedd's shoulder and gave him a gentle shake. The lad jumped and jerked away.

"Easy," Anton said, "it's only me."

Stedd swallowed. "Right."

"But you are likely to get yourself killed if you keep slipping into a stupor here in the wild."

The boy frowned. "It's not a 'stupor.' " Then he spotted the Thayans hastily divvying up provisions, or, in the case of those still wading ashore, making headway as fast as they could. "What's going on?"

"Lathander really ought to keep you better informed. There are more pirates." Anton pointed to the *Octopus*, which was now obviously heading into shore. "Hunting you."

Staring at the corsair vessel, Stedd trembled. It was one of those moments when he was all little boy without even a trace of the Chosen in evidence.

Anton went down on one knee in the wet sand to put himself at eye level with Stedd. "It must seem like it's never going to stop," he said, "but I promise, the bad part is already over. Nobody's ever going to tie you up, hang some filthy cursed trinket around your neck, or make you any sort of captive ever again."

Stedd managed a wan little smile. "Even you?"

Anton clapped his hand to his heart in imitation of an actor conveying distress. "It mystifies me how no one trusts my good intentions."

"No, it doesn't," Stedd replied. His smile widened. "What are we going to do about the pirates?"

"Run." Anton stood back up. "Unfortunately, we can't do it down the beach. We'll have to head farther inland and hope the rogues don't chase us."

"Why wouldn't they?"

Anton gestured to the dripping, tangled trees and brush beyond the beach. "Because that's Gulthandor. Just the thinning edge of it, thank the kindly stars, but still, harder traveling than the hiking you and I did on our way to Westgate, and by all accounts, teeming with ferocious beasts. If I know Mourmyd—the captain of the *Octopus*—he won't have the stomach for it. He's only bold within sight of the sea."

⬭

Short, bandy-legged, walleyed Mourmyd Jacerryl was a depraved murderer, thief, and slaver in the eyes of the world at large, but a toady in the presence of Evendur Highcastle. It was why Evendur always liked him—to the extent he liked anyone—and why they'd so often worked together to raid convoys and harbors across the Inner Sea. But now the Chosen found that the living reaver's interminable explanation, self-justifying and wheedling by turns, wore on his nerves.

"I wish we'd had a tracker to follow the Thayans into the woods," Mourmyd said, waving a scarred and weather-beaten hand. "But at least now you know where they went. That's worth some sort of reward, isn't—"

Even before Umberlee graced Evendur with inhuman strength, he could have grabbed a small man like Mourmyd and held him out over the circular pool in the center of the chamber without undue strain. Now, he could barely feel the other pirate's weight. The only difficult part was resisting the temptation to drop the fool into the midst of the dappled barracudas that rose slither-swimming from the depths in response to his will.

Mourmyd dangled limply as a hanged man from a tree. Either he was too shocked to flail and kick, or he realized that if struggling accomplished anything, it would only be to loosen Evendur's grip.

"Failure," Evendur gritted, "never deserves anything but punishment."

"Evendur—" the small man quavered.

"That's Captain, you filth! Or Wavelord! Or Chosen!"

"Chosen, then! Please, mercy! You *know* we would only have lost the trail if we'd tried to follow. Wasn't it better to return here quickly

185

to tell you what we'd discovered? And isn't it good news? The boy may well die in Gulthandor."

"You're a coward and an idiot." Evendur heaved the other reaver back onto the floor and shoved him away. Mourmyd lost his balance and fell on his rump. "But I did need to hear this news, and I suppose I also need to fight with the weapons Umberlee has given me. So I'm going to let you live."

The pirate with his cloudy left eye drew himself to his feet. His clothes were smeared with slime where Evendur had gripped them. "Thank you, Chosen."

"You can thank me by serving the goddess better than you have hitherto."

"Anything. Just tell me what to do."

"Go through the town and the docks. Tell the captains of Immurk's Hold that hunting the boy prophet is no longer optional. It's my command, and they'll sail with the tide to obey it or carry my curse, which is also Umberlee's, forever after."

"I understand."

"I want them scouring the southern shore from the point where the galley ran aground on to the east. And you, my old partner, are going to take control of Morningstar Hollows. It's where anybody trekking east through the northern reaches of Gulthandor would naturally head, and if they make it that far, you'll be waiting."

"Yes, Chosen." Mourmyd hesitated. "Is there anything more?"

"Yes, by the cold, green deep, there is! Send word to every port and lord who's bent his knee to the church. Tell them I'm levying warships and the crews to man them."

By any sane estimation, Evendur shouldn't need to assemble a fleet greater than the dozens of pirate ships already at his command. But if it turned out that he did, he'd have it. Because he mustn't fail Umberlee again.

Anton took what pleasure he could in the fact that the rain had eased up a little. Not that he was ever really going to be dry until he made it indoors again someday, but once a man passed a certain threshold of discomfort, even partial relief was welcome.

Then he twisted through the narrow gap between two trees, and his shoulder brushed the tangled vines clinging to the trunk on his right. Somehow, that minor rustling agitation transmitted itself all the way to up to branches interlaced over his head. They dumped the cold water trapped in their leaves and doused him. A goodly portion of it spilled down his collar, and he spat a curse.

Behind him, Stedd laughed. Anton rounded on him and the boy flinched.

Anton took a deep breath and forced a smile. "It's all right. I suppose it was comical if you weren't the one standing under the waterfall."

Stedd shook his head. "It wasn't *that* funny. I wouldn't have laughed, except I'm tired of the forest."

"*You're* tired. You and Umara are the landlubbers."

"The farm I grew up on wasn't like this." Stedd waved his hand at the towering trees, the dense thickets, and the boggy earth underfoot.

"Maybe not," Anton said. "Still, I'll wager you explored some sort of woods when you could slip away from your chores. Imagine how out of place we seafarers feel."

"Can't we go back to the beach?"

"With the Binder only knows how many pirate ships combing the coast for you?" Anton shifted the bundles slung to his shoulders and plodded onward; Stedd followed. "That would be unwise."

"But there's no one to preach to!"

"Try the zombies. They'll listen all day without complaining."

Stedd made a disgusted spitting sound to show that this time, he was the one who didn't think something was funny. He loathed the reanimated corpses and likely would have incinerated the repulsive but useful brutes with conjured sunlight if everyone else hadn't argued against it.

"Look," Anton said, "you've already done some preaching, and with luck, people remember what you said. Maybe they're even passing it along. Now it's Sapra that's important. Isn't it?"

"I suppose," said the boy with a touch of petulance in his voice. "But how are we going to get there in time when the going is so hard?"

"Wait." Anton turned back around. "What do you mean, 'in time'? Since when are we on a schedule?"

"I've been feeling it for a little while."

"How much time do we have, and what happens if you don't make it?"

"I don't know."

Anton snorted. "Of course you don't."

"I told you how it works! At first, I just knew I had to walk into the sunrise—"

"You do know the world is round, right? Not even a prophet can actually walk to the place where the sun rises."

"Still, I had to go east! Then, it was east to the Sea of Fallen Stars. Then, east to Sapra. And now I know I need to get there fast."

"Well, I don't know what to say to that, except that if Evendur or his followers catch you, you'll never get there at all. Of course, if you're telling me you can draw down Lathander's power to blast anyone who tries to hinder us, that's different, and I wish to the Nine Hells you'd mentioned it sooner."

Stedd shook his head. "I have power against undead and other things sunlight hates, but Lathander really means for me to be a teacher and a healer, not a warrior."

"Then you'd do well to listen to those who are warriors when we tell you—"

One of the Thayans cried out.

Anton pivoted to see the sailor recoiling from a thicket. Within the brush, half hidden, a long, dun-colored, four-legged shape prowled as though the vegetation was no impediment at all.

Anton snatched out his saber and cutlass and stepped to interpose himself between the beast and Stedd. The Thayan men-at-arms fumbled to extricate bows and crossbows from the wrappings and sacks that protected them from the rain. But by the time they managed it, the stalking form had disappeared.

A wand of some rust-red wood in her slim, pale hand, yanking the skirts of her robe free when they snagged on a fallen log, Umara strode over Anton and Stedd. "What was that?" she asked.

Anton shrugged. "This isn't my country, either, nor did I get an especially good look at the beast. But I believe it was a female lion. Gulthandor is supposedly full of them."

"Just an animal, then."

Anton grinned. "I realize Red Wizards are accustomed to hobnobbing with demons and the like and probably have high standards where ferocity is concerned. But I've heard stories about the lions of Gulthandor preying on men, and if the Great Rain has dwindled their food supply as it has humanity's . . . Still, the beast does appear to have gone on its way, so perhaps we don't need to worry about it."

"I agree we should be careful." Umara turned toward Ehmed Sepandem. "Everyone, stay alert," she called. "And let's put the zombies in a circle around the rest of us. Animals avoid the walking dead."

Once they had the marching order rearranged, they pushed onward. The cold rain pattered down. A woodpecker knocked on a tree, and a raven croaked. Helmthorn berries grew amid long black thorns, and the travelers risked sticking and scratching their hands to pick and gobble the tart indigo fruit.

Then, off to the west, something made a coughing sound. His voice half an octave higher than usual, a sailor asked, "What was that?"

"The same lioness?" Umara suggested. "Stalking us?"

"I don't know," Anton said. "It could just as easily be a different animal taking a look at us and then deciding to avoid us."

It sounded reasonable to him, but even so, the ominous noise had made him edgy, and as they trekked on, he wished all the living folk in the party could stay near to one another for purposes of mutual protection. Unfortunately, the hindrances posed by tree trunks, briars, and mucky ground repeatedly stretched out the procession no matter how often the wayfarers halted and regrouped. The best he could manage was to keep Stedd close.

He would have liked to do the same with Umara but recognized that as commander, she needed to confer with Captain Sepandem, prowl about looking for danger with her own eyes, and occasionally speak words of encouragement or correction to one of the common warriors. He took comfort in the thought that she was at least as capable of defending herself as anyone else in the company.

Eyes wide, glancing in all directions, the other men-at-arms shared Anton's jumpiness. Eventually, a marine yelped when a form sprang up right in front of him; he jerked his crossbow to his shoulder and shot. The bolt missed, and the brown quail he'd started fluttered on up into the dripping dark green boughs overhead.

His comrades laughed and catcalled. Glad to have something break the tension, Anton chuckled. Then, off to the left, brush rustled.

Anton whirled to see a male lion with a black mane and amber eyes springing from a low place in the ground. It charged past a zombie, whose shambling, swaying effort to intercept it was too slow, and at one of the living Thayans.

Arrows flew at the beast. One pierced its haunch, and the lion stumbled but then kept charging. Shouting words that rang like metal striking metal, Umara struck the animal with darts of blue light, but that didn't stop it, either. Anton ran at it even though he was unlikely to reach it in time for it to make a difference to the threatened man.

The lion sprang and carried its prey down beneath swiping talons and clamping, tearing jaws, reducing the Thayan's body to wet red ruin in a heartbeat. Then it abandoned its victim and raced back into the trees. Arrows and quarrels whizzed after it, but no more found their mark before the animal vanished.

Halting, Anton looked at the body on the ground, considered the unbloodied blades in his hands, and felt a frustrated urge to cut *something*. Looking just as angry, Umara said, "The cat wasn't put off by the zombie, it risked making a run at the whole pack of us, and then it didn't even carry away its kill to eat."

"Moreover," Anton said, "it's generally female lions that do the hunting, or so I understand. All of which suggests this wasn't a natural occurrence. Someone or something else is controlling the beast to extract Stedd from our midst. Possibly by slaughtering the rest of us until there no longer is a midst."

"One lion couldn't do that," Ehmed said.

"Which may be why we've already seen two," Anton replied.

"And the Black Lord only knows how many more are slinking just a stone's throw away," Umara said. "There could be a dozen, and we still might not spot them for all the brush and tree trunks."

"I wish I thought you were wrong." Anton turned and waved to Stedd. "Stick close to me."

Stedd obeyed, which unfortunately resulted in Anton leading him over to the mangled corpse so he could appropriate the dead man's crossbow and quiver of quarrels. With the head torn and crushed and viscera hanging out of the belly, the remains were a grisly sight

"Sorry," the Turmishan muttered.

Stedd sighed. "It's all right. I've seen a lot of dead bodies."

That made Anton feel worse, although he wasn't sure why. He gripped the boy's shoulder.

As the travelers trekked on, Anton repeatedly shouldered the crossbow, getting the feel of the weapon as best he could without actually shooting it or even taking it out of its sack. Until another beast, this one a lioness, broke cover and charged.

This time, everyone was expecting such an attack. Still, a couple Thayans froze at the sight of the onrushing predator with its long white fangs and claws. Most, however, shot, and Anton yanked his own new crossbow out of its bag, sighted down its length, exhaled, and pulled the trigger.

As the quarrel streaked from the end of the weapon, the lioness pivoted to retreat from the barrage it had encountered. As a result, the crossbow bolt caught it in the neck. The felid staggered three more strides then fell over on its side.

The Thayans cheered, and for a moment, Anton felt similarly inclined to enjoy the moment. Then the conviction seized him that if some wily intelligence was manipulating the lions like pawns on a lanceboard, then it had just sacrificed one minion in a gambit to achieve some hidden purpose.

He turned. With everyone else, even the zombies, looking at the lioness that had just perished, a second one was creeping in from the opposite direction. It was stalking straight at Umara and was nearly close enough for a final rush and spring.

There was no time to cock and reload the crossbow. Anton dropped that weapon, snatched out his saber and cutlass, and bellowed, "Watch out!" Then he charged.

Not that it felt like a particularly speedy charge when he had to heave his boots out of clinging mud, rip free of twigs and brambles, duck low-hanging branches, and dodge around mossy and vine-encrusted tree trunks. But fortunately, either his initial shout or his subsequent thumping, rustling approach diverted the lioness's attention. It whirled and bounded at him.

The beast covered ground faster than he had. He barely had time to shift to a spot where he had room to swing his blades, and then his foe was on him.

As he cut with the saber, the lioness leaped and spoiled his aim. Strewing rainwater as it traveled, the curved blade still sliced the cat's shoulder, but the result wasn't the lethal stroke he'd intended.

And the lioness was in the air! He dodged and cut again at the animal as it plunged down in the space he'd just vacated. The beast whirled and swiped at the saber, essentially parrying the stroke and nearly batting the weapon out of his grip.

At once, the lioness lunged at him, and he gave ground before it. Until a springy, many-pointed barrier—brush, by the feel of it— pressed against his back, and trees hemmed him in on either side. Despite his resolve to avoid it, the forest had boxed him in.

192

Well, he thought, if I can't use my feet to proper advantage anymore, my hands will simply have to do all the work.

As the lioness clawed, he met the attacks with stop cuts.

At first, the tactic worked. The saber cut deep, and the punishment kept the cat from striking home. He even slashed out one of its amber eyes. But he didn't kill it or make it relent, and after a breath or two, it caught the saber with another swipe and knocked it out of line.

It reared, exposing its chest and belly, and Anton thrust with the cutlass in the desperate hope of piercing its heart.

He at least felt the blade slide into muscle and scrape a rib. But then the lioness crashed into him and bore him down beneath it. The brush crunched as it gave way beneath their weight.

The cat's weight crushed him against the ground. Its remaining eye glared down at him, and the blood from its gashed countenance spattered down into his. More gore drooled from its mouth.

Pinned, helpless, Anton could only will the lioness to die. The ploy worked no better than he expected. The beast spread its jaws wide enough to engulf his head.

Then a spike or blade seemingly made of shadow popped out of the back of the lioness's mouth like a second tongue, stopping just a finger length before it would have pierced Anton's head as well. The vague shape gave off a perceptible chill during the moment of its existence, then withered away to nothing.

Fortunately, though, it had endured long enough to accomplish its purpose. The lion collapsed on top of its erstwhile adversary.

Anton struggled to shift the carcass and squirm out from underneath. Then, grunting, two of the Thayans rolled the body off him.

As he rose, the reaver looked around. Stedd was close at hand, and Ehmed Sepandem had evidently appointed himself the boy's temporary bodyguard in Anton's absence. Good.

And for the moment, no more lions were making a run at the travelers. That too was good.

Breathing hard, Anton gave Umara a grin. "I'm glad you didn't feel obliged to hurry."

The wizard snorted. "Whiner. I cast the spell in time to save you, didn't I?"

"What now?" Ehmed asked, an edge of impatience in his tone.

"That makes two dead lions and only one dead human," Anton replied. "And we wounded the only other beast we've seen. Maybe it, and any others like it, will give up."

"Do you really believe that?" the Thayan captain asked.

"No," Anton admitted. "Not if some lurking puppet master is driving the animals to hunt us. The best we can reasonably hope for is that there's only one lion left, but there's little reason to assume even that."

"If magic is controlling them," Umara said, "then perhaps that's what it will take to chase them away. Everyone, keep watch while I try something."

She pushed back her cowl to bare her shaven scalp and drew a long wand of some dark, mottled wood from a hidden sheath sewn in her robes. She took a long breath, then exploded into motion, whipping the rod through an intricate figure with tight, precise motions that would have done credit to a duelist. She finished by pointing it at the sky, whereupon she froze.

She remained silent and held the position long enough for Anton to wonder if she'd forgotten what came next. Then she started murmuring. The rhythmic lines didn't repulse him the way Kymas's incantations had, but they projected a noticeable pulse of energy that made him feel as though he was being prodded on each of the rhyming words.

Gradually, Umara's voice crescendoed, and as it rose to a shout, she lowered the wand, held it outward, and turned in a circle.

Crackling yellow flame leaped up where she pointed. Thayans recoiled from the heat, and Stedd goggled at the spectacle. When the wizard finished, a ring of fire encircled her companions and herself. Like the blaze aboard the *Iron Jest*, it burned fiercely despite the rain and the wet.

Except, Anton suspected, not really. A moment later, Umara confirmed his guess: "Don't worry. We're in no danger of burning up. This is an illusion. But fire ought to scare off wild animals if anything can."

She lashed the wand from left to right as though making a horizontal sword cut. With a roar, the ring of fire simultaneously leaped higher and rushed outward, seemingly setting brush and branches alight as it expanded.

Anton grinned. An onrushing threat like this should spook any beast, even if some warlock or demon was whispering in its ear.

But the fire had only traveled several paces outward when a thunderous roar reverberated through the forest. Reeling, all but deafened, Anton couldn't tell if the ground was literally shaking or if the prodigious noise had simply overwhelmed his sense of equilibrium. He did see that it extinguished the illusory conflagration as suddenly and completely as a man's breath could puff out a candle.

He staggered a step, caught his balance, then grabbed Stedd and steadied him as well. After that, he peered through the trees and the rain to find the power that had overmatched Umara's.

His eyes were drawn to a dot of flickering blue light amid the grayness. It had an indefinable but undeniable wrongness to it that made him want to flinch in the same way that Kymas's spells had made him want to cover his ears. He kept peering instead and determined that the glow appeared somehow attached to another quadrupedal and possibly leonine form. Then the enormous cat, if that was what it was, stalked into a stand of oaks and disappeared.

"What *was* that?" asked Stedd.

"The master of the pride," Anton replied. "Above and beyond that, I don't know."

"The light is blue fire," Umara said. "The chaotic force that maimed the world a hundred years ago. And if our enemy is bound to it, the thing is spellscarred or conceivably even plaguechanged."

"Does that mean your magic is no use against it?" Anton asked.

The Red Wizard glowered. "I'll kill it if I have to." She took a breath. "But I confess, if it remains content to harry us by sending normal lions at us, I won't complain."

"Is it trying to catch me to give to Evendur Highcastle?" asked Stedd.

Umara shook her head. "Who knows? It may have sensed your power and craved it for itself."

"Whatever it wants," Anton said, "it's not here to make friends." He looked up at the sky, or what little he could see of it through the tree limbs, and attempted the always-frustrating task of gauging the position of the sun despite the cloud cover. "We need to move. We'll want a better place to go to ground if the thing is still stalking us come nightfall."

They pressed onward. In time, they heard another cough off to the left. Men jumped, then craned and turned, searching for the source of the noise. Until a growl from the right answered the first noise and made everyone lurch around in the other direction.

From that point forward, coughs, snarls, and the occasional roar sounded periodically. The lions were demonstrating there were several of them still alive and shadowing their prey.

Once in a while, someone caught a glimpse of a brown shape slipping from one bit of cover to the next. Then the Thayan men-at-arms hastily raised their bows and crossbows and shot. Umara started an incantation, then broke off partway through when her target disappeared. The power she'd been gathering to herself dissipated with a sizzling sound and a crimson shimmer.

Anton took a couple hurried shots of his own before he realized what was going on. Then he called, "Hold it! Stop shooting. The lions are showing themselves to provoke us into wasting our quarrels, and Lady Umara her spells."

"May the Black Hand take it," Ehmed growled, "you're right. Everybody, do as the Turmishan says. Don't shoot unless a lion is making a run at us."

As the travelers resumed their trek, Umara came to tramp alongside Anton and Stedd. "I don't like the way our enemy keeps trying new tricks," she said. "Or anything else about this situation. We'd be better off taking our chances along the shore."

Anton pushed an eye-level branch out of their way. "It's a little late for that to qualify as a useful insight."

She frowned. "I wasn't finding fault."

"I know." He reached to touch her shoulder, hesitated for an instant, and then followed through. She didn't protest the familiarity. "I just . . . anyway, if we think it the wiser course, we can head back to the strand and try dodging Mourmyd Jacerryl and those like him. But we won't make it out of the forest before nightfall."

"And traveling in the dark with the lions lurking to pick us off would be suicide. You mentioned finding a safe place to camp."

Anton snorted. "Yes, being the master woodsman I am. I was thinking of high ground or a clearing. Something."

Now it was her turn to give him a fleeting touch on the forearm. "Maybe we'll still come to a spot like that before sunset."

Instead, they passed one blighted tree and then more, with twisted, knobby, arthritic-looking limbs and chancrous patches in their bark. Though Anton noticed, at first, he didn't care; he had more urgent matters to occupy him than the health of this particular part of the woods. But then, as the gray light filtering down through the canopy was growing even more anemic, he spotted a blue glow.

Thinking the lions' master had worked its way around ahead of the company, he snatched his crossbow from its bag and drew breath to shout a warning. Then he realized the azure light was only one of a dozen such flames flickering on the ground, in the midst of thickets, or in treetops without setting anything else on fire.

A warning was still in order, but one of the marines shouted it before he could: "That's plagueland!"

And so it was. A patch of earth where, a century later, the blue fire of the Spellplague still burned. Anton had never seen such a place before, but by all accounts, they were rife with peculiar dangers.

Umara glowered at the poisoned landscape. "Was the leader of the pride driving us here? Is it more powerful in plagueland?"

Anton shook his head. "If a Red Wizard doesn't know, how should I? I'm just glad we didn't blunder deeper into the area before realizing where we were. Look, we don't have enough daylight left to find a way around it. We need to make camp. We can chop brush to make barricades, and we'll want fires. Big ones, even if you have to spend some of your power to make wet wood burn like dry."

The wizard's lips quirked upward in a weary little smile. "I thought you weren't a woodsman."

"In my time, I've maneuvered around a port or two to attack by surprise from the landward side. Sadly, in this company, that makes me about as close to Gwaeron Windstrom as we're likely to come."

Chopping brush proved to be nervous work. Though he checked often and had Stedd standing watch as well, Anton kept suspecting that a lion was stealing up on him while he was intent on his task. But he and his companions finished building their boma before nightfall, even if it did look too low and flimsy to slow an attacking great cat for more than a moment.

The fires were somewhat more reassuring. Umara's words of command made the flames leap high and burn bright. They might actually serve as a deterrent . . . assuming the master of the pride couldn't extinguish a real blaze as easily as an illusory one.

Men faced outward, staring. Some gnawed biscuits and smoked fish, but at first, despite the exhausting day's march, no one tried to sleep. Everybody was too tense.

Snuffling and wiping at a runny nose, a sailor voiced the common expectation: "They'll come to finish this when it's full dark. Night is when a lion normally hunts."

And, Anton thought, the cats might well come from the direction of the plagueland, precisely because that was the one direction in which they hadn't revealed their presence during the day. So he kept watch in that direction, where the murk was like a desolate sky in which only a handful of blue stars burned. Of course, he thought wryly, even a handful was more than anyone in the vicinity of the Inner Sea had beheld since the start of the Great Rain.

The azure flames wavered like ordinary ones, and together with the blackness, that made it difficult to tell if they were doing anything else. But abruptly, Anton saw, or thought he saw, that one was growing gradually larger. Or rather, coming closer.

For an instant, he was certain he was seeing the unnatural blaze bonded to the master of the pride. Then the blue fire flowed straight through briars, dimly illuminating the closest stems and stickers in the process, and he perceived it wasn't attached to anything. It was drifting by itself like a will-o'-the-wisp.

That only made it somewhat less alarming. Anton turned to alert Umara in the hope that her wizardry could douse the flame. When he did, though, he spied Stedd, seated cross-legged among men who were too busy watching for the foe to pay him any mind, staring intently at the approaching glow.

Anton almost shouted at the boy, then remembered that the Thayan mariners didn't know Stedd the way he did, were already on edge, and might react with brutal dispatch to anyone who seemed to be trying to make an already perilous situation worse. He took the young prophet by the arm, hauled him to his feet, and led him to a spot as far from the others as the confines of the boma afforded.

"Were you pulling the blue fire closer?" Anton whispered.

Stedd nodded.

"In Asmodeus's name, why?" Anton had to make an effort to keep his voice down. "Blue fire isn't a toy! It could kill us in a heartbeat. Or twist us into forms so foul we wouldn't want to live."

"I wasn't playing with it! I was figuring it out!"

"Again, why? Never mind, I know. Because your dead god wants you to. Well, as usual, he has a wretched sense of timing. Help the rest of us keep watch, and you, Umara, and I can discuss blue fire in the morning."

The night wore on. The crackling, smoking fires burned down, and the company built them up again with more deadwood and Umara's cantrips. Safely above the reach of lions, an owl hooted, but otherwise, any animals in the area kept quiet. Despite the grinding tension, a couple weary men eventually lay down on the ground and dozed with their weapons under their hands.

Anton sat for a time, then stood up and stretched. His back popped. He took a drink from his water bottle, wiped his mouth with the back of his hand, and took a fresh look at the blue lights.

Then, like the world itself was splitting in two, a prodigious roar pounded out of the darkness. Dropping the bottle, he cringed from it. So did everyone else.

At least, he realized, the fires weren't going out. But wide-eyed men were stumbling, intent only on covering their ears, and surely, the lions were already charging.

"Fight!" Anton bellowed. The roar was fading, but even so, he wasn't sure anybody heard him.

"Fight!" Ehmed echoed, and then Umara did the same. Still, it didn't look like the rest of the Thayans were heeding the command. Meanwhile, bounding shadows converged on the circle of brush.

"Help us!" Stedd shrilled. He held out his hand to the east, and red-gold light pulsed across the campsite. Purged of panic and con-fusion, the Thayans gripped their weapons and came on guard just as the first lions sought to jump the boma.

Anton shot at the nearest target, a lioness, and the quarrel flew harmlessly over its back. The animal scrambled over the barricade and lunged at him, and, backpedaling, he hurled the crossbow at the felid's snarling face. It glanced off the beast's skull without slowing it even slightly.

Anton saw that his blades couldn't clear their scabbards before the lioness reached him, nor, with men and beasts battling on either side, could he evade by springing right or left. But his scurrying retreat had brought him to a point where a fire seared his back, and he hopped back into the yellow blaze.

He meant to keep moving right out the other side, but his foot caught on a piece of burning wood, and he fell down amid glowing orange coals and ash. The heat of the blaze closed around him like a fist and invaded his airways, too.

Scattering embers and scraps of burning wood, he rolled and flung himself clear of the fire. Then, gasping, taking stock, he decided he was likely blistered but not burned worse than that. His clothing wasn't on fire, and the lioness wasn't pursuing him through the flames. He felt a surge of relief until he realized he and Stedd were now on opposite sides of the boma.

He tried to reach the boy as expeditiously as possible, but there was no way to force his way through the press except by fighting. He slashed a lion's back legs out from under it while it was intent on a marine, and when its hindquarters dropped, the Thayan thrust a boarding pike into its vitals. Afterward, Anton managed four more strides and then had to clear his path by helping two other mariners kill a different beast.

So far, he and his companions appeared to be holding their own. But how many lions were there? Amid the howling chaos of lunging bodies and dazzling flame, it was impossible to tell.

Anton rounded the fire through which he'd rolled, spotted Stedd, and breathed a sigh of relief. Along with one of the zombies, Ehmed Sepandem stood so as to shield the boy from attackers. The leonine body on the ground in front of him showed he was doing a fair job of it.

But then a shape as long as Falrinn Greatorm's sailboat and as tall as the lowest yard on a square-rigger's mast bounded out of the darkness. Coupled with its hugeness, its mane of blue fire should have revealed its approach when it was still some distance away, but it seemed to spring from nowhere all in an instant.

The gigantic lion could have simply stepped over the thorny barricade in front of it. Instead, the beast trampled and crushed it, perhaps because it didn't even notice it was there.

Mindlessly impervious to awe or fear, the zombie lurched forward with boarding pike upraised, and the lion swiped at it. The attack ripped the animated corpse apart and smashed some of the pieces flat.

His sour face resolute, Ehmed stepped forward with a javelin in one hand and a cutlass in the other. Rushing forward to support him, Anton glimpsed a lioness lunging in on his flank.

The pirate pivoted, slashed with the saber, and caught the cat in the neck. The beast fell down thrashing, blood pumping from its wound.

The kill had only taken a moment, but when Anton turned back, Ehmed lay rent and squashed like the zombie. Head lowered, the lion with the fiery mane lunged at Stedd. It caught the boy in its mouth, picked him up, and ran in the direction of the other blue flames burning in the night.

Pointing with his saber, hoping someone would take notice and understand, Anton bellowed, "The boy!" Then he gave chase.

He saw immediately that he had little hope of overtaking the giant lion. The bounding strides of its long legs were too great. He forced himself to sprint even faster. Still, the beast lengthened its lead.

Then luminous scarlet netting glimmered into existence on the beast's hind legs, entangling them and apparently sticking them to the ground. The lion pitched off balance and fell.

Anton realized who must have cast the hindering spell. He'd lost track of Umara when the common lions attacked, but thank Lady Luck, she was still alive, had discerned his need, and had followed him to help.

Eager to catch the gigantic lion, he dashed onward. Zigzagging through the trees and leaping over fallen branches, he passed close to a blue flame glowing at the bottom of a pool of rainwater. Aches throbbed down his body from his left temple and the left hinge of his jaw down to his right ankle and the joints of his right toes.

He looked down at his arms. Bumps were swelling there. The plagueland had infected him.

He lurched around and spied Umara some distance behind him. She wasn't much more than a shadow in the dark, and he doubted she could make him out any better, but even so, her eyes widened at what she could see of his ongoing transformation.

"No farther!" he shouted, or tried to. His voice had changed, too. It sounded more like one of the lions coughing than the voice of a man.

But whether Umara had understood or not, there wasn't time to call again. He needed to reach the beast with the fiery mane while it was still immobilized. He ran onward.

For a few strides, he thought he was going to make it. Then, flopping on its side and twisting its enormous body, the lion brought the claws on its front paws to the mesh. It tore its bonds apart, leaped up, and bounded onward.

Once again, it started to extend its lead. Then, all but imperceptible in the darkness, a length of shadow burst up from the ground beneath it, whipped around its midsection, and jerked it to another halt.

It could only mean Umara had kept following despite Anton's warning. Otherwise, she wouldn't still have the beast in sight to target it. Hoping she wouldn't suffer for her tenacity, he sprinted onward and finally caught up with his quarry.

Unfortunately, by now, his steadily swelling tumors hurt even worse. Blocking out the pain as best he could, he cut at the lion's hind legs.

The creature lowered its head and spat Stedd onto the ground. Then it roared. The thunderous sound staggered Anton and shredded the shadow tentacle into nothingness.

But Stedd was now free and even unharmed by the look of him. As the boy clambered to his feet, Anton rasped, "Run to Umara!"

Stedd stumbled farther from the lion. Anton scrambled to position himself between the child and his monstrous abductor.

A huge paw with claws like cutlasses slashed down at him. He retreated and cut with the saber. The blade sent a fan of blood flying to mix with the rain. The lion snatched its foreleg back.

With a snarl, the beast pivoted to veer around Anton and chase after Stedd. The reaver hurled himself forward, straight at the enormous talons, fangs, and sheer crushing mass of the creature, and cut at its chest.

The saber sliced deep. Too deep, evidently, for the lion to ignore. It snapped around biting and clawing, and Anton recoiled. It wouldn't have been fast enough to carry him to even momentary safety, except that five luminous spheres, each a different color, flew at the cat's flank and discharged their power when they hit it, one vanishing in a blast of yellow flame and another bursting like a bubble into a cascade of steaming vitriol. The barrage made the lion falter for a precious instant.

Thank you, Umara, Anton thought. But now take Stedd and run. I'll hold back the lion somehow.

Slashing and dodging, he succeeded in doing precisely that for several breaths. But the knots in his limbs weren't just painful anymore. They were binding and grinding his agility away, and he thought fleetingly how strange it was to fight his last fight so far away from the sea.

Then he wrenched himself out of the way of another raking attack, and in so doing, spun toward the spot where he'd last seen Stedd. The lad was still there, give or take, hovering just a few paces away with a scowl of concentration on his face. Umara was there, too, reciting and whirling her hands in spirals. Anton inferred that when the boy hadn't fled to her, she'd run to him, and when he still refused to accompany her to safety, she'd resumed attacking the lion.

Idiots, both of them, but especially Stedd! Didn't he understand the blue fire would kill Anton even if the monstrous lion didn't? What in the name of the Abyss had happened to carrying out Lathander's mission?

But then again, why was Anton surprised that everything that had happened since he'd first met the allegedly holy child was coming to naught in the end? That simply made it of a piece with the rest of life. Grinning a grin that hurt his newly crooked jaw, determined to score at least one more attack on his towering opponent, he took fresh grips on the hilts of his blades.

Then Stedd raised his hands and called the name of his deity.

Red-gold light washed through the trees. Anton cried out as pain fell away from him in an instant, the sudden relief as shocking as an unexpected blow. He glanced at his arms and found that the lumps and knots were gone.

Meanwhile, the lion faltered and shuddered as the sapphire flame wreathing its mane guttered out to reveal the shaggy gold beneath.

When the last tongue of fire disappeared, it wheeled away from Anton to peer back in the direction of the camp.

Stedd dropped to his knees and then flopped onto the ground. Umara kneeled beside him.

Anton watched the lion for another breath—it had, after all, just been doing its level best to kill him—and then, still keeping a wary eye on it, he made his way to his companions. As he did, he noticed no blue flames were burning anywhere.

Stedd looked up at him with a certain smugness. "Told you . . . I needed to figure out the fire," he wheezed.

CHAPTER NINE

IT REASSURED UMARA TO HEAR STEDD SPEAK, ESPECIALLY BECAUSE the child had tried to be funny. He likely hadn't strained himself beyond endurance. Still, she asked, "Are you all right?"

"Just tired," Stedd replied. "That was . . . hard."

"Be ready," Anton said. "The lion's taking an interest in us again."

Umara looked around. Cleansed of the deformities that had been gnarling him into grotesquerie, Anton stood with his bloody swords ready to threaten the gigantic cat turning back in the humans' direction.

"It's all right now," said Stedd.

Umara's intuition told her the child was correct. The danger was over. But she'd be a dismal excuse for a Red Wizard if she dropped her guard before she was certain. She rose and slid her rustwood wand from her sleeve.

Moving slowly, perhaps to make peaceful intentions evident, the lion padded toward them, and as it did, it shrank. When it halted several paces away, it still stood as high at the shoulder as the largest draught horse, but was no longer the colossus that they had battled with steel and magic.

Despite the absence of blue fire shrouding its mane and its smaller stature, the creature seemed equally impressive, although now in a majestic rather than menacing fashion. Umara almost felt like bowing to it, and when it spoke, she wasn't surprised.

"I apologize," the lion rumbled. "I wasn't in control of my actions. Until the Chosen put it out, the pain of the Blue Fire maddened and diminished me. But I am sorry and shamed nonetheless, for the harm to humans and my own children, too. I can only seek to make amends. I've already commanded the other lions to stop fighting and run away. Now, I'm willing to use my powers to heal or fortify any in need of it, starting with you, Lathander's cub."

Anton raised his saber a hair, evidently to remind the lion he was standing armed and ready. "How kind. But I'd prefer you leave the boy alone."

"It's all right now," Stedd repeated. He tried to stand, then seemingly decided the effort was too much for him and settled for sitting with his back against the flaking bark of the nearest blighted tree.

Umara touched Anton on the forearm to ask him to rein in his belligerence, at least temporarily. To the lion, she said, "Who are you?"

"Nobanion," the beast replied, "or, if you prefer, Lord Firemane." He grunted. "Although that name feels like mockery now."

Anton cocked his head. "The lion lord of the forest? That's just an old story."

"Your great-great-grandsires knew differently," Nobanion said. "But then the world burned, and while I sought to protect a pride of my folk, a wave of blue fire swept over me. It left me as you first saw me, perpetually in anguish. Vicious and deranged." He turned his golden gaze on Stedd. "Until you cleansed me, and all this corrupted earth as well."

"It's time for the Blue Fire to go away," said Stedd, looking embarrassed by the creature's gratitude. "Otherwise, I couldn't have done it."

"You may have been insane," Umara said, lowering her wand to her side, "but it wasn't just delirium that made you attack us."

"No," Nobanion said. "In my time, I fought often against the Black-Blooded Pard and so won his hatred. Then the Lady of Mysteries died, and in the tumult that followed, he and I both suffered misfortune, but I fell farther. My agony enabled him to take revenge on me by subverting my will and enslaving me."

Anton smiled a crooked smile. "You're talking about Malar. Splendid. I've been thinking that a single divine enemy scarcely seems like enough."

"My hunch," Umara said, "is that the Beastlord is acting in Umberlee's stead now that we're away from the sea. From what I understand, they're both powers of savagery and destruction."

"Well," Nobanion growled, "he won't do it anymore, not now that you've restored me to myself. Not as long as you walk in my place of power."

"You'll protect us?" Umara asked.

"Of course," the lion answered

"Thank you," said Stedd, "truly. But we need even more."

"If it's within my power," Nobanion said, "you'll have it."

"We have to get to Turmish," said the boy, "and we aren't traveling fast enough."

"That can be remedied. Now, may I share my strength with you? There are men suffering beside your fires for want of the healing you and I can give them."

Umara looked to Anton. He shrugged and stepped out of Nobanion's way, although she noticed he didn't sheathe his swords. She came to stand beside him.

The lion lord lowered his head and licked Stedd with a tongue big enough to cover his whole head. Apparently, it tickled; the boy laughed and squirmed.

As she and Anton looked on, Umara murmured, "Surely, our new friend is at least semi-divine. If *he* can regain his former estate, that's a little more reason to believe Lathander actually has returned."

Anton smiled. "Belief is a wonderful thing. Or at least that's what people tell me."

Stedd had taken to riding on Nobanion's back with as little fuss as he might once have ridden the farm donkey or plow horse. Anton watched him bend down, hug the lion spirit's neck, and almost bury himself in the shaggy mane to avoid bumping his head on a branch.

It was remarkable how infrequently the boy had to do that. With Nobanion for a traveling companion, Gulthandor was a more welcoming place. Game trails wound through spaces where the trees grew farther apart, brambles didn't clog every pathway, and the ground, though not dry, didn't threaten to suck a man's boots off with every labored step. No doubt the lion spirit knew the best ways to traverse his own domain, but Anton suspected there was more to it than that. It was like the forest changed to reflect its monarch's desires.

If so, perhaps that explained the travelers' speed, not that mortal senses revealed any trace of it. Content to let Nobanion guide them, the wayfarers seemed to be hiking in a more leisurely manner than hitherto. Yet the spirit assured them they were actually crossing the forest as fast as riders on horseback might cross a plain.

Anton enjoyed the ease and peace of the trek. It was comparable to chasing Kymas's galley with Umara when, despite the various discomforts of life aboard Falrinn's sailboat, he'd once or twice caught himself wishing the journey could take longer.

But that interlude had ended when it ended, with life's usual lack of regard for anyone's wishes, and this one would, too. He told himself he'd be better off when it did.

Walking beside him, the hair on her scalp grown out to fuzz, Umara gave him a quizzical frown, and he realized he'd been tramping along in silence for a while. He tried to think of something to say, something that would mask the actual trend of his reflections, and then Nobanion came to a halt and lowered himself onto his belly, as was his habit when Stedd needed to climb on or off.

"This is as far as I go," the lion said.

"Already?" asked Stedd. Perhaps, his sense of urgency notwithstanding, he too had been enjoying the easy traveling.

"Yes," Nobanion said. "After a century of neglect, I have to tend to the needs of the prides and the forest as a whole. And my part in your undertaking is done. You'll see that, I believe, if you don't allow the sadness of parting to cloud your vision."

The boy sighed. "I guess I do." He ruffled his fingers through the spirit's mane as he might have petted a shaggy dog, then clambered down onto the ground.

The Thayan mariners regarded Nobanion with a touch of the same regret. That too was remarkable when Anton thought about it. They were hard men who in large measure justified their homeland's grim reputation, and mere days before, the lion spirit had led the attack that killed several of their fellows. Yet in the time since, his air of nobility had won them over. Or perhaps Stedd's steadfast eagerness to forgive and see goodness in everyone had inspired them to do the same.

Fools, the lot of them, Anton thought, and then Nobanion turned toward him and Umara.

"Stedd needs the help of everyone here," the lion rumbled. "But you two have known him longest and best. You, he needs most of all."

"Needs to do what?" Anton replied. "Do *you* know?"

Nobanion grunted. "No. But I have no doubt it truly is a charge laid on him by the Morninglord, and vitally important."

"Well," Anton said, "I've put up with the brat this far." He gave Stedd a wink. "I suppose I can tolerate him for a few miles farther."

"I already pledged to help him," Umara said, a bit of Red Wizard hauteur showing through even though she addressed a demigod, or something not far short of one.

Nobanion's golden eyes scrutinized them for another breath or two. Then he turned and padded back the way they'd come.

Anton blinked, or felt as if he might have, and in that instant, the huge lion disappeared. With his departure, even the trail back into the depths of Gulthandor looked suddenly indistinct and overgrown, like it was disappearing now that he didn't need it anymore.

Fortunately, the trail to the east remained as clearly defined and passable as before. And when the travelers glimpsed the brown ramparts of the Orsraun Mountains to the south, and later came upon a circle of the warty-looking mushrooms called spit-thrice, it was evident, to Anton at least, that Nobanion had kept his promise to see the human travelers safety to the limits of his domain.

That night, the pirate lay waiting while the campfires burned down and his companions snored and shifted under whatever coverings they'd contrived to keep off the rain. A sentry was also awake, but he wasn't looking in Anton's direction. When the moment felt right, the Turmishan rose silently, buckled on his saber and cutlass, and picked up the rest of his gear.

As he tucked his crossbow, quiver, bundles, and wadded blanket under his arms, his gaze fell on Stedd. The boy lay mostly concealed under a blanket, but his golden hair stuck out and gleamed even in the waning firelight.

Something clenched in Anton's neck and chest. He didn't know precisely what he was feeling, but that was all right because he didn't *want* to know. Scowling, he tried to will it away and feel nothing.

The sentry was looking away to the north, perhaps wistfully, considering that was where the sea was. Anton crept west, back up the section of trail the travelers had traversed before the light failed.

He soon reached a stand of beeches. Once he passed through, he'd be out of sight of the camp and vice versa. He felt a momentary urge to take a last look back and made himself quicken his stride instead.

When he reached the other side, he set down the articles he was carrying and started to roll his blanket. Then a voice asked, "Why?"

He dropped the blanket, pivoted away from the sound, and snatched for the hilts of his swords. He had them halfway drawn when he realized the disembodied voice was female and, in fact, familiar.

Umara wavered from invisible to visible, semitransparent and blurry for a moment, then locking into opacity and focus. The darkness hid the complex layered textures of her mage's garb and turned the red cloth black, but it didn't conceal her frown.

He took a breath. "I would have thought it beneath the dignity of a Red Wizard to play pranks."

"If I gave you a fright," Umara answered, "that's the least you deserve."

"Did you follow me out of camp?"

She shook her head. "I was waiting for you here. The moment you promised Nobanion you'd stay with Stedd, I knew you were lying."

He frowned. "Truly? I consider myself a pretty fair liar. What gave me away?"

"I don't know, exactly, and it doesn't matter. I want to know what you think you're doing."

"Surely, that's obvious." He smiled. "And don't ask how dare I lie to the great lion king's face and flout his will. Since this madness started, I've acted against the interests of Lathander, Amaunator, Umberlee, and Malar and lived to tell the tale. I don't feel all that inclined to cower in awe of a magical animal, no matter how impressive."

"I can understand that." Despite the rain, Umara pushed her cowl back. Anton had the feeling it was so he could see her fair-complexioned, fine-boned face more clearly. "Nobanion inspired considerable . . . respect in me, but he's not the sort of entity that ever allied itself with my order or my country. He's more like one of the animal spirits the witches of Rashemen send against us. So I don't feel inclined to grovel before him, either."

"Yet you mean to do what he told you to."

"I'm doing what *I* decided back aboard the galley. And with Kymas dead by your hand and mine, I don't have much choice but to see it through."

Anton sighed. "That's unfortunate. But I do see a choice."

"To walk back into Gulthandor alone? Even if you make it out the other side, what lies beyond? Westgate? Teziir? A boat back to Pirate Isle? There's only death awaiting you in any of those places."

"My ill-wishers will have to catch me first."

"But what's the *point*?"

"The point is that I've had my little flirtation with high and sacred matters. Now it's time to go back to being the man I truly am."

Umara hesitated then said, "Since I listened to Stedd, I'm a stranger to myself, too. It's not so much murdering my superior. With luck, that's the kind of thing for which a Red Wizard can be forgiven, and Kymas . . . gave me reason to want to dispose of him. But I'm disobeying Szass Tam—*Szass Tam!*—and gambling that somehow, it will come out all right. That's pure insanity, and it was comforting that I at least had another mad soul to keep me company as I went racing toward my doom."

The tightness in Anton's neck and chest was back. He covered the discomfort with a smirk. "You know just how to make prolonging our partnership sound appealing."

Umara drew herself up straight. "I'm a Red Wizard. You're an outlander and a pirate. Yet I just indicated I consider you a friend. Don't expect me to *plead*."

"I don't. But truly, you can't be shocked I'm leaving. I said early on that I would when the time was right. And later, when the matter came up again, I had the lion king of Gulthandor himself urging me to change my mind, with you, Stedd, and all the mariners looking on. Who wouldn't have said yes, whatever was truly in his mind?"

She sneered. "Coward."

"I prefer to see myself as tactful."

"*Why* won't you go back to Turmish?"

"People hate me there."

"People hate you everywhere."

"Once again, I'll observe that you truly do know how to persuade a fellow."

"Answer the question, curse you! After what we've gone through together, you owe me that."

Anton sighed. "Just . . . if Stedd needs the good will of the folk of Sapra, I'm the last man who should be standing at his side. Can we leave it at that?"

"No!"

Anton drew breath to tell her she'd have to. For after all, he'd never talked about what had happened in Sapra with anyone.

Yet it was no secret, at least not in the more populous parts of Turmish, and maybe he did owe Umara something. Or perhaps her badgering had simply worn him down.

"All right," he growled. "Turmish is a republic. It doesn't have kings or princes like many another land. But it has wealthy merchants who pretty much run the place under the watchful eyes of the druids, and my father, Diero Marivaldi, was one such." He smiled fleetingly. "So you see, snooty lady, in my fashion, I'm highborn, too."

"I'm not 'snooty.' I simply see no reason to behave as if I'm less than what I am."

"If you say so. Anyway, my ancestors and relatives weren't only merchants. Some would say we weren't even traders first and foremost. It was our tradition that every young Marivaldi serve in the Turmishan navy. Some fulfilled their obligations and moved on to command the family's commercial ventures. Others, finding a life of duty satisfying, remained with the fleet until old age beached them."

Umara nodded. "I'll hazard you expected to be one of the latter."

Anton blinked. "Considering all I've done to steal other people's wealth in recent years, I'm surprised you'd say that. But you're right. When I was small, tales of my heroic ancestors battling despicable pirates and sea serpents thrilled me, and any suggestion that I learn to pore over ledgers in a counting house or dicker over bushels of Aglarondan grain moved me to truancy and general rebellion."

Umara grunted. "As long as I was home, I never felt the need to rebel. My parents were delighted when I proved to possess a talent for wizardry. And from the start, I loved magic too dearly to even imagine applying myself to any other vocation. Although when I started to learn what it truly means to be a Red Wizard, the things expected of us beyond simply mastering spells and reading arcane lore . . ." She shook her head as though to clear it. "Never mind. We're talking about you."

"Alas, we are. In time, Turmish went to war with Akanûl. It was a squabble over tariffs and a scrap of border territory that wasn't good for anything anyway, but at the time, I believed my countrymen were fighting for the noblest cause in the history of Faerûn. That made me even more frantic to serve, and the sharpest spur of all was the example of my elder brother Rimardo. He was already first mate aboard a caravel and had acquitted himself gallantly in several actions at sea."

"And so you envied him."

Anton snorted. "Bitterly. When he came home on leave, I couldn't get enough of his stories, and yet, it maddened me that he was living that life and I wasn't. I may even have hated him a little."

"But your time must have arrived eventually."

"That depends on how you look at it. When I was old enough to enlist, I did. But by then, the petty war was ending as leaders on both sides realized it had never been worth fighting in the first place."

"Still, you were where you wanted to be."

Anton smiled. "As I said, only in a sense. I told you it's wealthy merchants who generally win election to the Assembly of Stars, and they keep a tight grip on Turmish's purse strings. Once we made peace with the genasi, the assemblymen decided the navy didn't need as many warships patrolling the sea. The country could save coin by putting some in dry dock."

Umara frowned. "Leaving you a sailor with nothing to sail?"

"Yes. For want of anything better to do with me, the navy made me a customs officer. It was a tedious life largely made up of the same sort of tallying and recordkeeping that filled me with loathing as a boy. And while I tramped around the docks with my chalk, slate, and abacus, I had to watch the warships that weren't in dry dock come and go with lucky wretches like Rimardo aboard."

"That would have galled me, too," Umara said. She ran her fingertips over her scalp as though the feel of the stubble annoyed her. "Still, if Turmish is anything like Thay, a new war is always on the way."

Anton sighed. "I actually did possess just enough sense to realize I should simply bide my time. But that time was so dull! To pass it,

I drank, gambled, and frequented the festhalls. As you can likely guess, I often found myself in need of coin, and although my father had plenty, I felt increasingly awkward asking him to toss some my way. He disapproved of wastrels, and my every wheedling visit made it clearer that was what I'd become."

"So you found a different source of gold?"

"Close, but actually, it found me. It turns out that smugglers study customs officials to discover who might be susceptible to bribery. In retrospect, my reaction was ludicrous, but at the time, I was astonished to learn that *I* looked corrupt, or at least, corruptible."

"But not so astonished you didn't agree to collaborate."

"Understand, my responsibilities seemed so petty, and so far removed from the heroic career I'd imagined for myself, that looking away while a few scoundrels moved contraband didn't feel like a true betrayal of anything. What did it matter if a few amphorae of Chessentan olive oil . . ." He sneered. "Listen to me blather. Next, I'll be making excuses for all the rapine and slaughter in all the years since."

"Just tell the story," Umara said. There was a hint of gentleness in her voice that he could only recall hearing when she was speaking to Stedd, and then, infrequently.

"Very well. At first, I allowed wine, copper ingots, lumber, and spices to come ashore untaxed. Eventually, though, I noticed stranger cargo. Boxes with peculiar symbols carved on the lids and something rustling inside despite a lack of air holes. Weirdly shaped objects that, wrapped like mummies, glowed a little even through the cloth. A moldy book with an iron stake sticking through the front cover and out the back."

Umara frowned. "I know that book."

"I thought you might. I didn't, but I was canny enough to recognize unsavory mystical artifacts when I saw them, and by chance, I learned they all were bound for a single buyer."

"Did that worry you?"

216

"It should have. But looking away was a habit by then. One piece of contraband was like another, so long as it dropped coin in my hand on its way to its destination."

"So in the end, what happened? Something obviously did."

"Indeed, and I suspect you heard something about the incident even in far-off Thay. It was quite spectacular, and a balor—I learned later that's what they're called—leading a pack of lesser demons seems like the sort of thing that would interest your folk."

Umara stared at him. "By the seven fallen stars! You were implicated in *that*?"

"Well, fortunately, not at first, not to anybody's knowledge. What with fiends laying waste to the city and striving to destroy the Elder Circle of the Emerald Enclave, who were paying one of their rare visits, we were all too busy fighting back to try to figure out what it all meant. This will make you laugh: Even I had no idea. As I stood with everyone else who could hold a spear or a sword, it never occurred to me that I was anything other than a loyal Turmishan officer seizing the chance to prove his mettle at last."

Anton sighed. "But afterward, when scores of folk lay dead, my poor, brave brother among them, and much of Sapra had burned to black sticks and ash, people wanted to know why. And the demons hadn't been subtle. It was no great trick to follow their trail back to the mansion of the assemblyman who'd called them forth from the Abyss."

"Why did he do it?"

"It was a coup, or the start of one. He wanted to do away with the republic and make himself king, but he knew the high druids wouldn't stand for it. So he tried to assassinate them with supernatural power that rivaled even theirs."

"Unless he was a master wizard, it was a fool's play. Even if it had worked, the balor would likely have ended up as the real king, and he, its plaything."

"It's a pity you weren't around to advise him. Anyway, it turned out he had a fussy habit of making notes on even the sort of deeds

217

and plans that one should never write about. The notes pointed to the smugglers who brought him the items required for the summoning."

"And under *duress,* the smugglers pointed to you."

"Turmishan interrogators aren't as fond of 'duress' as Thayans, but the knaves certainly would have given me up before they were through with them. Fortunately, I was Diero Marivaldi's son and an officer who'd fought well in the recent crisis. Folk in authority trusted me and spoke freely when I was around. Thus, I happened to learn the smugglers were about to be arrested just as the navy and the watch moved to round them up."

"And you fled."

"It was that or kneel at the headsman's block. I was as guilty as anyone for what had befallen Sapra. If I hadn't betrayed my office, it could never have happened. And once I was away, well, I was already on the outlaw's path. I figured I might as well keep walking it."

"Until it led you into piracy."

"Yes. I've heard that meanwhile, denied the satisfaction of seeing my head roll, Sapra turned its scorn on my father. His lifetime of honorable dealings counted for nothing against my crime, and he found it impossible either to trade or hold government office. He withdrew from public life and died not long after."

Umara stood quietly for a moment. Then she said, "Hm."

"I see my tale of woe affected you deeply."

"If I'd responded with a gush of commiseration—not that I'm suggesting I was inclined to—you would only have jeered at it."

Anton realized she was right. "Be that as it may, now you understand why I can't return to Sapra."

"No, I see I was right from the start. If people want to kill you everywhere, that's no reason to stay away from Turmish. You'll actually be safer there. Your brown skin won't stand out."

"My traitor's face will."

"Was it wearing the usual ridiculous Turmishan beard the last time anyone in Sapra saw it?"

He hesitated. "Yes."

"And that was years ago, in addition to which, I know a bit about disguise. It's part of the illusionist's art."

"Thank you, but it would still be too risky. I won't be responsible for the failure of Stedd's errand, whatever mooncalf thing it turns out to be."

"Stedd wants you with him, and not just because Lathander and Nobanion think it's a good idea. He had to forsake *his* family, too. They're back on the farm thousands of miles to the west where he'll never see them again. He needs *someone* to stand by him, and little though we deserve his trust, he's fastened on you and me."

"The more fool him, then."

Umara scowled. "If you don't want to return to Turmish, then don't. But at least be honest about the reason. It's not fear of the headsman's axe. It's shame."

To his own surprise, Anton nearly flinched. He forced a laugh instead. "You should ask the folk I've robbed and the widows and orphans of those I've killed if I seem like a man susceptible to shame."

"You may not feel it over anything Anton Marivaldi the pirate has done. But Anton Marivaldi the youthful customs officer is a different matter."

"How in the name of the Abyss would *you* know? Who ever heard of a Red Wizard suffering shame over anything?"

Umara scowled. "I'm tired of arguing. If you want to go, go." She pulled her hood up and headed into the beeches.

Anton told himself he was glad she'd given up. But he stood and watched her go, and when she was about to disappear into the trees and the darkness, he blurted, "Wait."

A while back, the travelers had started seeing axe-chopped tree stumps and other signs of human activity in the forest. Now, keeping low, Anton, Umara, and Stedd skulked from one bit of cover to the next. As far as Stedd was aware, there was no particular reason to make sure they got a look at Morningstar Hollows before anyone in the village sighted them. But after all the dangers he and his friends had passed through, he supposed caution was a good idea.

They reached a spot where the trees thinned out. Some distance beyond them, farmers were working bedraggled, rain-lashed fields.

Everything looked all right to Stedd. He started to straighten up, and Anton put his hand on his shoulder. "I wouldn't," the pirate said.

"Why not?" Umara asked.

Anton smiled. "If you squint, you might make out a couple white faces among the brown ones. And while Turmish doesn't forbid outlanders to immigrate, I don't see why they'd bother just to settle in a backwater like this. The village has failed and been abandoned so many times, it's a wonder even Turmishans keep rebuilding it."

"You think Evendur sent a force here to intercept us," the wizard said.

"It's a logical move," Anton replied. "I wish we could get a better look at the white men. But maybe we don't need one. If those are pirates over there, their ship can't be too far off. Come on."

They headed back into the forest, collected the Thayan sailors and marines who were waiting for them there, and then they all marched north, keeping to the fringe of the forest the while. After a time, they reached a spot where the rain-fed waters of the Inner Sea had advanced up a valley. There, a caravel floated with sails furled and several ropes mooring it to tree trunks.

Anton grinned. "Hello again, Mourmyd. My compliments on the skill required to bring the *Octopus* so far south on an uncharted and uncertain waterway, over submerged trees and who knows what else. My friends and I are in your debt."

"What are you thinking?" Umara asked.

"We steal the ship. Mourmyd surely didn't leave her unattended, but just as surely, he and most of his crew are lurking in Morningstar Hollows waiting for us to turn up there. We shouldn't have much trouble wresting *Octopus* away from whoever's still aboard, and

220

afterward, if any more of Evendur's hunters spot us on our voyage east, they'll mistake us for some of their own."

The Red Wizard smiled. "That is a good plan. I like it."

Stedd peered up at the two adults. "But what about Morningstar Hollows?"

Umara shrugged. "What about it?"

"If Mourmyd's pirates are there, doesn't that mean they took it over? Aren't they doing bad things to the people who live there?"

Anton sighed. "Now that you mention it, I'm sure they are."

"Then we can't just steal the ship and sail away. We have to help them!"

Umara frowned. "Your mission is our concern. We shouldn't risk it and you in a battle we can avoid."

"Helping people *is* my mission."

Anton turned to Umara. "You aren't going to talk him out of it. And why else are we here but to back his play, however feckless it turns out be?"

Umara glowered. "I didn't know when I was well rid of you."

Mourmyd Jacerryl was full. He made himself eat the last piece of roast chicken anyway, because the village woman who'd cooked it for him was watching.

Slender and long-legged, comely in the swarthy way of her people, the village woman didn't appear to be enjoying the spectacle, although she had the sense to try to hide her resentment. He wondered what bothered her more, that he'd ordered every one of Morningstar Hollows's few remaining farm animals butchered to feed his crew, or that he was gorging while her belly was empty. Probably the latter, he decided, with the food disappearing down his gullet right in front of her and the aroma of it hanging in the air.

He swallowed the last bite of meat, belched, and tossed the leg bone on the floor. "Well, that was rank," he said. "Filthy peasant food."

It had actually been quite tasty, and the woman likely knew it and took pride in her cooking. Still, she really had no choice but to mumble, "I'm sorry."

Mourmyd grinned. "Well, perhaps you can make it up to me. Take off your clothes."

The villager's dark eyes popped open wide, and then she shook her head. "No. Please, no."

"Do it."

"Please, no," she repeated.

She actually sounded like it would take more than simple verbal intimidation to coerce her, so Mourmyd considered his options. Straightforward rape was the obvious one, but in the wake of his meal, he wasn't feeling especially energetic. He turned to Gimur and said, "Help me convince her."

The pudgy sorcerer reached for a little jade carving of a nude and headless woman, one of dozens of talismans pinned or tied to his long gingery braids. It was the one he used to subvert a female victim's will.

The effects of such magic varied. Some women turned into docile sleepwalkers. Others grew timid, and the fear made them compliant. A few even became lustful.

Whatever the precise effect, the experience left the target feeling complicit in her own violation and filled with self-disgust. It was a subtle refinement to the basic torment, and Mourmyd liked to think he could be subtle when the spirit moved him.

Gimur spoke the first words of the spell. The fire in the hearth leaped higher, and a filthy smell filled the hovel. The village woman cried out and swayed, but Mourmyd knew she couldn't bolt. The magic already had her in its grip.

Then the shack's door banged open, and the *Octopus*'s boatswain, a hulking, olive-skinned half-orc named Borthog, burst in. Rain blew in along with him.

Something was clearly happening, and Mourmyd jumped up from the table. "Has the boy preacher come?"

"No." Borthog shoved the villager out of his way. "But there's fire to the north!"

"*What?*" North was where they'd moored the *Octopus*!

Mourmyd hurried out of the thatch-roofed cottage with Gimur and Borthog scurrying behind him. Other folk stood in the rain, looking northward where a column of smoke rose, stained yellow by the blaze that was its source. Unfortunately, Mourmyd couldn't see the fire itself or what was fueling it. Too many trees were in the way. But it certainly looked like the flames could be either burning the *Octopus* or at least dangerously close to it.

The loss of the ship would have been catastrophic under any circumstances. If it left Mourmyd stranded in a realm that had long since put a hefty price on his head, and where he'd spent the last few days committing new outrages, he was unlikely to survive it.

Turning to Gimur, he asked, "What can *you* see?"

The chubby sorcerer hesitated. His powers notwithstanding, he was leery of giving answers that failed to satisfy his captain. "No more than you. I'm not a seer."

"Then what in the Bitch's name are you good for?" Mourmyd pivoted to Borthog. "Turn out the villagers to fight the fire. Tell them that if *Octopus* burns, they will, too."

Like Gimur, Borthog hesitated. It gave Mourmyd the infuriating feeling that everything including his own crew was conspiring against him. He felt a momentary urge to draw his cutlass and start cutting.

Then Borthog said, "If you think it best. But it will take time to get the peasants moving. And if we don't *have* time . . ."

Curse him, the boatswain was right. "Then get the crew moving!" Mourmyd snarled. "I want them standing in front of me with buckets in their hands before I finish counting to twenty!"

It didn't happen quite that quickly, but once their officers started shouting orders, the pirates scurried to obey. Everyone understood the potential consequences of losing the caravel.

And while they all rushed through the woods, tripping over fallen branches, scratching and snagging themselves on brambles, and even bumping into tree trunks in the dark, Mourmyd prayed,

Please, he thought, great Queen of the Depths, let *Octopus* be all right! I came to this pesthole on your business because your high priest—curse him!—made me. Don't let me suffer because of it!

As the pirates approached the anchorage, wavering yellow light shined through the trees ahead. Heat warmed Mourmyd's face, and smoke stung his nostrils and set a man on his left to coughing. Near panic, the captain ran even faster, and his men did the same. Then they all faltered in confusion as they reached the strip of mud and weeds at the water's edge.

The first thing Mourmyd noticed was that the ship was all right, and the realization brought a surge of relief. But the feeling only lasted an instant, because the vista before him was uncanny.

The pillar of smoke he'd observed from the village still billowed above the treetops. But there were no flames underneath it, just a sourceless radiance that gilded the surface of the water. The odd thought came to him that the missing fire was like a detail a lazy artist might omit from a mural when he realized the layout of the hall would keep anyone from looking closely at that end of the painting.

Except that in this case, it was a detail nobody would miss until it was too late, and illusion had already lured Mourmyd and his men into an ambush.

He bellowed, "Trap!" But at the same moment, figures popped up from behind the gunwales along the length of the *Octopus* to shoot crossbows at the befuddled men on land.

Other quarrels streaked out of the darkness on the pirates' flanks. Someone screamed as he staggered with a bolt jutting from his face. Then, as soon as the barrage ceased, shadowy figures burst from cover to charge Mourmyd's crew with pike, axe, and sword.

Honed in many a fight, Mourmyd's instincts told him he and his crew had the ambushers outnumbered. But that changed almost instantly as his corsairs started to drop with their pails still in their hands and their blades still in their scabbards.

Mourmyd realized that even he was still gawking like a halfwit with a bucket in his grasp. He cast about, discovered Gimur in a similar stupefied condition, and lashed the pail into the sorcerer's ribs. Gimur yelped and lurched around.

"Do something!" Mourmyd screamed.

Gimur gave a jerky nod and gripped a talisman in the shape of a curved iron glaur horn. He howled and ripped the plait to which the arcane ornament was clipped right out of his scalp.

The sorcerer's scream became an ear-splitting blare like a call from a giant's trumpet. The ground shuddered under Mourmyd's feet but the shaking was even stronger where foes rushed in on the crew's left flank. There, trees swayed and rustled, and the oncoming attackers reeled and fell.

That gave the men of the *Octopus* a last chance to prepare them-selves for battle if the brainless scum would only take advantage of it. Mourmyd cast aside the bucket, drew his cutlass, and ran into the middle of them roaring, "Fight, drown you, fight!"

At least some of the reavers snapped out of their daze and reached for their own blades. Then a foe armed with a boarding pike rushed Mourmyd. Clad in the soaked, filthy uniform of a Thayan marine, the man knew how to handle his weapon, and for the next several breaths, Mourmyd had to devote his full attention to dueling him.

Finally, the pirate captain slipped past the jabbing, rust-speckled point of the pike and slashed the Thayan across the belly. The marine dropped the pike and, reeling, clutched at the wound to keep his guts from sliding out. Mourmyd pivoted away from him and looked around.

What he saw was cause for desperation. His crew were fighting back, but, taken by surprise, were doing so with just the side arms they wore habitually, not the full range of lethal gear they customarily carried into battle. Some only had daggers to pit against pikes and axes. It was rapidly proving to be a fatal disadvantage.

It might not be as disastrous if they had more sorcery strengthening them and blasting their enemies. Alas, Gimur was busy looking after himself. Jabbering incantations, he stood facing a tall, slender woman in a red hooded cloak across a distance of several yards. Her lips were moving, too, and she flourished a wand in broad, lazy sweeps above her head.

Orbs of phosphorescence appeared around the two spellcasters, bobbed and drifted sluggishly for a few heartbeats, and then dissolved. Streaks of light shot back and forth. Sometimes, they bent away from their targets, or simply stopped short. At other moments, radiant disks like shields flared into existence to block them.

In the flashing, flickering play of all that glow, hints of figures and faces appeared, vanished, and reappeared. A phantom lion sprang at a ghostly serpent, and a hovering expressionless mask of a countenance divided down the middle, flowed apart, and became two such objects.

Mourmyd lacked the esoteric knowledge that would have enabled him to comprehend much of what he was seeing. Still, it was clear Gimur was losing the arcane duel. His adversary appeared calm and confident, whereas he'd already yanked out several braids from his bloody scalp. That was a trick he only used when he needed to cast a spell more quickly and forcefully than normal.

The one cause for hope was that the Red Wizard appeared intent on her chosen opponent. Mourmyd surveyed the battle as a whole and found a path through the various knots of combatants that would enable him to circle around behind her. He started forward.

Then a familiar voice said, "Now, now. Let the mages have their fun, and you and I will have ours." Mourmyd pivoted to see Anton Marivaldi advancing on him with a bloody saber in his left hand and a cutlass in his right.

Mourmyd had to swallow away a sudden thickness in his throat. Generally speaking, he had faith in his own prowess and had vindicated that confidence in battle after battle. Yet he realized he didn't want to cross swords with Anton. Not on a calamitous night like this, when Tymora had so manifestly turned her back on him.

But maybe he wouldn't have to. Borthog, a boarding axe he must have taken from a fallen Thayan in his hands, crept up behind the Turmishan. Mourmyd need only keep Anton from discerning the half-orc's approach and the other captain would cease to be a problem.

Retreating, Mourmyd snarled, "You're a traitor! To your fellow pirates and our faith!"

Anton grinned. "Let's not belabor the obvious."

"I mean it!" Mourmyd said, still giving ground. "You've thrown everything away!" Meanwhile, Borthog slipped into striking distance.

But as the half-orc raised the boarding axe, Anton whirled. Either he'd known Borthog was there all along or had somehow sensed it just in time. Reflecting the rainbow luminescence of the mages' duel, his saber sliced into his would-be assailant's neck. Borthog collapsed with blood spurting from the gash and his tusked head flopping backward like it was on hinges.

But now Anton had his back to Mourmyd. Mourmyd charged.

Anton spun as he had before, sweeping the saber in a horizontal arc. Mourmyd parried and kept driving in. He thrust his cutlass at Anton's torso.

With his own cutlass, Anton shoved the attack out of line then, in a continuation of the same action, slid the weapon up Mourmyd's forearm, slicing it from wrist to elbow. Blood welled forth.

Mourmyd blundered on past his foe and wrenched himself around. He nearly dropped his cutlass in the process, then almost lost it again when switching it to his left hand.

Even the uninjured arm had trouble holding the blade steady, and that, combined with a sick, lightheaded feeling, told him his wound was bad. He was afraid to look to see how bad.

Even if it wasn't as serious as it might be, he had little hope of outfighting Anton Marivaldi with his off hand. Signaling his willingness to drop his cutlass, he held it out to the side and wheezed, "I surrender."

Anton hesitated. "Well, it *is* the way of Lathander to give even knaves like you and me a second chance. The boy would want me to show mercy."

"Yes," Mourmyd said.

"So I'm glad he isn't watching." Saber high and cutlass low, the Turmishan advanced.

By the time Anton brought Stedd from his hiding place to the anchorage, both the column of smoke and the yellow light Umara had created to counterfeit fire had disappeared. But the Thayans had kindled storm lanterns aboard the *Octopus*, and even in the rainy, overcast night, their glow sufficed to reveal not only the shape of the vessel but the bustle of activity onboard.

Anton paused on the shore to take in the sight. He felt himself smile.

Stedd peered up at him. "Having a ship again makes you happy," he said.

Anton snorted. "It ought to make you happy, too."

"It does." Stedd glanced to where a squatting sailor was sewing bodies into shrouds of sailcloth. "But I wish there'd been another way to get it. You and the Thayans, you hardly talk about it when one of us dies."

Anton shrugged. "Talking doesn't bring people back to life."

"I know, but . . . " Stedd shook his head.

"Warriors feel something when a comrade falls." Or at least, some did. Anton realized that prior to meeting Stedd, he hadn't experienced that emotion in quite a while. "But it's a bad idea to wallow in it. That goes for you, too. Either Lathander's cause is worth us risking our lives or it isn't. If it is, say goodbye to the dead and sail on."

"I guess."

"Speaking of sailing on, it shouldn't take long to ready the ship to head for the sea."

Stedd frowned. "I have to go into Morningstar Hollows first."

"Now, how did I know you were going to say that? Maybe Umara will want to tag along. She might as well. Now that the fighting's over, a lubber's of no use here."

The wizard did choose to accompany them, and as they hiked through the woods together, Anton realized that this time, the aftermath of battle had left him feeling peaceful, not restless and morose. With a scowl, he pushed the realization aside lest even thinking of the absent bleakness bring it surging back.

In the settlement, a motley combination of new or refurbished huts and decaying, uninhabited wrecks, a woman's corpse dangled from a sycamore maple, where she'd been hanging long enough for birds to make a meal of her features. Anton assumed Mourmyd had strung her up and left her as a warning to any villager who might be contemplating defiance.

There were also living townsfolk gathered on the common. Perhaps they'd heard the sounds of battle and were waiting to see who had won.

Umara waved two men—brothers, by the look of them, with the same shape to their broad noses and bony brows—forward. They peered warily back at her.

The Red Wizard gestured to the corpse. "I need you to catch her when I bring her down. Unless you don't care if she just crashes to the ground."

The brothers exchanged glances, then positioned themselves beneath the body's feet. Umara whispered to herself and crooked and uncrooked the fingers of her left hand. The rope supporting the dead woman unknotted itself, and she dropped into her neighbors' waiting hands.

"You can bury her in the morning," Anton said. "Her killers won't interfere for the excellent reason that they're dead now, too."

A couple villagers smiled. Others closed their eyes and sighed in a sort of private rapture of relief.

"Did the Assembly send you?" asked the taller of the brothers.

"No," said Stedd, "Lathander did."

Anton put his hand on Stedd's shoulder. "The boy here is the prophet who's been proclaiming the rebirth of the Morninglord. Perhaps you've heard something about that even here on the edge of the wilderness."

"Can he truly work magic?" asked a woman clad in dark, ragged mourning. "Can he create food?"

"Is that what the village needs?" Stedd replied.

"It's what everybody needs," the bereaved woman said. "The crops have failed. All Turmish is starving."

CHAPTER TEN

Turmishan gentlemen wore brimless drum-shaped hats and loose robes woven in bright patterns, and when Umara asked, one of the grateful folk of Morningstar Hollows had rooted around in a trunk, produced such a citified outfit, and presented it to Anton. The clothes felt strange after years away, but they ought to help him blend in, just as his beardless chin should keep him from looking too much like Anton Marivaldi the young naval officer, customs official, and despicable traitor.

It was his good fortune that in recent years, certain stylish fellows had taken to shaving, and the famous Turmishan square-cut beard wasn't quite as ubiquitous as it used to be. Traditionalists might frown at Anton in disapproval, but the mere lack of such a feature wouldn't make him seem peculiar and accordingly suspect.

Some gray pigment in his black hair and a hairline and eyebrows subtly reshaped with a razor completed his disguise. It didn't seem like much of a transformation to him, but Umara and Stedd both insisted he looked different. With Sapra growing ever larger in front of the *Octopus*, he supposed he was on the verge of finding out.

The harbormaster here had resorted to the same sort of improvisations as his counterparts in Westgate and elsewhere to cope with the rising sea. Many of the piers had a rickety, temporary look, and buoys alerted traffic to hazards recently submerged beneath the waves. In the city behind the waterfront, a few gray towers raised conical roofs above the surrounding buildings.

Anton glanced down at Stedd and was surprised to see a frown. "If you tell me Lathander didn't really mean for us to come to Sapra after all," the pirate said, "I swear, I'll toss you over the side."

Stedd smiled, but only for an instant. "It's not that."

"What, then?"

"The god sent me here to end the famine. I'm sure he did. But I don't know if I'm strong enough."

"You probably aren't all by yourself. But that's why we're going to recruit some help. So stiffen your spine. If I learned anything as a pirate, it's that the more dubious the venture, the more confident the leader needs to appear."

The clerkish adolescent port official who met the *Octopus* reminded Anton just a bit of his younger self. He didn't have quite the same martyred air of deeming his talents wasted on chores that were beneath him, but he didn't appear overjoyed that duty had called him forth into the rain, either.

Anton took a deep breath and then climbed down onto the dock. The official didn't shriek, faint, or snatch for a blade upon coming face to face with such an infamous malefactor. He simply recorded the names of the ship and its captain—Anton supplied aliases for both the pirate vessel and himself—and collected the mooring tax. Then he asked the ship's business.

Anton saw no harm in giving a truthful answer to that question: "My passengers are here to seek an audience with the Elder Circle."

The young man smiled a crooked smile. "Good luck."

"Why?" Anton asked. "What's the matter?"

The official hesitated. "It's not my place to gossip about the Emerald Enclave. Just . . . don't expect too much. And be careful passing through town."

Anton grinned. "I never do, and I always am."

Leaving the mariners to tend the *Octopus*, he, Stedd, and Umara headed into the city. The rain clattered down hard for a few breaths, then slackened for a while, then repeated the cycle. That, the gloom, the gaunt, haggard faces of passersby, and the empty marketplaces made Anton feel as if the city of his birth had never truly recovered from the night and day demons had burned and slaughtered a path through the heart of it.

But that was nonsense. Sapra had new problems now. He thrust thoughts of the past out of his mind and concentrated on watching for the danger the port officer had led him to expect.

Somewhat to his surprise, he didn't see any chalked tridents or other signs that Umberlee worship was on the rise hereabouts. Perhaps the Emerald Enclave, druids of Silvanus all, and the secular authorities who looked to them for guidance had taken a stand against Evendur's agents.

But he did see surly-looking outlanders loitering and sometimes even camped in public places. They all wore blue somewhere about their persons, and some periodically tossed powder into their camp-fires to make those burn a deep and unnatural azure.

Sitting on the rim of a fountain, five such fellows spotted Umara, Stedd, and Anton going past, conferred briefly among themselves, then rose and sauntered forward. Anton gave them a smile and put his hand on the hilt of his saber. Umara raised an arm gloved in seething shadow. The outlanders stopped short, then turned back around.

"Who are these people?" asked Stedd calmly. Apparently, after all he'd been through, he didn't find street-corner extortionists especially intimidating.

"Scar pilgrims," Anton answered. "Folk who willingly visit places like the tainted spot in Gulthandor for the wisdom and power they hope it will bring. Sapra is a way station for those who travel back and forth to the Plaguewrought Lands south of the Chondalwood. Turmishan merchants wring a lot of coin out of them, but we dislike one another even so."

"Why?" asked Stedd.

"Turmishans worship the Treefather and therefore Nature. Scar pilgrims court a power that poisons Nature. It's not a good fit."

To Anton's disappointment, it proved impossible to hire horses, mules, or even donkeys. Livery stables that still possessed such animals were keeping them close to make sure no one ate them.

He supposed it wasn't a calamity. The hike was less arduous than some they'd undertaken together, and it remained so even after the Hierophant's Trail commenced its climb into the highlands called the Elder Spires. Still, he was hungry and footsore when they reached their destination at dusk, and Umara looked as though she felt the same. Only Stedd, who'd walked thousands of miles since the day Lathander first spoke to him, was still fresh enough to gawk at the House of Silvanus with the appreciation the sight deserved.

Situated atop a sort of plateau, the supreme sanctuary of the Emerald Enclave was a structure of rough-hewn granite and wood, roofed but open at the sides. It sat on a little island in the middle of a pool pocked by plummeting raindrops. Hissing, the water plunged away in three places to become waterfalls that in turn gave birth to the Calling, Elder, and Springbrook Rivers.

Accompanying his father, Anton had twice visited the House of Silvanus as a boy, and despite his general boredom with religious matters, the scene had impressed him with its intimations of harmony, serenity, and hidden power. In and of itself, it still did, but the armed company camped near the pool struck a discordant note. A disparate lot, some wore the tabards of Sapra's city watch, some, the jupons of the Turmishan army, and some, the green and brown of the rangers who patrolled the wild lands in the enclave's service.

Anton turned to Stedd. "Does Lathander have any information to share about that crew?"

"What?" Stedd said absently. He was still gazing across the water at the sanctuary, and the pirate realized he had yet to notice the warriors.

Anton flicked the tip of his index finger against Stedd's temple. "Wake up! I know the view looks interesting, and probably more to you than it ever did to me. But there's something here we didn't expect."

"Right." Orienting on the men-at-arms, the boy frowned. "I don't know. Nothing's coming to me."

Anton sighed. "Of course it isn't."

"I see two options," Umara said. "Walk right up to the warriors and ask why they're mustering in a sacred, secluded place, or head on into the sanctuary. Either is better that waiting until a druid or ranger accosts us demanding to know why a Red Wizard is lurking about."

"I agree," Anton said, "and we came to confer with the chief druids, not their retainers. So . . ." He walked to one of the strings of steppingstones that meandered across the pool and then, despite himself, hesitated.

"What's wrong?" asked Stedd.

Anton grinned. "There's an old story that a guardian spirit will kill anyone who tries to cross with evil intent."

Stedd cocked his head. "You aren't evil."

"Maybe not at the moment. But suppose the water spirit judges folk by their past deeds. Or the color of their mages' robes."

"Stop blathering and go," Umara said.

The stones were flat and close enough to one another to make the crossing easy, and no guardian rose from the water to bar the way. But a druid with a bronze sickle hanging from his belt and a staff in his hand emerged from the interior of the temple to watch the newcomers approach. The staff had ivy coiling up its length.

As Anton stepped onto the island, the druid said, "What do you seek here?"

"An audience with the Elder Circle," Anton replied.

The druid grunted. "You've come at a bad time. They aren't receiving." His eyes shifted to Umara. "I mean no offense when I say I doubt they'd want me to admit a Red Wizard at any time."

"You may have heard something about Lathander's boy prophet." Anton indicated Stedd. "Here he is."

The druid's eyes widened, but then he frowned. "Anyone could claim that. I've heard of wandering charlatans with child accomplices who *have* claimed it."

"You're a priest," Anton said. "I trust you recognize holy power when you see it. Do something, Stedd."

Seemingly seeking permission, the boy looked up at the druid, and the Oak Father's servant nodded. Stedd stepped forward and wrapped his fingers around those gripping the staff.

Golden light glowed from the point of contact. The druid gasped, and, rustling, the ivy wrapping the staff put forth new leaves.

"Convinced?" Anton asked.

The druid swallowed. "I felt something, certainly. Something . . . bracing."

"Good," Umara said, "because Stedd's here to help you. As am I, who protected him on his journey."

"All right," said the man with the staff. "All three of you can come in."

Candles and watch lights illuminated the interior of the House of Silvanus. There were no doors or truly enclosed spaces, but the seemingly haphazard arrangement of stone slabs and wooden pillars and screens created something akin to discrete chambers and the possibility of privacy even so. It also made the place mazelike.

Fortunately, the travelers' guide knew all the twists and turns. With him leading the way, they soon reached a space that might have been a bard's living quarters, with a collection of musical instruments occupying much of the space and a carving of Silvanus presiding over an altar in the corner. A male half-elf and a human woman sat at a round table drinking from wooden goblets.

The half-elf had tawny skin, pale blue eyes, and curly brown hair touched with gray. A harp sat at his feet on the earthen floor.

The woman was tall with broad shoulders, fit- and formidable-looking despite her white hair and the wrinkles in her face. She wasn't a native Turmishan, but a life lived mostly outdoors had weathered her skin to nearly the same mahogany color.

Both drinkers wore druidic robes, and both looked vexed at being disturbed. Their scowls only deepened when they spied Umara.

"I know," Anton said. "She's a wicked Thayan, and her mere presence profanes this sacred place. Get past it. What matters is that the boy is Stedd Whitehorn, Lathander's Chosen, come to save Turmish in its time of need."

The half-elf and the druidess looked at him as though they thought he was making an incomprehensible joke. Then, apparently realizing he was serious, they turned their gazes on Stedd, who, suddenly all prophet without a hint of childish shyness or uncertainly in his demeanor, stared back.

Neither drinker recited an incantation or brandished a talisman, nor did Stedd evoke Lathander's light. But a heightening tension in the air, a feeling of crescendo without the actual sound, convinced Anton the druids were nonetheless using magic to scrutinize the boy, and he was opening himself to the examination.

And finally, the half-elf said, "It's true." His voice was a rich and resonant bass, and a little shaky now. "The Morninglord has returned."

"So the lad keeps saying," Anton drawled. "And presumably, you're two of the three people who most need to know about it."

"Yes," the half-elf replied, rising. "I'm Ashenford Torinblow, elder of the enclave. My friend is Grand Cabal Shinthala Deepcrest."

Anton introduced Umara and gave his new alias. Ashenford then thanked the travelers' guide, sent him on his way, and urged his new guests to sit.

Anton found it was good to take a seat, even better to savor a first sip of tart white wine, and best of all to realize that, whatever happened next, he'd accomplished his purpose. He'd conducted Stedd to his destination in spite of everything Evendur Highcastle, vampire wizards, and fiery giant lions could do to stop him.

"If we'd been expecting you," Shinthala said, "or if you'd simply come at a different time, we would have welcomed you as befits a Chosen. It wouldn't have been like walking in on a pair of topers grousing in a tavern."

"This is better," Stedd replied. "If you had a ceremony or something, I wouldn't know what to do."

Ashenford leaned forward. "Your friend here said you've come to save Turmish. Does that mean to end the famine?"

"Yes," said Stedd. "I can't draw down nearly enough light to do it all by myself. But when we . . . looked into each other, I saw you two are Chosen of Silvanus. If we work together, we can do something." He faltered when he seemed to perceive that, contrary to his expectations, the two druids didn't share his enthusiasm. Rather, the brief excitement his arrival had engendered was visibly wilting. "Can't we?"

Ashenford raked his fingers through his hair. "The Spellplague . . . diminished the druids of Turmish, even the Elder Circle. And even if it were otherwise, we'd need Cindermoon—the hierophant— casting alongside us to have any hope of accomplishing anything so ambitious."

Umara waved an inpatient hand. "Then get her. Stedd assumed he'd be collaborating with all three of you."

"It's not that easy," Shinthala said.

Anton sighed. "Somehow, it never is. You'd better tell us."

"The Blue Fire . . . burned Cindermoon on the inside," the white-haired druidess said. "Or maybe rage and grief over the harm it did to the land wounded her. But gradually, through the hundred years since, she's changed. She changed her very name from Shadowmoon to Cindermoon as if to proclaim that, so far as she's concerned, nothing is left of the world but ash. Her way of thinking has become spiteful and suspicious."

"In other words," Anton said, "she's crazy. But apparently, not enough that you felt moved to depose her."

Shinthala glowered. "Silvanus raised her up. It's not for us to cast her down."

Ashenford picked up his harp and set it in his lap. It seemed to ease him to feel it under his hands. "I'm not as convinced as Shinthala that that's truly the Forest Father's will. But either way, it would have been reckless to try any such thing, because for a long while now, Cindermoon's magic has been stronger than ours. Maybe because

238

she's a pureblood elf. She's still young, and although Silvanus's blessing lengthened our lives, Shinthala and I are past our primes."

"Look," Umara said, "if your Hierophant is . . . ill, that's unfortunate. But is she so addled she *wants* your land to starve?"

Shinthala scowled. "No, but she's already working on her own supposed answer to the problem."

Anton grunted. "Which brings us to the men-at-arms outside."

"Yes," the druidess said. "Hating the Blue Fire, she likewise despises the pilgrims who worship it, and at the moment, it's particularly easy to see them as a menace and an infestation. They can't buy provisions for the journey south, and even if they could, folk coming north report that the Plaguewrought Land isn't even tainted anymore. So, desperate and bewildered, they bide here and do their best to obtain food Turmishans need for themselves."

"So the obvious answer," Umara said, "is to slaughter them."

Ashenford nodded. "Starting with Sapra and working out from there."

"But that's wrong!" Stedd cried. "And it's Umberlee's way even if waveservants aren't in Turmish preaching it. When the news goes around that that's how your people are acting, it will help her win."

"I don't know Umberlee's intentions," the half-elf replied. "But I agree that massacring the pilgrims would be both evil and futile. Turmish would still be starving when the last of them lay dead."

"Then surely," Umara said, "Cindermoon will set aside her vendetta for another day if we can only persuade her that magic offers a genuine solution."

"You'd think so," Shinthala said. "And we'll try our best."

And fail, evidently, Anton thought. For he didn't see a trace of genuine hope in either her or Ashenford.

"I'll tell you how to 'try,' " Umara said, the edge in her voice betraying that the druids' negativity was starting to grate on her. "If your hierophant's insane, cure her."

"Do you think," Ashenford answered, sounding annoyed in her turn, "that Shinthala and I haven't offered time and again? It doesn't matter how tactful or oblique we are. Cindermoon doesn't believe anything's wrong with her, and any offer to pray over her or cast spells on her behalf only rouses the suspicious part of her nature."

"Stedd doesn't need her consent," the Red Wizard said. "He'll whisper an incantation, wave his hand, light will shine, and that will be that."

"I doubt it," Ashenford said. "Believing herself under attack, Cindermoon would resist the magic with her own power and will. It would be a struggle more like an exorcism than an ordinary work of healing."

"And a work we couldn't possibly perform unless we had her alone," Shinthala said. "As we never do anymore, not since she'd grown leery of us. She always has some sort of protectors hovering close at hand."

This is not my problem, Anton told himself. I did what I promised, and the boy and I are quits.

But it wasn't that simple. It was infuriating to think that Stedd might have traveled so far and braved so much only to fail in the end, and despite his better judgment, that anger goaded him to speak.

"All right," he growled, "we're going to have a two-tiered plan. First, you holy people will make an honest effort to talk Cindermoon into helping us. Because it doesn't matter if she's crazy so long as she cooperates. But if she won't . . ."

Arguing Ashenford and Shinthala past their misgivings as necessary, he told them as much as they needed to know. He confided the rest to Stedd and Umara after the druids departed to arrange a meeting with their counterpart.

When he finished, both the boy and the wizard looked upset. Their distress touched and irritated him in equal measure.

"It's unnecessary," Umara said.

"I hope," Anton replied, "the whole second part of the plan is unnecessary. But if not, this is what makes it work."

"But afterward—" Stedd began.

"What did I tell you after we seized the *Octopus*?" the reaver asked.

Stedd hesitated, not, Anton judged, because he didn't remember the answer but because he didn't want to give it. "That either Lathander's cause is worth risking our lives, or it isn't."

"And apparently, I believe it is." Anton grinned. "What do you suppose is wrong with me?"

At the center of the House of Silvanus was a circular space open to the sky. A ring of menhirs stood around the periphery, and just inside it, three granite thrones stood side-by-side facing the altar stone in the middle.

Cindermoon felt a pang of resentment as she, Shinthala, and Ashenford all took their seats. Granted, the founders of the Emerald Enclave had intended that three should preside here as equals. But for all their wisdom, the druids of yore hadn't foreseen the Blue Fire. The burned, broken land it had left behind needed a single decisive, clearheaded spiritual leader, one who could do what needed doing without having to take the opinions of lesser minds into account.

Perhaps one day, Cindermoon would be rid of them, but for now, she'd have to suffer through whatever charade they'd devised to trick her into abandoning her present course of action. She waved a copper-skinned hand that was dainty even for a female elf. "Get on with it."

"Gladly." Ashenford then raised his voice so it would carry to the other side of the open space. "Come forth!"

Three people stepped out into the yellow torchlight and the pattering rain. They were as Cindermoon had been led to expect. A blond outlander boy. A Red Wizard—more proof, had the elf needed it, that the other members of the Elder Circle were either idiots or willing to conspire with even the vilest blackguards to undermine her. And a strapping Turmishan warrior with a trace of gray in his hair and a blade hanging on either hip.

"Hello," said the little boy.

"This is Stedd Whitehorn," Ashenford said, "the Chosen of Lathander."

Cindermoon shook her head. "I don't see it."

Shinthala frowned. "Because you haven't tried."

"Please," Ashenford said, "look with the eyes of the spirit. That's all it takes."

Cindermoon was reluctant to do that because it required lowering her guard. But she also didn't want to appear timid or unreasonable, and at least she didn't lack for protectors. Loyal druids, rangers, and Drummer, a huge black bear that had been her companion since he was a cub, were all close at hand.

She took a long breath and emptied her mind of distractions, of anger, caution, and the clammy feel of the rainwater on the seat of her throne. Then, silently praying, she asked Silvanus to help her see.

At the same time, she sensed the boy—Stedd—revealing himself to the best of his ability. Their complementary efforts produced a sudden layering of her vision. She still saw the boy, but at the same time, she beheld a red and golden dawn, and with it came a surge of hope so keen and unexpected it made her laugh out loud.

When the revelation faded, she raised a trembling hand to her brow. "Treefather," she breathed.

"*Now* do you see?" Shinthala demanded.

It was the human druidess's eagerness to make Cindermoon *commit*, to manipulate and manage her, that jolted her back to her customary wariness. Yet she saw little choice but to concede the truth. To do otherwise might call her powers and thus her leadership into question.

"I do," she said. "Welcome, Stedd Whitehorn. The Emerald Enclave rejoices at the god of the dawn's rebirth."

"Uh, thank you." Stedd hesitated. "Did Ashenford and Shinthala tell you *why* Lathander sent me?"

"They claim to help end the famine."

"Yes. If we all work together, all the Chosen and the other druids, too, there must be something we can do."

"There is," Cindermoon said, "and I've already set a plan in motion to do it. I'll be grateful for any support you can give."

Stedd frowned. "You mean, the plan to kill the scar pilgrims?"

"Ah. My peers told you about it."

"Lathander wouldn't want me to help with that. I don't think . . . I mean, I *know* he wouldn't want *anybody* to just go kill hundreds of people."

Cindermoon's fingers tightened on the arms of her throne. Plainly, this was why Ashenford and Shinthala were so happy another Chosen had turned up. To their minds, the boy was another voice of equivalent stature to speak against her and dilute her authority. But by deep roots and green leaves, it wasn't going to matter.

"Then do the Morninglord's bidding," she said, "insofar as a child newly Chosen understands it. But please realize that although my folk revere your god, we worship Silvanus above all others. And *he's* decreed the pilgrims have to die."

Ashenford grimaced. "Shinthala and I are his Chosen, too, and we haven't heard him say any such thing."

"Then clean out your ears!" Cindermoon snapped. "Is the plan truly all that hard to comprehend? By purging Turmish of all who worship the Blue Fire, we'll magically cleanse the land of the last of the taint itself. That in turn will restore the enclave's strength. Then we'll use that might to feed the hungry."

Stedd shook his head. "You can't take the power from something so bad and use it for something good."

Cindermoon's fingers tightened on the armrests until they ached and she pried them loose again. "Boy, you're debating first principles with one who was already a druid *and* Chosen when your great-great-grandfather . . . never mind. I'll answer as your station if not your experience deserves. *You* couldn't turn death into life. But the Oakfather is the lord of *all* Nature, hunter and prey, dark and light. Druids can do things—difficult, ambiguous things—that dawnbringers and sunlords never could."

"Still," Ashenford said, "Lathander has returned in a time of turmoil. Surely, he has a thousand urgent matters to concern him. Yet he elected to send his first new Chosen here, to us. We'd be wise to consider what the boy has to say."

Cindermoon glared at him. "You'd be wise to heed what *I'm* telling you. The scar pilgrims are going to die. The Assembly of Stars has given its blessing—"

"Because you approached them without our knowledge," Shinthala growled.

"—and I've gathered warriors to carry out the campaign. You two can either help, and prove yourselves worthy of the rank you hold, or hold back and—"

Voices cried out. Drummer moaned and scrambled behind the row of thrones. Startled, Cindermoon jerked around on her seat and looked straight ahead.

While she'd been busy squabbling with her peers, a circle of wavering, somehow filthy-looking red light had appeared in the air. It was a window into a place where almost everything was on fire, including the damned souls shrieking and flailing in pits like mass graves and the giant soaring toward the breach between worlds.

Some trick of enhanced motion or warped time brought the balor to the window in an instant. When it did, Cindermoon could make out the pock-like scars on the demon's hideous face where her conjured hailstones had battered it, and the horn Ashenford had broken with a blow from an enchanted quarter-staff. She'd believed she and her peers had destroyed the demon utterly, but some power even greater than itself must have seen fit to resurrect it.

A beat of its bat-like wings carried it into the gateway, which now took on the aspect of a tunnel, and as it flew onward, some form of distortion made its massive body seem to slither like a snake's. Appearing suddenly, perhaps simply because the balor had willed them to, dozens of lesser fiends hurtled after it.

Cindermoon abruptly realized she'd lost a precious instant to consternation and had, at best, only one more left. She lifted her hand and drew breath to shout a word of forbiddance.

But before she could, Stedd Whitehorn shrilled, "Lathander!"

Red-gold light pulsed across the heart of the sanctuary, and the balor and the lesser demons tumbled backward like leaves in a gale.

Meanwhile, the mouth of the tunnel drew in upon itself like the contracting pupil of an eye. In a couple heartbeats, it closed completely.

The boy then pivoted to the Turmishan warrior who was supposedly his faithful bodyguard. Looking shocked at the sealing of the passage to the Abyss, the man stood with his cutlass in his hand. The short, curved blade still glimmered with a trace of the same dirty red light that pervaded the balor's domain. Evidently, it was the talisman that had opened the way. He must have surreptitiously eased it out of its scabbard when everyone else was looking elsewhere.

"Why?" cried Stedd. "Why would you do this?"

"Because a Marivaldi," the swordsman growled, "finishes what he starts."

With that, Cindermoon realized exactly which member of that once-respected family he must be, the only conspirator to escape after the near-destruction of Sapra and the Elder Circle. A ranger who likewise understood shouted to identify the dastard to one and all, "That's *Anton* Marivaldi!"

For one more instant, the traitor glared across the innermost sanctum at the trio on the thrones as though contemplating a suicidal charge. Then he whirled and ran back into the temple.

"Kill him!" Cindermoon cried, whereupon rangers and druids pounded after the fleeing man like hounds on the track of a deer.

Anton slowed for an instant to thrust his cutlass back into its scabbard. Despite tapers and watch lights, the interior of the House of Silvanus was dark enough that otherwise, the ruddy glow that Umara had conjured into the steel might have served as a beacon for his pursuers.

From the sound of it, he had plenty of them, and that was the idea, to lure all of Cindermoon's protectors away. He was glad that, in the aftermath of the catastrophe in Sapra, on the day preceding his realization that he was in imminent danger of arrest, curiosity had prompted him to go look at the body of the fallen balor. His description of its wounds had enabled Umara to produce a convincing illusion of the exact same creature. He'd judged that that, combined with the revelation of his own identity, would jolt the elf and her defenders into precipitous action if anything would.

Now he'd see if he could survive the consequences of his success.

Had it been possible to move in a straight line, he could have sprinted from the courtyard in the center of the sanctuary to its outer edge quickly. But it wasn't. The seemingly random placement of pillars and stone slabs supporting the roof and the lack of anything approximating a genuine corridor obliged him to veer repeatedly, until he wasn't sure he was even heading in his original direction anymore.

He *was* all but certain his pursuers were spreading out. It was what he would have done in their place to catch a stranger who was likely blundering back and forth in confusion.

He rounded a corner, and a wolf lunged out of the shadows. He wrenched himself aside and banged his shoulder into granite, but the beast's jaws snapped shut on empty air.

The wolf started to spin for another try, and he booted it in the ribs. That knocked it stumbling away and gave him time to draw his saber. As the animal gathered itself for another lunge, he decided on a cut to the neck. The curved blade was already in motion when he remembered druids were shapeshifters.

He spun the saber lower and slashed a foreleg instead. The wolf fell. He dodged past it and ran on.

He'd only taken three strides when a voice rasped words of power behind him. Instinct told him when to dodge. Spines like porcupine quills hurtled past him to stab into a wooden screen.

That's what I get for showing mercy, Anton thought. It would have served him right if the former wolf's barrage had hit.

Yet he showed mercy again when a ranger rushed out of the dark. Even though it took longer to sweep the other warrior's broadsword out of line, step in, and drive the curved guard of the saber into his face with stunning force than it would have to simply kill him.

Calling to one another, the voices of Anton's pursuers echoed. They sounded like they were all around him, and he could only hope it wasn't really so.

Three more turns, and then he burst in on a skinny adolescent girl in druidic robes who yelped and recoiled. Hostage! he thought, but no. If he took a captive, someone would hurry back to the Elder Circle to report the situation when his entire objective was to keep all their underlings away from them. He simply had to keep running.

When he raced on by without pausing, the young initiate found her courage and started an incantation. Fortunately, she recited the words slowly, like she had yet to fully master the spell, and he left her behind while she was still declaiming it.

An arrow flew past his head. Seeking only cover, he ducked into the narrow, unpromising-looking gap where two stone "walls" nearly met at an angle. That was the turn that finally revealed the pool, now black as the starless sky it mirrored.

Anton dashed out into the open, looked about, and saw that he'd apparently exited the temple ahead of any of his pursuers. And while people stirred among the lean-tos and campfires on the far shore—some sharp-eared soul must have heard the yelling inside the sanctuary despite the hiss of the waterfalls and the patter of the rain—they weren't yet doing so in an organized or purposeful way.

Anton judged that if he kept moving smartly, across the pool, past the camp, and on down Hierophant's Trail, he *might* actually get away. More likely not, but at least it was a chance.

He found the nearest string of steppingstones and started striding from one to the next. He reached the eighth one, and then an all but shapeless form surged up to tower over him. It seemed less a creature that had been lurking in the pool than a portion of the water that had formed into rippling approximations of arms, a head, and a torso; the liquid bulk at the center of it contained and concealed the next steppingstone in line.

Anton laughed. "You're confused. You're supposed to kill evildoers going *into* the sanctuary. But just sink back down, and I won't tell."

The water spirit raised its arm.

Stedd doubted that Lathander's blessings helped him lie any more convincingly. If anything, the touch of so much goodness ought to tangle his tongue if he tried.

Yet apparently, he'd played his part in Anton's trick convincingly enough. Because Cindermoon had ordered her guards to chase the pirate, and except for a couple woodsmen in brown and green, they'd all obeyed.

And in the aftermath, it seemed like the reemergence of a deadly threat from the past had distracted the little black-haired elf from current grudges. When her green eyes looked at the other members of the Elder Circle, Umara, or Stedd, it was without the clenched mistrust he'd sensed before.

Maybe we could persuade her now, the boy thought, but really, he knew that hope was too faint for even a Chosen of Lathander to depend on. He and his companions needed to stick to the plan.

Umara plainly agreed. Seemingly peering in the direction where Anton and his pursuers had disappeared, she had her back to the three thrones and their occupants. That enabled her to whisper an incantation and crook and cross her fingers into mystic signs without Cindermoon spotting it. The spell plunged the two rangers into slumber; their legs buckled beneath them and dumped them on the ground.

At the same moment, Ashenford and Shinthala scrambled off their stone chairs, pivoted to face Cindermoon, and started chanting. The half-elf held out his hand, a sickle appeared in it, and he spun it over his head. Like a ghost plant growing in midair, the suggestion of holly, with toothy leaves and little red berries, formed around the white-haired druidess. Stedd could even smell it.

Because Stedd didn't know how to subdue people without hurting them, he had to leave it to his two new druid friends to overcome Cindermoon. They should be able to. They had her outnumbered, and they'd caught her by surprise.

But then, with a roar, Cindermoon's bear rounded the line of thrones. The illusory demons had scared the animal off, but apparently not far and not for long, and the sight of mere human beings working magic wasn't frightening enough to keep it from trying to protect its mistress.

A swipe of its claws jerked Shinthala's leg out from under her and dropped her on her back. The phantom holly vanished, scent and all. The bear reared over her.

Stedd threw out his hand and cast brightness into the beast's beady eyes. The light was harmless, but, startled, the bear flinched from it.

That gave Shinthala time to cast more magic. She spoke, and her voice came out as a high, inhuman throbbing. Her manner reminded Stedd of someone ordering a naughty dog off a bed.

The bear shuddered as though struggling to resist the druidess's power to command it. Then it wheeled and lumbered back the way it had come.

Stedd spun back around. Without support from Shinthala, Ashenford had failed to render Cindermoon helpless; instead, he himself strained against vines that had burst from the ground to wrap around him. Now on her feet like her peers, her delicate face with its slanted eyes and pointed chin furious, the elf turned toward Shinthala and swept out a hand that was suddenly covered with insects. As her arm snapped out straight, the conjured hornets took flight.

A fan-shaped blast of yellow flame engulfed the wasps halfway to their intended victim. When the blaze guttered out a heartbeat later, there was nothing left of them. Her fingers smoking, Umara shifted to face Cindermoon dead on.

Cindermoon twirled an upraised hand. Visible chiefly by virtue of the raindrops it caught and spun, a cyclone twice as tall as a man howled up from the ground. It charged Umara like a bull, snatched her up into the air, and flung her into one of the menhirs. Something *cracked*, and the Red Wizard collapsed like a rag doll at the base of the stone.

Stedd stared for a heartbeat, then remembered that here was something he *did* know how to do. He scurried in Umara's direction.

As he bent over her, he glanced back at the fight. Kneeling, the blood from her clawed leg pooling around her, Shinthala conjured a huge boar halfway into being.

Then Cindermoon shouted, "No!" and shook her fist. The blurry, misty semblance of a hog vanished.

Stedd reached out to Lathander and drew down his light. Setting his glowing hands on Umara's shoulders, he poured the power into her.

Ashenford flailed his arms, and his bonds, now dry and brittle, started to break apart from the top down. That freed his hands to start a different spell, but his legs were still immobilized when the whirlwind roared at him and engulfed him. His chanting ended in a cry of pain.

Cindermoon snapped her fingers, and the cyclone vanished, dropping the half-elf to the ground. Stedd just had time to wonder why she'd thrown away such an effective weapon, and then she made a beckoning gesture. Thick gray fog billowed out from the spot where she was standing, a cloud the whirlwind would have blown apart.

In a heartbeat, the fog spread far enough to swallow Ashenford and Shinthala. Only Umara and Stedd were beyond its reach, and he was sure that only he saw when a huge owl flew up from the middle of it.

Without a doubt, the bird was Cindermoon. She'd been holding her own against her assailants, but had apparently decided even so that it was foolish to go on fighting them all by herself when she had a little army of supporters within easy reach.

Umara's eyes fluttered open. Stedd pointed at the owl. "Please!" he said.

The wizard jumped to her feet so fast, she knocked him aside. She rattled off words that felt like needles jabbing him.

A shadow tentacle like the one that had grabbed Nobanion shot up from the ground to snatch at the owl. It flicked harmlessly past just under the bird's talons.

With a noise that was half grunt and half snarl, Umara rose onto her toes with one arm straight above her head. She looked like someone straining to reach something on a high shelf. The tentacle stretched just a little more and whipped around Cindermoon's avian body.

Umara lashed her arm down. The length of shadow jerked the shapeshifter to the ground with a violence that made Stedd wince. He hoped the Red Wizard remembered the idea was to help the hierophant, not smash her to bits.

The fog vanished as either Shinthala or Ashenford made it go away. Then the two of them, Stedd, and Umara hurried toward the spot where Cindermoon lay bound. She was mostly an elf again, although she still had some feathers here and there, and her legs were too short for the rest of her.

Stedd was relieved to see that although unconscious, the hierophant was breathing and not visibly mangled. Still, Shinthala frowned at Umara and said, "That spell you just cast was true black magic."

"Like Anton said," the Red Wizard snapped, "get past it. How's your leg?"

"I'll worry about it after we tend to Cindermoon."

"Fair enough. You healers do that. I'll stand guard and keep the tentacle tight."

Stedd, Shinthala, and Ashenford knelt around the elf. Stedd placed his fingertips against her temple and drew light and warmth

251

into them. Shinthala murmured under her breath, and Ashenford crooned a song as gentle as a lullaby. Druidic magic suffused the air with the scent of verdure.

Then *denial* as sudden and vicious as a punch in the throat rocked Stedd backward. His head rang, and for a moment, he couldn't catch his breath. When he finally did, he saw that Shinthala and Ashenford looked just as shaken as he.

"What happened?" Umara asked.

"What we expected," Shinthala replied. Her voice was thick, like she'd bitten her tongue. "Cindermoon's not awake in a physical sense. But she does know when someone tries to touch her psyche. Or her madness knows. And it's fighting back."

"Then overcome the resistance."

"Thank you, we remember the plan," Ashenford said drily. He looked at his fellow healers. "We need to do a better job of coordinating. Shinthala, you and I will sing the Hymn of Still Waters. Stedd, you invoke Lathander's light when we reach the word 'peace.'"

Anton took a hasty retreat. No combat maneuver was more basic, but it felt chancy when he was blindly backing down a string of wet steppingstones and not a continuous surface.

Still, he managed to set his feet where he'd intended to, and the water spirit's blow fell short. Fingerless like a mitten, its enormous hand slapped down in the space he'd just vacated and splashed apart. But when the guardian raised its arm back up from the surface of the pool, the hand was intact again.

Anton had his doubts that even an enchanted saber could hurt a being capable of reforming itself like that, but he reckoned he had to try. He lunged and cut before the hand could swing up out of range.

The blade splashed through its target, which seethed, rippled, and dropped some of its liquid substance back down into the pool. The agitation spread up the spirit's arm in diminishing convulsions.

Anton grinned. He'd at least hurt his adversary. He just couldn't tell how much.

Hoping to land a cut to his torso, he lunged again. But the spirit flowed backward like a wave sweeping across the surface of the sea, and the attack fell short. The entity then riposted with a horizontal swipe.

Thanks to his aggressiveness, Anton was in too close to defend by retreating. He pivoted and slashed.

If his first attack had hurt the spirit, then the stop cut had likely done the same. But the creature's arm kept spinning at him anyway, and as it did, it expanded. A sheet of water like the sort of wave that swept mariners overboard during a tempest bashed him from head to toe.

The impact was hard enough to bruise and bloody him. It also knocked Anton off balance and left him teetering on one foot, and only part of that foot still atop a steppingstone.

In a normal battle, falling into the pool might not be disastrous. It shouldn't be all that deep if it had steppingstones sticking up out of it. But if, as Anton sensed, *all* the water was in some sense his opponent, it seemed like a bad idea to end up submerged in it to the knees or the breastbone. Wrenching himself sideways, he regained stability.

As soon as he did, he hurled himself forward. Once again, the water spirit flowed backward. But it didn't react as quickly as it had before, and the saber caught it across what, in a man, would be the stomach.

Losing cohesion, the whole entity plunged toward the surface of the pool. Only for a heartbeat, though, and then the liquid mass of it surged up and put on form once more.

At the same time, someone shouted, "There he is!"

The voice came from behind Anton, where the sanctuary stood. But when it startled him into glancing around at something besides the water spirit, he saw that a dozen of Cindermoon's pilgrim hunters had assembled at the other end of the chain of steppingstones as well.

Sighing, he wished they'd let him finish his duel with the water spirit, just so he'd know if he really could have won. But he supposed he couldn't expect them to share his curiosity.

Hoping the elemental spirit wouldn't instantly smash and drown him, he lowered his saber and turned to face the druids and rangers in front of the temple. "I surrender," he said.

"Is he allowed to do that?" a young druid asked.

"Cindermoon said to kill him," an older one replied, whereupon the woodsmen around him drew back their bows. No doubt, on the other shore, other archers were doing the same.

And just like that, plunging into the pool became the *only* option. In the highly unlikely event that the ploy enabled Anton to dodge flights of arrows while the spirit somehow failed to kill him, either, he'd swim to the top of one of the waterfalls and see if he could survive a ride bouncing from rock to rock all the way to the bottom.

He flexed his knees, and then a female voice cried, "Stop!" And everyone did. It was, after all, a voice servants of the Forest Father were accustomed to obeying.

Cindermoon strode from the temple. She glowed from head to toe with green phosphorescence, presumably to make it easier for her subordinates to orient on her.

Stedd, Ashenford, Umara, and Shinthala trailed along behind her. The Red Wizard was moving stiffly. The snowy-haired druidess had a bloody leg and hobbled with the aid of a staff.

Clearly, Anton's confederates hadn't had an easy time of it. But their scheme must have worked.

Anton shot Stedd a grin, but the boy didn't return it. Rather, his mouth tightened.

All right, Anton thought, we might as well find out to what extent your worries are justified. He inclined his head to the shining elf. "Lady Cindermoon."

"Please, call me Shadowmoon," she replied.

Anton smiled. "With pleasure."

The hierophant didn't return his smile, either. "Anton Marivaldi, the Assembly of Stars itself long ago judged you a traitor and condemned you to death."

"Yes, and started a fashion. In the years since, a number of places have sentenced me to death *in absentia*. Which is all right. I couldn't have offered much of a defense had I been present."

"Nonsense!" Umara snapped. "Tell these people you weren't privy to the real traitor's plans! You had no idea the talismans you helped smuggle could be used to summon a balor!"

Anton sheathed the saber and walked slowly back toward the Red Wizard and the four Chosen. "Would that explanation win me leniency in a Thayan court?" he asked. "Would it soften your heart if demons had butchered your loved ones?"

"Whatever happened years ago," said Stedd, "you brought me here to help Turmish. You helped save Lady Shadowmoon and stop the Emerald Enclave from murdering people." He looked up at the hierophant. "That has to be worth something!"

The elf frowned. "It is, Chosen, and I don't desire your friend's death. How could I when he just risked his life on my behalf? But the enclave can't simply flout the judgment of the Assembly of Stars, certainly not in a matter as serious as this. Anton Marivaldi must answer for the malfeasance that resulted in the balor and all the piracy against Turmishan vessels in the years since."

Stedd shook his head. "It isn't fair!"

"You know better," Anton said. "So set it aside and concentrate on finishing Lathander's business."

Clearly pondering, Shadowmoon bowed her head and toyed with one of the carved wooden buttons running down the front of her gown. Finally, she said, "While we can't overturn the assembly's sentence, I don't see that we're obligated to carry it out here and now. I recommend that when the time is right, we escort Anton Marivaldi to Alaghôn and turn him over to the assembly. He can plead for mercy, and I'll speak on his behalf." She looked to Ashenford and Shinthala. "Does that meet with your approval?"

"Yes," the half-elf replied.

"I agree, too," Shinthala said.

Shadowmoon turned back to Anton. "You heard the plan," she said. "Will you cooperate? Will you swear to remain with us for now and surrender yourself to the assembly when we command it?"

"I swear it on my honor," Anton said.

Shadowmoon inclined her head. "Then we'll treat you like a guest and not a prisoner. And with that decided, we need to take up the greater matter before us: how to feed the multitude who are starving."

CHAPTER ELEVEN

THE LEAN-TO LEAKED. ANNOYED BY THE TRICKLING AND DRIPPING, Umara tried to rearrange the weave of branches over her head and only succeeded in making matters worse. "The Black Hand take it," she growled.

Lying beside her, Anton chuckled. "You'd think rangers could build a better shelter."

"I don't suppose they could have, really. Not one that this rain couldn't find its way through. When I get back to Thay, I'm never going out in foul weather again."

"We could still watch the ceremony from inside the sanctuary. The rain hasn't worked its way through that roof."

She shook her head. "I don't want to try to make out what's happening from the other side of the pool. I want to be up close."

It surprised her to learn that the Chosen's ritual wouldn't take place inside the temple. But as Ashenford explained, the entire plateau was sacred to the Oakfather, whereas only the easternmost patch of land could be considered holy to the Morninglord. Thus, it made sense to perform the rite where the petitioners would find it easiest to draw power from both gods.

There were plenty of them to do the drawing, too. After Shadowmoon canceled the massacre of the scar pilgrims, she'd dismissed most of the rangers and other warriors from her little army. But the Elder Circle had summoned additional druids to gather in their place, along with a miscellany of nature spirits and forest creatures. Sprites the size of mice flitted on dragonfly wings, and treants towered over everyone else, remarkably easy to mistake for actual trees with their gnarled, asymmetrical bodies, crowns of leafy branches, and bark-like skin, shifting ponderously when they moved at all.

The company had assembled to perform a work of magic greater than Umara had ever witnessed or likely ever would again. It would be priestly magic, not arcane, and beholden to the forces of Light and Nature rather than those of those of the Pit, and thus, in no way her sort of power. But she meant to drink in the spectacle and learn all she could nonetheless.

The ceremony should commence soon. At the moment, everyone was waiting for Stedd to announce that, behind the wall of gray thunderheads to the east, the sun was rising.

Umara turned back to Anton. "You wanted to watch this, too, didn't you? That's why you haven't already run away."

The pirate drew back. "Wizard, you insult me. I gave my oath."

He was only able to maintain his air of affronted dignity for a moment. Then a snort forced its way out, and she laughed with him.

"You're right, of course," he said. "Naturally, I want to see how this all works out. But once it's over . . . " He gestured in the general direction of Hierophant's Trail.

"I suspect Shadowmoon actually intended for you to flee."

"Then she won't be disappointed."

"You don't suppose the Assembly of Stars might actually pardon you?"

He grinned. "In their place, I wouldn't."

She took a breath. "Well, then, we'll smuggle you back aboard the *Octopus* and safely out of Turmish."

Anton hesitated. "If someone catches you helping me, we're liable to end up facing the headsman together. Even if we don't, you'll still have forfeited any good will you may have generated on Thay's behalf. And from what you told me, that's the one prize you can offer your superiors to make up for not bringing home a Chosen."

Umara made a spitting noise. "Please. You already saw me trick Shadowmoon herself with an illusion. I can fool any Turmishan if I put my mind to it. Druids and such have their talents, but Thayan magic is the most sophisticated in the world."

Anton laughed. "Certainly, Thayan arrogance is the most egregious."

"You do realize I'm offering to help you."

"I know, and—" His head turned to the druidic spellcasters and their allies. "We can talk about this later. I think the ritual is starting."

He was right.

Standing at the brink of the drop-off, closer to the hidden sunrise than anyone else, Stedd extended his hands to the eastern horizon, and they bloomed with gold and crimson light. He turned and thrust them at the ground. Lines, circles, triangles, and more complex figures spread outward from the spot he was indicating, writing themselves on the ground in light.

Standing to the west of her collaborators, Shadowmoon began a kind of slow, twisting, pirouetting dance in place. She made the contortions look as effortless as they were lithe. To the north, Shinthala looked upward and muttered; the clouds overhead rumbled and flickered as lightning stirred inside them. In the south, Ashenford stroked arpeggios from his harp.

Traceries of light flowed from the druids' positions across the ground to interweave with the figures Lathander's power was drawing. But the new designs were green instead of yellow or ruddy, and more freeform, their shapes hinting at the uniqueness of every leaf on every branch or every bend in the course of every stream rather than the perfect roundness of the sun or the flawless arc of its daily progress across the heavens.

Trained to construct every pentacle with geometric precision, Umara winced at a sloppiness that, had a Red Wizard committed it—perhaps because he was drunk—would have proved either futile or suicidal. But the Elder Circle's figures smoldered with a power that, so far at least, they seemed fully able to contain.

A droning began. It sounded so much like a deep tone from the Thayan pump organ called the zulthoon that Umara might have mistaken it for one had she not known no such instrument was anywhere nearby. Eventually, she realized the treants were groaning out the hum as accompaniment to Ashenford's harp.

One or two at a time, the other celebrants joined in, sometimes singing, sometimes chanting, sometimes contributing by other means. A barefoot, dirty, and nearly naked druid—a hermit, Umara suspected—beat out rhythms on a pair of femurs. Sprites hovered in a cloud to merge the whine of their wings into a piercing chord. A spindly horned man with enormous eyes and ears simply exploded into a run of eight ascending brassy notes, leaving not a speck of flesh nor a drop of blood behind.

By rights, it should have all combined into cacophony, but somehow, beauty emerged instead. What Umara chiefly noticed, though, was vibration resonating through her bones as mystical energy accumulated.

The glowing designs grew larger than the space taken up by those who created them. A straight line of rose-colored luminescence shot into Umara and Anton's lean-to and out the back. Figures and sigils even wrote themselves on the surface of the pool, maintaining their forms thereafter despite the constant flow to the tops of the three waterfalls.

Then the storm clouds to which Shinthala had been muttering answered as clouds had never answered any mortal spellcaster before. The sky—the world—blazed white with so many lightning bolts that it was impossible to see the individual strikes or, in fact, anything but brightness. The accompanying crash was so loud that it scarcely registered as noise. Rather, it smashed sensation and thought into chaos. Even though Umara had had some notion of what to expect, for a moment, she feared that she was dying.

She wasn't, though, and when her head resumed working, and she blinked the dazzle out of her eyes, she saw the rain beating down harder than it had in all her time on or near the Sea of Fallen Stars. The pounding drowned out whatever singing and chanting was still going on, and gray veils of falling water obscured objects only a few paces away.

The Great Rain had caused Turmishan crops to fail and produced privation around the Inner Sea. Thus, it had at first astonished Umara to hear that the Chosen's solution to the famine involved bringing down even more of it.

But Stedd was certain that, contrary to appearances, the rain was neither a force of pure destruction nor a weapon forged by Umberlee to impose her creed on the region. It was how one part of the world was mending the damage inflicted by the Spellplague.

And if the Great Rain was fundamentally a kind of healing, then master healers should be able to nudge it to work faster and finish restoring the natural order in Turmish. With luck, that truly would raise the Emerald Enclave's magic to its former potency, and then the druids would be strong enough to undertake another great work.

That was the plan, anyway. Lying on her side in a lean-to with the torrential rain blinding and deafening her, Umara couldn't judge how well it was working. "I'm going outside," she shouted.

"What a bad idea," Anton replied. But when she crawled out, he followed.

The rain pummeled her, stinging her nose, cheeks, and chin. She tugged her hood farther down and looked around.

Standing in the open, she could see and hear better, albeit only somewhat. The patterns of light on the ground had stopped expanding, presumably because they were complete. Reduced to a vague silhouette by the downpour, Shadowmoon still danced, and at least some of the other celebrants were still intoning their incantations; a trace of their voices whispered through the rattle of the rain.

Umara drew breath to yell, then thought better of it. She offered Anton her hand, and he smiled and took it. She led him toward the drop-off.

As they made their way, the sky repeatedly flashed white, and booms and crashes shook the tableland. Umara realized the clouds were producing some of the most prodigious thunderbolts she'd ever seen. But they didn't make her flinch, not after the supreme violence of the initial blast. They simply felt like one detail of a still greater power at work on every side.

Unfortunately, even when she reached the spot where the ground fell away, she still couldn't tell if that power was doing what the Chosen intended it to. Once again, the rain obscured too much. She could make out some of the nearer peaks composing the Elder Spires, but that was all.

"Seven black stars," she growled in annoyance, and could barely even hear herself. But then the pounding of the rain abated, if not the roar. Surprised, she looked around and found one of the treants looming over her and Anton. The leafy branches that spread out above the creature's face blocked some of the downpour.

She and Anton weren't the only folk to whom the tree man was providing a sort of shelter. Several of the winged sprites perched in its lower branches.

"Thank you!" Umara bellowed.

The treant smiled, its mouth bending slowly. It extended a huge, bark-covered hand.

Umara hesitated, then took hold of a bark-covered fingertip. Anton gripped another.

The wizard wondered how long a polite treant handclasp was supposed to last. Then images surged into her mind.

Her immediate impulse was to defend against psychic intrusion, to snatch her hand back from the treant's and sear the creature with a burst of fire while she was at it. It was the prudent way to react when anybody sought to touch one's mind uninvited, and besides, the contact reminded her of Kymas riding in her head.

Yet another part of her—the part that had decided a measure of trust was possible even with outlander pirates, farm boy prophets, and druids—doubted the treant meant her harm. So, telling herself the contact was neither an attack nor an intentional violation, she focused on the visions and perceived them clearly.

When she did, she realized that either by virtue of its participation in the ritual or simply because of some inherent bond with the land, the treant could see farther than she could. In fact, it discerned what the rain was doing across the length and breadth of Turmish, and it wanted to share that knowledge.

The storm fed streaming floodwater that gnawed at the base of the peninsula that was home to the House of Silvanus and Sapra. Already eroded by months of rain, soil and even bedrock crumbled, falling away to form a gigantic ditch. Scattered steadings and hamlets slid and tumbled into the gulf. Umara hoped the folk who'd lived therein had abandoned them. If not, well, the druids had sent messengers to warn them.

Plainly, even after a year of torrential storms and even given the climactic fury of the current one, the collapse was occurring with impossible speed. But as the Chosen had realized, the Great Rain was in its essence a transcendent mystical force, not a mundane one, and apparently, it could do impossible things.

When the channel across the peninsula opened, the sea came rushing in to fill it. Smiling, Umara could only assume that even Umberlee was powerless to stop it, for the Queen of the Depths surely wouldn't approve of the results.

Before the Spellplague, the Emerald Enclave had ruled a holy island called Ilighôn as its particular domain. With the straits reopened, Ilighôn was reborn.

The reshaping of land and sea brought a rush of spiritual power. Green light rippled and flickered in the sacred pool known as Springbrook Shallows. Treants laughed and danced with slow, swaying steps in the meeting place they called Archentree.

Then Umara's benefactor looked farther afield. Once again, the sea was advancing, but this time, it wasn't racing down a newly created channel. It was rolling over a long expanse of shore and drawing ever closer to a gray stone city.

"That's Alaghôn!" Anton shouted. "The capital! Before the Spellplague made the waters recede, it was a great port. Now, it can be again."

That's assuming the water knows when to stop, Umara thought. But in truth, she expected that it would.

The treant shifted its clairvoyant gaze. Now Umara beheld patches of plagueland in the south. Pounding down, the rain extinguished Blue Fire as easily as it could have doused ordinary flame.

Then the visions faded, and the wizard found herself wholly in her own body and limited to her own perceptions once more. She was clutching the treant's finger and Anton's callused hand tightly, and the reaver was squeezing back. For some reason, she found herself reluctant to let go of him.

She did, though. The rain wasn't falling nearly as hard as before, and the lightning and thunder had abated. She and Anton no longer had any reason to cling together like timid children.

All around her, the druids and their allies had an exuberant look; despite their exertions and the stinging drenching they'd just endured, they experienced the same exhilaration as the enormous dancers in Archentree.

Grinning, Ashenford struck chord after chord from his harp. Shinthala wore a kind of satisfied sneer, like the magic just concluded was an adversary she'd wrestled into submission. A centaur galloped, his hooves throwing up mud, and the sprites that had sheltered in the foliage of Umara's treant friend flew into the air and whirled around and around one another.

But Stedd made a little gasping sound that almost sounded like a sob.

Anton and Umara both pivoted to the boy. His golden hair dripping, Stedd winced and held up a trembling hand to signal that he was all right.

The adults hurried over to him anyway. "What's wrong?" Anton asked.

Stedd shook his head. He looked unhealthy and spent, with discoloration like bruises under his bright blue eyes. "Nothing."

"Tell me!"

"It's just . . . There are three grown-up Chosen and all these other druids and creatures to draw down Silvanus's power. There's only me to draw Lathander's. And this new . . . well of strength we just dug. It's for them, not me. It doesn't give me any extra power. But don't worry. I can do what I need to."

"I'm sure you can," Anton said, "when you take up the work again tomorrow. The druids can stop for today and give you time to rest."

"No, they can't." Stedd pointed to the glowing lines and symbols at his feet. "The designs and the . . . things the designs tie together . . . won't last until tomorrow. Lathander says that when folk start a big, complicated work of magic, they need to push through to the end."

"That's true," Umara said, "but perhaps the others can finish without you."

Stedd sighed. "You know that *isn't* true."

Umara and Anton exchanged worried looks.

The boy scowled up at the pirate. "You told me to concentrate on finishing Lathander's business."

Anton scowled. "Would it sway you if I took it back? No, plainly not, stubborn brat that you are. Do what you have to, then. But be careful."

"All right, everyone!" Shadowmoon called from her station to the west of everyone else. "Prepare yourselves. We have to press on."

Umara squeezed Stedd's shoulder. Then she and Anton moved back to stand with the treant.

The ritual resumed in the same incremental fashion in which it had begun. The Chosen at the cardinal points started conjuring in their various fashions. Stedd looked to the eastern horizon, prayed, and a golden glow lit his body from within. Shinthala murmured

265

words that made the toes of her bare feet lengthen, burrow into the earth, and root her in place. Shadowmoon danced, and Ashenford harped. And gradually, over the course of the several breaths, the rest of the celebrants joined in.

Umara felt the intricate design on the ground pour out the power it had amassed. Or perhaps the luminous figure could more accurately be described as a lens focusing an ongoing torrent of spiritual energy rising from the Morninglord, the Treefather, and their worshipers. She suspected both descriptions were true in their way, and neither was sufficient.

However the magic functioned, she and her companions were about to find out if it was equal to the colossal task before it. The treant offered its hand, and she took hold of a fingertip as she had before.

The first vision showed her the forest called Mielikki's Garden. The conjoined powers flowing outward from the Elder Spires rose through the trunks of the oaks. Branches sprouted acorns in a matter of moments, and hungry squirrels came bounding shortly thereafter.

Similar visions followed. Silvanus was the Forest Father, and whatever the celebrants had intended, the magic quickened the wild places first. Fortunately, plenty remained to revitalize plowed fields and orchards as well. Barley and beans sprouted and grew tall in fenced squares of mud and weed that peasants had abandoned in despair. Blossoms burst forth from apple and cherry trees, then fell in blizzards of petals as fruit supplanted them.

Umara sensed that Stedd had been correct: The other Chosen couldn't have brought forth this bounty without him. The druids could summon the vitality and fertility Silvanus embodied. They could even direct it to farmlands that under normal circumstances were the province of Chauntea the Earthmother. But to flourish, the wheat and rye, the carrots and peas, the peaches and strawberries also needed an infusion of the sunlight the cloud cover had so long denied them.

Fingers closed around Umara's wrist and pulled her hand away from the treant's. "Look!" Anton said.

She did and caught her breath. Stedd was on fire!

No, she realized an instant later, he wasn't. But the radiance shining from his body had brightened from a dawn-like glow to a blaze. Squinting, she could barely make out the human form inside the light or even stand to look at it directly.

"Is that the way it should be?" Anton asked.

For the most part, Umara still didn't comprehend the inner workings of the ritual. But she feared she could guess the answer to the pirate's question. "He may be channeling more power than he can handle."

"Then this ends." Anton started forward.

Umara caught him by the forearm. "You can't," she said.

"I touched the tree man's hand again, too. I saw there are already new crops in the fields."

"Still, if you interrupt the ritual, the change may not stick. And Stedd wouldn't want that, no matter what."

"To the Hells with what he'd want," Anton answered. But he didn't try to pull away.

The ritual seemed to stretch on endlessly. Umara supposed that was because her wonder and curiosity had given way to apprehension.

Finally, Shadowmoon shouted, "It's done!"

The celebrants stopped chanting, singing, drawing shrill harmonies from beating transparent wings, or making any other sort of sound. The enormous glowing design on the ground vanished.

Stedd's corona winked out at the same moment. Its departure left his body looking utterly emaciated, as though the magic had melted every ounce of fat and most of the muscle, too. He turned to Anton and Umara, tried to smile, and then pitched forward onto his face.

Evendur Highcastle sensed that elsewhere the rain had fallen with exceptional fury for part of the day and then subsided to what, in these times of perpetual rain, was normal. But on Pirate Isle, the storm had changed in certain respects but raged on even more violently than before.

Thunder boomed, and lightning repeatedly struck the highlands above Immurk's Hold. Avalanches spilled down the mountainsides, and wildfires burned. Surveying the scene from the battlements atop Umberlee's temple, his vestments flapping around his spongy flesh, Evendur speculated that it was the wind that kept the fires going in defiance of the rain. The same screaming gale burled huge waves at the island to maul and toss ships at anchor, crash against the rocks, and fling spray high into the air. It tore the thatched roofs off huts and taverns or knocked them down entirely and tumbled the wreckage away.

The wind was also a voice, though Evendur suspected he was the only one who understood it. It had called him forth to stand in the tempest and attend his deity.

Umberlee kept him waiting long enough to watch a galley pound itself and the dock to which it was moored to pieces, and the handsome old house called Teldar's Rest slowly list until it toppled. Then, finally, she deigned to appear to him, although he felt her anger like a hammer blow before he actually recognized her countenance for what it was.

Her face was the sea. The *entire* sea, or at last as much of it as he could see from his perch. Two faraway lighter patches were her glaring eyes, while the breakers defined her snarling mouth. Somehow, her features maintained their fundamental constancy even though the water was in constant storm-tossed upheaval.

The instincts of a Chosen told Evendur the Queen of the Depths came to him in this guise because no lesser form could contain or express her wrath. An instant later, the sheer force of that anger shattered the walkway under his feet and much of the temple facade beneath it. He and countless shards of blue-green stone fell down the cliff face toward the waves below. He slammed into an outcropping, bounced off, and smashed down partly on and partly off a boulder protruding from the foaming surf.

"I warned you," she told him. Louder now, deafening, her voice was both the roar of the wind and the hiss of the waves, and it held gloating laughter as well as rage. Perhaps he should have expected as much. She was the drowner of sailors and the breaker of ships, and every opportunity to torment and destroy excited her.

Instinct prompted him to try to drag himself all the way up onto the rock. He couldn't. He was still aware and undead but as incapable of movement as any ordinary corpse.

The alternating push and suck of the waves shifted his center of gravity and tipped more of his body into the water, immersing his legs up past the knees. He kept slipping a bit at a time until he slid wholly into the water.

The waves bumped him into the waving seaweed on the side of the boulder. Then a riptide seized him and dragged him away from shore.

He wondered what Umberlee had in mind. She could feed him to sea creatures willing to eat carrion, or scrape him through corral reefs and cut and pull him apart a bit at a time. But he suspected she meant to dump him back where she'd found his drowned corpse to deliver a more protracted initial torment. Whatever punishment she intended, it could only be because she'd decided he'd failed her yet again.

Previously, Evendur had deemed it wise to remain mute in the face of her rage. But he sensed that tactic would no longer serve. His only hope was to convince her he could still achieve her ends.

But how? He sensed his paralysis was no impediment. Linked to him as she was, she could still hear his voice if she condescended to do so. But what was he to say? He struggled to frame some sort of argument, and finally, the words came to him.

"Fine!" he snarled. "Cast me away! *Surrender!*"

He felt the pressure of the rip current diminish for a moment, as though his insolence had startled her. Then it swept him onward.

"I know what your holy books say," he continued. "The mighty Queen of the Depths *never* surrenders. But maybe it isn't true. Because I'm still your champion, and if you take me out of the contest now, you're abandoning the Inner Sea to Lathander."

The racing current tumbled him.

"Leave me in place," he pleaded, "and I can still win! I'll bring together every iota of the church's might into a great armada and lead it against the boy and any who dare to stand with him. Whatever miracle he's worked, I'll unmake it. Whatever hopes his magic and preaching have raised, I'll dash them. And when I've done all that, and drowned him in your name, no one will doubt your supremacy any longer!"

Suddenly—and rather to Evendur's surprise—the riptide ebbed away to nothing. He felt something in his upper back grinding together, and strength surged back into his hulking frame.

"Kill *everyone*," Umberlee hissed. "Everyone but those who grovel before me. Turn the green sea red if that is what it takes."

Then the crushing sense of divine presence disappeared.

Evendur kicked upward until his head broke the surface. The howling, hammering storm was already subsiding into just another gray, rainy day. The harbor was half a mile away, an inconsequential distance for a fellow who could swim like a shark.

Anton put his hand on Stedd's brow. That morning, it had been cold. Now, it was hot. The temperature swung back and forth for some reason the druids had failed to explain in terms a pirate could understand.

The boy's eyes, vividly blue even in the subdued light of the House of Silvanus, fluttered open. "Papa?" he croaked.

Anton winced. "No, Stedd, it's me."

"I *wanted* to say goodbye. But you wouldn't have believed. You would have tried to stop me."

"Your father's not here. I'm Anton. Try to remember."

"I wanted to say it! I promise!" Stedd squirmed under his blanket like he was trying to sit up but couldn't manage it.

"I believe you," Anton sighed, "and everything's all right. Why don't you drink some water?"

The earthenware cup was ready to hand. But in the moment it took him to pick it up and turn back around, Stedd had lapsed back into unconsciousness.

Anton felt an urge to throw the cup at one of the granite slabs bordering the space that served as Stedd's sickroom. He settled for growling an obscenity.

"At least he woke up," Umara said.

Anton gave her a sour look. "Is that what you'd call it? Why doesn't he have a druid sitting with him all the time?"

"I'm sure they check on him often."

"Even if they do, why aren't they healing him?"

Umara took a breath. "You heard what Shadowmoon said. This isn't an ordinary sickness amenable to the usual cures. And in any case, it does no good to grouse at me."

Nor was it fair. "Sorry."

"It's all right." She cocked her head, listening to the drumming on the roof. "The rain's slacking off. Let's get some air."

As they negotiated the turns of the sanctuary, a structure that, with familiarity, had come to feel less labyrinthine, he said, "I'm not truly angry with the druids or the boy, either."

"I hope, not with yourself," she replied.

"No!" he snapped. "With Lathander. Surely, *he* could help Stedd. But now that the boy's served his purpose, his god's tossed him away like a broken tool not worth the mending."

"In Thay, we expect spiritual powers to favor the strong, not help the weak."

Anton snorted. "Whereas I used to think they don't truly care about anybody. Then Stedd nattered on and on about hope and goodness until, perhaps, he blathered the common sense right out of my head. Well, now I have it back."

They stepped out under the gray sky. Anton took stock of how hard it was currently raining, and then, on impulse, squashed his drum-shaped Turmishan hat flat and tucked it in his sword belt. His hair was going to get wet, but he got tired of having it covered all the time.

Then a white horse and a rider in green and brown scrambled onto the plateau. The steed was lathered and rolling its eyes, and Anton wasn't surprised. He wouldn't have cared to take a horse up the steep last leg of Hierophant's Trail, certainly not at any kind of speed.

But the ranger in the saddle showed no consideration for his mount's weariness or frazzled nerves. He dug in his heels and urged it onward to cover at a gallop the remaining distance to the edge of the pool.

"The Elder Circle!" he half shouted, half gasped in a way that showed he was nearly as exhausted as the horse. "I have to speak to the elders at once!"

No doubt impressed by his urgency, druids came scurrying to assist him. A couple took charge of the horse and started to relieve it of its saddle. Others conducted the ranger across one of the chains of steppingstones.

Umara looked at Anton. "Whatever it is, I don't care," he said. Then they followed the ranger and his escorts back into the temple.

Once apprised of the woodsman's arrival, the Elder Circle opted to receive him in a relatively spacious area where, on other occasions, Anton had watched older druids instructing novices five and six at a time. It was less imposing than the circular space at the center of the temple, but it was also drier, and the cryptic symbols daubed on upright surfaces gave it its own air of mystery and magic. Sometimes, they seemed to change when a person wasn't looking, although afterward, Anton could never identify what was different.

A bench carved into one of the stone slabs afforded Shadowmoon, Ashenford, and Shinthala a place to sit. Everyone else—the ranger, those who'd brought him in, and curious souls like Anton and Umara who simply wanted to find out what was going on—stood.

The woodsman was a barrel-chested fellow whose bushy beard had grown out enough to lose any trace of a straightedge cut at the bottom. He bowed deeply but so quickly that the gesture of respect nevertheless felt perfunctory. "Elders," he rasped.

Shadowmoon waved a dainty, copper-skinned hand, and the skinny adolescent girl who'd tried and failed to smite Anton with a spell emerged from behind a screen carrying a stool. A boy perhaps three years older than Stedd followed with a wooden cup.

"Something is clearly distressing you," said the elf. "Sit, drink, and tell us what it is."

But the ranger didn't wait for the seat or the cup to deliver his tidings. "We're going to be attacked."

Shadowmoon's green eyes widened. "Please, explain."

The messenger dropped onto the stool. "This comes from another ranger, Vonda Pisacar. You know her?"

"Of course," Shinthala said. "As well as we know you, Mareo Calabra."

"Then you know she likes to patrol the wild lands along the coast. She was doing that west of Sapra, seeing what the sea had swallowed and what was still above water, when she spotted what she thought was likely a pirate ship anchored offshore."

Probably one of Evendur's, Anton thought, still hunting Stedd.

"Vonda wanted to find out what the ship was up to," Mareo continued, "and she's friendly with the merfolk. She knows a tune to whistle to call them if any are nearby. Well, one was, and she asked him to swim out and eavesdrop on what people were saying aboard the ship. He got there just in time. The pirates were making ready to sail."

"Where to?" Ashenford asked.

"To meet up with other ships. Pretty much all the ones from Pirate Isle but extra, too—warships from places like Westgate sent because the church of Umberlee demanded it. The undead wavelord people talk about is supposed to lead them all to Turmish to destroy Sapra and everything else they can get at."

"This is retaliation," said a druidess with a sparrow perched on her shoulder and feathers adorning her three long braids, "for running off the waveservants when they tried to set themselves above us."

"There's more to it than that," Shinthala said, "but the whys can wait until later." She looked to Mareo, who was finally taking a drink from the cup. "I trust this same news has gone to Sapra and the Assembly of Stars."

Mareo swiped the back of his hand across his lips. A stray drop of red wine dribbled into his whiskers even so. "To Sapra, yes, and it's been sent to Alaghôn as well. I just don't know if it's arrived yet. A messenger can't get there by land anymore." He grimaced. "And warriors on the mainland can't just march here and reinforce us."

People muttered to one another in dismay, and to his own surprise, Anton stepped forward. "You don't need the army anyway," he said. "You should meet the enemy at sea and sink them before they ever come within catapult range of Sapra."

Mareo nodded. "I suppose that's the strategy to try."

"Why do you sound so pessimistic? The Turmishan fleet is as capable as any on the Inner Sea."

"So I've always heard tell," Mareo answered. "But the navy says some of the ships are far away on various errands. Even if they somehow hear about the trouble, they likely won't make it back in time. And as for the rest . . . " He shifted his gaze back to the three elders. "Please understand, I don't mean any irreverence. I'm thankful there's food now. Everybody is."

"But . . . ?" Shinthala prompted.

"Well," Mareo said, "it wasn't exactly a *gentle* miracle, was it? Not the first part. Silvanus and, I hear, Lathander made the rain fall harder than ever before, and the sea bashed ships in Sapra Harbor around as it rose. Some are damaged too badly for the shipwrights to repair them in time to meet the pirates."

"But what you don't understand," Anton said, "is that the storm also strengthened the Emerald Enclave. If Turmish doesn't have enough ships that are fit to fight, magic can take up the slack."

Shadowmoon sighed. "Not necessarily."

Anton rounded on her. "Lady, you told us that when your holy island was reborn, it renewed your strength." By all the Hells, clinging to the treant's finger, he himself had watched it happen, even if he lacked the knowledge to make sense of very much of it.

"It did," Ashenford said. "But then we spent the land's strength and our own. We didn't weaken ourselves to the extent that your poor young friend did, but the results were somewhat similar. We need time to recover."

"You may not be at your best," Anton replied, "but it will still be three Chosen against one."

"Fighting on the sea," the half-elf said, "which is his place of power, not ours."

"Even if the pirates come ashore," Shinthala said, "a port like Sapra is at best neutral ground. The same is true of the farmland that keeps it fed. But I may know how to beat the raiders."

Ashenford turned in her direction. "How?"

"They surely want to kill us. And Stedd Whitehorn. They may enter the forests to get to us." The wrinkled, white-haired druidess smiled an ugly smile. "Then we'll have them."

"No," Anton said. "That's the wrong play."

Shinthala's smile twisted into a scowl. "Why?"

"Various reasons, but the main one is what your scout Vonda found out. Evendur Highcastle's changed his strategy. He's not hunting other Chosen anymore, and that means he won't take the bait you're dangling. Once he breaks the fleet, destroys Sapra, and burns the crops here on the island, he'll sail along the coast wreaking the same kind of havoc with impunity. There won't be anyone who can stop him."

Shadowmoon folded her hands and stared down at them as if the answer to every vexing question could be found there. At length, she said, "Captain, I swear to you on the scepter of Queen Amlaruil that the druids of Turmish will aid in the defense of their homeland."

Anton's mouth tightened. "But you won't give all you could, will you? You'll hold something back. Even though that could make the difference between winning and losing."

"Please believe," the fragile-looking elf replied, "that we of the Emerald Enclave care about the folk of the towns and farms. We've always looked after them to the extent our path allows. But our *true* purpose, decreed by the Treefather himself, is to protect and nurture the wild lands. Thanks to you, Lady Sir Umara, and especially Stedd, we have the chance to do that more effectively than we have in a century. It's a chance we mustn't squander."

"What about Stedd's purpose?" Anton asked. "His god ordered him to keep the Umberlant church from becoming the supreme power around the Inner Sea."

"Silvanus doesn't want that, either," Ashenford said. "But he also judges there's little danger of the goddess of the sea extending her influence into the forests."

"He might be surprised," the reaver said. "He should visit a ship-yard and take a look at just how much timber the carpenters use. But never mind. I can see I'm not going to sway you, so I'll thank you for your hospitality and take my leave. If I head out now, I can be in Sapra tomorrow. I'll help repair a damaged warship and sail with her when she puts to sea."

"Did you forget you're our prisoner?" Shinthala asked.

Anton blinked. Caught up in the passions of the moment, he actually had.

"I think," Shadowmoon said, "that in light of his recent service to the land, and the matters of great urgency that will soon pre-occupy the Assembly of Stars, we need not consider him such any longer."

"I agree," Ashenford said. "By the First Tree, if the assembly ever even finds out he was here in the first place, I'll answer for it."

THE REAVER

Shadowmoon looked back at Anton. "There," she said, "you're free to do as you please. But as one who's come to think well of you, I recommend you *not* go to the fleet. A disguise allowed you to walk through Sapra without being recognized. It won't keep mariners who knew you in your former life from doing so if you seek to work right alongside them, and then, no matter how honorable your present intentions, the navy will kill you for the man you were."

Anton laughed even though he felt like something was grinding on the inside. "If that's the way of it, then fine. I've already wasted too much time fighting for causes I don't have a stake in."

◄◯►

On Umara's previous visit, Sapra had seemed sluggish with hunger. Now, the port felt frantic, echoing with the sawing, chopping, and hammering of the shipwrights and smells of the smoke and pitch that likewise figured in their labors. Men of the watch were swinging mallets, too, erecting barricades at certain key points in pessimistic but realistic anticipation of the Umberlant raiders coming ashore.

Some townsfolk nailed shutters closed in an effort to make their particular homes secure, or drilled ineptly with spears in possibly unsanctioned militia companies. Others pulled carts, pushed barrows, or carried bundles or squalling babies as they headed out of town.

Umara wondered where the latter thought they were going. If it was the half circle of farmland around Sapra, that wouldn't be far enough. If it was the forests beyond, she doubted many of them knew how to forage or avoid natural hazards. How would they have learned when, from what she understood, the Emerald Enclave had always discouraged intruders? Sometimes, it had done so violently.

She imagined the bewildered horror of the fleeing townsfolk if the same servants of Silvanus who'd worked magic to feed them yesterday ended up slaughtering them tomorrow because they frightened a bear cub or trampled a sacred wildflower. Many a Red Wizard would

277

have found the potential irony humorous, but she didn't. Perhaps she'd been away from Thay too long.

"I keep thinking," Anton muttered, "that we should have brought Stedd with us."

Umara glanced at him. "You said the pirates won't venture into the forests to try to take him, and the druids said they'll kill them if they do."

"I remember." He detoured around one of the deeper puddles in the street. "Just as I realize neither of us knows how to nurse a sick child. I suppose that after months of first hunting the boy and then helping him, it just feels odd to walk away and leave him behind."

"For me, too."

"But to the deepest of the Hells with how it feels. We got the stubborn whelp to Turmish. Now, I'm going to concentrate on what *I* want."

"Which is what?" she asked.

He hesitated. "A new ship, I suppose. Somehow. Put me ashore in Akanûl, and I'll figure it out."

For a moment, she felt disappointed but didn't know why. What had she expected him to say?

They walked on. Four men came striding in the opposite direction, and then, evidently taking note of her red cloak and robes, stepped aside into a puddle to let her and Anton pass on the higher, drier part of the cobbled street. Less intimidated or simply intent on his errand to the exclusion of all else, a boy pushing an empty barrow ran past a few breaths later, and the wheel and his pounding feet threw up water to splash her.

Though the two boys didn't look especially alike, the incident made her think again of Stedd. She told herself she wasn't abandoning him. He himself had said that he—or his god—wanted her to return to Thay.

Then she and Anton rounded a corner, and the pirate hesitated. Fearing someone had recognized him for the fugitive he was, she cast about to locate the threat. But no one was gaping at them, reaching for a weapon, or making a hasty retreat, and after a heartbeat, Anton simply tramped on. Now, though, he scowled and quickened his stride.

"What's wrong?" she asked.

"Nothing," he replied.

Only somewhat reassured, she kept on studying their surroundings until she finally realized something. While none of the nearby shops and houses looked clean and new—months of unrelenting rain had torn tiles and shingles loose and flaked paint off walls—nothing looked unmistakably old, either. Which made this street different than the last one, or many another in Sapra.

"This is a part of town the demons destroyed," she said. "Where everything had to be rebuilt."

"Yes," Anton said.

"And it bothers you to picture it burning again."

"No, because I don't let things bother me if I can't do anything about them. And Shadowmoon, curse her, was right. The navy wouldn't let me help defend Sapra even if I were stupid enough to volunteer. And our one ship, without an assigned role in the battle plan . . ." He stopped in his tracks, and his brown eyes widened.

"What?" Umara asked.

It only took him a few breaths to explain. The idea seemed cunning and madcap in equal measure. Just the sort of trick she'd expect him to devise.

She smiled. "Let's do it."

He blinked at her immediate acquiescence. "You're serious?"

"Why not? We've seen that Evendur Highcastle can be hurt, and at least inconvenienced by having a ship sunk out from underneath him. If luck favors us, we could tip the scales." She smiled. "Then I can go home and say, 'No, I didn't capture a Chosen for sacrifice. But I did stop the waveservants from becoming the dominant power on the Sea of Fallen Stars and threatening Thayan interests. That's worth something, isn't it?' "

"Will the crew be game?"

"They have been for everything up until now, and I'm still a Red Wizard. They'll do as I command."

Energized, Anton and Umara hurried onward. But as they neared the ramshackle collection of piers that was Sapra Harbor, and she spotted a battered fishing boat sunk to the gunwales in the shallows, it occurred to her that for all she knew, the *Octopus* might be in much the same condition. If so, she and the reaver would have no way of putting their plan into effect. In fact, if the Turmishan fleet lost the battle at sea, they'd be stuck on Ilighôn when Evendur's armada descended on the island.

She sighed when she saw that she needn't have feared. Floating at its mooring, the *Octopus* had sustained some damage to the rigging but was essentially intact. She started down the dock.

Anton gripped her forearm. "Look at the men mending the yards and cordage," he said.

She did and realized none of them was a sailor or marine who'd sailed with her and Kymas from Bezantur. They were strangers, clad in the green uniforms of the Turmishan navy.

"The thieves commandeered our ship!" she said.

Anton nodded. "With so many of their own disabled, I should have anticipated it."

"What do we do?"

The pirate grinned. "The next move is fairly obvious, isn't it? Our men must be somewhere, perhaps squatting in one of the scar pilgrim camps. We start by rounding them up while the navy kindly finishes making repairs on our behalf."

Anton headed down the benighted pier with as little noise as possible. That was only sensible. But he resisted the urge to stay low or slip from one bit of cover to the next. Even in the rain, that would be foolish behavior for an invisible man moving through the dark.

He knew because he couldn't see any trace of Umara stealing along just a pace or two ahead of him.

She popped into view, though, at the same instant the lookout in the bow fell victim to her spell of slumber. She skulked up the gangplank, and Anton followed.

Anton crept astern and positioned himself beside the hatch leading into the captain's cabin. Umara lifted a storm lantern down from its hook, climbed up into the bow beside the sentry she'd put to sleep, and waved the light back and forth in the air.

The signal brought the rest of the Thayans sneaking down the dock. Twenty men couldn't do so as quietly as she and Anton had alone, but the mariners made it onto the ship with only a little noise.

In their hands were scraps of lumber, lengths of chain, and other improvised and pilfered weapons. The Turmishan sailors had confiscated their boarding pikes, cutlasses, crossbows, and such when they'd taken possession of the *Octopus*, and maybe it was just as well. Anton didn't want his crew killing anybody, nor should it be necessary to achieve the current objective.

The Thayans' clothing was different, too, but that was of their own choosing, or rather, Umara's. She'd ordered them to discard their ragged crimson uniforms and put on whatever they could scrounge amid the current crisis. The results made them appear like a tough-looking but otherwise nondescript company of tramps, which was pretty much the desired effect.

They and Umara surrounded the hatch beneath which the rest of the Turmishans were sleeping out of the rain. The wizard murmured too softly for Anton to hear and swirled her hands in sinuous patterns. Phosphorescent green vapor billowed into existence around her fingers, most of it clinging there, a few wisps trailing as she made the mystic passes. Some of the other Thayans flinched from a stink Anton was too far away to smell, but if it bothered Umara, no one could have known. Her expression of calm concentration never waivered.

She nodded to a sailor to signal that her incantation was coming to an end. He stooped and lifted the hatch.

Umara spoke the final word and thrust her hands down at the opening. Luminous mist streamed down like the steaming breath of a dragon turtle.

Anton could imagine the noxious fog abruptly filling the hold. The putrid reek would wake the sleepers, and the cloud would blind them. Overwhelmed by nausea, many would simply lie where they were and puke. Those with stronger stomachs would struggle to reach uncontaminated air, but even they would blunder on deck coughing and retching with their eyes full of stinging tears, in no condition to withstand the foes awaiting them.

The Thayans subdued the sick men with brutal efficiency and, almost certainly, satisfaction. As they'd complained, the Turmishans had played a trick of their own to dispossess them of the *Octopus* without even giving them a chance to fight for her, and now they were paying them back.

Of course, they couldn't do so altogether quietly, without the occasional outcry or crack of wood bashing somebody's head, and suddenly, the hatch to the captain's cabin flew open. Still invisible, Anton stuck out his foot to trip the officer when he rushed out with a sword in one hand and a buckler on the other arm.

The captain crashed down on the deck. His hands and arms reappearing in a surge from the fingertips upward, Anton moved to dive on the other man's back, pin him, and choke him unconscious.

But his opponent, a burly man with a slab of forehead over deep-set eyes and a touch of silver in his square-cut beard, wrenched himself around and slashed. Anton just managed to jerk to a stop in time to keep the sword from slicing his belly.

No one was that fast without magical assistance. The swordsman must have drunk an elixir or recited a charm before coming through the hatch.

Anton stepped back and reached for the hilt of his saber. His opponent started to scramble to his feet. Anton rushed him.

The move startled the Turmishan captain and made him falter for half an instant. Then he tried to put his point in line.

By then, though, Anton was already safely inside his reach. He plowed into his adversary, bore him down beneath him, and made sure the back of the bearded man's head hit the deck hard. The impact slowed the naval officer down but didn't stop him struggling. Using the heel of his hand, Anton hit him in the nose, smashing it flat and banging his head against the deck again, and that knocked him unconscious.

Panting, the pirate turned and looked toward the bow. The Thayans were just finishing up the task of subduing any sailor who'd made it out of the hold.

That left the incapacitated men still below, who'd recover quickly as soon as the foul vapor dissipated. Hoping to deny them the opportunity, Anton had instructed the Thayans to attack as soon as the glow of the mist winked out, and he himself was the first man to leap down the hatch.

There was just enough light left to reveal a pair of figures rushing him with blades. He swayed back to avoid a slash to the head and parried a thrust to the chest with his cutlass, a better weapon than a saber for tight quarters like these.

He bellowed, rushed the Turmishan sailors, and made cut after furious cut. He needed to drive them backward and clear the space under the hatch so the Thayans could start dropping after him.

The sailors gave ground for a moment, then pushed back. The one on the left tried a thrust to the face. Anton slipped the attack, stepped in, and hammered the cutlass's guard into his assailant's jaw.

The remaining Turmishan cut at the pirate's flank. Anton pivoted and swung the cutlass down just in time to parry. Then a Thayan smashed his foe over the head with a piece of board.

From that point onward, it was easy. Superior numbers overwhelmed the one or two other Turmishans who'd recovered sufficiently to fight.

Afterward, still hurrying, some of the Thayans hauled up the gangplank or manned the halyards to ready the *Octopus* to set sail. Others bound and gagged the prisoners, whom they'd put ashore or set adrift when they had an opportunity.

Watching the latter operation, Umara shook her head. "It would have been easier just to kill them."

Anton chuckled. "I was just thinking the same thing. But Stedd wouldn't have approved."

CHAPTER TWELVE

Dwelling in the House of Silvanus, preoccupied with Shadowmoon's mental deterioration and other threats to the wild lands that a blade couldn't answer, Shinthala had in recent years seldom worn her scimitar. But the weight still felt comfortable riding on her hip.

She still felt at ease in her old war cloak, too, but had taken it off for the moment. The enchantment it bore made her appear a half step away from her actual location, an advantage when enemies were trying to aim blows or missiles at her but inconvenient on the rolling deck of a warship with crewmen scurrying back and forth. Even in the bow and the stern, there was nowhere to stand that was truly out of the way, and the poor fellows kept jostling her, then cringing and stammering apologies as if they expected her to strike them dead or turn them into frogs.

She'd retrieve the cloak when the enemy armada appeared. Hoping to catch a first glimpse of it, she squinted out over the waves.

But it was Shadowmoon and Ashenford who wavered into view before her. It was like she was looking through a hole in the air and the House of Silvanus was on the far side, except that the opening didn't have clearly defined edges. Rather, the shadowy space around the other elders blurred by degrees until it was indistinguishable from the backdrop of gray cloud and falling rain.

Shinthala sighed. "I suppose it was too much to hope the two of you would believe I was off meditating."

"This is unnecessary," Shadowmoon said. "We arranged for druids to sail aboard every ship."

"And if we were going to send our followers to fight the Chosen of Umberlee," Shinthala replied, "on the open sea, no less, it was only right for one of the Elder Circle to share the danger."

"But you're needed here," Ashenford said, and in his voice, Shinthala heard the fear of losing someone who'd been a friend and sometimes more for over a hundred tumultuous years.

But she couldn't speak to that now, only to their duties and the choices they entailed. "Even without me, the Emerald Enclave's magic will be at least as strong as it was before Stedd Whitehorn came to us. The restorations of the island and—forgive my bluntness, my friend—of Silvermoon's sanity ensure that."

Ashenford shook his head. "Still—"

"There is no 'still,' " Shinthala said. "The more I thought about it, the more I realized Anton Marivaldi was right. We do need to fight these waveservants and pirates, and we won't be able to lure them into the forests. So we'll just have to meet them on the water."

Shadowmoon smiled a sad little smile. "Of the three of us, sister, you were always the one who relished a battle."

"Then let me have one," Shinthala said. "Why not? If I die, how much has the Emerald Enclave truly lost? I don't have elf blood in my veins, and the Treefather's gift of long life is running out in me."

"We'll do everything we can," said Shadowmoon, "to send you power and luck from here."

"I know," Shinthala said. "But do me one more favor. Bring Stedd to the circle."

The elf cocked her head. "If you think there's a point."

"There might be. My judgment tells me we who serve Silvanus should help fight this war. But in the deepest sense, it's Lathander's struggle, and perhaps if his Chosen is present when you're casting magic to oppose Evendur Highcastle, that will finally rouse the boy." Shinthala smiled at Ashenford. "Or perhaps he'll simply respond to the sound of your harping. I always did."

"The boy will be there," Shadowmoon said. "May the Forest Father keep you." She waved a tiny copper-skinned hand, and she and Ashenford vanished, just as Shinthala was about to take what might well prove to be a fond last look at them.

With a snort, the white-haired druidess returned to playing lookout. She fancied her sight was still keen despite her advancing years, but even so, a young man in the fighting top partway up the foremast spotted the enemy's sails before she did. "Pirates off the bow!" he shouted, his voice breaking. Just audible despite the distance and the rain, a sailor aboard the nearest caravel to starboard shouted the same thing.

It had seemed to Shinthala that *Delise's Needle*, the ship she'd chosen to ride, had made extensive preparations for battle before ever leaving the harbor. Still, the lookout's warning triggered bursts of activity both on deck and aloft. Some of it, like the artillerymen fussing over ballistae and catapults, was comprehensible even to a landlubber. Other procedures were not.

But in all cases, the haste seemed to reflect taut nerves rather than necessity. The Umberlant fleet was still far away. Refusing to succumb to her own anxiety, Shinthala watched its upper sails, then the lower ones, and finally the hulls of the vessels appear above the waves before she fetched her cloak and whirled it around her shoulders.

Perhaps that momentary respite from standing and staring did her good. For when she looked out over the rail again, she noticed gray shadows gliding beneath the waves in advance of the Umberlant ships. One raced straight at *Delise's Needle*.

Muttering a charm of seeing, she studied the oncoming form, and then she perceived it as clearly as if she were swimming alongside it. It was a long, slender fin whale, gray-brown on top and paler on the belly, and magic crawled in its head like worms. No doubt that was the source of the rage or compulsion driving it toward the warship.

Fortunately, a whale was an animal, and in theory, druids had power over all beasts, even those of the sea. Shinthala held out her hand and called her sickle with her thoughts, and it leaped into her grip all the way from her personal quarters in the Elder Spires. She whirled the bronze blade in ritual cuts as she rattled off words of command. Holly—ghostly to others, she knew, but real to her—flowered around her and filled the air with its scent.

She felt her spell start to close around the whale's mind like a hand, then something—the original enchantment impelling the animal, no doubt—slapped that notional hand away hard enough to break its fingers. The resistance spiked pain between her eyes. She was still reeling from it when the finback rammed the ship.

The jolt hurled her sideways, and for a panicked instant, she imagined she was about to tumble into the sea. Then the rail caught her.

She took a ragged breath and looked around. Clutching crossbows and javelins, sailors peered over the sides waiting for the whale to make another pass at the ship.

Maybe Shinthala should let them try to kill it, blameless though it was. But if she did mean to try again to calm the finback with magic, it would be counterproductive for her allies to cause it pain.

She cast about and her eyes fell on Thieron Astorio, the other druid onboard, a small barefoot man whose armor of dyed leather scales was fashioned to make it look like he was wearing a coat of leaves. His staff in one hand, Thieron clung to a forestay with the other, an indication that he hadn't found his sea legs any better than she had.

Still, he looked calm and was an initiate of the Circle of Air, far advanced in the mysteries, and that helped Shinthala make her decision.

"Don't attack the whale!" she bellowed to the crew at large. "Give me another chance to send it away!" She looked at Thieron. "Druid! I need you!"

Weaving a little, he ran to her.

"We're going to control the whale together," Shinthala told him. "I'll destroy the magic that's making it attack us. When you sense that giving way, cast a spell of friendship."

"I understand," Thieron replied.

They peered at the sea but for a moment couldn't find the whale. Then, perhaps realizing they'd lost track of the finback, a sailor shouted, "It's to starboard!"

Dodging around a ballista and the artilleryman waiting to shoot it, the two druids hurried to that side of the bow. The fin whale was turning for another run at the caravel. This time, it meant to ram her amidships.

Shinthala shouted words of negation and swept her sickle back and forth while once again, holly grew around her. She imagined the cruel power driving the whale to batter the ship without regard for its own well-being as a chain. Her counterspell was rust, pitting the links and crumbling them away.

This time, she was ready for the waveservants' magic to fight back. Still, it nearly slapped her away. But then she felt the power of Ashenford, Shadowmoon, and the other druids in the House of Silvanus streaming like a river in the sky. She seized it, melded it with her own, and stabbed with the result.

The magic slithering inside the whale's head withered away. And, as Shinthala briefly sensed, somewhere aboard one of the pirate ships, a priest of Umberlee screamed in pain and blood gushed from his nostrils.

But despite its liberation, the finback, likely angry and confused, was still coming. Thieron recited the spell of friendship, and it emerged as a nasal moan unlike anything Shinthala had ever heard.

But strange as it sounded to her, the finback understood it. Instead of ramming the caravel, the animal dived and passed underneath.

Sailors cheered, and Shinthala was happy enough to contribute to their morale. But she suspected they might not be so exuberant if they realized just how difficult it had been for two allegedly mighty druids to counter Umberlant magic here at sea with the will of the Bitch Queen's Chosen reinforcing it.

This whale had been Evendur Highcastle's opening move, a way to soften up the Turmishan fleet before it and his own armada even came together. He likely had worse in store. But Shinthala could only counter threats and smite targets as they presented themselves. She looked around and spied a ship to port under attack by some sort of marine hydra swimming alongside it. Half a dozen heads atop serpentine necks struck at the men on deck with a motion that reminded her of hands picking berries.

She tried to free it of the coercion that controlled it. Another man died while she chanted, and this time, the Umberlant enchantment proved too strong to break.

She needed to try something else, quickly, while there were still living crewmen left aboard the beleaguered ship. She thought of using her affinity with lightning, but she'd already decided to hold that power in reserve. Instead, with a single murmured word, she invoked another of the Oakfather's gifts, a bond as close as kinship with the elemental spirits.

Flapping the sails behind her, a whirlwind howled into existence above the sea. A water spirit might have served her needs even better, but she feared the Chosen of Umberlee could turn such an entity against her.

The living whirlwind rushed at the hydra, buffeting but not quite capsizing the ship it was attacking in the process. The wind engulfed the beast in its murky spin and lifted it out of the water. The reptile roared and thrashed for a moment, and then the forces at work in the vortex tore it apart and flung the heads and other pieces in all directions.

Shinthala grinned and looked around to determine where to send the spirit next.

Cursing, Anton peered at the ships around him. Even for a veteran sea warrior like himself it was difficult to locate his quarry amid the chaos of an engagement being fought over miles of water in the gloom of the overcast and the rain.

He could see a great deal. In some places, whales, sea serpents, and krakens still assailed the Turmishan fleet. In others, Turmishan and Umberlant vessels hurled flaming catapult shot, volleys of crossbow bolts, and shimmering bursts of magic at one another. Two ships had already come together, the deck of one of them packed with combatants. Every few moments, a body fell over the side.

But Anton couldn't figure out which ship Evendur was aboard, and hadn't been able to determine the Chosen's location previously because the *Octopus* had only joined the pirate armada at the start of the day.

As far as he'd been able to tell, none of the reavers had regarded the ship's tardy arrival as cause for concern. Why should they? They recognized Mourmyd Jacerryl's vessel as one of their own, and they knew contrary winds and other hindrances could prolong any journey over water.

Anton hoped the familiar sight of the ship would fool Evendur just as effectively, and that would allow those aboard the *Octopus* to attack him by surprise. Because that was the only way to sneak up on him. Umara's wizardry couldn't veil something as big as a caravel.

Nor, Anton reflected, did it seem to be good for much else at the moment, even though she muttered and gestured away, her index finger writing runes in crimson glow on the air, her telltale red garb put aside for nondescript mannish garments of brown and gray. "Anything?" he asked.

She shook her head. "Not yet."

"If anyone had told me that a Red Wizard of Thay couldn't locate something as stuffed full of magic as the Chosen of a god . . ."

"The problem," Umara growled, "is too much magic. Druids or waveservants on every ship, all praying at once . . . I'm doing the best I can."

Anton found a smile for her. "I know. Sorry."

"Turmishan galley off the port bow!" a man in the rigging bellowed.

Anton pivoted in that direction and saw that, indeed, a ship much like the one the Thayans had abandoned off Gulthandor was heading toward them. Worse, the oars were speeding it along fast enough that the *Octopus* couldn't evade it. The wind had been blowing erratically as spellcasters on both sides struggled to bend it to their purposes, and at the moment, only a feeble breeze pushed at the caravel's sails.

Anton didn't want to fight Turmishans but had no way of convincing them that the crew aboard the *Octopus* was anything other than the motley band of corsairs they appeared to be. He turned to Umara. "Can you hold them back without hurting them?" he asked.

"Perhaps." She pulled the rust-colored wand from her belt and swept it back and forth as she chanted rhyming couplets. Anton had the feverish feeling that he could *almost* see what the tip of the rod was sketching on the air. His vision seemed to splinter around each stroke.

Still, he didn't know what she was conjuring until the long crimson creature with its piscine tail and body and horned, half-human face surfaced midway between the *Octopus* and the galley. Even then, he didn't know exactly what it was, an accurate representation of some huge demon fish that swam the seas of the netherworld or simply a product of Umara's imagination.

Whatever it was supposed to be, the phantom swam at the galley as fast as the Turmishan ship's oarsmen pulled it through the waves. The creature's fangs gnashed as though it couldn't wait to start chewing through the hull.

Men on the galley cried out in alarm. An officer shouted commands. Anton grinned. But then another voice—a druid's, mostly likely—shouted, "Ignore the beast! It isn't real!" And with that, the huge fish with the demon face started to flicker, present one instant, absent the next.

Umara whispered words that made Anton feel as though he were choking. Her fingers clenched on the wand, and blood trickled down her wrist as if she were gripping a blade.

The flickering stopped. The demon fish veered left an instant before it would have collided with the galley's ram and sped on down the vessel's starboard side. The gnashing fangs, its momentum, or a combination of the two, snapped off one oar after another.

The creature hadn't quite finished when the druid bellowed words that made it vanish and stay vanished. But by then, the galley was crippled. Anton judged that even a puny breeze would enable the *Octopus* to leave her behind before the Turmishans collected their wits and ran out replacement oars.

He turned to Umara and asked, "But it was an illusion?"

Breathing hard, she smiled. "Some illusions are more illusory than others."

"Evidently. Nice work." As the *Octopus* left the galley in its wake, he resumed his peering. And then he spotted a ship, small in the distance but still impressive to knowledgeable eyes, to the northeast.

She was impressive because she was a galleon. The large ships with their long beaks and lateen-rigged mizzenmasts were rare on the Sea of Fallen Stars, and no captain from Pirate Isle commanded one. Some coastal lord—an Impilturian, judging from the lines of the vessel—especially eager to curry favor with the church of Umberlee must have sent her when the waveservants put out the call for reinforcements.

Anton pointed. "That's Evendur."

"How can you tell?" Umara replied.

"You met the arrogant son of a hag. Can you imagine him commanding anything other than the biggest, grandest ship in his fleet?"

The wizard smiled. "When you put it that way, no."

"Neither can I." Anton raised his voice. "We're going after the galleon off the port bow!"

A sailor frowned. "With the wind the way it is, it could take all day to catch her if we can do it at all."

"I'm a pirate," Anton replied. "Catching other ships is my trade. You Thayans just do what I tell you." He ran toward the stern to take the helm.

Evendur Highcastle grinned as he watched a Turmishan caravel whose masts and sails were masses of fire. Some artilleryman shooting burning shot or bowmen loosing flaming arrows had managed to set them ablaze despite the rain, and now the ship was doomed.

Or so he assumed. But then he felt magic stirring on the caravel as some druid completed a spell, and all that flame rose higher into the air, clear of the rigging, and flowed into the form of a gigantic yellow hawk. The elemental spirit looked around, and then, with a beat of its wings, hurtled not at the pirate ship that had set the caravel on fire—that vessel had evidently moved on to seek another fight—but at Evendur's own galleon the *Fury*. Crewmen cried out in alarm.

Evendur spoke to the sea and told it to manifest a spirit of its own. Gray-green water heaved and became a colossal squid, which then snatched for the hawk with whipping tentacles.

Steam burst into being as water and fire came together. The burning spirit ripped with its beak and claws. But still, the squid dragged it out of the sky and then beneath the waves. Clinging to life, the hawk continued glowing for a breath or two, and then the light went out.

That left the spellcaster who'd dared to send the fire elemental against Evendur's own vessel. The undead pirate focused his will on the portion of the sea under the caravel and raised it up like a hill. The Turmishan ship slid down the swell and capsized.

And just for an instant, Evendur felt lightheaded. He gripped the rail to steady himself, and the pressure made liquescence slough away from the firmer flesh underneath.

That instant of shakiness was a reminder that he'd been using his magic freely, and even the might of a Chosen had limits. Now that it was too late, he realized he could probably have killed the druid on the caravel with more finesse. As opposed to squandering the power necessary to destroy an entire crippled ship that, except for the spellcaster onboard, was unlikely to play any further role in the battle.

But Evendur had been annoyed. Because, while he had no doubt he'd win the conflict in the end, nothing was happening as he expected.

For starters, he hadn't anticipated fighting this fight at all. The Turmishans weren't supposed to know he was coming. Still, it hadn't dismayed him to watch them sailing and rowing out of the east, because his fleet was bigger.

Unfortunately, that wasn't proving to be an insurmountable advantage because some of the ships under his command had proved reluctant to engage the enemy. Pirates liked to think of themselves as fearless masters of the sea, but in fact, they commonly survived by attacking vulnerable targets and avoiding dangerous foes like the Turmishan navy, and maybe some were still operating according to the same principle. And perhaps the sailors from Westgate, Lyrabar, and the other coastal ports resented being ordered to fight on the side of the same corsairs they'd always considered murdering scum. Maybe, unlike the nobles who'd sent them, some had heard the Lathanderian message and doubted Umberlee's supremacy.

The situation wasn't as bad as it could be. As far as Evendur could tell, none of his ships had fled or surrendered. Even the reluctant ones fought when a Turmishan vessel forced the issue. But a number seemed to be hanging back in the hope that Umberlant magic would carry the day.

Evendur despised them for their lack of zeal. But he had to admit theirs was a reasonable expectation. The waveservants, after all, were fighting at sea and in their goddess's holy cause. What else should they need to make them invincible?

But even that wasn't playing out in the straightforward manner it should. The druids' control of natural forces allowed them to resist the magic of the sea, and the Emerald Enclave was a notoriously warlike religious order, constantly taking up arms against loggers, settlers, and other despoilers of their sacred forests. Whereas some of Umberlee's clergy were battle-seasoned, but others were not.

Evendur's own mystical strength would still have tipped the scales, except that the Turmishans had brought a Chosen of their own. He could feel the presence of his counterpart like the *idea* of a mighty oak, rooted and massive, looming somewhere ahead.

He needed to kill Silvanus's Chosen, and then, surely, the Turmishan defense would crumble. Striving for a more precise awareness of the elder druid's location, he concentrated, and some burgeoning faculty inside him pointed like the needle of a compass.

He ordered the *Fury* onto the proper heading, and, barking a word of command, jerked the wind back into her sails when some other spellcaster sought to redirect it for his own purposes. A Turmishan ship changed course to intercept the galleon, but fortunately, he had sahuagin swimming around her like outriders, and when he spoke to them in their own snarling, burbling tongue, magic carried the sound to their ears.

The shark men converged on the enemy vessel and, dropping the tridents that would otherwise have hindered their climbing, swarmed up the sides to attack with fang and claw. It was a suicidal assault, but it kept the Turmishans busy while the *Fury* passed by, and shortly afterward, the ship of the Treefather's Chosen emerged from the grayness and the rain.

Unlike Evendur's vessel, she wasn't a galleon or a grand galley, either, just a caravel. Still, she was plainly a formidable warship, not that it would help her now.

For now *was* the time for all the brutal, sudden, overwhelming strength that Evendur could muster. He roared a word of power and shook his boarding axe at the caravel. A wave reared up behind her, taller than her mainmast, then crashed down on top of her. The water felt like his own prodigious hand, first trying to swat the ship to splinters, then to grab whatever was left, roll it over, and drag it to the bottom.

But to his irritation, the magic of the enemy Chosen opposed him. He hadn't caught his foe by surprise. Druidic power attenuated the force of his blow and weakened his grip. When the attack ended, the caravel was still floating upright.

He knew why. For an instant, he'd sensed two additional Chosen of Silvanus. They were ashore somewhere but still lending power to their ally.

Yet even so, that first attack had nearly succeeded, and he saw no reason to allow his foe time to recover the strength to withstand another. Seeking the Treefather's Chosen, he studied the enemy ship.

The small man in armor that looked like a coat of leaves was almost certainly an accomplished druid. But it was the woman beside him, white-haired but still straight-backed and sturdy-looking, who was plainly Chosen; Evendur could feel the spark of divine power smoldering inside her. Glaring at her, hissing a curse in one of the secret tongues of Umberlee's worshipers, he willed her lungs to fill with water. Nearly invisible in the rain, a streak of shimmer stabbed at her.

But the magic missed by a finger length. It was like the druidess wasn't truly standing where she appeared to be. If so, a spell of clear sight might wipe away the deception.

But before Evendur could start casting one, she raised a bronze sickle over her head, and ghostly red flowers bloomed around her like a picture frame. She slashed the curved blade down and bellowed, "Oakfather!" Somehow, the shout was also an ear-splitting thunderclap, and at the same instant that she roared it, the world blazed white, and the undead pirate shuddered in burning agony.

Silvanus's Chosen had struck him with lightning! He recognized the pain and spastic paralysis from when the two Red Wizards had used the same force against him, but their efforts had been puny compared to what the white-haired druidess had called down from the sky.

When the pain released him, he found himself sprawled on broken planking, in some danger of dropping through into the hold beneath.

His ears rang, and patches of his putrid flesh were burned black and smoking. His high-collared sea-green cape was on fire.

Clambering to his feet, he stripped the burning garment off his shoulders and waved it like a flag for the druidess to see. Because he suspected her mastery of lightning was her deity's special gift to her and her greatest weapon. And he wanted her to know right away that it wasn't enough to stop him.

Meanwhile, catapults arced projectiles back and forth, some ablaze, some balls of cold stone and iron. Ballistae and springalds shot their darts, archers their shafts, and crossbowmen their bolts.

Some missiles found their marks. Wood crunched, and men fell thrashing and screaming. But many missed. The rain had soaked hemp and flax strings and sinew cords to the detriment of both range and accuracy.

Evendur realized he didn't mind. As magic hadn't decided the fight and artillery and bows weren't getting the job done, either, he'd just have to do it by leading a boarding party onto the enemy ship and hacking down its defenders with axe and cutlass. And why not? That was the pirate way.

He bellowed his orders, and other voices relayed them the length of the galleon, to the mix of reavers, soldiers of the church, and Impilturian sailors who now made up the crew. The helmsman adjusted the ship's course.

Boulders fell like the rain, ripping sails, cracking into spars, breaking cordage, and crashing onto the deck, a few smashing men to pulp and spatters in the course of their descents. The conjured barrage was another worthy effort on the part of the druids, but once again, not devastating enough to arrest the *Fury*'s forward progress, especially when Evendur didn't really even need the rigging. If necessary, the sea alone would sweep the ships together.

Still, he hated having bits of his splendid new vessel battered into kindling, and he retaliated by bellowing Umberlee's name and spinning his boarding axe in a circle. The water under the caravel copied the motion, churning into a whirlpool that spun the Turmishan vessel and shook a crewman and a catapult over the side.

As Evendur would have wagered, the druids managed to quell the maelstrom before it capsized the caravel or dragged it under. But the quelling took time, and when they finished, their ship no longer had any hope of keeping away from its foe. The crew scrambled madly to prepare to repel boarders; the whirlpool had shaken and tumbled any previous arrangements into disarray.

The *Fury's* archers and crossbowmen obliged them to do it under a hail of shafts and quarrels. And as the two vessels came side-by-side, other pirates threw grappling hooks then hauled on the lines that now bound the ships together.

Because the galleon stood higher that the caravel, some boarders would slide down those ropes. Evendur, however, simply leaped before the corsairs pulling on the ropes had even finished their task.

His strength carried him across the gap, and he thumped down on the caravel's quarterdeck. For this moment, he was alone, every one of his followers left behind on the galleon, and his enemies would never have a better chance to attack him. But, goggle-eyed, the closest Turmishans froze.

No doubt someone had warned them what to expect, but even so, Evendur's appearance—hulking, slimy-rotten, the lightning burns surely only adding to the horror of it—had balked them. Laughing, reveling anew in the gifts the Queen of the Depths had given him, he struck left and right, cleaving the skulls of two dark-skinned mariners with square-cut black beards.

That jolted the remaining Turmishans on the quarterdeck into motion. But at the same instant, timbers groaned as the two hulls bumped and ground together, and the first of Evendur's crew jumped and swarmed after him.

He let the newcomers handle the Turmishans left in the stern. He had a white-haired old woman to kill, and he gazed out over the main deck to determine her current location.

Once Anton managed to maneuver the *Octopus* squarely astern of the galleon, the same strong, steady wind that Evendur had likely called up to speed his own vessel aided the one behind her as well. The reaver called the Thayan helmsman back to his post and trotted to rejoin Umara in the bow. She scowled at the ship ahead.

"Ready?" he asked.

She snorted. "Are you? Back in Sapra, the fact that neither of us has ever managed to hurt Evendur Highcastle very badly failed to persuade me that we should stay well away from him henceforth. Now, however . . . well, let's just say I'm still game, but I see both sides of the argument."

Anton grinned. "I'm sure you've devoted some thought to the question of how to hurt him worse."

The tattooed wizard nodded. "I have one or two ideas. They involve other spellcasters wearing him down as much as they do some cunning masterstroke on my part, so let's hope the druids have been fighting fiercely. What about you?"

"When we fought before, I sliced him up a little, but I never cut his hand off his wrist, a leg out from under him, or the head off his shoulders. This time, I'm going to work on the assumption that dismemberment will stop pretty much anything, even an undead Chosen."

"When I was a mage in training, I had to accompany a band of troll hunters into a swamp. The creature killed two of them after it had already lost an arm and a leg. Then it grew the arm back."

Anton laughed. "Thank you. What a perfect thing to say to bolster my morale. Remind me, why are we doing this?"

Umara smiled. "I thought you knew."

Peering through the rain, Anton studied the galleon. As far as he could tell, no one aboard the larger ship was alarmed at the *Octopus*'s approach. If Evendur's men had even noticed, they must believe that Mourmyd Jacerryl and his cutthroats were coming to lend them a hand.

In time, Umara said, "They're in range for a blast of fire if you want one."

"Tempting," Anton replied, "but it wouldn't be like my incendiaries all detonating at once in the bowels of the *Jest*. It's unlikely that one attack would sink her. So let's creep at least a little . . ." Squinting, he leaned forward.

"What's wrong?" Umara asked.

"I know you can't see much of what's happening aboard the galleon from here, but try."

Gripping the rail, she leaned out over it like he had. "I see . . . scurrying."

"That's one word for it. We knew Evendur was chasing another ship. He caught her. Now his men—or most of them—are boarding her."

"Then we can't set the galleon on fire lest the blaze spread to the Turmishan ship as well."

Anton nodded. "Exactly. What we *are* going to do is lead a boarding party of our own."

The galleon held the captured Turmishan warship on its starboard side, so the *Octopus* steered for the port side. As Anton and his comrades made their approach, his nerves felt taut as the string of any cocked crossbow or ballista, and he studied the larger vessel for a sign that he was sailing into a trap.

But there was none. There was only the rattle of the rain and shouts, screams, and the clanking of blade on blade, the latter sounds muffled by the galleon's bulk.

When the *Octopus* reached the proper position, Thayan marines lifted grappling hooks, but Umara raised a hand to tell them not to throw. She then murmured a spell, and the end of a coiled rope on deck reared like a serpent. It rose up and up until it was as high as the galleon's railing, then looped around it and tied itself off, without the telltale thud a grapnel would have made.

"I'm first," Anton said. He took hold of the coarse hemp line and climbed hand over hand.

When his head reached the level of the deck above, the clamor of the battle washed over him. As he'd expected, the enemy had left half a dozen men on the starboard side to shoot crossbows bolts and fling javelins into the melee below as targets presented themselves, and, more importantly, to keep any Turmishans from clambering aboard the galleon and causing trouble.

But, Anton thought, that effort had failed. Because he was a Turmishan, and he was about to make a lot of trouble.

He drew his saber and cutlass and skulked closer to the third man in line. Meanwhile, Umara clambered up the rope and over the rail. He winced when her foot bumped audibly against the gunwale, but none of the Umberlant warriors noticed.

A moment later, though, the first man in line, the one in the galleon's forecastle, turned his head, perhaps to call something to his comrades. When he did, he must have glimpsed Anton or Umara at the periphery of his vision, because he jerked around to goggle at them.

The man bellowed, " 'Ware—" then collapsed as Umara rattled off a spell of slumber.

Unfortunately, even an unfinished warning sufficed to make the other crewmen turn around. Anton rushed the nearest, beat the javelin in his hand out of line, and sliced him across the belly. The Umberlant warrior fell.

At the same moment, something, pure instinct, perhaps, told Anton to duck. He did, and a quarrel whizzed over his head. The next man forward had shot a crossbow at him.

Anton looked around, found a crate of javelins, grabbed one, and threw it. It caught the crossbowman in the chest, and he toppled backward.

Anton spun back around to see how Umara was faring. She gestured to indicate the men who'd made up the aft portion of the line. All three lay motionless, slain or rendered helpless by her wizardry.

302

He flashed her a grin and pivoted to starboard to look out over the battle below.

As best he could tell, nobody had noticed the skirmish aboard the galleon, and small wonder. Locked in the jostling press of a shipboard melee, the combatants below were far too busy with their own killing and dying.

Evendur was easy to spot. Hulking and hideous, he was fighting on a less crowded patch of deck—less crowded, perhaps, because he'd experienced so little difficulty slaughtering most of those who dared to face him. A white-haired woman with a scimitar in one hand and a bronze sickle in the other fought him with a nimbleness that put many a youthful man-at-arms to shame, but even so, the relentless sweeps of his glowing axe were pushing back into shrouds, halyards, and sheets that threatened to entangle her like a net. The moment they did, the wavelord would chop her to pieces.

Anton couldn't allow that, because the old woman was Shinthala. His final conversation with the Elder Circle had led him to assume none of them would sail with the Turmishan fleet. But plainly, one had, and she might well be its best hope for victory if she could escape the present onslaught and get back to casting spells.

An attack of some sort had littered the galleon's deck with stones and lengths of snapped cordage that had previously secured and controlled the yards on the mizzenmast. Anton ran, leaped, and caught a dangling rope.

His weight rotated the yard to which it was attached, and even when the spar jerked to a halt, he kept swinging out over the deck of the Turmishan caravel like a pendulum on a string. When he judged the moment was right, he released his grip.

He thumped down hard, but that was all right. He hadn't broken or sprained anything, and he'd come down more or less where he'd intended.

Evendur jerked around to face him. If possible, the dead man's features were even mushier and seemingly incapable of human expression than during their previous encounter, but the way he faltered conveyed surprise even so.

Anton grinned and drew his saber and cutlass. "Well," he said, "here we are again."

Stedd didn't mind that someone had carried him to the circle of stones in the center of the House of Silvanus. He'd been too hot, and the cold rain felt good on his upturned face.

But he did mind the chanting. It made it hard to doze. And the force that throbbed in the ground in time with the words was even more disturbing. It struck echoes in the core of him and reminded him that he too could channel power.

He flinched from thinking about such things because the last time had hurt him so badly. He shifted on the wet grass, trying to squirm his way into sleep, and then a radiant figure appeared, more vivid than any sight had ever been before, even though Stedd's eyes were shut.

He opened them in surprise and the newcomer remained as before, a smiling, handsome, youthful-looking man, with blond hair, golden skin, and the trim, long-legged build of a runner clad in princely robes of crimson and blue. Strangely, none of the druids, not even Ashenford and Shadowmoon, seemed to notice the interloper standing the middle of their ritual.

Trembling with a joy so keen it almost felt like terror, Stedd took a long breath. "You never showed yourself to me before."

Lathander smiled, and somehow, that simple change of expression communicated his message as clearly as words: You weren't ready to see me before. Now, you are.

The Morninglord then waved his hand, and a golden shimmer trailed from his fingers. Stedd gasped as strength and well-being surged through him. Suddenly feeling too exhilarated to keep lying down, he scrambled up, and none of the druids noticed that, either.

For a moment, grinning, he imagined Lathander had accelerated his recovery purely out of kindness. Then visions poured into his head, first a panorama of battling warships and sea creatures seen from high above, and then a closer view of three particular vessels locked together. Anton, Umara, and Shinthala were in that fight. So was Evendur Highcastle.

Stedd sighed. "I was supposed to beat Umberlee by ending the famine. But the fight's not over, is it? Because she and her Chosen haven't quit."

Lathander inclined his head.

"All right." Stedd swallowed. "I want to help. But how can I?"

Lathander proffered a golden mace. Stedd was certain the god hadn't been holding anything a moment before. But he was now, and surely, it was Dawnbringer, the weapon he'd wielded in all his great battles against the lords of darkness.

Stedd hesitated. Chosen or not, he felt unworthy to touch such a holy thing. He was also afraid it would be too heavy for him, and he'd drop it in the mud.

But since Lathander wanted him to take it, that was what he did, and without any fumbling. Dawnbringer was light as a stick in his hands.

"All right," Stedd said, "I've got it. What am I supposed to do with it?"

Another image of Anton flowered before his inner eye.

Though his face was slime and tatters, Evendur somehow managed a recognizable sneer. "You're nothing," he growled. He flicked the boarding axe, its edge glowing a poisonous green as it had aboard the *Iron Jest*, like he was brushing away a fly.

The gesture made water explode from empty air. The stinging blast splashed Anton and knocked him backward onto his rump. A warrior of Umberlee's temple rushed him to spear him with a boarding pike.

Anton blocked with the saber, hamstrung his attacker with the cutlass, and leaped to his feet as the other man went down. It only took a moment, but, left unhindered, Evendur might have only needed a moment to dispose of Shinthala.

Fortunately, Umara had seen fit to hinder him. She'd cast her spell of the five colored orbs at him, and the discharges of fire, acid, and other destructive forces made him recoil.

That gave Shinthala the chance to take note of her surroundings. Instead of blundering back into the running rigging, she slipped nimbly through and put the lines between Evendur and herself.

Anton charged before the spheres of light even finished flashing out of existence. As a result, a screech stabbed pain into his ears and made his teeth clench, but he reached the Chosen of Umberlee in time to slash at his knee from behind.

The saber cut deep enough to shear through muscles and tendons and cripple any living man. But it didn't cut through bone to take the swollen, oozing limb completely off, and Evendur didn't fall. Rather, he whirled and cut. Anton jumped back barely in time to keep the boarding axe from smashing in his ribs.

The dead man pursued him with the luminous axe poised for a strike to the head. For three steps, Anton retreated on a straight line, then pivoted on the diagonal. The shift caught Evendur by surprise, and he failed to defend as the saber bit into his extended arm.

Once again, the blade sliced deeply. Anton felt it scrape bone, but it didn't cut through. Evendur didn't even fumble his grip on the axe, just snapped it out in a short, vicious cut of his own.

Anton parried with the cutlass. The clanging impact tossed him backward, and his back foot came down in water or blood. He slipped and floundered off balance.

Evendur stepped in, then stiffened as darts of blue light pierced him from overhead. He glanced up at Umara, who still stood at the railing of the galleon, and growled, "Drown." The wizard reeled backward out of sight.

Hoping to take advantage of the undead pirate's distraction, Anton lunged and tried a head cut. But Evendur hadn't lost track of him, and his axe blocked the saber. Anton shoved closer and stabbed with the cutlass for the other corsair's glazed, sunken eye.

Evendur jerked his head down, and instead of catching him in the orbit, the cutlass sliced a flap of slimy flesh from his brow. The injury intensified the putrid stench that emanated from him even in the rain, but it didn't make him falter. He pushed with the axe even though it was still hooked on the saber blade, trying to shove through Anton's guard and bring the glowing edge to his face through pure brute force.

Reflex made Anton push back. It only took an instant to feel it was the wrong choice. He couldn't match Evendur's strength. But before he could spring backward or twist aside, the axe pressed into the side of his face from jaw to temple, then hitched upward to split the skin.

The gash itself was a superficial wound. Anton had suffered worse in the midst of battle and kept on fighting. But the luminous poison in the axe head filled his lungs with what felt like frigid brine. He fell down retching.

Evendur raised the axe, and a small man in armor that looked like a coat of leaves shouted words that made thorny vines grow from the deck and try to coil around the living corpse. Evendur spat black sludge, the briars vanished, and a huge hand made of water rose from the sea, snatched the little druid, and yanked him over the side.

Meanwhile, Anton struggled to stand. He made it to his knees, but he still couldn't breathe, and another spasm of coughing wracked him. The convulsions spattered the deck with blood from the gash on his face.

"Fight *me!*" Shinthala called. Evendur pivoted to face her, then stiffened.

The druidess's eyes shone like lightning. Phantom serpents crawled through the ghostly holly that surrounded her, and streaks of a different grayness shot through Evendur's body.

Anton just had time to realize the undead pirate was turning to stone before he wasn't anymore. His inherent mystical strength had resisted the petrification. He snarled and brandished his axe, and a ball of silvery phosphorescence flew from the head of the weapon.

It missed Shinthala by a hair but discharged its magic when it was right next to her. The blast of pale light froze puddles on the deck and plummeting raindrops, and painted the left side of her body with frost. The holly and snakes vanished, and she toppled. The newly-made hailstones clattered around her.

Black spots dancing at the edges of his vision, Anton struggled again to rise. But something went wrong and he flopped back down on his belly instead.

As he did, Evendur stumbled slightly and gripped a tack. He only held on for an instant, though. Then his unsteadiness, if that was what it had been, passed, and he appeared as formidable as ever.

Certainly, he must seem so to the Thayan mariners. As Anton had intended, they'd followed him and Umara onto the galleon and then started jumping and sliding down onto the Turmishan warship in an onslaught that, in any normal battle, would quickly have turned the tide against the enemy. But now, with no spell-casters left to oppose the Chosen of Umberlee and Anton likewise helpless if not dying, the men still peering down from Evendur's magnificent ship hesitated.

Then someone rasped, "Keep going! Kill the scum!" The voice was so hoarse that it took Anton an instant to recognize it as Umara's. She'd somehow managed to free herself of the drowning curse, but not before coughing her throat raw.

Evendur looked up at her. "Your men have better sense than you," he said.

Umara sneered back at him. "They'll follow where a Red Wizard leads." She stepped back, spoke a word of power, ran at the rail, and leaped.

Magic made her jump like a grasshopper; she cleared the obstruction and landed forward of Evendur in the caravel's forecastle. Encouraged by her example, her countrymen resumed their attack.

But Evendur laughed. He ripped the dangling flap of flesh loose from his forehead, exposing a patch of bare skull, and started toward her.

Stedd now understood what Lathander wanted him to do—or at least he hoped so—but not how to do it. The fight was out to sea, and he was here.

Then the god gestured to draw his attention to the chanting celebrants inside their circle of stones. A column of hazy green light rose into the air above them. When it was taller than the tallest tree, it started turning west and ultimately became a verdant thread winding across the slate-gray vault of the sky. Thanks to the Morninglord's unspoken guidance, Stedd realized it was like a river of power the druids here were sending to their counterparts in the battle. And a person could swim down a river.

Stedd squared his shoulders. It was something he'd seen Anton and the Thayan fighting men do when they were about to start some hard or dangerous task. Then he moved to the center of the circle, still without any of the druids noticing him. He settled himself, stared up at green phosphorescence, and wished himself to the middle of what he imagined to be a tangled mass of dozens of warships attacking one another on the Sea of Fallen Stars.

Nothing happened.

So then he pictured Anton and Umara. They were his friends, and he wanted to be with them.

That made something happen. The emerald luminescence suddenly felt different, almost as if Stedd were above it instead of the other way around. It was like the pond back on the farm, daring him to jump from the high overhanging willow branch, or like a steep, snowy hillside challenging him to make a running start with his toboggan pressed to his chest.

Shadowmoon turned in his direction, and the slanted eyes in her delicate face widened in surprise. "Stedd!" she said.

He thought about pausing to explain what was happening. But now that he could feel the green current, he felt an urgency, too, as if he were running out of time to do whatever it was he needed to. Hoping the elf would understand, he gave himself over to the power.

He shot up faster than an arrow, faster than he'd ever imagined anything could fly. In a heartbeat, the druids were tiny as bugs below him. The moment after that, he'd left them, the House of Silvanus, and the whole flat mountaintop behind.

There was barely time to note the courses of the island's three rivers, peer down into its forests, or note the locations of Sapra and the half circle of farmland that supported it as he flashed along. Then he was hurtling over the sea.

He had the notion he ought to be afraid, but his flight was too exhilarating, and now that he was in the midst of it, he could *feel* the river of emerald light bearing him up. It was as real, as mighty and trustworthy, as anything in the world.

At least until it started to thin.

He noticed the change first as a slowing down. The current wasn't pushing him along as forcefully as before. Then he realized the storm clouds above and the waves below didn't look as green, which meant the verdant haze surrounding him wasn't tinting them to the same degree. After that came a sense of giving way that made him think of plants withering, or the bottom tearing out of an overstuffed sack.

Maybe the problem was that, distracted by the thrill of flying, he wasn't concentrating hard enough anymore. Once again, he fixed his mind on Anton's face.

Unfortunately, it didn't make any difference. He kept on slowing down, and the trace of green that was left continued fading.

Apparently, his loss of focus wasn't the problem. Rather, something was interfering with the flow of the Emerald Enclave's power.

And Stedd couldn't do anything about that. He didn't have the ability to channel the Treefather's magic; he was just riding it. Nor did he have any idea how to use Lathander's gifts to achieve a comparable effect.

THE REAVER

Drifting like thistledown on the faintest of breezes, his heart hammering, Stedd peered at the sea far below. It seemed that even though Evendur Highcastle and all his waveservants and pirates had failed to catch him, Umberlee was going to get him after all.

Umara rattled off words of power, whipped her hand like she was throwing an ordinary knife, and a blade made of flame streaked from her fingertips. Without even breaking stride, Evendur blocked it with a twitch of his axe.

Two Thayan marines scrambled to flank the undead pirate. As Evendur split the skull of the one on his right, the one on the left drove a boarding pike into his torso, but that didn't even make him flinch. Using his off hand, he grabbed the pikeman by the throat, jerked him off the deck, and gave him a single brutal shake. When he opened his fingers, the unfortunate mariner dropped with a broken neck, whereupon Umara decided she liked being cornered in the forecastle of the caravel about as little as she'd ever liked anything in her life.

Not that she'd seen much choice but to jump aboard the Turmishan vessel. Assuming it wasn't already too late for them, she'd needed to distract Evendur from the stricken Anton and Shinthala. And the Thayan men-at-arms had required a leader's display of boldness to keep from losing heart.

That didn't alter the fact that she'd just broken one of the fundamental rules of combat wizardry: stay well clear of the melee. Worse, she'd done it while battling the most formidable foe she'd never faced.

With the overcast blocking the sun, shadows barely existed. Still, she found the vague gray streak below a yard. Hissing and snarling words of command in one of the languages of Thanatos, she turned it black and brought it writhing up from the deck in the form of a tentacle.

The shadow whipped at Evendur to coil around him and bind him in place. But before it could, a wave leaped up and crashed across the deck. It didn't even make the Chosen stumble, but it washed away every trace of the tentacle as though it had been made of ink.

Evendur continued his advance. A few more strides would bring him to the forecastle.

There were two companionways connecting that elevated position to the main deck. Perhaps Umara could dart down one while the dead man was climbing the other. But by itself, that elementary trick would only keep him away for a few extra breaths at most.

She rattled off a different incantation and swept her hand in a horizontal arc at the end of it. A half dozen duplicates of herself, each mimicking her stance and movements perfectly, appeared around her.

Evendur glared up at her. "Oh, *that* spell," he sneered. He brandished his axe, and another tower of water heaved up from the waves. Umara realized he intended it to smash across the forecastle, obliterate all her decoys, and bash her in the process.

But it didn't. Instead, it lost coherence and poured back down to merge with the rest of the sea.

The attack had failed because Evendur had for the moment exhausted his ability to channel Umberlee's might. Somewhat encouraged, Umara hurled another burning knife at him.

Raising his axe, he blocked that missile, too. Clearly, his physical prowess was a different thing than his ability to work miracles, and despite the gashes and burns various foes had inflicted on him, he still possessed it in full measure.

Evendur started scrambling up the companionway to starboard, and Umara and her illusory twins scurried down the steep little flight of steps to port. He whirled, sprang back onto the deck, rushed her, and closed to striking distance a mere heartbeat after she finished her descent.

Caught by surprise, she hesitated, and the boarding axe flashed out. Fortunately, it struck one of the phantom Umaras. The illusion winked out of sight like a bursting bubble.

Retreating, the Red Wizard spoke words that shot a pang of pain through the core of her. She was transforming a bit of her own vitality into a force that was anathema to the undead.

She thrust out her hand, and white light flashed from it. Bits of Evendur's flesh charred and sizzled, but he didn't even appear to notice. The axe swung, and this time, it chopped at the right target. Umara snatched her hand back lest the weapon clip it off.

Still backing away, she conjured flares of flame and lightning, a lance of ice, and then, in increasing desperation, wrapped herself in a veil meant to befuddle Evendur by making it seem that she too was undead. He just kept coming, the axe popping her duplicates one by one. It was pure luck that it hadn't cleaved real flesh as of yet.

Umara refused to acknowledge the truth for as long as she could. But when she found herself down to her last decoy and had all but exhausted her own power, it became inescapable. It didn't matter that Evendur was presently unable to draw down his deity's magic. She still couldn't stop him.

The blast of magical cold had chilled Shinthala to the bone. The frost encrusting the left size of her body was freezing her still, and she suspected she had frostbite underneath it.

Yet even so, the cold scarcely mattered. The squeezing in the left side of the chest, the pain jabbing through her left arm, and the grinding aches in her neck and jaw hurt worse and alarmed her more. Being a healer, she understood what they meant. The shock of the initial chill had sent an artery into spasms and made it impossible for her heart to do its work.

Ashenford and Shadowmoon were right, she thought. None of us should have come here. All I've done is throw away my last few years and whatever good I could have accomplished with them.

And then, as if to validate her despair, she felt the torrent of magic that the druids in the House of Silvanus sent through her attenuate. In a few moments, it dwindled from a river to a trickle.

She knew it was her fault. Her participation was necessary to draw Silvanus's magic here, where it was needed, and her stuttering heart had disrupted that process as summarily as it had ended her efforts to destroy Evendur Highcastle.

Paradoxically, though, the realization that her failure was even more complete than she'd first imagined replaced her despair with resolve. Because she wasn't the only one who'd depended on the power coursing down from the Elder Spires. The druids aboard dozens of ships, faithful servants of Silvanus who'd trusted an elder of the Enclave to lead them, were relying on it, too, and by the First Oak, they were going to have it for as long as she lasted, even if that was only a breath or two.

She wheezed a prayer to Silvanus. Perhaps it helped a little, but her debility made a shambles of the precise pronunciation and cadence spellcasting generally required. It was mostly by pure stubborn will that she reached into the eastern sky, gathered the power diffusing there, and drew it pouring down like a waterfall once more.

Something else poured down with it. Through dimming eyes, she saw a blond-haired little boy appear before her. Stedd Whitehorn looked as surprised as she was.

Stedd had done enough healing to sense that Shinthala was in a bad way, and that even if he saved her life, she likely wouldn't be able to fight anymore today.

The thought flashed through his mind that with the battle still to win, that might be a reason *not* to spend any of his power helping her. It was a coldblooded choice he could imagine Anton or Umara making.

But he wasn't them. He squatted down beside the old woman, put a luminous hand on her shoulder, and murmured, "Lathander."

Warmth flowed from his flesh into hers, and her clenched jaw relaxed. That would have to do for now. He took his hand away, straightened up, took a first good look around, and gasped.

He'd seen a lot of fighting since the start of his travels but never before dozens of men locked in hand-to-hand combat aboard a ship. It was so crowded! He was lucky Shinthala had fallen amid ropes connecting a mast and its sails to the deck. They made a little clear spot amid the clanking, grunting press that had likely kept him from being knocked down and trampled the moment he arrived.

At first, the frenzied hacking and stabbing confused him, and though he peered around desperately, he couldn't spot Anton. But then a pirate pushed his opponent backward, momentarily opening a gap in the tangle of fighters and revealing his friend sprawled on his face beside the starboard rail, where the side of a bigger ship loomed over the one they were aboard.

Clutching Dawnbringer, dodging this way and that, Stedd darted through the mass of combatants. A blade glanced off a shield and he had to jerk to a stop to keep it from hitting him in the face. A heartbeat later, he sidestepped to avoid the jabbing point of a poorly aimed pike. Then a retreating Turmishan sailor bumped into him and knocked him staggering.

But his smallness let him slip through narrow gaps as they opened up. It also likely kept warriors busy fighting foes their own size from paying him any mind. Certainly, none of Evendur's followers seemed to notice that here was the very boy for whom the church of Umberlee had offered a huge bounty, in easy reach at last.

When Stedd finally reached Anton, he saw that his friend's head lay in a pool of blood flowing out faster than the rain could wash it away. The pirate wasn't moving and maybe not even breathing. The boy flung himself to his knees beside him, put his hands on Anton's back, and sent light, warmth, and vitality streaming across the points of contact.

For a moment—long enough for Stedd to feel a pang of alarm—nothing happened. Then Anton jerked and gasped in a breath. That started him coughing, but when the fit ended, he raised his head without difficulty.

"Stedd," he rasped. "First, I couldn't catch you. Now, I can't get rid of you."

"Lathander sent me."

Anton swiped blood from his face. The cut underneath looked as if it had been healing for a tenday. "I guess he wants you in at the finish."

"He wants me to give you the power to kill Evendur." Stedd held out Dawnbringer only to see it vanish from his grasp. He gasped in dismay.

But then he realized it was all right; the mace hadn't entirely disappeared. Rather, it had melted into a red-gold light that settled into the reaver's saber and cutlass and set them aglow.

Something about the process drained what was left of Stedd's own mystical strength, and when it was done, he slumped down panting. "Are you all right?" Anton asked.

"Yes."

"Then keep yourself that way." The pirate sprang to his feet, looked around, and started pushing toward the bow.

Having spotted Evendur, Anton would have liked nothing better than to charge and attack him instantly, but with the deck crammed with combatants lurching unpredictably back and forth, it wasn't that easy. He had to weave, backtrack, and periodically kill someone to make his way toward Umberlee's Chosen.

A waveservant pivoted toward him and thrust with a trident whose tines seethed with some malignant blue-green glow. Anton parried with the saber, stepped in, and drove the cutlass into the sea priest's guts. Shortly thereafter, a pirate who'd sailed aboard the

Iron Jest two or three years back bellowed, "Traitor!" and sprang at him with a falchion. Anton cut first and sent his former crewman reeling backward with a face split down the middle.

At least such hindrances gave him a chance to test his weapons now that Stedd had blessed them. The differences he discovered had more to do with the way he perceived and reacted than the simple heft of the blades. At certain moments, the men around him almost seemed to move sluggishly because he was so keenly aware of every tiny preparatory motion and the attack that was likely to develop from it. He felt fresh, strong, and clearheaded.

Clearheaded enough, certainly, that he hoped to deny a monstrosity like Evendur Highcastle any semblance of a fair fight. He pushed his way far enough forward that he could come at the dead man from behind.

As he did, he belatedly discerned that it was Umara Evendur was trying to kill with sweep after sweep of his axe. Glaring defiance, an oval shield of reddish glow floating in front of her, the slender wizard struck back with darts of blue light, but Anton's instincts told him she couldn't withstand her attacker for much longer.

It's all right, he silently promised her. You kept him occupied long enough. He charged with the saber poised for a stroke to the neck.

Unfortunately, despite the muddled cacophony of the battle and the rattle of the rain, Evendur heard—or in some other fashion, sensed—his would-be slayer's approach. He spun around, parried with his boarding axe, and the two glowing weapons rang together. The dead man then started to riposte, and Anton took a retreat.

Evendur, however, didn't follow through. Instead, he hesitated to peer at the rose and gold gleaming in Anton's blades.

Anton grinned. "Do you like it? It's a gift to you from Stedd."

Though he scarcely had a face left, just eyes sunk in pulp and oozing rags, Evendur managed a recognizable sneer. "That little turd-smear of sunlight's not enough, Marivaldi. How could it be? My deity rules these waters, and yours is just a sad little memory."

"I don't think so," Anton replied, "but either way, it doesn't matter. Because the gods aren't standing on this deck, we are, and I was always ten times the fighter you were. Now that I finally have blades that can kill you, I recommend you jump overboard and swim away like the ridiculous fish the Bitch Queen has made of you."

Evendur bellowed, sprang, and chopped so explosively that even though Anton had been trying to provoke him, and had the sacred light pent in the swords to sharpen his reflexes, he nearly failed to respond in time. But only nearly. He hitched backward, and the axe with its glowing green edge whizzed past short of his chest.

Before the Chosen could ready the weapon for another blow, Anton slashed low. The saber, its blade more scarlet than gold at this particular instant, sliced the side of his opponent's knee.

To Anton's disappointment, the weapon still didn't take the limb off or even drop Evendur to the deck. But it made him flail and stagger, and, hoping to score again while the dead man was off balance, the Turmishan spun the saber up for a head cut.

The Chosen somehow whipped the axe high in time to block. Metal clanged, and the sword glanced away.

Evendur then took a retreat to steady himself and reestablish his guard. It seemed to Anton that he limped just a little.

The Turmishan grinned. "Fighting's isn't as entertaining when the other man can hurt you back, is it? At least, not as entertaining to cowards."

"I just wanted this," the wavelord replied. He stooped, used his off hand to snatch a cutlass from a corpse's flaccid grip, and then advanced. The boarding axe shifted back and forth and high and low, threatening the same sort of attack it had made before. He held the short, curved blade well back as though he only expected to use it in the clinches.

But Anton read a certain coiled readiness in the hand that gripped the sword. Or perhaps it was simply because he himself customarily fought with two weapons that he sensed Evendur's true intent. Either way, he was willing to gamble that when the dead man next attacked in earnest, the axe would feint to draw a parry, and then the cutlass would flash out to deliver the killing stroke.

Though retreating, Anton allowed his adversary to take longer steps and steal distance. Then the axe whirled at his head.

For safety's sake, he took one more half step backward. But he didn't block, and, not waiting to see if he would or not, Evendur charged with the cutlass extended.

Anton dropped to one knee and the attack passed over him. As Evendur was now too close for the saber to strike to best effect, the Turmishan used his own cutlass to make another cut at the dead man's leg. The attack landed where the first one had, slicing the initial wound deeper and grating on bone.

An instant later, Evendur slammed into him. The impact jolted Anton, but the Chosen tripped right over him.

Anton whirled to find that, as he'd hoped, the wavelord lay sprawled on his belly. The Turmishan leaped to his feet and cut.

He managed four slashes before Evendur wrenched himself around and struck back with the axe. It was a clumsy blow, but one that still would have taken Anton's leg off if he hadn't hopped backward.

Evendur heaved himself to his feet, plainly favoring the damaged leg. Anton circled, obliging the dead man to pivot on it, feinted low, then cut to the forearm. The saber scored, but when he tried to pull it back, it stuck in the wound.

He started to pull harder, but at the same moment, Evendur dropped his cutlass. Apparently unafraid of any resulting harm to his fingers, he grabbed hold of the saber blade and jerked Anton closer. The boarding axe spun at Anton's ribs.

Anton couldn't parry. One sword was immobilized and the other was on the wrong side of his body. He let go of the saber hilt and dropped to the deck. The axe streaked over him then looped up for a chop straight down.

Anton rolled and fetched up against somebody's legs. The axe crunched down beside him. He scrambled and grabbed the haft before Evendur could jerk the weapon free. Then he drove the point of his cutlass into the crook of the dead man's elbow.

Still clutching the axe, Anton tried to drag himself closer for a cut to the groin. But with a snarl, Evendur heaved the weapon up and away, breaking his enemy's grip, and staggered backward.

That at least gave Anton the chance to spring back to his feet. Meanwhile, Evendur dropped the saber and shifted the boarding axe to his off hand, evidence that the stab to the elbow had done some good.

Anton shouted and sprang, and the Chosen reflexively retreated away from his adversary's fallen sword. Anton hooked it with his toe, kicked it into the air, and caught it.

He shot Evendur a grin. "That's better." Then he attacked in earnest, and his foe did something he'd never seen him do before, either before the end of his natural life or after. Umberlee's Chosen gave ground steadily, one hobbling retreat and then another, fighting defensively because his wounds and Anton's aggression left him no choice.

Perhaps recognizing that his master was losing the duel, a waveservant lunged in on Anton's flank. The reaver twisted out of the way of a trident stab and slashed, shearing into the sea priest's side. The waveservant's knees buckled, and his weapon slipped from his fingers.

Unfortunately, even though the exchange had only required an instant, the need to dispose of the cleric perforce relieved the pressure on Evendur and gave him a chance to come back on the attack. As Anton pivoted back toward his true foe, he was ready to defend and accordingly surprised to find that the undead pirate had kept on retreating, opening up the distance between them.

"I win!" Evendur spat, and with that, the sea roared. A wall of water reared up over the port side, and the caravel listed to starboard.

Anton realized it no longer mattered that he'd been prevailing in the clash of blades. The dead man had lasted long enough for his magic to renew itself and was now about to capsize the ship.

Evidently, he had no compunction about drowning his own followers if it would kill Anton and his allies as well.

Anton charged. The deck kept on tilting beneath him, nearly costing him his balance. Other warriors reeled in front of him, and he had to dodge around them. Meanwhile, Evendur kept backing away, although his crippled leg prevented him from moving as fast as his pursuer.

Anton staggered into what he hoped was striking distance. Only just, but the deck was slanting so steeply that in another heartbeat, he wouldn't be able to advance at all. He took a final bounding stride.

The mass of water to port crashed across the caravel, battering and blinding him, hiding his foe in a blast of stinging gray. He cut at the spot where Evendur's neck had been an instant before.

He thought he felt the saber connect with something. Then the wave tumbled him off his feet and wrapped him around the pulley at the foot of a line.

For a moment, he thought that was where he was gong to die. Then he had air to breathe, the deck was tilting back to port, and, gasping, he realized the ship hadn't quite reached the tipping point after all. Perhaps being grappled to the galleon, which in turn was bound to the *Octopus*, had slowed the process. There had been no way for Evendur to capsize one ship without channeling sufficient power to overturn all three.

Anton looked to see what had become of Umberlee's Chosen but could only find part of him. It wasn't immediately apparent where the severed head had rolled or washed to. Fortunately, the motionless body showed no signs of imitating the dismembered but still spry troll of Umara's recollections.

The wave had staggered everyone, but the Turmishans and Thayans recovered first, or maybe Evendur's demise robbed his followers of their fighting spirit. In any case, a couple more Umberlant warriors fell to their opponents, and then the rest threw down their weapons and cried for quarter.

Stedd and Umara headed for Anton, the blond boy running, the slender, shaven-headed woman pacing with the deliberate dignity of a Red Wizard, even though her soaked, slapping garments made the affectation vaguely comical. "Did we win?" asked the boy.

Breathing hard, Anton waved his saber—the dawn light in the steel now fading—to indicate other ships still fighting in the distance. "The Turmishan fleet still has to deal with all those other enemy vessels. But even so, yes. We just won the battle." He grinned. "Well, I did, mainly. But I'm generous enough to share the credit."

EPILOGUE

AT FIRST, ANTON DIDN'T KNOW WHAT HAD AWAKENED HIM. THEN he realized it was silence.

For months, he'd slept despite the sound of the rain, sometimes hammering, sometimes accompanied by the crash of thunder, sometimes merely pattering, but always present in one form or another. Now it was gone.

He scrambled out of bed and started pulling on his clothes. He was only half finished when someone rapped on the door. "Come on!" Stedd called through the panel.

"Why?" Anton replied, just to be contrary, but he didn't get an answer. He suspected Stedd had already scurried on down the hall to bang on Umara's door, and sure enough, that was where he subsequently found him, fidgeting outside the Red Wizard's room while she finished donning her robes.

When the three of them exited the house the city fathers of Sapra had loaned them, they found fresh threats, denunciations, and obscenities chalked on the facade. Because Anton had ended up fighting side by side with Turmishan sailors to defeat the Umberlant armada, a couple of his old comrades had recognized him, and now the whole town knew he'd returned.

Fortunately, Shinthala had insisted he'd atoned for past misdeeds, that he had, in fact, played a pivotal role in averting disaster, and men-at-arms from the fleet backed up her assertion. As a result, the city authorities had opted not to arrest him.

But it was a decision that infuriated some, and while Anton wished it were otherwise, he didn't blame them for their continued animosity. Folk who'd remained ashore hadn't seen him do any of the things that had allegedly benefited Turmish. They hadn't even seen the enemy armada. They *had* seen demons slaughter their loved ones and devastate their city, and afterward, their hatred of the one responsible party to escape justice had had years to fester, while accounts of the outrages he committed as a pirate kept it fresh in their minds.

No one was glowering, spitting, making signs against the evil eye, or shouting "Traitor!" or "Demon worshiper!" at the moment, though, even though dozens of other people were rushing out of doors. Everybody was too busy gawking at the changes in the weather and the sky.

Water still dripped from eaves and branches. But those were the only droplets falling, and in the east, the massed clouds were breaking up, admitting light that dyed them salmon, rose, and yellow.

Stedd fairly danced with excitement. "Do you see? Do you see?"

Anton gave him a look of mock annoyance. "Isn't this the time of day when you're supposed to keep quiet and meditate?"

"Not today! Lathander doesn't mind if we watch together!"

"Because now your task truly is over," Umara said.

Your task truly is over . . . The words gave Anton an unexpected empty feeling. Trying to shake it off, he asked Stedd, "So, what will you do now?"

"Go back to the House of Silvanus for a little while," the boy answered. "Shinthala says I can, and the elders have been Chosen for a long time. Even though they're Chosen of a different god, they can teach me things."

"Just don't go around saying you think Lathander is as great a god as the Oakfather," Anton told him. "They'll stick you in a wicker man and burn you."

Stedd rolled his eyes at an adult's attempt to be funny. For all his precocity, it was the first time Anton had noticed him behaving less like a little boy and more like an adolescent. Well, if he'd grown up a notch, it was understandable, considering everything he'd been through.

Umara gave Anton a smile that seemed a little wistful, as though she too felt almost sorry their mad endeavors had reached an end. "What about you?" she asked. "What comes next for Anton Marivaldi?" And to his chagrin, he didn't know.

He liked Stedd. Perhaps he'd even come to love the boy in somewhat the same way his older brother had loved him. But Stedd didn't need a scoundrel watching over him anymore. A notorious character lurking about might even prove an embarrassment when it was time to found a temple or whatever it was he'd end up doing, and anyway, Anton couldn't imagine devoting any more of his time to religious matters. This one interlude notwithstanding, it wasn't in his nature.

Which didn't mean he saw a better option. His past infamy likewise precluded making a respectable life for himself in Turmish or nearly anywhere around the Sea of Fallen Stars. Nor, even had he wished it, could he return to piracy. The corsairs who'd escaped the defeat of Evendur's armada knew he'd fought against them, and they wouldn't forget.

What was left, then? Umara recaptured his attention by frowning and narrowing her eyes as she awaited his answer, and then, at last, a possibility occurred to him.

He took a breath. "Wizard, we don't do too badly working together. What would you think about taking a sea captain into your service? Somebody needs to teach you lubberly Thayans how to sail your new galleon home to Bezantur."

Umara hesitated. "You understand, no matter how cleverly I claim to have done good work for my country, I can't disguise the fact that I failed to accomplish what Szass Tam sent Kymas and me to do. Stedd's god says I may escape punishment for that. But he doesn't guarantee it, not for me nor anyone who helped me in my dereliction of duty."

Anton grinned. "If I'm taking a stupid chance, how is that different than anything else we've done together?"

Umara slowly returned his smile. "When you put it that way, I don't suppose it is."

A few paces away, a little girl riding on her father's shoulders squealed at some new bit of splendor revealing itself in the sunrise. Anton, Umara, and Stedd lifted their eyes to see what it was.

ACKNOWLEDGMENTS

Thanks to Fleetwood Robbins, James Wyatt, Liz Schuh, Shelly Mazzanoble, Nina Hess, and all my other friends at Wizards of the Coast; to my fellow Sundering authors Ed Greenwood, R.A. Salvatore, Troy Denning, Erin M. Evans, and Paul S. Kemp; and to my agent Andrew Zack for all their help and support.

ABOUT THE AUTHOR

Richard Lee Byers is the author of over forty fantasy and horror novels, including sixteen set in the Forgotten Realms® world. His short fiction has appeared in numerous magazines and anthologies, and he writes a monthly feature for the SF news site Airlock Alpha. A resident of the Tampa Bay area, he is a frequent guest at Florida science fiction conventions and spends much of his free time fencing and playing poker. He invites everyone to Friend him on Facebook, Follow him on Twitter (@rleebyers), add him to your circles on Google+, and read his blog at http://rleebyers.livejournal.com.

FORGOTTEN REALMS®

Also by Richard Lee Byers

BROTHERHOOD OF THE GRIFFON
The Captive Flame
Whisper of Venom
The Spectral Blaze
The Masked Witches
Prophet of the Dead

THE HAUNTED LANDS
Unclean
Undead
Unholy

THE YEAR OF ROGUE DRAGONS
The Rage
The Rite
The Ruin

THE PRIESTS
Queen of the Depths

THE ROGUES
The Black Bouquet

THE WAR OF THE SPIDER QUEEN
Dissolution

SEMBIA: GATEWAY TO THE REALMS
The Shattered Mask

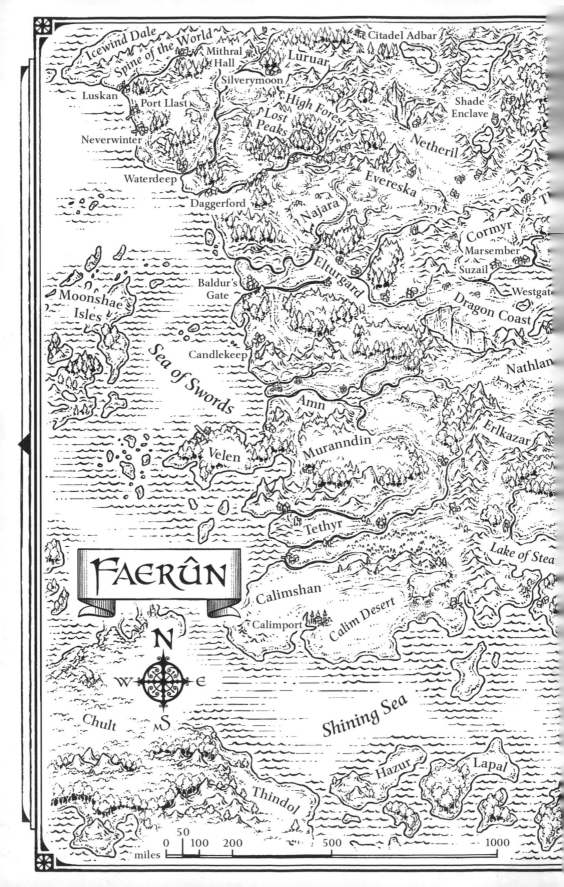